I0564601

THE THOUGHT BAZAAR

A novel by

RICHARD LAWRANCE

(c) copyright : Richard Lawrance 2009
email: lawrance.richard@gmail.com

ISBN: [978-0-9808575-2-8]
Publication Date: 10/2011

FOR CHRIS

WITH THANKS TO
GARY, GEOFF AND JIM

SYNOPSIS

Rhea Barnett has lost her mother but, despite a healthy period of grieving with her family, is unable to resolve her feelings. Believing the problem is with her personal belief system, she travels to India seeking spiritual plurality. There she meets an Australian who is unlike any male she has met before; empathetic, seemingly in touch with himself and his spirituality. And, as Rhea discovers, his sexuality. But it is not long before Rhea uncovers in Reiner the same insecurities and instabilities with which she is so familiar in the English males of her past. In the end she leaves him, stoned and dancing around a self-immolating backpacker on a beach in Southern India, and travels on to join her best friend Belinda in Australia.

There Rhea completes a novel she has begun to find during her travels through India, in which a young member of the resistance in the Third World War, Michael teams up with the punk Bozzo and heroin addict Sheena to plan a revelation to the world of a multinational corporate plot in collusion with global government. In the process, the hapless Michael falls in love first with Sheena, and then with Bozzo. And then discovers that the story he thought he was in is about as far from the centre of the narrative as he could have imagined.

23 October.
On the Train to Gatwick:-

My mother is dead. Sounds dramatic, but I haven't done this for a while. I can remember at school beginning each New Year with a resolution that I would keep a diary every day. Then a week and a half later . . . (Not true. The year I met Aidan I had a consistent and committed flurry of self-disclosure. But then, ah - my heart flung itself to the far corners of the universe and glowed there with passion and a future.)

My mother's death worries me because, as it runs past my memory's all-seeing all-knowing (all-singing and all-dancing) eye, it all seems so incredibly funny. I remember during Media Studies we once conducted a semiotic analysis of those black and white home and road safety adverts they made during the early 60s. Being party to my mother's demise was like playing a role in one.

Picture: We are all sitting down at the table for a good old family Sunday lunch. Brook has come up from Nottingham with Janaka and the kids, Verda is looking anorexic, and Fleur is brimming with radiance. Dad is depressed because the new head of the NCB wants him to do a lockout job on the mines. You can hear him say, through the crackles on the soundtrack;

"He said, If Murdoch can do it in Wapping, you can do it in the mines. Freeze the bastards out."

Then he shakes his head and clasps it ruefully in both hands.

"I don't know," he says, "It's just not my way."

Scenario: a family in the throes of a domestic crisis. A family inattentive of daily details. A family consumed by the weight of the world. Cut to Janaka, smiling with infinite Indian solicitude. Just as my mother screams from the kitchen.

We all rush in/out at once. The fat from the roast potatoes has spilt onto the stove and caught fire. But it has also splashed my mother in the process, and it is a question of which crisis to attend first. And, being a typical North Country family, despite our diverse (and considerable) competences, we dither. Dad gets water but, instead of throwing it on the flaming fat - which we later learn wouldn't have been the right thing to do anyway - he throws it onto my mother's arms - which we discover was not the right thing to do either.

Meanwhile the normally cool Brook picks up the flaming roast potato dish, promptly burning her own hands in the process. But! Brook is not totally unseated by the confusion. She does not drop the fragile glass dish onto the ground, where it will smash and burn our feet. (Camera engages in filmic elongation as family look from Brook and suspended flaming dish to the ground beneath, where copious feet shuffle ineffectually.) Instead she spots the sink and hurls the by now intensely painful dish towards safety. Unfortunately for all of us, upon impact with the porcelain sink (which would fetch a fortune in London secondhand shops) the fat leaps skyward, allowing those treacherous flames their prise upon our all-too-flammable imitation lace kitchen curtains.

Suddenly there are arms everywhere, trying to flagellate gymnastic demons of conflagration with tea towels, which themselves catch alight and take flight. Fire replicates itself with cancerous intensity, and people flee in its midst. Janaka is on the phone to the police while my father tries to tell him everything is under control. Sisters flit from room to room like leaves in a tornado, searching for buckets which never materialise. Hitherto unsuspected brooms fall from unseen crevasses with unnerving alacrity. Only my mother and I seem to think there is nothing to panic about. Here I am leading her out of the kitchen with

calm purpose. And my mother is saying;
  "I knew I should've bought fireproof curtains."

I nod sagely.

Next minute, bodies are backing away from the kitchen, shielding faces with arms as flames reach menacingly towards them. Yes, Yes, call them, my father yells half over his shoulder to Janaka, who is holding the receiver as if it is an alien object he does not quite know what to do with, but which will probably reveal the ultimate truth of its existence any second if he is lucky. Brook is already hurrying the children from the house. Verda is hurtling downstairs with an armful of blankets which she and my father comically flap at ghosts of consumed air whilst retreating from the intensifying heat. And before I know it, we are outside the house, and the sound of fire engines whoop-whoops in from the distance.

Then there is the ashen look of horror on my father's face. Oh no Oh no, he is saying. The briefcase! At first we think he is succumbing to an irrational burst of sentimentality. Brook reassures him there will be others. Even though we know this one is irreplaceable. Made from the hide of a young bull he reared on a farm he was evacuated to during the war, and was taught to tan himself. But it is our mother's sudden agitation that informs us of the truth. Oh Aaron, no, she is saying, no. Oh God. Oh God. Do something.

But my father is trapped like granite in his mountainous Capricornian implacability. He looks all of the ten years he is senior to our mother, and more. Neighbours are gathering with concern, both for us and for the safety of their own homes, and suddenly my mother wheels upon them. DON'T JUST STAND THERE YOU WOGS! she screams, DO SOMETHING! HELP, FOR GOD'S SAKE! Immediately Brook is trying to restrain her. I am half-grinning apologetically to our shocked neighbours. Fleur and Verda are stunned. We have never seen our mother like this before. She is fighting Brook. No, no, she says. I move in to help. My father fumbles on the edges of the action. In a moment of unanticipated stillness my mother catches sight of him. Get them, you STUPID MAN! she yells. He blusters. Oh god, I'll do it myself, she says. And before we know it, she is a pair of fluffy fake tiger skin slippers flipping towards the house like two aging bunnies fleeing the farmer's gun.

Nobody tried to stop her. Brook ran forward a bit crying, Mum! But more a: Mum, don't do that now, the Fire Brigade are here. For at that moment the shiny, red metal engines gleamed into our street and hoses volumed out like snakes. Black-clad men in penile helmets made themselves busy. And my mother ran into our burning house and was never seen alive again.

The irony is that with her went the documents that could have saved my father's career. The Coal Board couldn't have planned it better if they'd tried. Compassionate leave. Full pay. Dropped the embezzlement charges. Slap on the back and Your job's there whenever you need it. Then they gradually slip away. An honorary (as in, non-voting) position on the local management committee, and a fat payout. Gently does it. But decisively. They have it all worked out, these boys.

Ronald was at the funeral. Looking so sombre. So solicitudinous. And my blubbery father, accepting his condolences as if he was a friend. I study him across the grave and I can't stop thinking, Where do you put it? I want to ask him there and then. He treats me as if nothing has ever happened. As if an economics degree, Masters in Computing and PhD in Business Management changes things. As if flashy cars, Yves St Laurent suits and French champagne make him okay. As if, when he looks at me, I am supposed not to remember the fifteen year old boy who played Doctors and Nurses with his father's best friend's eleven year old daughter. Who had me stripped naked for 'examination', so that my little buds stood out firm in the chill air of the bedroom while he rubbed his hands along the insides of my thighs towards the downy tuft of pubic hair I was so secretly proud and yet afraid of. And even now I can feel those deep and strange emanations within me. Encompassingly corporeal, opening out again and again, as if they would go on forever. Even though it was

7

only for an instant. Immeasurable, yet tangible. Just beyond my understanding. And I looked up at Ronald with such trust.

Am I really supposed to look at him now and not see the man who wants to engineer my father's removal from the mine his father founded? Am I not supposed to make the connection between Ronald's appointment as finance manager of the colliery and the sudden emergence of cooked books from my father's office? Am I not supposed to see his hand, moving like a surgeon's knife through the hierarchic complexities of upper and middle management to cut out promotion for a select few with my father's demise? Who? We'll never know, because there is, of course, a full scale 'review'. And the strike.

And I was supposed to marry him once. I shudder at the thought of it. Shudder at my naivety. At the willingness with which my family constructed me not as a child or a teenager but as property, as the object of familial bonding, the catalyst for a two-family merger. Ronald was to 'have' me. And I wanted to marry him. I wanted the inevitability of that future, of love, of security and comfort and home and all of those displaced moorings of identity. Thank God for an independent education. Independent of the family, anyway.

So here I am, leaving England for the first time in my all-too-short life. And I don't really know why. My mother lies beneath an oak tree in an obscure country churchyard adjacent to the village in which she was born, somewhere in the middle of nowhere in the North of England. We take such antiquities for granted, don't we - villages, old churches, country parks, locks and moors - having romped all over the world quashing everybody else's. (Antiquities, that is.)(Do they have locks and moors in India?)

Not that there was much left of my mother to bury. A few old bones. Not even the ashes. My father had them. Kept wandering towards the burning house once he realised she wasn't coming out, firemen deflecting him and shouting at us to look after him. Verda and Fleur were sobbing uncontrollably.

I was still calm. I genuinely thought she would come out.

Once it was all over, they allowed him in amongst the wreckage. When they brought him out again, he was rubbing my mother's ashes into his hair.

He sort of collapsed into himself then. I mean, we all did. Lots of sobbing and hugging. Dad held off until the funeral, but as the coffin was lowered into the grave he too joined the rest of us in unmitigated grief. Then he didn't stop. Just sort of amorphously blobbed on into this fawning, slobbering womaniser, pawing everything in vaguely sympathetic but definitely female form that came near him. He was like a big bath bun soaking up endless quantities of compassion. It was embarrassing.

No, it was disgusting. And that's the problem. I don't think of him with affection at the moment. I think of him with anger. I remember a stubborn man refusing to go back into his burning house (a house he had equally stubbornly refused to leave despite my mother's well articulated desire for a home commensurate with our means) to fetch the documents that would save a reputation my mother had worked so hard to help him establish. He stood there and watched her go. Mum always used to call him an old goat when she was annoyed (which was often), and that's just what he looked like then. With his fleshy face and wispy white hair and silly goatee beard; an obdurate, stupid goat.

I know I am displacing my own anger. Because I didn't lift a finger to stop her either. And I'm feeling guilty because I am leaving him after he specifically asked me to stay. But Verda and Fleur are coping fine - anorexic, but fine - and Brook comes up on a regular basis. She only has to run her fingers through his troubled locks and he hasn't a care in the world. The hairdresser's touch. Although she's always been able to do it, ever since we were kids. With everybody, not just dad. Even Mum used to succumb to Brook's watery hands. Name-fulfilment? (And the Art of Transcorporeal Ecstasy. A short

9

radio play by Someone Who Still Listens To Radio Plays.)

And so I am snaking my way along the backbone of England, finding it not so easy to control my pen upon the gently rocking page while the trees outside scrape the underside of this country's rather mucky, pallid sky. There's a lot of rubbish in the air about Britain just now. And it gathers around the bases of the trees symbolically - abandoned cars, unstuffing mattresses, old washing machines. People walk through it oblivious; people with dogs, couples having illicit affairs, lonely pensioners, and children - hundreds of children with only the myth of private enterprise and an unwarranted optimism for a future.

Everyso often toothless banks of suburban backyard gape out of the landscape. They gather momentum. They increase. Until London howls its helpless illusion of opulence up to the bleary-eyed, already winter-wet sky from its rear ends. And the sky can drizzle only parsimonious tears for them while the Iron Maiden walks amongst the clouds. And I flee to - what? Wash myself in someone else's quashed antiquities? While my mother runs forever into the mountainous fire of her consuming glory. (I think I might need to do something about this metaphor business.)

*

Gatwick Airport:-

A spec of dust clings to the aluminium grill of an air-conditioning duct, a current of turbo-fanned air threatening to flush it into the atmosphere from behind. The grill is covered with such debris of rarefication, wrapped around the alloy spars like weed about rocks at an ocean outfall.

Suddenly our spec is dislodged. Like a subatomic particle that has just made the quantum leap. Or a seed lifted from a flower by the breeze. There is something imperceptible about the event. As if the fine line between internal decision and external determination has been lost, and nothing found in its place. The separation between action and existence is blurred.

Even once it takes flight it seems to have seminal volition, caught within some giant, unseen industrial plant, distracted by irrational starts and caprices factitious in nature. Addled through levered traps, presses and pistons of aerial coercion, it leaps into the spiralling updraughts and downdrafts of invisible separation towers, is ousted sideways along horizontal production line shifts to finally emerge as the completed, but irreducibly incomplete, product.

I'd like to say this is a metaphor for Britain today, and how I feel about leaving it. An allegory, perhaps, for our loss of heritage and fictional nationhood, the emptiness of ideology as a cogent political force other than post-industrial capitalism, and the chimerical insubstantiality of hegemony. I could bring in the IRA bomb blast in Bond Street last month, and describe how the occasional disruption knocks commodity clean off its rails, but how the machinery soon reconstructs itself and the spec of dust-to-be travels on. But in fact I'm simply watching a spec of dust because I have three hours to kill before my delayed departure becomes an ordinary, plain, straightforward undelayed departure. And I never did understand metaphors.

But there's more. This particular spec of dust is destined for the highly-polished shoe of a middle-aged family man, standing amidst wife, three young children, and a hasty assemblage of handbaggage flanked by the inevitable see-through polythene carrier bags of Duty Free. Altogether, they form a rock in an accelerated film of Life On Earth: The Gatwick Paradox. Human activity teems around them. People are flung to extremes of emotion by separation or reunion, where they hold their feelings like dead foetuses, unable to comprehend. Their bodies are lakes of compassion, full to the brim. Any ruffling of the breeze might displace uncalled-for tears through disused ducts. Any rumbling of the earth beneath might suddenly empty them without warning.

11

But our family are past this stage. They are together. They have said their goodbyes. Their minds are numb and waiting, immured once more against the vast capacity for feeling upon which they so immeasurably sit. And our spec of dust approaches their reflective foothills like a drunk, uncertain of his (or indeed her) reception.

I think I like airports. They seem such wonderfully reductive places. They take everything away from you - possessions, relationships, emotional attachments, even nationality potentially - and deposit you in an environment over which you have absolutely no control. Once you've passed through immigration, there is no going back. Only the not-unreasonable possibility that, several enclosed concourses, incubated tubes of light, and passages of time later, you will emerge at some preordained Other End, and take up life in earnest once more. Resume responsibility for yourself. Oblivious to the fact that you have touched the heavens and come back again.

For the now, the bounties of the commodity-bearing world are yours, offered up by gentle pools of glassy light and tasteful sales staff with well-manicured hands. Departure Boards sporadically update your fate, and you await the smooth injection of drink, food and mood muzak onboard. If I were an existentialist, this would be bliss. (If, as an existentialist, I could believe in bliss, of course.)

What differentiates the family here from the environment around them is not so much their sociality as their independence. They are together. But their interdependencies are as intact as their awareness of their powerlessness. They are bound by fear and confusion, not security and strength. They are not solid. But then, neither are rocks really, I suppose. (I can't remember my science here. The actual mass in matter is ten to the minus billion billion billion etc?)

Of course it is distinctly possible that this is just an act of projection. Because I don't see my own family as particularly together right now. We present the semblance of unity, but inside I fear we are falling apart. I wonder if death does that to families generally? Already I miss them separately. I miss Brook. I miss my father, in a contradictory sort of way. I remain fond of my two younger sisters. But I feel nothing for my mum. And that disturbs me. Has disturbed me for some time.

I cried and cried when she died. I didn't think I would ever stop crying. But now I don't feel anything. And, worse, have serious doubts as to whether I really liked her. Ever.

At university the feminist line was that the patriarchy wields power even in the domestic unit by virtue of its capacity to go 'out' into 'the world'; to have social as well as financial mobility in the dominant superstructure it creates for itself. Men have power in the home simply by virtue of the fact that they are men who can leave the home. The personal is political.

Sounds like an old idea even as I write, but I remember being unable to buy it at the time because my own experience was so contrary to the ideology. In our house, my mum really was the strong one. Not just in the power she managed to find by supporting dad, or feeding him covert advice or manipulating him from the bedroom, but manifestly. In the apparent workings of the family, in her evident intellectual pragmatism, in her active engagement with his working life, she ran the family. She didn't exactly run his mine, but nor did she want to. She just told him when he was wrong, or when his advice was bad, or a decision was ill-timed. She did not go 'out' to work with him, but then I never got the impression that she wanted to, or would have if she could. Her skills were in fact better suited to an advisory role. She would have made a good policy adviser or strategy consultant to a managing director in the corporate sector, or perhaps even the National Coal Board itself. But then she would also have been subjected to intra-company dynamics, which would have threatened the role she was able to fulfil from the house, where my father quietly nursed the loss of his father's business to the black heart of nationalisation.

Now that I think about it, I wonder whether it was her relative youth that gave her that edge over my father. A certainty about him. Of knowing somebody that was just that bit behind her generation. The woman of the fifties as opposed to the man of the forties. It sounds perverse, I know, but he seems so 'old school' from the years before the second world war put paid to old school tie, hand-shake gentlemanliness. Whereas she was from the progressive generation. The lets-rebuild-the-country, the socially as well as geographically mobile, the future is ours, we could reach the moon generation. My mother seemed to have her power relations extremely well worked out.

Dad, on the other hand, was almost paradigmatically male. Not in the more conventional sense of The Dominant Male, but the converse. He was the always-ready-to-give-the-other-chap-a-second-chance type, the advocate of give-and-take, it'll-turn-out-right-in-the-end, fair's-fair. Loving. Idolised mum. Always a healthy dollop of affection for us kids. And all because he could afford it. His position as head of the household, and 'man', mine manager, allowed him the luxury of concessions. He was (is?) in ideological terms the worst offender. Because he wasn't stupid. I'm sure he could've been a right bastard when circumstances dictated. (Why am I talking about him as if he's dead too?)

My family was not, as it were, consonant with the mould. Any more than I am. For I know I have the education. I know I am more conventionally attractive and more socially articulate than my older sister. And yet I want to be Brook. Always have. I want to hold people's heads over white porcelain and run the rivers of England through their hair; albeit aided by the Water Board and the marvels of modern plumbing. I want to run deep and strong, have children so easily and complement every aspect of my life as if I were born to it. Instead of feeling like air; substanceless, fairylike, off with any movement in the space around me.

14

What was it all for, the years of study and career-building? To systematically dismantle my material life? Give my wardrobe away. Sell off my stereo and processor. Put my university notes and books and shoes (why shoes?) into store. All I own fits into one small pack - so small I could have taken it onboard as hand luggage.

But instead I have chosen to check even that in, so that I sit here, dressed almost entirely in white, with next to nothing on my person by my passport (tucked into my natty passport pouch which hangs from one shoulder under the opposite arm, tight) and my travellers cheques and ticket (in a super-secret money belt strapped about my comfortably thin waist). And of course this beautifully bound leather writing bureau. My one luxury.

I'm not sure why I have chosen writing. I haven't written anything seriously since I was at university. And even then, I question my commitment. Certainly life as a journalist was never mine. And with Hi DIE it was only ever submission-writing and press material. So is that what I mean, I wonder, by 'seriously'? That the writing should be mine? A couple of abortive poems at university. Diaries that never took off at school. And yet it seems to me that I have always written.

Not in the conventional sense. Not as an academic or a novelist. Stories bore me. (Contrived stories bore me. I like listening to people.)(Come to think of it, when I say contrived stories I mean men's stories. It's the male authors I've read who need the artifice of structure, closure and overview.)

I'm a good letter writer. Or so Brook says. But I'm not here to write for other people. I'm here because as I approach 'here' any sense of 'writing' or being 'a writer' abandons me. What I thought I would say is not what I want to say. What I want to say is not what I actually say (read 'write'). And certainly not what I would say (read 'speak'). What emerges on the page is something quite new and unexpected. A part of myself I don't quite know well enough. 'Here' is a refuge, where I am able to exist beyond all I seem unable to be

15

or do in what they call 'the real world'. And I think I need to be here a lot longer than the real world normally permits. Which is why I think I'm probably going. And perhaps why I didn't want anyone at the airport to see me off. I don't really know what happens next. And that not knowing is fine. Tempting. Even delicious. (What, Biblical imagery so soon?)(This self-commentary could become tedious, Rhea.)

*

On The Plane:-

White for purity, I suppose. No, but I do want a sort of cleansing. In my light, cotton wrap-around top and cheeseclothy drawstring pants (Rhea is wearing a fine summery outfit with…). But good ones. Leather sandals. Dressed for the weather I hope to find upon arrival, rather than the drab, rotting-mattress farewell of London.

But my knitted patchwork shawl for warmth on the plane, that's coloured. Multicoloured. So I don't look entirely as if I'm on my way to some spiritual university to discover nirvana. (If, that is, it hasn't been discovered already.)

Mind you, I still felt overdressed as I got on the plane. All of these beautiful, dun-coloured hostesses with their nut brown eyes, in subdued saris of mauves and pinks. A taste of what's to come. And the Air India emblem stencilled all over the interior of the cabin.

The Jumbo is so plastic inside. All vacuum-pressed, as if it's fresh out of the mould. Outside, people are fiddling with the metal skin of the plane, inserting tubes and disconnecting others. It's even more like a humidicrib than the departure lounge. And inside, it can't be insignificant that people are all arms up, coats and cardigans flapping like vestigial wings as they stuff luggage into overhead lockers in awkward, if ummeditated, pre-emptive worship.

16

So, a spiritual quest. My life has always moved with such linearity. Where did we get this idea from anyway; chronology? Not that I think everything is pre-determined, but it does have a narrative quality. I could be telling my own story right now, I feel so alienated from myself. A woman standing on the edge of somebody else's anger. Although of course the anger naturally has to be mine.

I want to find an alternative. Somewhere I can feel both anger and love at the same time. Believe in both good and bad, right and wrong. The world we live in - the world I live in - seems to make so much out of rationality. Everything is either/or, for or against, with or not, black or white, war or peace, strike or caress - no, never the last one. Not for men, anyway. And I think that's the problem. Somehow a male subsumption of the intellectual domain has combined with their alienation of self to produce a generalised ethic in our (patriarchal) society of rational appropriation. If you can say it, or understand it in words, then it's yours. Which means that if you can define it, and others, they are yours too.

I seek a culture in which there is a plurality of thought, where logical pluralism is the norm, where traditionally conflicting ideas and feelings can co-exist, subtended by some broader concept. But not a transcendent one. Not yet another form of hierachic ordering.

The plane's moving. Four hours late. A strike by baggage handlers, we're told. Although it was initiated by air traffic controllers. It's only when the lower strata of the workforce take the initiative that the public get to know about it.

So the airport is now embedded in lights. Lights of the suburbs around. Constellations of greens, reds, blues and golds within, glistening away like gems in the velvet breast of night, here on the chasmic edge of the world's largest city.

And we are accelerating. Rumbling down the runway to a hearty surge of engines. I could be exploding, pressed back into my seat as I am by

17

the advance; but I'm not. Pale flashes of a distancing existence punctuate the stream of darkness beyond the other side of the cabin. The interior lights dim. And beside me, we are airborne.

The wing over which I sit scythes gems from the blackness below. Reins of vapour whip back over the stretching metal surfaces in taut, aerodynamic curves. My Jumbo is both cumbersome and beautiful. It is hauling the spangled breast of England into the night sky: Blake's chariot, but inlaid with jewels, not fire, lifting me into the oblivion of my future. Terrific, isn't it?

*

Somewhere Between Abu Dhabi and Bombay:-
Almost there. The last stop was one of those austere Muslim citadels somewhere in the middle of the desert. You see them in films. White walls suddenly climb out of the sand in the distance; although these days their cool shadows and curves contain the latest in modern technology. Minarets point to the sky like a cross between ornate pencils and medieval rockets, but probably hide a Scud missile or laser-powered radar.

All we get to see is this huge dome of an airport terminal (we've flown mostly through darkness), tiled with viridian and lit from below. It was like being underneath the skeleton of a giant mushroom; or on the inside of a green hill looking out. Weird place.

Nothing in terms of Duty Free. So bleak. And these white-frocked businessmen swept silently by with pristine, air-conditioning composure. Cut you to shreds with a single, righteous glance. A frightening gentility, Islam. I had to hug my shawl to disassociate myself.

I've been missing my father during the flight. Not enough to shed a tear over. More of a tortuous sadness. I went round to see him the night before I left (which was, of course, last

18

night - seems so distant already). Prior to a riotous all-night party at Belinda's. I preferred it that way. Go out with a rage, and slip Dad in beforehand. Just pop in and say "Bye!", all cheery.

As it was I interrupted an intimate interlude with a lady friend. I had known of her before. Married to one of the firm; those men who had so systematically avoided my father like the plague since Mum's death. And here she was.

I used to think of my father as a mountain. A soft, cuddly one, admittedly, but still mound-like and large-framed. More solid than my mother; even though she was the one with the strength. He was the one full of emotions and gentle passions, with a granite mantle of sagely knowledge. As if millions of years of geomorphic history grumbled within him. Especially after Sunday lunch!

But now both passion and rock have gone. He's like jelly. Red and wobbly. And this woman had come round to try to staunch the gaping wound in life he has become.

She was a beautiful woman. Late middle age. No attempt to cover the years in her face, nor the supple wattle of skin about her neck. Save a string of large but delicate pearls. Her breasts had similarly fallen, but she was not thrusting them into amazonian twin cones like so many of those '50s women. They simply sat softly in the folds of her pleated frock, itself yoked with restrained dignity and lashed modestly in at the waist.

They were eating venison, which my father had undercooked, and to which his visitor had added fresh herbs at the last minute. Deep red juices seeped onto their plates like wine, irrigating a juniper sauce. It made me hungry.

And my father sweating, his linen napkin falling from his chin, with embarrassment or excitement I was unable to tell. I couldn't help imagining him blundering into this woman that night, like an elephant trampling someone else's flowers, his mouth

19

searching for the herb-laced nipple to pull upon milk he would never find.

And would she forgive him, as he shuddered and whimpered too soon? Why do we always stroke their backs and caress their flaccid calves and coo soothingly? Although I suppose we don't do that, my generation. We have been bred side-by-side, boys and girls. We are equal. The boys of my era are overcoming performance trauma and confronting the pre-eminence of penetration. Even so, I know I've cradled an almost-stranger's head and murmured, "It's okay. It's okay."

He cried when I told him, Dad. Just stood there at the table, having introduced me to a lady whose name I have already forgotten, while streams of water ran uncontrollably from his welling eyes. I am supposed to be his favourite. Which I've never understood. He's so much more like Brook. I take after Mum, if anybody. Or so they say.

Poor old Dad. I just had to go. Leave him to his oceans of tears and face suffused with emotion. Except around the neck, where he so valiantly failed to hang himself recently. (The light cord snapped, leaving him with a ridiculous scar that comes up blue when his blood pressure rises. We still have to go out of the room to laugh.)

And now here am I shedding my own. Tears. I should've known they were in there somewhere. Big blobs of salty water falling onto the page as I write. The guy next to me doesn't quite know what to do about it. He's trying to concentrate on his business papers, but I know he's aware that I'm crying. Ah well, roll on breakfast, eh?

*

Dawn over Abu Dhabi is something else. Deep pink against the immutable white facades, strengthening to a rich gold that sent grey shadows shafting across desert waves as the sun rose.

I am looking forwards to arriving in India. Excited about the prospect of being on my own at last. I have given myself a year. Fifty two weeks - well, fifty one now. They cancelled my first flight last weekend. I was going to do the trip through Europe - Magic Bus, hippy trail, Middle East - but I know where I want to go, so why beat about the bush?

Acclimatise in Dehli for a few days then head off up north to Nepal for the trekking. They say it's the best way to start. Not too hot, but sunny. Friendly people. Food okay. Water straight from the Himalayas. I've promised myself that I will be in a new place every week. Although what 'new' means I've left myself to find out. There is so much of India to cover. And so much of me I'd like to 'step out', as it were.

But, here's breakfast. An omelette-type thing. Not astoundingly Indian. I should've had vegetarian, as Belinda said.

*

24 October.
Bombay:-

So. I am in India. Not quite as I had expected; but pleasantly so. We were so late out of Gatwick, a number of us missed our domestic connection to Dehli. So Air India have put us up in what appears to be their company hotel. (The Air India insignia meticulously tiled into the base of the circular swimming pool about which the hotel is built is, I think, bit of a giveaway here.)(And the fact that they've named the hotel - The Centaur - after it.)

We are just the other side of the airport. Although you wouldn't know it, judging by the vehicular gymnastics we had to go through to get here. It's pandemonium out there. People everywhere; on bicycles, on Lambrettas and Vespas, inside three-wheeled autorickshaw-type-things (that look like the old electric milk floats but in miniature and with lawnmower engines), crammed into the ubiquitous black and yellow taxis, hanging off the buses, and cheerfully packed into brightly coloured trucks that look like post-colonialism's rival to the breakfast cereal packet. And they all seem to be bundling simultaneously around the same corner, or up and down the same street at the same time, or any combination of the above, with no regard for any such mundane concept as the Rules of the Road. It's a stunning place!

Mind you, you do get just the mildest taste of what's to come on the plane as you land. As soon as the wheels vaguely touch the tarmac, every body on the plane of remotely Indian origin suddenly rises to the overhead lockers with preordained automatism, unpacks and, like a film speeding up, flocks to the nearest exit as if their lives depended on it. These are people who, up until this point, have conducted themselves with the same exemplary decorum displayed by everybody else lulled into soporifia by the hypnotic routines of international air travel. But for some reason, arrival HOME . . .

And the airline staff do nothing about it. Just continue with their own on-arrival procedures. Disarm doors and cross-check. Pack away the grub. Switch off the seatbelt sign.

Even though more than two thirds of the aircraft hasn't been anywhere remotely near a seat for the last ten minutes.

In the arrival hall I could already feel the warmth. And new smells - I can't quite put my finger on it yet. A combination of fresh moist soil and dust, or dew-laden bark and sun. Heavy, acrid, slightly weighted with humus, yet fecund. It's exciting.

But in the crush it was oppressive. For I soon found out why everyone was in such a hurry to get off the plane. The arrival hall was packed. You could see it from the immigration queues. Which were, mind you, a phenomenon in themselves. Ten times the size of their not inconsiderable British equivalents. And it was our turn to stand out, The Foreigners. The only ones foolhardily optimistic enough to be craning our necks to see what was happening up front. Like faulty genes in those endless lengths of DNA passively awaiting replication.

And they moved so slowly - I was tempted to say at a snail's pace, but I'm actually reminded of Verda's pet tortoise eating lettuce; so purposefully masticating a steady inroad into the leaf, yet oaring at the ground as she eats and so forever pushing the lettuce leaf away at the same time. Not that I think we had any chance of pushing India away. But it had that sense.

Whereas the Indians themselves seem quite placid. Until they reach the counter. Then the perspiration starts to bead on their lips, and they begin to fidget and fumble, gesticulate and defer, as if they are preparing at any second to sign the confession and take the cup of poison. (Or whatever the Indian equivalent is.)

It is a sense of agitation which, once I got beyond the barriers, is everywhere. Suddenly I am awash in this sea of people, each seeking some idiosyncratic and particular goal which bore little relation to the body as a whole. Like excited molecules in a volatile colloid, each looking for its required bonding to acquire equilibrium, or that next quantum leap, without ever finding it.

In the midst of which, I felt so pale and flabby. A phospholipid aspiring to fatty tissue, but still at the 'milk' stage, suspended and not quite sure where to go next. I felt unclean, and was aware of the rivers of alcohol still coursing through my veins from my send off the night before (two nights before?).

As for our tortoise, it turns out to be still under construction; the Bombay International terminal itself, a monolithic but incomplete rectangular mountain of concrete, covered at the extremities by a fine net of bamboo scaffolding about which lithe, brown-skinned bodies clamber skilfully. Its two giant paws stretch out cumbersomely either side of the existing terminal, clawing their way through the low-rise low life of India that teems around it as if some incongruously geometric obstacle has been thrown down by the Gods to test them. And tested they are, eddying out in whorls and curves created by the ill-fitting edges of this leviathan (wrong imagery again) threshold to the Rest of the World.

Although perhaps I'm being too eurocentrically paternalistic about this. Perhaps the Indian Gods really do exist, and have stuck this factitious rock down here on the end of some giant metaphysical swizzle stick by which they mean to mix up all of the Indian castes and racial groupings below into a sort of Cosmic Cocktail. Taking up where Ghandi left off, now that Indira has snuffed it as well. The Rest of the World just sort of leaps in through the gaps in the rock, like aliens through fissures in the time frame.

Nup. Too romantic. I'm just glad the airline handled our transfer to the hotel. I couldn't have coped with the sudden intensity of negotiation. Even as we stood in line for the bus, our Air India 'minder' was beating off the touts like lepers. And once we got out on the road it was bedlam.

Although one area we drove through was strangely deserted. It looked like a housing estate under construction - that same concrete infill with great, ungainly holes where the windows were supposed to be. But so sweaty in the heat that it looked as if a cholera epidemic had hit the place ten years ago and nobody had been near it since.

Reminded me of Thatcher's England in the North, but in reverse. There, the uninhabitable council estates are boarded up and empty because the original population have all gone down south to find out where all the money is. Here, those escaping poverty are yet to arrive. Or so it seems.

The hotel itself is a tall, smooth, white oasis in the midst of the diesel and monoxide chaos. A fortress. Capitalism defending itself from the Bombay squalor. Yet in the middle of it, the aqua-blue pool with its half-man half-deer, surrounded by trellises and pergolas adorned with bougainvillea, soft mats of lawn and huge pots of tropical ferns and small palms. And the jogging track around the roof, where international businessmen can maintain their physical alertness so that they can make that crack decision at the burr of a telephone and transform the lives of millions. A sanctuary of Indian corporate enterprise.

Well, I've had my complementary shower in my complementary room (only for the day; we fly out at 6.00 tonight). Now I'm off for my complementary breakfast, and perhaps a stroll through the hotel shops before my complementary lunch. Now should I be experiencing strong ideological reservations about my seeming willingness to engage so readily in such bourgeois decadence?

*

Down in the courtyard, a family are preparing posies of small, pale orange flowers for a wedding tonight. And bunches of a plant that looks like spring onions without the onion. Seems to be a family business. Even the youngest has a plastic spray canister with which he wanders round moistening the foliage, as the sun climbs to its zenith in opposition to the aquamarine centaur-archer below.

They must be privileged to work here. As, presumably, must be the family

25

who have employed them. That is, the clients who have hired the hotel for the wedding. Not so outside. As I strolled out front, the chaos seemed to close about me; although presumably it's from this same chaos that individual livelihood spawns.

Like the two guys who sailed towards me as soon as I stepped from the protective ambit of the hotel compound. They were riding one of those old women's bicycles with handlebars, one pedaling, the other sitting. They could've been gay, the ease with which they touched each other and hailed me, allowed their limbs to fall effortlessly about each other, embraced the air with each gesture like a balmy breeze from the desert. Physical lyricism.

And verbal. Where was I from, they wanted to know. Sweden (why Sweden?), Australia, San Francisco, London? (London, I say. Or near London, I correct myself clumsily.) Ah, they say, suddenly blessed with insight from the beyond, I am a golden lady, blessed with sunlight. I have come down from the sky.

My first instinct was actually to believe them. It was such an unashamedly beautiful image. But then, it was also so obvious. Did I like India? Well, I haven't had much of a chance to find out yet, I joke foolishly. Do I like Indian men? Would I like a drink? (It's as if they are offering to buy me one.) Did I have a licence? No, I don't drive. Sorry? Oh, a liquor licence. No, but I hadn't had any trouble in the hotel so far. Would they care to join me?

They grin and nod, but it is clear as we approach the hotel entrance that they are uncertain, and unwelcome. The beefy, turbaned, thigh-booted doorman steps towards us. My companions frown. Perhaps they had better not, they suggest. Must I defend them? Will we begin our class defence here? Who am I kidding? We will come again tomorrow, they say. But I won't be here to- . . . They wave and tack off back down the road, waiting perhaps for their next victim - fair word? Potential client, perhaps. No, they just lads. But so different to what I'm used to - the stiff, self-conscious, inarticulately loquacious English 'lads', with their easy turn of phrase, handy quip, neat trap of words, intellectual

26

sleight-of-hand, but basically no idea what to do with 'it' next. These guys seemed all the way.

So much safer up here, with my half-Indian half-European moonlike slice of the sky down below, my air conditioning, and my complementary lunch to digest. Although what I mean by 'safer' is anybody's guess.

*

Bombay-Dehli: In The Air:-

I'm not sure about my use of the term 'chaos' above. There is something abstract and existential about it; mythical, but only in the rational domain of eurocentered 'Western' thought. I don't know whether it's something to do with the heat and humidity, but the effect here is more and more of a fever. It is active, and debilitating. It grows on you, makes you hot, swells and sweats and confuses you, is conducive to hallucination etc..

At Bombay Airport, for instance, we were supposed to identify our luggage. Although we are not told this until we have stood in two separate, seemingly unmoving queues in order to check in and be allocated a seat (why they couldn't have performed both operations at the same time is, of course, unexplained). This, mind you, is after running both from the terminal entrance to the first queue, and from the first queue to the second queue, because the complementary shuttle bus has delivered us so late that we must hurry. Despite the fact that the queues themselves are not. And neither was the bus that brought us here.

Nevertheless, hurry we do, running to identify our luggage. Security men in white boiler suits everywhere. Ushering us up and down stairs, into the hot outside below the insulated concourse above. The land of fumes and baked concrete, oil slicks and luggage. Instant organisation; until we get to the loose array of portage apparel. Then the sense of purpose

27

totally disappears again. What are we doing? Why are we here? Who's in charge?

I point to my bag three times before anyone will believe that one small backpack is all I have. One member of our party does not even wait for the white boilersuits. He hauls his somewhat more substantial backpack out of the pile and places it into the loading skip himself. This man, I think to myself, has done this before. He goes under the unlikely name of Godfrey. I had afternoon tea with him, and he certainly talks like a returning veteran.

Another terribly-terribly military type does the same, although not with his own hands, naturally. Issues commands and instructions in a loud voice instead. Neither of these two seems to trust the Indians a bit, and their racism is infectious. I do not depart until I have witnessed the exodus of the skip, complete with luggage, for the jumbo I have personally divined to be 'ours'; this despite insistent arm-flappings and urgings by non-boilersuited Air India staff. Godfrey waits for me at the doorway. To make sure I am safe, I think.

So we slip oleaginously into and out of a chaos that has connection, contiguity, contagion and absurd twists of dissonance. One minute things move towards making sense, next second meaning has disappeared. It would be easy to lose your grip here. On the way to our aircraft we pass through three distinct, heavily armed security checks - khaki-cloth and gun barrels steely with air conditioned precision. Yet down the clanketty metal-grid stairs onto the tarmac anyone could've joined us; hopped over the fence from the squats on the far side of the airfield, slipped onto our ratty old bus and plopped a quick thermonuclear device into someone's handluggage. So inconsistent. But then, isn't that what I'm supposed to be looking for? If one can equate (I can equate) inconsistency with pluralism.

In the air, everything is Air-India-smooth once more. Hot meal. Free wine. Cleaned air. And my first sunset over India. Soft pink. Like icing with just a dash of cochineal. Over an almond fruit cake perhaps.

*

The Janpath, Dehli:-

I've realised what it is. It's those moments in a fever where you keep coming to and from consciousness, entertaining the wildest, hallucinatory dreams. But in India, the dreams are the reality. It's only in moments of rest that sanity returns; and then only to be pulled from beneath you like a rug, to tumble you out onto the choleric world of insanity once more.

As we arrived in Dehli, everything seemed fine. Soft landing. Godfrey and I chatting inconsequentially. Until we noticed that we were taxiing away from the airport terminal, and had been doing to for some time. Then we come to a halt out in the middle of nowhere, in our personalised parking bay of flashing lights and quartz halogens hastily convened by three walls of airport service vehicles in varying shapes and sizes. Our captain comes over the intercom and asks us to disembark through the forward exit in an orderly fashion. There has been a bomb scare and the aircraft has to be thoroughly searched.

The cabin crew seem more concerned than we do. One of them goes white and has to sit down. Some of their colleagues were killed recently in an mid-air explosion.

As for the passengers, that Indian panic that was evident on arrival in Bombay is remarkably absent. We stand in the aisles patiently, placidly file out and wait in our queues for transport. Even once onboard the fleet of modern, airport buses that appear out of the night, we have to wait until it seems every other transport is filled. Nobody is to have an unfair advantage. If the Jumbo goes up, we'll all go with it. And I can't help looking up at this multimillion dollar machine and thinking: the flight crew must have known this for well over half the journey.

Inside the terminal, the same pukkah gentleman who ordered his baggage onto the plane at Bombay is almost single-handedly responsible for getting the luggage carousels going. He doesn't actually have any immediate success in populating them with luggage, but he does get them going. (The airport staff are busily trying to convince us to come back tomorrow. This could take all night. And we are arrivals. God knows how the poor bastards in transit on their way to London are coping!)

He then leads us bravely off in search of the EATS bus, known to Godfrey and myself through our Fodors and to Mr Military by virtue of its acronymic source - Ex-servicemen's Airport Transport Service. Reputedly the cheapest airport shuttle service in India, one can understand why: the vehicle is miles away from the arrivals hall and, when we find it, its engine is ticking over but the cab itself is driverless.

Nevertheless we climb onboard, stake a claim as it were, and Mr Ralph Nestor Wiseman (as our leader turns out to be named) asks Godfrey and I to mind his bags while he goes off to rustle up some local initiative. He was here in the war, you know, and the only way to 'get things done around here' is to 'raise hell', 'stir these fellows up a bit'.

While he is gone, the driver arrives anyway, and Godfrey and I rapidly deploy an entire year's course of Le Coq mime in order to prevent our redoubtable chauffeur from whisking us away into the night, Ralph Nestor Wiseman-less.

Then there is the mad bus battle for a hotel. I had planned to head straight for the level of accommodation I knew I could afford to last out the year, but Godfrey and Ralph Nestor persuade me to give myself a break on the first night.

"The place can be a bit of a shock," says Ralph, "Best give yourself a fighting chance."

Fighting chance seeming to be the operative term here. The first reasonably priced hotel we come to, the plan is I guard the bags by the door of the bus while Ralph Nestor confounds the driver with military logic and Godfrey dashes in to see if there are any rooms. But the second I step from the vehicle I am besieged by an army of veritable orcs and dwarves.

They all seem smaller than me, and all surround me with a storm-ravaged forest of potentially pillaging arms. I know a good hotel, this way this way, you want to change money, my brother has a taxi - one chap actually grabbed my pack and started walking off down the road with it. If Godfrey hadn't returned with a swift "No go!" my entire worldly belongings would have disappeared into the maelstrom-humidity of the Indian night. "Now you know how a white corpuscle feels in a flu epidemic," Godfrey says; a seemingly meaningless comment until you understand, as I now do, that Godfrey trained as a (wait for it) vet. (Where do they get these guys from?)

Back on the bus, Ralph Nestor Wiseman, last remaining Pillar of the British Empire, discovers that his wallet and passport have been stolen from his document pouch. Which he does not understand because the pouch was with him all the time, except when he left it under our care on the bus at the airport. When, we reassure him naively, it did not leave our sight. (Which it didn't.)

So that when we get to The Janpath, which is next on the circuit and does have rooms, although at 100Rs more than Ralph Nestor Wiseman assured us they would be (465Rs - they probably realise not many places will take us in at this hour), we have to stand beside the Ruins of British Colonialism and watch him telephone the airport hopelessly, trying to get somebody else to locate his proof of identity and entire travel budget while the no-fuss welcome-back-to-the-haven reception staff look on with just that over-obvious trace of we've-seen-this-one-before. And part of me can't help but recognise what a superb con job this stunt would be, if Ralph were in fact not quite the epitome of imperial rectitude he seems.

But he seems genuinely flustered, our champion, dismounted and tweaked by his jolly handlebar moustache: Welcome back to India, Mr Wiseman! It is so fitting to be seeing you again. Am I getting paranoid? Or just tired. Nevertheless I've dropped a Puritab into the water in the thermos jug here in my room, just in case.

Cleaned my teeth in it. And tomorrow is, after all, another day, Scarlet.

*

25 October.
I hope Godfrey isn't going to be a problem. He's seeking a perfect union with a woman, and I get the horrible feeling I might be a potential bonding opportunity. Luckily he's on his way to some spiritual university in Rajasthan.

He's one of these tall, pre-Raphaelite types with long, fine hair who simply sail along with the wind. But behind that soporific plummy voice and conciliatory eyes I'm sure there's a tiger of a man bursting to leap out upon the slightest manifestation of platonic devotion that just might make me THE ONE!

And there we'd be, bound to the renunciation of all material possessions and earthly desires for each other, in mutual pursuit of the spiritual purification of love. Godfrey would be as strong as a bow for me, true as an arrow, as certain as the spheres - but only one string. Drat! So easily cut. There'd just be that little last relationship which hurt him so much, and not quite resolved . . . And of course the ultimate universal intelligence would just happen to be masculine, wouldn't it? In a non-sexist sense, of course. (Of course!)

No thanks. I haven't travelled 10,000 kilometres just to start mothering another wounded, pro-feminist male on an ongoing rebound. (These guys seem to slip from one ideologically sound incarnation of masculinity to another like schizoid masochists in a shooting gallery. Kill me! No, kill *me*! I'm even worse!)(Excuse me, but aren't you the same person?)(Who, us?)

We journeyed across Dehli together this morning. Crammed ourselves into one of those miniature 'milk float' tri-scooters and tacked out into the vehicular chaos. We both needed to find accommodation within our respective

32

budgets. If I am to make my (now) 51 weeks I have to be able to bed down for around 20Rs a night. Godfrey is the same. He is only here long enough to meet up with a friend who's been bumming around up North. They were travelling together before Godfrey had to return home to 'raise fresh capital', as he puts it.

He really is a vet. Although he's been working more in the conservation field, it seems. Saving wild boars, lions and (wait for it) tortoises. In England! In those big game parks, apparently; like Longleat. I asked him about the tortoises and I still don't understand. Some vaccine is being developed from them that can save the world; he didn't quite get around to explaining what from, but it sounded very interesting and if I were still a journalist I'd . . . probably be avoiding him like the plague! Can't have been too successful, whatever it is, because now he's come to India to try his hand at saving the world by thinking about it instead. As in, meditation. Some sort of spiritual Think Tank.

Anyway, out and about at last. Away from the humidicrib of air-conditioned airports, planes and hotels and into the hot dust of India, and the ever-present diesel fumes. Ah, life at last! A crow picks pink flesh from a dead rat in the shadow of the endless Western hotels that line Janpath. As we approach Old Dehli we pass what seem to be some military barracks protected by an iron grill fence and an expanse of lawn. And while khaki power parades there, ordering its rows amongst the giant, green leaves, in its stormwater effluent at a roadside corner around which most of Dehli seems to be bundling, brightly coloured women are washing clothes very khaki in colour! And getting khakier by the wash, it seems!

Everywhere washing is drying along the roadside, moulded onto chairs, railings, beds, walls - in fact, any available surface - by the friable combination of sun, monoxide and dust. One old man is lying on one of the oversized rush-matting footstools that pass for beds here, his nose at car exhaust level. The mud wall behind him can only act as a fume and sound trap, and he's inches away from the traffic. Getting into his lungs would be like reboring a mine shaft.

Meanwhile, the driver seems to be taking us for a ride and a half. As soon as we get in it's 'change money?' And 'good hotel? Better hotel?'. But Godfrey has somewhere in mind. 18 Rs. I can't find it anywhere in my Fodors, but the driver manages to circumnavigate the Red Fort three times before we reach it.

Our legs creak as we bundle out of this ridiculously cramped little machine, but if the journey was a rude awakening, the hotel is even worse. Walls the colour of the toast I had for breakfast - grey (supposedly white) bread just blanched under the grill. The rooms aren't filthy. Just bare. Old, sweaty concrete. A single window, shuttered on the outside and barred at the embrasure from within; no such thing as glass here, it seems. A single, metal frame bed with rusting springs and a mouldy mattress that sags in the middle. A chair which looks like someone had a go at stripping it back once but gave up. And a warped veneer cabinet beside the door, on which sits the predictably cracked enamel handbasin and jug. When we arrive, the proprietor shows us a homemade register in which satisfied customers have written comments of approbation. I find it hard to imagine why, although Godfrey seems perfectly happy. Asked for his 'usual room'.

I do, however, have an almost en suite shower, of sorts. My room is up an almost external stairwell - as in, it's the only one up here - and on the narrow (unlit) landing outside my door is a deep porcelain sink with no plumbed outlet. The water just empties all over your feet. And beside this is a shutter-doored closet (even less lit; as in, pitch black when the door is closed) containing nothing but a nozzle at shower height, and corresponding tap at hip level. Doesn't look as if it's been used for years and smells like a male urinal, so God knows what goes on in there. I'm none too keen to find out.

So here I am. 18 Rs a night. This is how I will live for the next 51 weeks, so I'd better get used to it. Nothing to even drop my puritab into. Have to break out my plastic bottle. Even then I wouldn't trust the tap water. But there's a kiosk down in the

34

courtyard that sells Coca Cola and mango juice etc.. So I might just have to indulge. Godfrey says that machine-capped bottles are usually okay. Can't help wondering if I'm much different from my transcendental guide here, putting myself through some sort of cathartic, masochistic purification by penury.

*

Godfrey's just come up to see if I want to go sightseeing. I am half-inclined to get out into it, but not with Godfrey. I'm actually feeling incredibly tired. They say it happens when you do finally and completely get away. A presage of ennui. No. A chance to be myself, more like. Although the one probably does precede the other, after all that *trying* you have to do back 'home'.

*

I can't seem to settle. I haven't eaten since breakfast and I don't trust this water. And this room is so hot, still and bare I keep waiting for a rat to scuttle along the wainscotting. Not that there *is* a wainscotting. And the shutters look like they haven't been opened in centuries.

I don't want to be in Dehli. I'd rather be north, where it's cooler. If I'm going to stay in dives like this, I might as well be looking out over Mt Everest or something. I went down the road to the Old Dehli Railway Station to see if I could buy a ticket, but it might as well have been a mountain itself. As in, insurmountable and impenetrable. Suddenly a problem where one wasn't before.

I knew there would be queues, and petty frustrations with officials. I'm used to that from home. No wonder the colonial liaison between the English and the Indians lasted for so long; they have the same natural affinity with the rigours of institutional formality and petty power-broking. As if the self cannot be made secure without these ongoing, incremental accretions in bureaucratic inscription.

35

But I didn't get as far as the booking office. I didn't even get inside the station. I just stood at this cavernous entrance, looking at a flora of kurtas, lengas, lungis, saris, salwars, and kameezes being thrown into life by a forest of brown limbs and crowns. Turbans of varying primary colours bobbed about upon an uneven, constantly moving canopy of black hair. I could barely see the battery of platforms and - my god! - steam trains beyond. It was like looking back into the Dark Ages.

Or one of those picture books you used to see as kids, where a plethora of locomotives fan out from some indeterminate one of any number of glass-domed Victorian stations. Why were we as a nation so obsessed with burrowing through mountains to emerge, soot-stained and grinning, on the other side with a lump of coal and a steam train?

Anyway, I couldn't enter the mountain. It was like, I got this far today. Maybe tomorrow I will go inside. The day after, buy the ticket. And so on. This is not me.

And on the way back it was the same as the walk there: beggars everywhere. Just pawing at you. Upturned hands working inwardly bent fingers as if they were trying to crack nuts from thin air. I felt such a coward, but surely it's a matter of give to one and you give to them all. And I really don't have the money to spare.

One poor kid had nothing from the waist down. He was propelling himself beside me on a low, flat trolley pretending to be a pop star, with a Coke bottle for a microphone. It was like walking through a horror movie in which nice things keep turning into nasty things as you approach them, and the city becomes a wood and the wood turns into evil greeblies and craggy mountains rise out of nowhere and turn into even bigger evil greeblies that tower over you menacingly!

So calm down, Rhea. This is not a fairy story and you're going to be okay. This is just a passing phase, as my mother would say. (Oops! Hallo mum.)

36

*

Well, Godfrey turns out to be a saviour after all. I was having a bit of a weep, I don't know why, and he turns up on the doorstep and invites me out to tea. I was so glad to see him. I am beginning to realise how important company is going to be on this trip. It doesn't have to be in-depth, hot-off-the-press, up-to-the-minute intimacy; just companionship. People whose cultural heritage you can assume for a while.

He took me to a street-side cafe around the corner and I ventured a small, selective sample of the local fare. I know I am bound to get sick eventually - everybody seems to - but not until I have at least acclimatised a little. One thing at a time.

I found it hard to eat. As in, put food in my mouth. And yet when I did, it was so tasty. I wonder what there is within myself that will provide the resources for me to cope with this new and obviously different culture. You don't understand how different until you encounter it.

Godfrey, meanwhile, was reassuring. He told me that, under Rajiv's socialist government, they in fact have a sheltered workshop scheme designed specifically for the beggars so that they can earn a healthy living with dignity. They opt for the streets simply because they can make more money that way; not only from guilt-ridden us, but from the still caste-ridden Indians: as in, forty years after Ghandi's Children of God and the rich still pay to keep the Untouchables at bay.

He also told me not to worry about the railway station. When he first arrived in India, half-an-hour in the streets was as much as he could handle. Then it was back to his room for three hours to summon up the energy for another foray. That was the way Belinda said to do it as well, now I come to think of it. I guess I just thought I'd be different. (Sorry Bee.)

*

I can't stop crying. I don't know why. It's my family. I wrack until it seems I can squeeze no more pain out of my body and then I give birth to a sentence. And with it comes an image of one of my family. And the sentence is one I want to say to them. Like 'Sorry' to Brook for leaving her with Dad. And 'It's alright. I love you,' to Verda. I want to look into her eyes, take her by the shoulders and tell her squarely that she'll be fine as long as she stops hating herself. It isn't mum. She ate like an anorexic before. It just got worse after mum died.

There are no words when it comes to Fleur. I just want to hold her. The image that comes is of her eating Dad's begonias by the back door, and him being furious because they were the only thing he'd ever successfully managed to grow. Little Fleur looks up at the booming shadow of her father, pink and purple petals plastered about her mouth, and says, "Pretty?". And Mum comes out and whisks her inside before Dad has the chance to do anything else. It was one of the few times I ever saw him really angry.

To Dad I just keep saying sorry, sorry, sorry, I had to go. And he stands at the door, blubbing, with his aging-breasted ladyfriend standing vulnerably at the table behind him. But another part of me is furious with him for not helping himself. Why isn't he coping with this? Why are we still doing it for him? Yet he seems so helpless. And I love him. So I grip myself in spasms of tears, unable to fathom where such virulent emotions come from.

Then there is the locket of my mother's hair that he pressed into my hand at the funeral. I told him I didn't want it. She gave it to him. A gold locket shaped like a droplet in which my mother had placed a lock of her hair. There is an inscription on the back: 'To my dearest Aaron.' Sounds so Edwardian, yet this was after the war. It's amazing the way the language of sentiment takes so long to catch up with the language of reality.

I still can't find anything to say to my mother. That's what hurts the most. I just clutch this borrowed locket and cry and cry and cry. And get angrier and angrier and angrier in my frustration. In the end it's my father I want to shout at. "You stupid bastard!" I want to yell at him. "Why the fuck did you let her go back inside?" Even though we were all there. We all could have stopped her. And probably didn't for the same reasons as him. Disbelief. Not quite comprehending the action and its full implications. A sense that common sense will prevail. I still don't understand it. So I keep crying.

I am not averse to a good cry. I am used to allowing something to build up inside me until it feels like my entire insides are weeping, and then letting it out with a good howl. Afterwards I have a sleep, or go for a refreshing walk, and feel much better.

This is not like that. There is no problem which becomes clear, or which passes, or which remains the same but now manageable. With this, just as I reach the end of one catharsis and am suitably wrapped up in foetal position to slip away in the hope that tomorrow will indeed be another day, up from the querulous caverns of my belly comes another sorrowful convulsion and, with it, another set of imprecations which overtake my brain.

And in the midst of it I am thinking: where is Rhea? Am I so insubstantial that I have nothing to match this plethora of generalised others my teeming ego seems to fling at me with such relentlessness? It's like I am under siege; but I am myself the sole source of the assault force. It's me driving me nutty.

But there, writing about it restores rationality to her rightful throne of irreligious perspicacity for a while and I am in control again. Reality has a semblance independent of me after all. Here, in India. Where tomorrow I will, of course, find some amazing substitution for my quixotically insubstantial past. Tomorrow, Scarlet, tomorrow.

*

I can't sleep. Every time I am about to drop off, I wake up with a start. As if I don't trust myself even to rest. Now I can't stop shaking.

I can hardly write. I've never been like this before. Never. I can't stay here.

*

Sunday, 26 October.

I think I am going mad. I couldn't stay at that hole a moment longer. I tried every relaxation technique I know, but I was shaking uncontrollably. So I jammed everything back into my pack and bowled out onto Chandri Chowk.

That was worse. Packed with traffic and bodies. Like walking into somebody else's delirium. And shuddering at the entry. It was all I could do to bundle myself into the nearest autorickshaw, insist on the metre, and head on back to Hotel Janpath; clutching my pack to my chest as if I were about to have a miscarriage.

Luckily, as we got to Janpath itself I recognised the Ashok Yatri Niwas, where Godfrey had tried to get us in last night. So I got the driver to drop me there.

The foyer was almost empty. I couldn't believe my luck. It would only have been around nine o'clock, but they had rooms coming out of their ears. Made me wonder what the story had been last night, when they were suddenly so full. Anyway, I took a room on the top floor, as far away from the chaos below as possible.

Even then I couldn't sleep. So I went downstairs to find something 'safe' to eat. There was a coffee shop affair with other backpackers, which was reassuring. But the only thing I could trust on the menu was ice cream and fruit salad. The fruit salad came out of a tin and the ice cream tasted like Walls, which was comforting in a funny sort of way. Like having a sore throat when you're a kid. Even swallowing was difficult. It didn't hurt. I just couldn't do it properly.

Back upstairs, I started imagining my father was dying and was psychically calling me home. I would have phoned him there and then, had there been a phone in the room. Instead I started making these insane plans. Like, I would join a dance company here in Dehli. They were bound to want my experience from the experimental scene in Britain. Offer my services as an education officer. There was an international professional puppet company somewhere in Dehli too. I could approach them. A dance perspective. Community penetration. PR as they've never known it. I used to be a journalist, you know. Maybe I could get a job on the English language newspaper too. Arts writer.

So it went on. I had my whole life planned out by the time I finally fell asleep. Probably with another one to follow. Then I dreamt about Dad.

He was emerging from our house, which was burning down again. He lurched from side to side, like Frankenstein, carrying mum's body in his arms. Except that she wasn't mum. She was a Vivian Leigh look-a-like, with falling red tresses and a white muslin dress which draped the ground each lurch.

Dad was crying. His hair was alive with fire and tears just seemed to fly from his cheeks. At first they were tears of anguish, but they became tears of rage. My father started stamping. But not like a child. Like Frankenstein. Stomping from side to side in a slow, rhythmic circle, my mother joggling in his arms like a stuffed dummy. It was a dance, and in the end my father was stomping so hard it was shaking the camera on the film set. People were fleeing him. Flames cowered before him.

Suddenly in leaps Godfrey, dressed as a Ninja. He is plying Dad with those little ninja discs. Dad reels and staggers like King Kong, blood bursting from his wounds. Until Ninja Godfrey delivers a deft salvo in a deadly configuration that carves Dad's body into fifty different pieces. They fly out in all directions with piercing whines and I wake up in a cold sweat. I must ring Dad!

It sounds funny writing about it now. But in the dream it was horrifyingly real. When I woke up I had no idea where I was, gripped by panic. I thought for a moment there was someone in the room with me. A man. But then, in the thin light growing outside, I could hear a muezzin calling from nearby, and I realised it must have been his voice that came whining into my dream as Dad's exploding body parts.

Now he sounded so peaceful. A voice from the desert. And beneath him I could hear the city starting up. People moving things on wheels or in thin, swinging metal cannisters. Rickety trucks rattling into motion. The early morning chuckle of voices trickling through rising rituals. Occasionally one calls to another. Gradually, that background inner ear burr called 'city' gains strength, and I feel secure.

Until I go to the window, and remember that I am on the top floor of one of the tallest buildings in Dehli, my windows are closed and there isn't a mosque for miles. So the shakes start again. Not so violent this time; just a quivering in my internal organs. But constantly. I am not cold.

Downstairs, I try to eat breakfast. But what little toast gets through my unsalivating mastications seems to want to come up rather than go down, and in the end does neither. All I can take is tea.

I think I ought to call a doctor, but am afraid that he will put me away, stick unsterile needles into me, dose me up with impure medicines, pass on infections under his fingernails, be unclean, certify me as insane. And I will be trapped in an institution in India forever, feeding on cockroaches and wasting away from dysentery and yellow fever and cholera and typhoid and nobody will ever be able to find me because nobody knows where I am. Not even Godfrey, who thinks I am still sleeping upstairs in a dive on Chandri Chowk. Then I really will lose my mind.

But I suppose there's the rub. The fact that I am aware that I could lose my mind is at least some indication that my mind is still intact to lose. I sit here looking at myself in the mirror and want to

42

laugh. As if someone in there is winking out, grinning and saying "I know you're in there - somewhere!" And I'm out here, going mad in India. Nicky-nacky-noo.

*

27 October.

I ventured out today. Decided it was time I started following Belinda's advice. A little foray into the chaos and then back to the hotel. One step at a time. So I went down Janpath in search of the post office. Hoping for a letter. Absurdly, because I've only been away five days. I must learn to cope. I can't afford fifty one weeks at Ashok Yatri Niwas prices, reasonable though they may be. I'd be lucky to make fifty one days!

But I'm feeling so lonely already. I found myself wandering down the street hoping irrationally that Belinda's face would emerge from the bobbing stream of features constantly coming towards me. "Oh, Rhea, at last! I knew I'd come across you eventually. I couldn't bear to think of you here all alone. I just had to come."

It was from her I was hoping for the letter. We've always been friends. Parting was never an issue. Then there we were at my farewell, three o'clock in the morning, pissed as peacocks, sobering up in each other's arms. Well, I was sobering up in Belinda's arms. She was growing mournful. Saying how much she'd miss me. I looked up and there were these giant tears in her eyes, glinting in the dying firelight. And I finally understood that I was going, and that it meant more to my best friend than it did to me.

Then she looked at me. It only lasted for a second, but it was a gaze so deep; as if the full gulf of the night had opened between us, but across it was a direct communion of the warmth within each of us, that *was* each of us. The night and the thread of 'us-ness' interwove, were inextricable, and could have replicated themselves again and again. We could have gone on from that moment forever, begetting and begetting it and its components over and over.

And all the while there was Belinda's softness and fullness, so thoroughly of flesh and structuring, bones and person. I wanted to immerse myself in her. It's funny, I've always thought of marriage as a male domain of proprietorship, but in that moment I think I understood what it was we as women bring to it. For this was far from innocent. It was the night that was clear, purer than pure. Vast and comfortable. I liked being there. With B. If ever we were created, I thought it might have been there. In the weft of those two states of being.

Then B's usual hail-and-hearty self returned with: if she got really lonely, she'd chuck in Hi DIE and come out after me. And we were back with the mundane again. I don't know if she was even aware of the moment.

But I'm sure she is responsible for me being here like this. It was she who rabbited on about the plurality of Indian society, the exhilaration of the contradictions, the temples and palaces in contrast to the peasants and beggars and so on. "Hard, but rewarding," she said.

She never talked about not coping, though. Spoke instead of drinking fruit milkshakes and lassi, discovering safe restaurants by watching where other backpackers ate, travelling light with a pack that was easy to throw on and off trains and buses.

But then, she was younger than I am when she did this. And was travelling with an upper class shit of a boyfriend called Lord who'd 'done' India before. One of those well-parented bastards of the 70s who could well afford to slum it for a while, knowing that Daddy was there to bail him out if he 'got into trouble'. Or to finance further education when he 'got home'. In the old days his ilk used to 'travel in Europe' or 'travel The Orient'. Now they stick a pack on their backs and play Hippy for a while.

I never understood how B put up with him. Eventually he 'gave' her to one of his University mates at a party and then dumped her because of his consequent jealousy. "It's not your fault, B." etc. Men really do seem to go to ridiculous lengths to extricate themselves from relationships to which they have self-obligated. Pity they have to fuck us over in the process.

I wish it could've been that simple with Aidan. We seemed to drag on and on for so long, neither of us knew how to end it. Neither of us wanted to. No consuming conflagration of vitriol and betrayal for us. No violent personal schism wrought by divergent values. Just the growing gulf of years, interests, and independent experience. Does it always happen that way with first loves?

Speaking of first loves and the docile Aidan, I saw my first sacred cow today. On Janpath, following my Fodors in the wrong direction to the post office, I passed an empty cart with odd pneumatic tyres being pulled by a longhorned Brahmin bull. It had sagging white skin and was travelling on the wrong side of the road, against the flow of traffic. The old Indian supposedly 'in charge' kept up a continuous verbal patter while his limbs danced ineffectually about the bull, tapping it with a thin cane. The whole routine seemed intent on persuading the bull to cross to the right (as in, the left) side of the road, but the bull just plodded nonchalantly along flicking flies from its ears, chewing on nothing and towing this empty tray. And the entire flow of traffic simply moved around it without a murmur. It was just as Belinda said: the whole of India makes way for the cow, and the cow is oblivious to the concession.

I have also discovered Marsala Dosa. It's a sort of light, mushy pumpkin curry which comes in a cross between a giant pancake and a taco shell, which I think is what we call paratha back home. They serve it in the restaurant downstairs. It is very easy to eat and eminently safe. Even so, it sits on my stomach. Lassi is better, but I am still not passing anything but water.

In fact, I am feeling fairly weak. And I can't stand the freedom with which Indian men keep latching their eyes onto me. B didn't tell me about that either. Perhaps it was because she was with a man. But they look at me as if I am not there; at me is worse than through me.

45

As if they are mentally undressing me not out of lust but because I am not worth the effort of considering in any other manner as a passing object. I hadn't expected this; to feel so objectified. Literally.

And everyone wants money from you - beggars, salespeople, hotel staff. They don't seem to consider that you can be on a budget too. I suppose that's understandable. I am, after all, a 'Westerner'. And I am feeling better today. Even though I dreamt of Dad again last night.

This time he was berating me as if I was Mum. Demanding to know why I had died on him. How could I do this to him? I, his wife! "What of your duty?" he kept saying. "What of your DUTY?" Louder and louder, as if he thought the word DUTY would bring me back to life. His face was getting more and more suffused with anger.

But I wasn't dead. I kept trying to tell him, even though I was lying in the coffin already dressed and ready to go to my grave. How could I explain being here like this, and then tell him I wasn't dead? He'd be furious.

Eventually I got fed up with my own guilt, stood up in the coffin and yelled at him, "It's not my fault, you miserable bastard. How do you think I feel? I'm the one who's dead!"

He reacted as though he had heard me, but I knew no sound had issued from my throat. I could feel the beginnings of sound coming from somewhere, but they hadn't filled out the words I had articulated. They were coming from afar, like a host of ghouls flocking to my vocal chords, closer and closer until I awoke with a strangled cry. It was dark outside, and I could hear my muezzin again, voicing the call to prayer.

*

28 October.

I have met a man. An Australian. I don't mean in a romantic sense. I can't work out whether I find him more comforting or frightening, but he's nothing if not compelling. And certainly unexpected. Enough to help me take my mind of myself for more than a couple of seconds, anyway.

I was making my second tentative journey down Janpath this morning, this time in the right direction but away from the Post Office, towards the centre of town - or what appears on the map to be the centre of town. I was still feeling fairly shaky, but was determined to overcome this chimerical obsession with 'Messages from Home'.

I'd only got as far as the Hotel Imperial (eminently colonial, white plaster walls and bougainvillea-gladed gardens) and there were these two hippy-types rolling hysterically around under a giant banyan tree. I immediately recognised Godfrey, and was tempted to walk on past. But he saw me.

"Rhea!" he called out, pointing at the man beside him and laughing uncontrollably. Then he looked at the man and pointed at me, pointed at the man, looked at me, called "Rhea!" again and waved me over, still laughing. It was like being invited to step into somebody else's movie. I felt one of those inward shivers, but smiled, probably quizzically, and stepped up anyway.

And sure enough, once I did, so I became part of the narrative. For Godfrey then started pointing at his shoes instead, looking at us both, laughing. It was his companion who had to begin the exposition.

"He's had shit on his shoe," he said.

I looked down, but all I could see was a pair of Reeboks which someone seemed to have splashed with a watercolour wash to break them down for a production. Godfrey was laughing anew, which intensified my feelings of alienation. Like being stoned and getting a touch of the paranoias.

"I've just paid 20 Rs," spluttered Godfrey finally, "To have a man throw shit on my shoe!"

47

I smiled again at both of them as they laughed, wanting to be party to their joke but still not certain about being in their film. I stood there behind my smile, while Godfrey narrated his way through the loops and whoops of his anecdote, wondering: where's the punchline? Should I laugh yet? Watch for them to laugh; they'll give me the cue.

Godfrey and Weiner - I presume this guy here is the one he's come to Dehli to meet - are walking down the street when out darts this brown youth with a cloth in hand, pointing at Godfrey's shoe. Is this the joke? No. They laugh, but not culminatively. Because there, as clear as daylight, is this perfectly placed dollop of shit, declares Godfrey. Now this is really funny, but I still don't understand why. Until Godfrey explains, "You could see as plain as anything that it had been thrown down from above. It was just sitting plum on the top of my brand new, all-leather Reeboks, which I'd bought especially."

Now I can see what's funny. Godfrey's brand new Reebooks have been soiled from above. But there's more.

"I just couldn't believe it. All of these years of coming to India, and some little street urchin pulls this one on me."

And more.

"Of course, he has the boot polish. I was so bemused I stood there and let it happen. Out comes this sort of off-ochre coloured gunk. He wipes the shit off with his conveniently-to-hand rag, of course. Then I ask him, is he sure this is the right colour? I mean, I can see it's not, but I just let him smooth it on and rub it in. I knew it would never come off.

"Then - oops! The laces have broken. How did that happen? Luckily he has a new pair which, miraculously, match the new diarrhoeic colour scheme of my Reeboks. By now Weiner was asking the price, and this well-practised little grub was making ha-ha jokes about 1000 Rs; so that when he finally asks 57 Rs, it is such a precise amount!"

"I wanted to pay him for his sheer aplomb, but Weiner was having a great time by now. Suddenly he was the gruff foreigner. 'Twenty,' he says, and the boy looks at me as if to say, 'C'mon! Is this guy crazy or what?'. But I shrug and say, apologetically, 'He's the cashier.' And hurry off after Weiner, who is already marching off down the street.

"But this guy is still with us, dropping price as he goes. And Weiner keeps sternly spitting out 'Twenty!' without even looking at him, while I grimace and shrug and say 'He's the cashier'. I knew Weiner was trying to string him out until we got to Connaught Place, because we both knew the boot boys there charge 5 Rs at the most, and we could just ask one of them."

I've never really thought about jokes before, but being outside one trying to get in was like watching it unravel on an autocue. Firstly, it assumed I shared the same cultural milieu. Secondly, it presumed I would devalue the same objects. It being, I suppose, the position of the joke teller, the anecdotalist. Godfrey and Weiner. The whole narrative proceeds on the basis of cultural premises which are introduced only to be reversed, or contradicted.

Godfrey's culminating reversal was when the boot boy finally decided they were gay. "You want boys?" he asked? "My brother has a place." "I just couldn't contain myself," guffaws Godfrey, "And there's this little rat running alongside us saying, 'What's so funny? What's so funny? Only 30 Rs."

At the same time I too was wondering: What's so funny? Are they gay or not? Apparently not. And so the joke ends by commenting on itself. What's so funny?

"Then you started to smile, didn't you?" Godfrey says to Weiner. "So I gave him twenty bloody rupees and told him to nick off," says the Australian; for that was the first time I properly heard his accent.

Of course I laugh at the punchline; but part of me is empathising frantically with the young Indian, while another part is wondering: are B. and I like this when we laugh together? Surely our intention is to share an experience we might find in common, not to invite group membership by excluding and thus nominating 'others'? Yet other women also tell jokes in this chauvinistic way. So perhaps 'patriarchal' is a better description of them than 'masculine' or 'male'. Or are they universal, jokes of this structure?

All of this I am thinking or aware of thinking in the instant that Weiner, still smiling, turns from capping the anecdote in that uniquely Australian laconic way, extends his hand to me and says, "G'day, I'm Weiner." Just like that. As if Godfrey, his narrative, and the entire collocation of experiences that had constituted reality for that coherent period in meaningful time and space, had been a pot boiler for this self-introduction to me. I felt so important. So focussed. So much the centre of an attention to which I had been entirely alien up until that point. It was a powerful act.

Yet despite my awareness of this, as he touched me I all but collapsed. It was the first time anyone had touched me in six days - anyone I felt I could trust, anyway - and I wanted to melt. His hand was so firm and slender. Sure veins snaked across the ridges of his phalanges in soft mounds. His wrist moved effortlessly about articulate carpals. His palm was so warm against my lifeless grip, it seemed to pass energy right into me. I almost cried.

And probably would have, had the Australian not followed with, "You don't look too good." An observation that enabled me to say, "No, but I'm fine really," and for it to be the truth. I was fine, really.

Even then he didn't dwell on it. Went on to explain, "It's for his sins, you see. He has dared to tread on Indian soil wearing the pure white hide of the sacred cow, so he has been well and truly divinely done over." So that was the joke. Suddenly I was apprised of the situation, in the scene, part of the story. Godfrey was wearing new prized leather shoes, but leather's source, cows, are prized in

India as sacred. So Godfrey got a divine one in the veritables. Right.

It's funny, I've had guys trying it on before with endless 'familiarity' tricks. Intimations that they know this or divine that about you. The sudden empathetic gambit that hits the mark, makes you think they have the magic understanding your little girl always wanted of her father. Eye games, proximity moves, etc.

But when I smiled at Godfrey's anecdote, at last free to respond with genuine warmth to the friendship these two obviously shared in their adventure, Weiner's eyes became crystal clear. I could have stepped into them. For he wasn't coming forward. Moving in. He just maintained the same smile and rolled easily on to the next equally apposite topic. "You hungry? We know a great 'safe' place to eat."

Mirthfully placing the "safe", but then removing any barb, just to be sure: "We always get so paranoid about 'safe' places to eat. I'm sure it's the same with you. I think it's because we've all had the experience of being deserted on a lone bed in a rundown hotel in the middle of nowhere, cascading just about everything from any conceivable orifice and thinking we are going to die, wishing we already had but hoping like crazy that we pulled through." So that we all had something to laugh about together. And I felt easy enough to venture; "Oh that's not my problem. I'm clogged up at both ends."

"That's a new one," he said. But without judging. Just interested. Accepting.

I am making too much of this. I guess it's nice that he doesn't need me, or seem to. I feel no compulsion whatsoever to confirm or 'support' him as a man. I mean, here's Godfrey in pursuit of his ideal woman. There's Aidan with his desire to be supportive and pro-feminist, but needing my support in the process. Whereas Weiner was more interested in the chana and biryani they serve at The Embassy restaurant on Connaught Place (which was, indeed, 'safe'!) than in me. Or in Kathmandhu (where he was supposed to meet Godfrey)(Godfrey was late), where he can roll dope off leaves in the forests and smoke chivums 'like they're going out of style'. He says he saw God up there, but I don't exactly get the impression he is serious. The only sober notions he seems to carry with him from that place are: it's close to the Himalayas, and it's supposed to be where Shiva's bull - the original sacred cow - came from. But he immediately counters any sententious impact these disclosures might bear with the prompt dismissal of Kathmandu as, basically, one massive dope den for bombed-out second-generation hippies like himself.

And he does indeed look the part - dreadlocks, hol(e)y t-shirt, and the grime is so ingrained it's hard to tell the difference between pigment and piazza. He talked about a place in Australia called Nimbin, where they seem to have discovered Woodstock about thirty years after everybody else and are still getting over the fact. Except they never gave up their day jobs, so the place is now riddled with accountants and systems analysts who all drive to Sydney for their week's work, then come home to their renovated bus on some commune for the weekend, smoke dope and get the munchies until dawn - which, of course, they share with someone meaningful.

I'm being cynical, I know. In truth, I've never met a real live hippy before. They were already history before my time. "Woodstock" was a film we analysed in Cultural Studies. I've probably always secretly nurtured a desire to be one. Free love, interpersonal liberation, sexual exploration, truth. It's all a myth, I know. The hippies were probably as fucked as the rest of us. But I think I'm more aware of my own constraints in relation to the aspiration - the 'all of me' I could never let go as an adolescent.

This goes back a long way in me, this sense of what will happen if I let go. I can remember myself as a child. Quite young. Might even have been one of our first trips to the seaside. I am standing on basalt-ish porous rock, which is sticking up from the sea in a shelf of craggy, quirky protrusions. I am thinking of it as a forest. I have meticulously picked my way out from the shore, from knot to knoll, fantasising a journey through an enchanted wood. Even though, of course, I am largely above it, I am still in it in my imagination.

A twin pair of knobs in the distance are the horns of a young doe, and I am anxious to reach her and make friends. But before I can, my mother calls me from the shore. She sounds very cross, but her crossness makes me anxious rather than afraid. In other words, *she* is anxious. I can't see why at first, but as I look for my way back to reassure her I realise that the sea has risen. My return route is uncertain.

In my mind at that time there are two features I remember clearly about my situation. The first of them is that the sea has not come in. It has come up, through the rocks, from the ground deep down beneath. The other is my sense of my mother as a star. Dad is just Dad, worried, lumpish and ineffective beside her. But my mum's face shines out from the rest of the scene in that awful contortion of panic and trying-to-sound-calm-and-commanding. She was so much younger then. So much younger than dad. And there was such certainty in her youth. "Come on Rhea, just step where I say." Always looking back to that face, beaming out in every direction. A star on the horizon of my forest. And I cannot reach her. But am trying.

This evening, after we had eaten and wandered around the back streets, Weiner, Godfrey and I arrived back at Connaught Place. It was dusk. An eerie mist separated the buildings, as if the hot dust that permeated the day had been trapped in the air like a colloid by the encroaching chill of nightfall. Through it, the pale street lights of Dehli accumulated a sourceless strength.

From this emerged a line of implacable Brahmin cows, all white, all with their humps flopping to one side or the other, and all drooping their ears. They plodded with preordained immunity, as if they carried invisible divinities along this same route every night of the year, a mundane prefigurement of destiny. And the whole of evening-settling Dehli parted to let them through.

53

Suddenly, amidst this almost cosmic placidity, Weiner gives a whoop of delight and runs at the file of cows. The cows, equally affronted, are completely unsure how to react. Some stumble sideways, some back off, others jog around in short circles, trying to locate the source of this vital immanence. Instantly, they are a pack; and Weiner is lost from view amongst them.

But Godfrey is smiling beside me, as if he already anticipates some uproarious outcome. And sure enough, after a moment or two, Weiner comes riding out of the herd on the back of the biggest, whitest Brahmin bull of all. After all his pontifications about the reverence with which the animal is held by the local culture, here he is, the bucking bronco riding out of the Yee-ha West. He was amazing. Frightening, but amazing.

It took those locals present a while to fully comprehend what was actually happening. It was the bull itself that finally provided the key to their understanding. It grasped far more readily the implications of its predicament and lost no time in running amok. Incensed Indians then began running around it, waving staffs and fists at Weiner and shouting inflamed abuse in Hindi.

My only frame of reference here is Bacchanalian, but the swarm of impassioned tent-cloth and stick-limbed chaos that drove Weiner from Connaught Place was far from revelling. On his last pass, the mad Australian yelled maniacally to us, "Off into the night!", his eyes wide and matted hair flying about his face.

"There goes another major international incident," said Godfrey. And the unwieldy entourage disappeared into the concrete gloom like ghouls between the gravestones. "Shouldn't we go after him?" I asked Godfrey after the dust had stabilised. "He'll cope," Godfrey replied, and invited me back to their room for a number to await the interloper's return. I declined.

Now if that was 'letting go', I'm not sure how much I admire it. On the contrary, I am left remembering the last male I spoke to with any conviction in

England. It was at B's, during my last night party. One of those tall, lanky London types with mop Oxford bags hair bailed me up in a doorway, gazed meaningfully but somewhat drunkenly into my eyes, and I thought: here we go, another I-know-what-you-re-thinking type. But instead he said to me: You're the one who's going, aren't you? I said I was, and smiled. (Flirting? Last minute fuck? Not sure. Not really me.) And he blurted out: And what do you think of Thatcher? Is she a feminist or is she a feminist? And I just laughed. I laughed and laughed. Told him to fuck off, still laughing, ducked under his arm and left him there in the doorway, gazing after me with a beery, unfocused frown. These boys! and their notion that, if you can articulate an argument and 'win' it on your own terms, then you own the idea. That you are somehow 'right'. They're mad. I'm not saying that's what Weiner reminds me of, but his actions tonight - the act of cultural appropriation - I mean, I laughed too. But not comfortably. Far from it.

*

5 a.m.

I have discovered the dubious delights of Bed Tea. You can book it the night before downstairs. It costs a meagre 2 Rs and is delivered to your room between six and seven the following morning. So I doubt that its financial benefits are great at either end of the transaction. Indeed, the tea they serve in India (it's called 'chai') is so sweet and boiled-milkish that its arrival at the top floor is likely to be a thankless task all round.

I ordered my first sample last night; something to aid the internal passage of biryani and chana, which was sitting pretty heavily on my stomach. So that when I emerged from my first good night's sleep since leaving England to an insistent rapping on the door, it was not without some justification that I anticipated an imminent delivery of my morning cuppa.

It was still dark outside, but this did not enlighten my fumbling progress to the still-repeating door to mumble, "Yes?" at the inch or so of wood before my barely mobile lips.

The reply was inaudible, so I mouthed "Bed Tea?" through the door, accompanied by my first realistic attempt at vocalisation. "You want Bed Tea?" came the response, loud and clear. "No, later," I replied, cognisant now either that it was still dark outside or that I was still tired, I wasn't sure which.

I went back to bed and looked at the clock. It was 4.20 a.m.

Moments later, however, the knock returned, persisted for some seconds, then ceased. There was a pause. Then it recurred, this time at the door next to mine. There was movement within. And whispers. Like Alec Guiness and the Lavender Hill Mob sneaking in and out of other people's houses. And it began to dawn on me that in progress was an early morning call for my next-door neighbours, off to catch a first-light train or international dawn flight. So I drifted back off to sleep and went with them, pulled into the night sky in my star-spangled Air India chariot by some cosmic ad maker towards an ethereal post-materialist (but eminently capitalist) bliss.

Just as I was dropping off, a couple of cleaners arrived to make up the now-vacated room. And suddenly it might as well have been the middle of the day. They banged and clattered and crashed and told each other jokes in loud voices. It's a crazy place, India, Rhea. Tell me it's you and not me.

*

29 October.

I should be doing some solid Jungian analysis of my dreams. That was, after all, why I started trying to remember them in the first place. Now I can't seem to get rid of the blessed things. Party tricks. I'm sure that if dreams really do contain information about your current psychological concerns, it's only natural that your subconscious is going work them over doubly hard to fob you off. After all, it's got its own position to think of, hasn't it?

The dreams I've been having since I left England are like a party of unemployed jongleurs out for a picnic. Whoopee, cop this one lady! Just joking! I was awoken by my phantom muezzin again this morning from yet another dream about Dad. This time he was dressed like something out of the Arabian Nights, sitting on a cloud smoking dope from a hookah, his current lover by his side, reviewing the autorickshaw troops. The troops are led by the evil Ronald, baring his teeth like the Red Baron. I was trying to warn Dad that Ronald was plotting a coup (no voice again) while Dad grinned and winked back at me, pointing to his lover secretively to suggest that she was really my mother.

So go on, how do I feel about clouds? What do I associate with them? The Red Baron? Hookahs? I'm sure it is all sending me up. Especially when in rides Weiner on a bull, dressed up to the nines like some voodoo witch doctor, eyes red with rage. Scoops me up on the end of his trident, twirls me about above his head and carries me off; while I'm frantically (still voicelessly) trying to indicate my father, whom he should be trying to save. As in, he should understand automatically the chivalry I require of him; but he just grins obliquely up at me as if I must be loony. (So I feel alienated from my Dad as a symbol of role-confused sexual freedom, hate the aggressive and appropriative Ronald in me, and want to be fucked by a Weiner. What's next?)(Don't tell me, the bull does it, right?)

Next minute Weiner and his bull are charging through the Yatri Niwas's foyer towards the lift. We're not going to fit in, I try to tell him (still

57

voiceless). Luckily, at the last minute he realises and mounts the stairs. The stair well seems to go on for ever (well, well, well!), but at the top someone is calling "Bed tea!", and knocking at a door I know is mine. We just have to get there. But I know also, however, that the bull will expire from exhaustion long before then.

Luckily, Belinda arrives behind us. She claps her hands to spur the bull on, saying to me; "Come on, Rhea! Bed tea for you! Then it's time to throw you out of the window and lock you in the lift." She knows these are two fears of mine; windows and lifts. She is trying to jolly me along. "No more chana and marsala dosa for you. Just waking you up with bed tea, throwing you out of the window and locking you in the lift! Twice every morning!"

I'm not sure I believe she is really there, but when I arrive at my door she is standing in the middle of the room. "Bee!" I cry, "You're really here!"

She smiles, and I want to run and hug and kiss her. But she compels me into stillness. Light emanates from behind the frizz of her hair. She is telling me, without speaking, that everything is alright.

Someone is knocking at the door behind me, but I am not interested. For Belinda is opening her mouth like an angel. I expect the sound of an angel to emerge, but instead comes the muezzin's call, long and clear. And I open my eyes to daylight, feeling as if I have been singing the night long.

The point (problem?) is that the muezzin is real. I really hear him/her. The dreams are real when I'm in them. So endlessly inventive and creative – isn't that so much closer to the real than what I engage with during supposed wakefulness, where I am always one step behind what is happening around me? Closer to being me. Who's to say that is not reality and this is actually the dream?

*

58

I've been to the toilet! I know it's not exactly a world-shattering event, or even agreeable reading, but it's certainly a welcome relief after seven days of etc. etc.. Must've been the chana and biryani. Or Belinda 'singing' me in the night; like the Australian aborigines used to. (Although I never could quite work out at school whether that was something they did now, or something they did once before they were wiped out. Then of course at university we learnt that it was almost the latter; the remaining Australian aborigines were now urbanised. Only the Tasmanians were wiped out totally.)(Today we learn that there are a number of Tasmanians who dispute that they are extinct, along with a number of tribal aborigines who don't take too kindly to being thought of as urbanised.)(Wasn't anthropology supposed to fix all of this for us?)

Whatever the cause, I've never been so pleased to see a few miserable brown nuts of excreta drop into the porcelain translucence of a toilet bowl. (Lucky they were mine, eh?)

*

Godfrey and Weiner 'called' for me today! It was almost like the good old days when guys used to 'happen by' on a Saturday afternoon. When they weren't at the football, of course. (Come to think of it, when I wasn't at the football.)(Not that that was ever much really. Dance classes were on Saturdays. When I look back on it, I am amazed my mother supported them into my teens, she was so against me making a career of it. I'm sure I would've gone professional if she hadn't harped on so much about university and the need for a career. What good has political science and sociology done me anyway, apart from the journalism?)(What good has journalism done me, apart from a suburban weekly and an introduction back into dance!)(Did my mother die feeling she'd been duped by fate? When she heard I'd got the job with BBC Education she was so pleased. Next minute I had joined Hi DIE! Does her soul turn her slowly over the spit of her own grave, roasting with slow

59

anger?)(That's not very funny really, is it? Why aren't I dreaming about my mother, if dreams are so important?)

Anyway, their pretext was that Weiner wanted to apologise for his behaviour the night before. But since they found me in the restaurant downstairs, they were able to make a joke about me eating tinned fruit and ice cream for breakfast into the bargain. They invited me to the Lakshmi Narayan temple, just around the corner they said.

Turned out to be a bit of a walk, but worth it. The temple surprised me. It was new. Ish. 1938. Yet in the same garish colours as the older ones in the literature. I obviously hadn't thought of Hinduism as a contemporary religion; but then, why should it be any different from Christianity, spawning its little red brick God kennels across the suburbs during the 60s and 70s in an effort to rescue itself from postmodernist oblivion? (Without inordinate success.)(Well, Sunday school was all they got out of me. And a handful of coloured prayer book leaves. Sad in its way, isn't it?)

As for plurality, I've got a horrible suspicion Hinduism is going to turn out to be as patriarchal as the rest of them. This temple, for instance, is supposed to be devoted to Lakshmi, one of the three female aspects of the Hindu divine triumvirate; yet the whole place seems far more concerned with her male equivalent, Vishnu (The Preserver) and his counterpart, Shiva (The Destroyer).

There is some sort of ideological justice in the fact that the Creator (usually Brahma, who is also masculine, according to a shamefaced Weiner) was in this case a massive black woman called Dhurga. But basically all poor Lakshmi got was a slip of a shrine and hundreds of - wait for it - swastikas! Hitler, meet your mum! Although these are apparently the originals. According to Weiner, Hitler reversed the direction of his so that they ran anti-clockwise. I seem to remember a similar story coming out in the Hitler Was A Black Magician (And So Was His Dad)(Please Buy Our Records) rage during the 70s. The original symbol, however, actually represents the sun; which is refreshing, I suppose.

There was a quote I liked from the Bhagavad Gita (13/15) on GOD, however;

> *It is without and within all beings and constitutes both animate and inanimate creation. By reason of its subtlety, it is incomprehensible; both at hand and far away.*

There is a tactile elusiveness about this concept: lovely yet ungraspable. Such a contrast to outside. Young soldiers shouldering rifles, standing along the roadsides, scattered through parks, sometimes even at restaurant doors, casually. Just like anybody else; shaking hands with their friends, nodding to acquaintances, smiling, pleased they are gainfully employed. But what would it take to make just one of them empty his whacking great rifle into a human body?

Interesting; I've scribbled here, 'Krishna is God incarnate. That is, not the Son of God, or God, but God in a human form.' And again; 'Hinduism is not revealed, it is prescribed by Krishna, in the Bhagavad Gita.' Mind you, what Krishna actually says in the Bhagavad Krishna isn't exactly free from ambiguity. One is supposed, for instance, to abnegate one's sense of self. But does that mean to have no concept of self? Or to defer the one one already has? The self put aside.

Which may sound more approachable than good old Christian self-denial, but surely it is still an unrealistic and fundamentally repressive principle? To defer one's sense of self is to defer also one's sense of sentience and knowledge of place. The logical extension is to seek non-being. To be not-here. Which is not only epistemological rubbish, it also incapacitates political action.

> I am spirit
> I don't want to be here

Given the problematic nature of 'here'. That's what it says. Enlightened understanding is uncommunicable; a non-verbal experience or state. Convenient, isn't it?

61

In fact, the Bhagavad Gita seems to be something of a grandiose patriarchal hoo-ha. It is all the one speech, delivered by Krishna to a semi-deific hero called Arjuna, who's suddenly got a case of the wobblies on the verge of battle. (And who wouldn't?)

Although in this case, of course, he's not simply scared. Great Skies Above no; it's Grand Compassion, because he doesn't want to kill all of these lesser mortals with his all-powerful weapon. So Krishna, standing there on the chariot beside him, spends endless pages enumerating a litany of cosmic principles which, I understand from Weiner, amount to little more than: GET OUT THERE AND KILL THE BASTARDS!!!!! Which, in the end, of course Arjuna does.

There seems to be great sentimentalisation of male grandiosity here. Women in popular Hindu mythology seem to have no purpose other than to be wooed, caught, entrapped, raped and otherwise assailed by every manner of evil giant, warrior, King or demon imaginable. Like Sita, the incarnation of Lakshmi whose story is depicted in a frieze of pre-DC Comics vintage on the walls of the Narayan Temple. The epitome of purity, Lakshmi voluntarily incarnates herself specifically to allow herself to be captured and raped by the evil mega-demon Ravana so that Rama, the incarnation of her godly consort Vishnu, can dash in to rescue her and, in doing so, rid the cosmos of the otherwise indefatigable bad guy. Now there's self-abnegation!

You can see it on the film billboards too. They all show men in anger, men in terror, men in action, men of righteousness; while the women are either being violated, beaten or adoring in the background. If they are in the foreground at all, it is only to be chucked under the chin by some patronising lover, or to defer their eyes demurely. And I'm not paranoid. Weiner notices them too. So where is all of this counter-oppositional plurality, B.???

*

30 October.

62

Had my first 'dreamless' night last night. Slept right through. Until the ubiquitous Bed Tea, which even beat my muezzin this morning. All to the good, as Godfrey and Weiner were going to take me on a guided tour of the entire colonial history of India in one day. Which I thought was nothing if not ambitious.

We rattled all the way to the edge of town (15 kms) in an autorickshaw - or 'Shiva's Chariot', as Weiner calls them (with reason: apparently all of the rickshaw drivers in Dehli come from either the Punjab or Kashmir, the foothills of the Himalayas, which is where Shiva is supposed to live). To Qutab Minar, a complex of Moghul structures at the centre of which is a tower built in 1193; to commemorate the victory of Qutb-ud-din over the last Hindu stronghold in Dehli. The first Moghul conquest of India. Interesting that the complex encloses (i.e. appropriates) a C5th. Hindu pillar made of iron so pure it has never rusted. Far more impressive technologically, but lost against the grandeur of the 73 metre Qutab Minar itself.

We then hurtled all the way across to the other side of Dehli to the Red Fort, via Jami Masjid; not only the largest mosque in India but, according to my erudite tour guides, the best example of architecture by one of India's last Moghul emperors, Shah Jahan. I'm beginning to understand just how androcentric Islam is. Back home head scarves and neck-to-ankle cover seems to be as far as it goes, but here it's six feet behind the man, look at no-one and, in some parts of this mosque, you aren't allowed at all without a male relative.

The Red Fort next door was clearly built (1638-48) around the mosque to protect it, with its red stone and mega-tablet battlements looming over the now-dry moats (in which squatters nest). So brutal and offensive in its defensiveness. Yet inside you can still find delicate inlaid designs of precision-cut agate, coral, tigers eye and turquoise. And the myriad of emptied latticeworks where subsequent marauders have plundered the prized gems. While the ceiling of the emperor's lounge escapes unscathed, remaining impossibly made entirely of silver.

It is such a shock to learn that so much of the iconography I have always associated with India is not, in fact, Indian. All of these spiked domes and minarets, red stone walls and jewelled marble interiors were brought here by Moghul conquerors. And after them, what should we find slap-bang in the middle of the Red Fort but the obdurately rectangular Victorian architecture of a British garrison, complete with colonial verandahs.

Trust us to simply walk in and co-opt the existing vestiges of power. Our own inveterate history of occupation must have taught us the art of economy in imperial enterprise. The British never conquered India. We just established trade links then moved the army in to protect them.

Meanwhile, outside both British and Moghul enclaves, the rest of India seems to muddle along. Amidst the crush of coaches, taxis, auto- and cycle-rickshaws all battling to escape the clutches of imperialism, an island of squats sits oblivious. From our bus (Godfrey and Weiner decided even Shiva's Chariot would be too expensive in this traffic), we watched one old chap thread his way through the conglomerate of vehicles, ascend the bank to a handy copse, glance around to check no-one was looking, and squat down to relieve his daily load. As if not being able to see us meant that we couldn't see him.

When he'd finished, he whipped his hand around to wipe his bottom with a piece of red cloth wrapped around his middle finger. Complete with bow-tie, it looked as if he was a child who 'had a hurt'. Weiner says it's a permanent fixture. Their equivalent to toilet paper. Take it off to wash it occasionally. Always eat with the other (right) hand.

Then three little girls came over to our window, hands out, toothy grins, for - baksheesh? No, chocolate, of course! So I gave them some. Which wrought the predictable give-to-one-and-give-to-all condescending jibes from Weiner and Godfrey. But they were wrong. The girls scampered back to their island of makeshift housing and proudly showed their spoils to - who should turn out to be their

64

father? - our defecating gentleman. His daughters pointed us out, and he smiled his toothless smile and waved to us. That was all. No flood of money-grabbing locals.

There was a certain dignity about the father. He looked so much older than a father of their's ought to be. So gravely purposeful when sneaking off to his toilet, yet when he smiled, almost angry , but at the same time surprised at the emotion. Frightened eyes beneath a dowdy red turban falling to one side. And his daughters lined up before him, chocolate blackening their white teeth while their bodies faded already, one into its red dress, the next into its white, the last into its black. Dusk was already claiming them for the night as our bus finally pulled away.

Weiner and Godfrey introduced me to another 'safe' eating house - the Sona Rupa, on Janpath. A sort of vegetarian family restaurant. I actually enjoyed the food for once. But now it's time for bed. My hand aches from writing. I should go back to shorthand. (Which is a joke. I couldn't read it even when I was using it every day!)

*

So much for sleep. Who should come a-knocking at my door just as I was dropping off but 'the lads'. I thought it might have been my bed tea dream making a comeback, but no. There at the door were Weiner and Godfrey, each with a bottle of Indian whisky under one arm. One was already half empty. Godfrey slurred something about not usually doing this, but I couldn't draw him on whether he meant getting drunk or waking up young women in the middle of the night. Although it turned out to be only about ten o'clock! (Thank goodness my better habits are returning.)

It was reassuring to have people drop by. When I was with Hi DIE, it happened all the time. Living in group households, there was always someone knocking at your door. Perhaps I'm not meant to live alone. (Now then, Rhea; who is doing the 'meaning' here? Placing it in the passive only makes you the victim of the plan; it doesn't obviate the need for an organising intelligence.)

They had another excuse for the visit. They wanted to invite me to Varanasi with them, to see the Ganges. Apparently it's where Shiva (Weiner seems to have this thing about Shiva) became an ascetic after being freed from Brahma's head; which was, even more apparently, affixed to his hand. Why? Because he had cut it off, of course.

According to Weiner, Brahma and Shiva were having an argument about who came first. Shiva tried to show that he was the original by cutting off Brahma's head. Brahma proved him wrong by making the latter stick to the former's hand until he capitulated. Which he did. In Varanasi.

Which is why the Varanasi is the number one tourist destination for India's entire population of saddhus; they are all Shaivites, on a permanent pilgrimage which inevitably ends up with a dip in the Ganges, either alive or in ashes.

I asked Weiner which method he was planning. He said he was in the running for a lease on one of the holes. Although you cannot become a Hindu (you have to be born one i.e. it is not a revelatory religion), Weiner reckoned (he does a lot of 'reckoning', Weiner) he might qualify as honorary Shaivite on the grounds that he had the neck for it.

I hadn't noticed this before. He wears a neck scarf all the time. But beneath it is an amazing birthmark that covers most of his throat and neck. It's like a bright purple map of the Euro-Asian Continent. 'The Blue Necked One', he announces; it's what Shiva's name means in Hindi.

He continues to fascinate me, Weiner. Later on, once Godfrey had dozed off, he started to talk about the categorical sexism of Hinduism. In Hindu cosmology, for instance, the female aspects of the threefold deity are created not just by the male aspects but by their gazes i.e. the very instrument of masculine appropriation and objectification. (So no wonder Indian guys feel so free with theirs.)

In the myth, Brahma is disturbed by the darkness besetting the

66

universe, and so summons Shiva, who in turn summons Vishnu by thought (thus representing the actual chain of command?). From their three 'refulgent gazes' (!) a celestial virgin is formed of 'cerulean'. They do not recognise what they have formed, and so ask her what she is. "Sirs," she says, "Do you not recognise your own omnipotent energies?" And promptly appoints herself Goddess of Three Times (past, present and future), Preserver of the Universe, and divides herself into three - one for each of our lucky deific aspects; white for the pure Brahma, red for Vishnu and black for the ominous Shiva.

"Now if that isn't a cosmic prescription for male projection, I don't know what is," said Weiner, "Not only is the objectifying nature of their own gazes the very mechanism of the creation of femaleness, but, once created, the women automatically do the men's work for them i.e. are a virgin - promise of untainted property - and divide themselves up as marriage fodder into the bargain. This is how Hinduism understands the genesis of the female aspect. Pathological patriarchy."

It was like hearing my own thoughts bounce back at me. No defensive aggression or mea culpa what-can-I-do about it. Just straight down the line analysis. Then he turns around and caps it with;
"It's all bullshit, of course. Just the boys being scared of the dark. Or Brahma being scared of Shiva."

Apparently in a prior Hindu myth Brahma creates Shiva from the quality of darkness. After emerging from the cosmogenic egg, the first quality Brahma becomes aware of is darkness, so he creates Shiva from it. Only then can he discover awareness (by confronting the objective reality of another; a competitor?) and thus create individual consciousness. Thus, Weiner argues, consciousness is an afterthought. A cosmic rationalisation. The baseline of patriarchal construction is fear. Fear of darkness. Fear of the unknown. (Jung's misoneism.) Fear of all that you are. Or aren't. ("Although basically,

67

Brahma just wanted a mate," says Weiner, with characteristic Australian litotes.)

Weiner has this theory that men devote so much of their energies to constructing the outside world (i.e. knowledge, buildings, technology, authority) with rationality because they need to compensate for the emotional void within them. The more they construct and rationalise the material world around them, they emptier they are becoming inside.

"The whole scientific ontology of time and space is one giant mega-myth, a rational-empirical construction to metaphorise the existential void of darkness at our centres," he said. "A darkness that produces nothing, but through which, from time to time, almost perhaps without reason, certainly without cause, violence erupts. Like a gap in the doorway to something unimaginably, arbitrarily dreadful. Inside we are nothing but the occasional cypher for irrational malevolence. And it worries us."

There was something profoundly unredeeming about this position. There was no forgiveness in it. I literally shivered. One of those someone-has-just-walked-over-your-grave shivers. As if the part of me that was listening had suddenly dropped into the void that was the centre of this man, and the rest of me was watching it drop away into nothing. Like there was no coming back.

For someone whose analysis of patriarchy was so incisive, his conclusions were awesomely rational. Or irrational, as the case may be. Luckily he was drunk. And so was I a bit. And the Godfrey we had assumed to be asleep lifted the clamp of gloom by murmuring, with his eyes still closed;

"You've been in India too long, Reg."

"Reg?" I said. It turns out that his real name is Reginald. He calls himself Weiner because it's his second name, and he prefers his ethnic identity. "Any ethnic identity," he said, "but ocker." Ocker being, evidently, the iconic Australian larrikin. He even called himself Ion for a while, after a Greek friend of his at school. "I thought it was a wonderful name. Meant 'the moon'. But every bastard kept calling me Ian. Ian! So I gave it away." (His father is in fact German, but wanted to give his Australian-born son a local epithet. So he annointed him with the most un-Australian equivalent to his own name, Rainer. "Nobody in Australia's called Reginald! I kept telling him, but the bastard wouldn't listen. So I came to India instead. Maybe he'll hear it from here!" - pause - "Mind you, he hasn't yet." - a further pause - "I haven't really written to him, you see.")

Anyway, it made me laugh. So I kicked them both out, still smiling; Weiner looking disgruntled, Godfrey quietly amused, and both with a remaining half-a-bottle of earth-shatteringly bad whisky to finish between them. It's the night's turn to receive their assiduities. I'm for slumber.

*

31 October.
I rang home today. Just to let Dad know I was okay. Went through my first bank ritual to do so. B's warnings were no exaggeration. Forty five minutes and three counters just to get change! I don't care if the rate's not as good, it's the hotel for me from now on.

Typical Dad. He didn't want me to 'cut short my holiday', but he was 'worried about Fleur and Verda'. Verda still isn't eating and Fleur is sleeping around. I told him that if he thinks Verda's bad, he should meet the Jainists in India: they're so vegetarian they wear special raised shoes to avoid treading on ants. As for Fleur, it's the springtime of her life and men are simply drawn to her like bees to the honeysuckle: is that so bad? (He can't argue with that; he was always telling us how he sang about 'You Are My Honeysuckle/ I Am The Bee' to mum when they first met.)

Meanwhile, Brook is having 'tests' at 'the hospital'. He doesn't say what sort of tests or which hospital, but automatically reckons she's got AIDS because she's being doing hair at a hospice which cares for HIV patients. I know he's just overdramatising to try and make Daddy's Girl dance on the other end of the telephone line, but the news is disturbing nevertheless. Brook was looking pretty tired before I left, especially with the added burden of Dad. I know it's her choice to step into the River-of-Strength breach, but Mum never made any bones about Dad's melodramas when she was alive. Just dismissed him publicly as an old worryguts. Brook's not like that. She plays the still-waters-run-deep line; accepts all and says nothing. And I'd hate for her to be internalising his stress to her own cost medically. I get the feeling there was something going down between her and Janaka, too. But nothing I could put my finger on.

As for Verda, she just needs a bomb under her. (I was going to say a good screw, but that's unfair.) I must write to her. And Fleur. Avoid sisterly contraception advice. (What eats roots, shoots and leaves? A Weiner joke. Took me a while to get it; 'roots' is Australian for bonking.) Meanwhile, Dad's new woman, Stella, seems to have moved in permanently, so it can't be all bad. Just shows the imperviousness of his sensibility, that he tries to make me pirouette into Brook's role from nine and a half thousand kilometres away. He should have known that I was never trained to pick up the soiled linen.

There was a postcard from Belinda at the Post Office, which was a joy to my heart. She says a man she met at my farewell is pursuing her at work because he wants to become more sympathetic to feminism! I can't think of anybody more uncomplicated and straightforward than B., yet these guys always come along and pedastalise her. This time ideology is the plinth. (But then, isn't it always?)

She also reminded me about this dance company she knows here. Their artistic director visited Hi DIE before my time, but the work sounds interesting. Combination of dance and puppetry. So this is my commitment: I'll contact them tomorrow. Short term goals. One day at a time.

Weiner gave me a lecture on parsimony this afternoon. Found him and Godfrey at the United Coffee House on Connaught Circus, looking decidedly under the weather. Spent a week's allowance on last night's binge, so the spiritual purification of the Ganges has to wait for a while. And yet Weiner chooses to warn me against exchange rates in hotels and the cost of the Ashok Yatri Niwas; as if I hadn't thought of it already. Just another man, in the harsh light of day (or in this case, the low wattage of the United).

*

I am writing myself. Re-reading this, I find it hard to recognise myself at times; especially the dramatic swings of personality. I seem aggressively feminist, even misandrist, and yet I know I'm not. I like men. Need them. Have loved some. Still do, I expect. And yet here I am tearing through the trappings of patriarchy, at both macro (urban, national, cultural) and micro (personal) levels, like a brace of anarchistic saw-teeth on the rampage.

The woman I am here is not the person who collects puppets from different folk cultures and hangs them around her walls at home. Who goes to jazz ballet classes and likes to dance to chamber music in the lounge when nobody else is in. Who goes shopping for leg warmers and outrageously large jumpers and woollen mittens in winter, and used to go hiking in the Pennines with Aidan. (Maybe that was what kept Aidan and I together for so long. Nobody else seemed to do it.)

But there's more to it than that. As I put my thoughts and feelings down in this form onto this page, I automatically give them a narrative, a passage through time. Which means that I give the same structuring to those who enter them, like Weiner and Godfrey, and B., my family. I am not representing these people in reality - certainly not their realities - but as they contribute to mine, or my construction of mine. I am not being written into Weiner and Godfrey's stories; they are being written into mine.

Yet does this only happen as I write? I am not aware of doing the same in my head in the present, and yet I must, surely. Narrative is so symptomatic. Jokes, anecdotes, day-to-day conversations, they all recount events in a chronology that

71

automatically says; listen to it in this way. But always in the past. By the time I become aware of the events enough to be narrating them, they have happened. There is no such thing as reality. I am perpetually making it up. I am a writer, whether I like it or not.

The difference between male writing and female writing, however, seems to be that when men write, they either write and expect you to accept it as truth, or else tell you that they are going to do so and then expect you to analyse it as truth. Writers like Fowles, Marquez, Eco do this all the time: Hey, it's really me writing. Do you believe it? (P.S. Aren't I clever?) Whereas women writers seem to be able to combine the two. There is a sense of consanguinity and humility about the text that opens out to you, says Yes come in and share this with me. It's not serious really, although of course it is.

I'm generalising of course. All I know is that being a journalist knocked the stuffing out of the writer in me. Journalism always fills itself with such self-righteous hoo-ha about ethics and objectivity, yet its commodification of words just shot my will to write meaningfully to buggery. You cobble it together according to house style and end up feeling like someone else's cultural latticework. And the 'someone else' certainly isn't the reader!

No-one is trying to control me like that when I write here. Yet when I read this, I am aware so strongly that I am trying to control myself through these pages. I am 'coping'.

Maybe I should throw caution to the wind and actively contrive to rewrite myself, instead of allowing myself to be written by some spiritual or cultural quest in the 'outside world'. The problem with a spiritual quest is that it puts a rationally comprehensible but nevertheless lyrical plug into a hole that is emotionally, affectively bottomless. Instead of dealing with the emotions themselves. Which are what the hole is full of anyway. I think that's what Weiner's 'void' misses. The 'construction' metaphor is great, but we could just start dealing with the feelings, couldn't we?

*

1 November.

Strange to see eagles and vultures in the city. The eagles wheel in circles before my window, climbing invisible towers of hot air. While the vultures flop about the feathery canopies below, alongside the crows, awaiting some unhappy carnage beneath, where India hives itself out amongst the dusky trunks. Life teems underground. Above, the dusty verdant veneer rolls on, broken only horst-like by architectural monuments to disappearing tyrannies.

Poetic? Metaphoric. Badly. Weiner says Dehli is like walking around a series of picture postcards. A Monument Capital, like Canberra, in Australia, he says as if Imight not have heard of Canberra in Australia. A shrine to history before history has even occurred. And he could be right. It was constructed solely to serve as seat of government, all designed by the same man (Herbert Baker), took 20 years to complete (1911-1931); they started at the Presidential Palace and worked outwards, fitting in Old Dehli as they went. I took my first trip out that way today, alone, clutching my passport pouch under my armpit. To the Sri Ram Centre. To visit Parvati. (Tried phoning. Hopeless.)

I don't know what I expected of them (Parvati), but they certainly weren't it. Something traditional, I think; Bharatnatyam or Kathak or somesuch. Whereas in reality they are extremely contemporary. Well-versed in their local traditions, but eclectic in approach. Attempting to redefine and combine established disciplines in order to develop new, culturally appropriate forms. And why not! How stereotypically colonialist of me to expect an artefact. Belinda had already briefed me.

They use puppetry more than I had imagined. Body mask, face mask, head and full body puppets, rod and marionette, cloth-and-light, shadow - all integrated into any one work. And much emphasis on the dance drama. They are reworking the Ramayana at the moment. I sat in for a while.

73

They are an extraordinary instrument, puppets. Inanimation is their natural state. Lifelessness. It takes one of these black clad human forms to bring to them into being. Which means a company can play an endless range of characters; sometimes two or three at any one time. People, animals, symbols - even ideas. (I am the idea you are about to have; how do you feel about it?) And size is no obstacle. From the largest to the smallest with a single lighting cue. And vice versa. A giant emerges from a dwarf. A boar from a tortoise. It's the ideal form to deal with the magnitudes of a Hindu myth.

We have no equivalents back home. Alfred and his Cakes. Little Red Riding Hood. Or any of the folk myths we laughingly call our own simply because they manifest themselves in a language we can understand. I sometimes wonder at our sense of history. Language seems to bind it with an unholy unity. Yet we've had nothing of a scale to match this since Beowulf. (Except the Celts. I keep forgetting the Celts. The Chuchulain Cycle etc.)

The company mostly seem to be from Rajasthan. Equal gender mix. Keen to meet me, but seemed to find it hard to understand what an education/publicity officer might do. Even though they are fully funded by the Indian Government and tour schools as well as regional centres, the majority of their work is inhouse. Nataraj, their a.d., says their audiences are too large and too poor to play in anything smaller.

The Ramayana is their major production for the year. There is a major Indian festival coming up called Diwali - the Hindu New Year. Some of the women in the company have the most beautiful intricate decorations inked into their hands; Mehndi Mande. They have invited me to an outdoor performance of the same myth tonight; called the Ram Lila, by an amateur company.

It's good to be back in a familiar context.

*

Ram Lila:-

• family parties come out of the closet, complete with chrome-clad stacks of hot food and chapati, cushions and collapsible chairs, saris, kurtas, jeans, clutter and gesticulation. An ordered anarchy comes and goes throughout the evening, marshalled only by the lengths of string they've pegged into lines to delineate price divisions.

• naked bulbs dance around the perimeter like a cheap petticoat. Above, stars are strained through the aerial Dehli dust like spangles in a cheesecloth cloth canopy. Trees jostle for a place on the horizon, silhouetted by the street lamps and traffic battling it out for primacy in the illumination stakes beyond. Only when the show starts do the FOH lamps throw our chlorophyllic pantheon into surreal relief. The Indians really know how to do this, outdoor performance: there's an earnest yet haphazard sense of let's get out there, get this up, get it on and go to it: we'll pick our way through the performance later.

• and what a cosmic conglomerate of categorical patriarchy. If the Gods could lift the flap of our heavenly tent and peek in, what would they see? Straight-backed heroes stride majestically about the stage, quivers and bows like vestigial wings, effortlessly repelling one affront of evil after another. Mostly from women. The king's wife wants her son to be the heir instead of Rama. The mega-demon Ravana's sister is more ugly, bitter and twisted than the big bad guy himself, who can at least stand up straight. Even the heroine, Sita, feints and swoons, protests and submits as divine bait to urge arrow-backed Rama to rout the naughty-plus Ravana. My Rajasthani puppeteers insist they don't believe in it. They just come here to please their parents. Or Nataraj. They aren't sure which.

• Transcultural parallels:
- He Who Masters The Charmed Weapon - Arthur pulls the sword from the stone; Rama proves he's the boy for the job by stringing Siva's bow;

-   Where This Arrow Falls - is where Robin Hood lies in final rest; is where Rama and his buddy will spend their fourteen years in exile; (is where William Tell's son gets an apple for a brain?)(Sorry, son. I missed.); Cupid and his shaft of desire;
-   The Sacrifice - Snow White sacrifices self-esteem for seven dwarves; Cinderella sacrifices the same for two ugly sisters; Cassandra sacrifices herself for Agamemnon's folly; Persephone sacrifices herself for her mother's freedom; where does the list end? But Sita sacrifices herself not for her lover, but so that he will conquer evil, reunite the opposites - that's interesting;
-   The Bitch - sorry, should that read Witch? Where do I begin!

These myths need to be completely rewritten, from the inside out, so that their symbols and motifs can be re-contextualised i.e. their obsessively patriarchal connotations transformed.

*

Auto-rickshaws are the last thing to die down at nights (at around 1 a.m.) and the first thing to start up in the morning (3 a.m.). There is only 2 hours of peace in a night.

*

2 November.
Parvati's bhopa player brought his two wives in today. They sat against the wall and sang from beneath their veils while he performed this amazingly sexual song in which he would suddenly lunge towards you with a "Whoooa!" such that you had no alternative but to respond in kind. Took me back to begin with. It was so refreshingly earthy and alive, when I think of our sedate folk sessions at university; or even worse, those maudlin hole-in-the-head late night Dylan/Cohen suicidefests Aiden used to take me to. (He didn't even like them. Just thought he ought to.)

He was a bit like a puppet on a piece of metaphysical elastic. His twin wives were his puppet master. But that is too fanciful. The women were full of toothless shy smiles. They admired their bhopa player, relished his freedom to launch himself so boldly into the public foray. There was no rewriting history here. Who am I to do it, anyway? For these people. For myself, perhaps.

Devi showed me some Kanchipudi, which is the dance of the North. Again, much eye-fluttering and demur obeisance to the (obviously taller) male deity. (Whoever said Siva was big?)(He might have been quite a small chap. One of those little men who always get so angry because no-one takes any notice of them. Which was why he danced his dance that shook the world. Bit of a small man's tantrum.)

Water-pouring was an interesting motif. Both refreshing and calming to watch. Made me thirsty. In another motif Devi held one finger up above her head and, with the other hand, held the opposing foot off the ground. It was an odd pose; full of lumps. Refined, with poise and sophistication, yet slightly off-balance, quizzical. Asking a question of transcendence or spirituality or the ether - whatever. The air. I liked it. Enchantment as a question.

Death: when a performer leaves a puppet whose character has died, the other puppets acknowledge the performer's going. It is as if she is a spirit. I find that heartwarming, unifying. I would like to die in my bed like that.

One of the Rajasthani puppeteers, Kama, has invited me to visit his home tomorrow, to meet his family. He lives in a colony of artists, he says, at the end of a bus route. I checked it with Nataraj, and he seems to think it's fine. Kama has been showing me his rather dilapidated snapshot portfolio of previous Parvati tours. They've been around, this company: Japan, Sweden, Australia - better than Hi DIE ever managed!

I don't quite know how to explain that I'm not really in a position to help him at the moment, but I've got a horrible feeling he'll turn on a meal he can ill-afford and go to great lengths to welcome me. We're meeting at the bus stop outside the centre tomorrow morning. I've got the collywobbles again.

*

India seems to be so good at organising chance meetings. I went to The Embassy for a light meal tonight -priding myself, I think, on venturing out alone - and who should be there, menus in hand, but Weiner and Godfrey. They both seem to have recovered from their Trial By Fire(water). Godfrey was adamant he had been fine all along. It was only Weiner who spent an eternity brooding under the mountain of his own hangover. According to Godfrey.

They both expressed an immediate interest in my journey tomorrow, so I invited them along. I don't know how politic that is in terms of Indian face and protocol, but I know I'll feel a lot happier if somebody else is there to eat the food and share the experience. I made a joke about them acting as my official food tasters. I hope this is okay, though.

*

3 November.
Only Weiner actually turned up this morning. Godfrey was off 'chasing some woman', according to Weiner. Another bid for the perfect relationship? I don't know Weiner well enough to venture onto this agenda with him. Meanwhile, Weiner set off on the wrong foot from the start, warning me not to expect too much. "These Indians" often make such invitations, he said, but "they" don't expect you to accept. He did qualify that, if the invitation was genuine, it was a privilege indeed, to be able to visit a local in their own environment. But his scepticism was thinly disguised; and Kama was, of course, there.

I nearly died when we arrived. On our way there, Weiner talked about an artists colony he lived in in Sydney, where they all rented space in an old warehouse and curtained off their studios etc.. I suppose I had built up an expectation of something similar. I

78

certainly didn't expect a mud village! Squatting on the northernmost edge of New Dehli, residential high rise springing up all around it, next to a crude cross between a canal and an open sewer. "The source of the Ganges," said Weiner. I thought he was serious for a moment.

There was rubbish everywhere. Faecal waste; human as well as chicken and goat. Half-starved dogs staggered everywhere, weaving their way through the invisible upturned ribs of death. None of these houses seemed to have any toilets, and the water was obviously drawn from a communal supply. "The government are going to make us move," Kamadeva explained, "Into blocks of flats. Because of the sanitary conditions. They say criminals hide here. But our new homes are south of Dehli, and it is too far to come to work. Many of us will not go."

Kama's place was, however, spotless. His "missus", as he called her, had swept it within an inch of its sunbaked life. Not that there was a lot to sweep. You couldn't even stand up fully. The whole family seemed to sleep in this one ten-by-ten mud house. There was a yard out front, 'fenced' by a one foot high dried-mud wall. There the chickens strutted about, along with the occasional goat (for milk), but the cooking was done inside. Over a small wood stove in "the missus' corner". Light came in through a narrow slit of a window just below ceiling height all round. And the door. And in another corner was a raised (also mud) platform which I gathered was Kama's bed. The rest sleep where they can find a space, I presume.

Mrs Kama had, as I feared, gone to great lengths to cook us a meal. Her veil was draped over a delicious-smelling pot as we came in. She offered us that same, toothless fragment of a smile as Bhopa's wives when Kama introduced us. She looked so much older than Kama. And I wondered whether that was due to an actual age difference, or merely her end of the bargain. She had obviously dressed up especially for us. They all had.

79

Meanwhile, meticulously cleaned metal plates gleamed at the ready. (Just two, for us.) Kama sent out immediately for some Campa Cola, and Weiner and I were sat in pride of place, on the edge of Kama's 'bed'.

Kama's daughters (and they were many) looked like they'd survived on the smell of a lettuce leaf (Weiner's phrase) for weeks. But such beautiful features. They took it into their heads to dress me up in a gold lame Rajasthani wedding dress. Gauche by European standards, I suppose, but magnificent in its own right. Trouble was, I already had on my overalls, and became readily hot and flustered. Not helped by Kama, who kept referring to Weiner, grinning obscenely and suggesting that the dress was for sale. I felt a bit like meat at an auction. Fortunately, Weiner diplomatically declined.

Kama then brought a young puppeteer to perform for us. She was a 'woman manipulator', Kama said; apparently a bit of an oddity in the village, "Because her husband is no good," confides Kama; "Too much arak." So this extremely young (for a wife) woman twirls her homemade puppet through a dervish-type dance, accompanying herself with some sort of reed in her mouth and bells on her wrist. The street puppets here all seem to perform fairly stock functions: they fight, dance, or perform simple tricks.

Before lunch, we went on a tour of the village. I've never seen so many craftspeople gathered in one place, let alone so close to an urban centre the size of Dehli. In fact, I've never seen such craftspeople period. Not from a true folk tradition, anyway. There were dollmakers and puppetmakers, potmakers and ornamental-clayworkers, metalworkers. It was like discovering the cornucopia of every Indian trinket you've ever come across. At every house we visited, little stools were brought out and a range of goods displayed for our inspection.

Weiner says they are most likely country drop-outs who've come to the city to feed off the tourist trade. Not the genuine article, so to speak. But they looked pretty genuine to me. (What's 'genuine' anyway?) I wasn't sure whether we were supposed to buy or not. Everybody, it seemed, was either Kama's friend or a member of his family. But at the end of each viewing he asked us if there was anything we liked, and said it would be brought to the house later.

"I don't like dealing with money in this way," he protested, "It is not the purpose of your visit. But these people, they make the living, you know."

Nevertheless, much as Kama tried to identify himself with us, Weiner insisted on asking how much all the time. I eventually settled on some little puppets for Brook's kids, because I liked them as much as to compensate for Weiner's obstreperous tourism. Meanwhile Weiner chose a grotesque mask with skulls hanging from it, and offended Kama further by insisting on possessing it there and then.

Then we got to the artists themselves. A girl contortionist balanced a full glass of water on her head whilst threading her body through the most snake-like postures. Bhopa's son mimicked the same suggestive dance I had from his father yesterday, with comic accuracy. An old woman performed a balancing act in her front yard with her daughter (granddaughter?), on a board across a rolling block. Reminded me of Mao's maxim: Women hold up half the sky.

These, however, all proved to be a warm-up for the main event, as we were mysteriously led into a high-walled compound which looked like a former mission. Chairs miraculously appeared from nowhere and an entire show unfolded before our very eyes. A young man broke rock slabs with his forearm. A sword swallower flipped the third blade as he slipped it down his gullet, 'to show that he was the full quid', as Weiner puts it.

Then came a man accompanied by an army of monkeys, who performed a multifocal tour de force of acrobatics which ended in an aerial bridge stretching from one arm to the other in a huge, primate arch, across which one of their number after another scampered in rapid succession. "It's Hanuman's bridge to Ceylon," said Weiner, "In the Ramayana." And Kama beamed. For once Weiner had said the right thing.

81

These were followed by a fire-eater who juggled flaming torches, about which a team of acrobat dwarves leapt and somersaulted. The fire-eater then fired flaming arrows from a mega-bow, which the dwarves also vaulted around, caught with their teeth and performed any number of other death defying feats.

The final act of the show strode into the space wearing a flowing cape, brahmanical thread, and not much else, announcing himself as "Mahadeva, of Maharastra!" His first trick was to remove the thread, revealing it to be a snake; which was a pretty impressive start as far as I was concerned. But "probably stoned" was Weiner's predictable scepticism. Reckoned Mahadeva was too dark to be from Maharastra. "I'd say he was blacker than an abo's armpit, if it wasn't such a disgustingly racist comment." Which it was. Although I couldn't help smiling.

Meanwhile, Mahadeva was balancing a set of five lethal-looking blades bound together by a knot of cloth on a pole some ten feet above his head. Next instant, in one movement he whisked the pole away, turned and threw himself face down such that the blades pinned his lower quarters, narrowly missing his genitals and rather pert posterior.

Next minute he was up, flamboyantly unravelling the instrument of his near-deflowering in mid-air to unleash five healthy machetes, which he was instantly juggling. Other implements of death were thrown in from the sides, until he had aerial some ten or twenty axes, cleavers, knives, swords - he even had the giant bow twirling in there somewhere. And caught them all, one by one. "Haircut, anyone?" said Weiner, aside.

Then Mahadeva's four sturdy assistants were summoned, while the principal limbered up. Obviously a big number, this one. He pulled his hair for us to see. "Strong hair!" he said beefily. (Even though he was in fact quite a thin, wiry man.) And the assembly echoed, "Strong hair," in case we hadn't heard. I was loving this, but at the same time it was starting to take on the proportions of an old silent movie. What with Weiner and his asides.

Mahadeva rubbed what looked like ash into his greasy, gangly locks and instructed each assistant to grip a generous handful. Holding them by their belts, he began to spin around and around until their feet lifted from the ground. As he span faster, their bodies lifted away from his. Eventually, he released their belts, so that they were all whirling around his head, secured only by their grip on his own hair (I could understand the need for the ash now!), like a human helicopter. I'd never seen anything like it. Twenty limbs and five heads spinning in the one human agglomerate. Our own attempts back home to revitalise dance with performer-centred, community-based praxis pale by comparison. This was so grass-roots. At one point Mahadeva had them forming a ruff-like wave around his neck, a living carousel!

Suddenly, the aides were released. As one they all leapt backwards, like a film in reverse, simultaneously landing on their feet. Each grabbed one of the original blades and threw them in to the still-twirling Mahadeva. He caught them one by one and threw them back out. Somehow a fifth was added and before you knew it, the five of them were juggling five blades through Mahadeva, who continued dervishing in the centre. It was mesmeric. Even as I resummon the image, I can't figure out how he did it. The man seemed like a constant fountain of blades, forever spinning and repelling all comers.

The next instant, we were back into living technicolour, as Weiner danced into the middle of this sea of spinning knives. He had donned his mask of skulls and was hippy-high-legging right out of Woodstock around the twirling Mahadeva. Mountain Man! Clapping under each leg.

The first Mahadeva was aware of it was when the knives stopped coming. The assistants were simply uncertain. Didn't want to hit the Westerner. As Mahadeva slowed, he tried for a while to join in with the yee-ha-ing Weiner, but it soon became clear that Weiner was dancing alone. The smiles dropped from faces all round. Everyone was looking at Weiner's feet. Being a Maharastran,

Mahadeva was of course a Muslim. It is an insult to bare the soles of your feet to a Muslim.

I couldn't be sure that was what destroyed the atmosphere so utterly. It could simply have been Weiner's obvious disrespect for the event. But Mahadeva moved away. People started packing up props. It was horrible. One minute we had all been part of a mountainous, unified event. The next, it was dissipating, falling away into its component parts. Kama's face was ashen; whether with rage or shame I couldn't tell.

Back at Kama's house, the meal was indeed truly delicious; although I had difficulty bringing myself to eat much. Not so Weiner. He was wolfing it down. I should have guessed then this was a man with the munchies.

During the meal, Kama seemed to regain some of his self-esteem teaching us to say, in Hindi, "We are all one big family." But when it came time to settle up, Weiner again embarrassed us all by insisting on haggling. In front of Kama's family and neighbours.

I bought the "woman manipulator's" puppet at a good price (for her), as well as my presents for Brook's kids. When we parted at the bus stop, Kama asked me to send him a transistor when I got home. As in, radio.

I was livid with Weiner. Argued with him all the way back to town. He said he had been stoned, but I said that was no excuse. He should at least have enough respect to acknowledge cultural difference, if not indeed show a little intercultural sensitivity. He'd been in India too long for that one, he claimed. He wasn't an Indian, so why should he try to pretend to be one. But haggling was fine because they did it. These people have become too accustomed to anthropological imperialism, apparently. We "Poms", it seems, don't know we are born. We feel so guilty about lording it over the colonies all those years (he speaks of it as a past state), we can't see beyond our own self-effacing I'm-sorry-we-ripped-you-off noses.

I am, I gather, culturally bound, ethnocentric. Kama was making "big bucks and big notes" out of our visit, I am to understand now, and as such was exploiting us no less than any multinational corporation.

I did attempt to point out to my informant that there was just the mildest difference between the global significance of Kama's appropriation of the middleman role and a transnational company's pantheonic command of national economies, but Weiner wasn't listening. Third World poverty was a guilt construction of unwilling beneficiaries of capitalism like myself. While I am busy sentimentalising my pity for an imagined oppressed global class, the Tribe of Nations called Europe is busy trying to dismantle the national boundaries they constructed one hundred years ago in order to convince themselves they were real countries now, because the capitalists they were trying to keep in/out have outgrown them.

"You think of yourselves as important," he railed, "I come from a country whose original culture goes back a minimum of 53,000 years. More like 200,000. It took the combined efforts of Europe and, particularly, Britain a mere 200 to 'civilise' that almost out of existence. The locals've got wise to it now, thank Christ; but yous bastards still don't understand that the world isn't necessarily the way your few miserable square kilometres sees it."

The long and the short of it is, I don't know how I'll be able to look Kama in the face. I can't get the images out of my mind, both in the mission compound and again in his home, when Weiner laughed at Kama for suggesting he buy the Rajasthani wedding dress for me. Like someone had thrown in a thunderclap and it had stuck.

*

4 November.

Awoken by my muezzin again this morning. It's like being in a progressive barn dance in reverse, this place: one step forwards and two steps back. And somewhere along the way, we all change partners.

I'd been dreaming about Dad again. This time he'd gone into the house to rescue Mum, but came running out with his hair on fire. Kamadeva is there trying to put it out, but he has no water. "Where is the water?" he keeps saying, "Where is the water?"

In confusion, he grabs Brook's skirt and tears it off her. Wraps it around my father's blackening cranium like a turban. But I can see Brook has no underwear, so I tactfully stand in front of her so that the firemen can't see. "It's okay, Rhea," she says, "I'm married." But I can tell by the sound of her voice that she is mortified.

Meanwhile, as fast as Kamadeva swaddles my father's head, Dad unravels it. He staggers towards me, blubbing "Look what they've done to my head, Rhea! Look what they've done." And sure enough, he's had plastic surgery, and his cranial dome is a petrified torrent of dermal weals.

Suddenly, everyone has deserted us, and I don't know why. I turn around, and they have all formed a crowd around Mahadeva, who has arrived on a peacock juggling his manifold implements of death. He rides through the crowd and juggles them over my father's bared pate. Kama is grinning and nodding, both giving approbation and seeking it. As in: This will do the trick, will it? But I'm not sure. Of course it's a magic ritual, but one of the axes might still fall and split my father's skull.

The arrow which then pierces my father's skull from one temple to the other, however, does not come from Mahadeva. I look to the source of the archer, but see only Weiner sitting with his back to us. It is a game we have been playing. I creep up behind him and playfully cover his eyes with my hands. But Weiner isn't playing anymore. I feel instant heat glow from beneath, and snatch my hands away. Weiner turns, and his brilliant, blue eyes have been replaced by two smouldering hollows. He opens his mouth, and from the pit of his stomach, it seems, a huge lick of fire leaps out.

He turns away. He wasn't meaning to scorch me. He is being sick. Vomiting fire. All over my parent's home. Which is suddenly in its terraced row before him like a scaled-down model. I try to yell at him stop, my parents are inside having Sunday lunch. But my diaphragm flaps on emptiness. Nothing will come from my larynx. And when it does, it is this thin, reedy voice, flying in from the distance, as if to a freeze-frame in a video clip. Out of the cosmos comes my voice, to fill my throat with full song. And I wake with a start, the sound of my voice still ringing in the room in the hotel in which I am staying, ringing out into the darkness beyond. I am my muezzin.

*

5 November.

Image: a young boy tends an emaciated cow by the side of the road. The cow lies in its own day-old waste, skin and bones. The boy listlessly thrusts a few strands of straw at its mouth, but the cow does not respond. It barely has the strength to involuntarily flick its ear into the cloud of worrisome flies that have become its aural cosmos. Above, a vulture circles, waiting for the inevitable death. And another New Dehli urban peasant is about to lose his livelihood.

Higher still, however, the eagles have found a column of rising air. They spiral lazily from one level to the next, forming this giant kite of cosmic grace in the sky, there to receive the souls of those corporeal hosts who will expire that day.

*

Nat dispelled any illusions I might have had about India as a Third World Country today. I'd always imagined a nation dependent on foreign aid, rich in tradition but devoid of the technological and cultural wherewithal to pull itself out from the bottom of the global economic dung heap. According to Nataraj, however, thirty five years of Nehru-styled socialism have made India self-sufficient in all of its basic produce. There is actually a surplus of rice, which is distributed to the poor for free. The country has its own car (the Ambassador), it's own motor scooters (the Bajaj), it's own motor bike (the Enfield) and it's own bicycle (the Hero, would you believe?). It manufactures its own drugs for a highly sophisticated, if thinly spread, Western-style health system; again, free to the poor. (Mind you, what counts as poor here is difficult to say. How poor do you have to be?)

I remember phenomena like the transistor-radio-for-sterilisation campaigns from the sixties, but Nat says these were as much a product of the Western press as instruments of government policy. He also said the notion of India as a country was mythological. India has only ever been the Hindu religion, he says, and that changes from town to town, village to village. It has no unifying core; only central ideas. It's the conquerors and colonists who have imprinted the stamp of national unity on the place. The Moghuls with their spires, domes and Islam, the English with their Victorian architecture, capitalism and Christianity. It is only to them that India is one place, one culture.

"Even after Ghandi united the country, Hindus fought Muslims, Muslims fought Hindus, Sikhs fight for the Golden Palace and the Tamils seem to fight everybody."

The Tamils are from the south, around Madras and Sri Lanka. Nat says I should be in town on the day they commemorate Indira's assassination. There's not a cab to be found, because all of the taxi-drivers are Sikhs, and Dehli is still convinced it was the Sikhs who killed her. I asked him what he thought, and he replied nonchalantly, "Did the CIA kill Allende?" As in: Is the Pope a Catholic?

He says there is no such thing as tradition in India anymore. "Culture is up for grabs," he says. Nevertheless, he recommended a festival of Indian folk performers which the Academy is hosting this week. "We do it to maintain our *own* sense of our culture," Nataraj explains with almost mischievous delight. "Although yes," he admits, but still with high mirth, "We do have a little more to maintain than you might in London." I told him I wasn't from London. I like Nat.

Kama, however, couldn't look at me today. The rest of the company were friendly, but I felt they were embarrassed by my presence. On the ground, then, I think I may have outworn my welcome with Parvati.

*

LOK UTSAV

- Kanjar Dancers from Rajasthan - like an earthbound fireworks display of swirling skirts. Such energy, and a startling array of bold colours. My puppet! At one point their drummer came on, making the same lewd, sexual thrusts towards them as Bhopa at Parvati. And the women responded, not coquettishly but sexually, rhythmically. Dancer and drummer engaged in individual ragas of dance and percussion. I found it very arousing.

- Chirkulan dancer - glides around the performance space at speed balancing what looks like a 4-tiered brass cake stand on her head bearing 30 burning lamps. The light of the world? A mountain of light. Loading and unloading them must be a feat in itself, let alone carrying the weight. Women would've made the world like this, loading and unloading lamps, each new light revealing a new face. Not some male god with his golden egg, darknesses and refulgent gazes!

- One Kathakali dance is performed by pre-pubescent virgins entirely behind a curtain so that no-one can see it! We just know that they're executing the dance, presumably perfectly. Now who's that for?

- An old woman from Gujarat sings Kutch folk songs wearing the costume of a young girl, emphasising her (aging) breasts and hips. So odd against the wrinkled skin and missing teeth, she vivaciously fluttering her eyelids and tilting her head - she was obviously singing sexually suggestive songs about her husband! An old man who manifests not the slightest glimmer of sexuality throughout; just the same, bland, egg-headed concentration on the dholak on which he accompanies his wife throughout.

- And who should appear as the climax of the evening but . . . Mahadeva, of Maharastra! The performers we saw at the colony turn out to be his troupe, specky cossies and the lot: the fire-eaters, the dwarves, the monkeys. Mahadeva did a new act, on top of juggling his endless axes, bows and knives; wearing a fine, pleated and waisted skirt, he started dancing a sort-of dervish; just kept spinning around and around; unravelled part of the skirt to reveal a piece of cloth into which, as he spun, he made various animals - a peacock, an eagle, a brahmin bull, a rat. Then his aides started to throw in the axes and knives again, and he started to juggle those at the same time as making his cloth origami. With the aides juggling over his head at the same time the whole scene was one of this spinning manufacturing of woven life with a constant heaven of weapons seemingly suspended overhead. I can't describe it - he was astounding. Hit of the show. They must've been brought up especially for it. All the more reason why Weiner's behaviour would've embarrassed Kama. We had been privileged with a personal preview.

*

6 November.

• Humayun's Tomb - built on an original structure begun by a previous ruler: how does it come about that sometimes conquerors destroy preceding iconography and yet at others build within or upon it? What determines that cultural decision?

• Raj Ghat - inscribed on the gate to Ghandi's tomb:

> *"Recall the face of the poorest and most helpless man who you may have seen and ask yourself if the step you contemplate is going to be of any use to him, will he gain anything by it? Will it restore him to a control over his own life and destiny? In other words, will it lead to swaraj or self-rule for the hungry and also spiritually starved millions of our countrymen? Then you will find your doubts and yourself melting away."*

I found this profoundly moving. Weiner saw it as a sop to ideological mobilisation, weakening the possibility of political action by sentimentalising and individualising it. I told him he was fucked. He wanted to know why I was crying. Once I told him, he wanted to have my emotion. Trouble is, I gave it to him. Why do we keep doing this? Although he's a mercurial case, Weiner. He was knocking on my door this morning before I'd even had time to drink my bed tea. Very sheepish. Full of apology and contrition. Yes, he knew it was his fault. Yes, he was aware that he had tried to 'take the argument off' me, 'rationally appropriate it'. It was a male and patriarchal trait, but he didn't know what to do about it. Not that he was apologising, he took full responsibility etc.

And I believed him, unfortunately. We actually sat down and had the first reasonable conversation I think I've ever had with a man on the subject. At least he wasn't playing games, as in playing contrite, playing the surrender of power, playing the born-again passive. He was the one enunciating his culpability, but with a straightforward acceptance of responsibility. Refused to accept blame, which I think I respect. We reject the guilt trip, after all. But when I tried to raise the issue of the foot-pointing with him - part of me still suspected he did it on purpose - I could tell straight away that it had been working within him. He was genuinely upset, in retrospect. And there was the Sorry Little Boy. Always too late, boys! Always too late! But I'm having tea with him tonight. Is this out of sympathy, because his best friend's off chasing the perfect relationship? (Oh give yourself a break, Rhea.)

*

8 November.

Well, I seem to have discovered sex again. Although it was never quite like this. We haven't been out of bed for two days. The only reason I'm here now is because Weiner's taken a break to collect

91

some things. Although I must confess (I must stop confessing)(and musting) that I'm glad of a bit of space to myself. This is all rather sudden.

We have discovered we have something in common. Dance. Although Weiner actually *did* the deadlies, as in danced. Was a dancer. In, believe it or not, Australia's only Dance-in-Education company. (Down in Tasmania, of all places. No wonder no-one's ever heard of it!) He's also done some work with tribal aborigines. They all come down to some sort of Aboriginal dance centre in Sydney, and Weiner worked on an exchange there. Sounds really interesting. The idea of working with people for whom ritual and dance are still actually integral to daily life, as in spirituality: living history.

We've also done the feminist bit. I was afraid to begin with it would be one of those I've-always-wanted-to-understand-will-you-help-me trips, but he turned out to be a seasoned 'pro-feminist male'. (I didn't even have to point out that a man can't actually be a feminist!) He had a relationship for a while with an aboriginal woman in Tasmania who left him to join a radicalesbian collective. Sounds like they gave him a hard time. That and trying to survive as the only non-gay male in a dance company. He kept talking about 'empowering' the women, which rang alarm bells for me - a bit mea culpa We-can't-give-it-away Power-at-bargain-prices. But he's the first male I've ever met who's the one telling *me* that all men are potential rapists. He's a bit hung up on personal pronoun defenses ("It's a bit pedantic, don't you think? Trivialises the power of the ideology") and direct action ("I'm not easily convinced that the personal is political."), but we got over it for the most part. When I asked him what he was doing in India if he was so committed to social action, his answer was asceticism. And redistributing his hard-earned savings where they could actually be of use. Now if that's not personal direct action . . . (didn't really buy that bit.) He also lived on his own block of land for a while; selectively logged it, built his own log cabin with the help only of his redoubtable combi, organically farmed all of his own vegetables, even recycled his own waste - great stuff! Although I can't quite work out who was collectively benefiting from that little piece of direct action. (India, I guess. He's lived here off the sale of his land ever since!)

I've found myself talking about my mother for the first time since the funeral. I was trying to explain why I've been having these panic attacks. Admitted, as much to myself as to Weiner, that I might have been going mad for a while there. And it was because, I think, I'm starting to understand, at a fundamental level, what it is to have never really liked her, or known her, and she has already gone. It's not as simple as guilt. It's always been so accepted that I'm like my Dad. My relationship with Mum, or lack of it, has never mattered. She was always the one who pushed me; that was all. But part of me was waiting for the chance, I think, to get to know her. To get to know that part of her in me. And now it's too late.

So I cried. I cried lots. But at least it was with someone this time. Someone who didn't try to shut me up, thank god. He also pointed out that my father seems to have done his fair share of pulling on the old heart strings. I told him about my phone call last week. "And I suppose he used to bounce you up and down on his knee?" said Weiner. I found the suggestion of a sexual connotation to my relationship with my father rather confronting. But understandably so. It's naive of me never to have seen myself in such terms. Dad must have had as much a say in making me 'his', after all. Passively active as it were.

As for Weiner, he's very sweet. And I don't mean that matronisingly. I expected him to be so cool and adept sexually. Whereas in reality we ended up in bed more by default. We'd had such a long night of talking and confessions, when we came to part he went to give me one of those we're-in-the-profession-together community artsworker type of hug. It was so clumsy and he so surprisingly vulnerable for the intellectual sceptic he presents most of the time. We just sort of didn't let go. We kissed a bit and he stayed a bit, then stayed a lot. And we made love beautifully; but the second time.

*

93

9 November.

There's something deeply and darkly magical about Weiner. One minute he's madly sending up the "poms", as he calls us, and the next minute he's quoting poetry to me as we make love. He's the only man I've ever met who can tell me I am as beautiful as the moon, and I simply believe him. It's like, I suddenly can't believe myself. And yet I do. I can accept that I am as he sees me. It's rather wonderful, in an unabashed, innocent sort of way.

Ralph Nestor Wiseman called today. We didn't know who it was at first. Weiner and I were making love - in full flight! I was just slipping into that semi-conscious state where my mind slides down to my centre somewhere and intense images rise up to meet it in hot waves. Then there is this knocking on the door which comes from so far away. And I'm just reaching my orgasm. And it's sort of an oh yes, yes, yes but no, no NO! SOMEONE'S AT THE DOOR.

Now I'm not terribly loud when I cum (not that I know of, anyway), but Weiner is. And I mean LOUD. And he always comes when I come. So I'm saying No, no, there's someone at the door, trying to pull myself back to consciousness, and Weiner is bellowing "Wha-wha- What?" like a bull on – whatever bull's get off on. Suddenly he opens his eyes too, and there he is, thundering back from wherever he goes to, scrambling mentally to pull together the bits and pieces of cognition that serve as his conscious apprehension of reality. Hi guys! It's *now* time! "What is it?" he says, gripping me in a kind of crazed panic, still coming. (Of course I'd already lost mine, bugger it.)

We could have been in one of those Carry On movies. The next minute we are hopping around with one leg in our jeans, an arm through a blouse etc., frantically trying to get dressed because it's our wife/lover/husband/best friend at the door. And to begin with Weiner genuinely thinks it is Godfrey.

"Pretend we're not here," he says, sniggering and hiding (unnecessarily) under the covers.

Godfrey is expected any minute crowned with failure, because he's off mooning after the same woman he was after before. She is apparently having an affair with a local lad, and Godfrey is hanging around desperately hoping he can "be there for her" when the affair (which he naturally thinks is doomed by its very cross-culturality) ends, to "pick up the pieces" - her, presumably, amongst them. The Valiant Knight, the Faithful Knight, the Devoted Knight, the Knight of Perseverance. Whereas, of course, Weiner is expecting the Defeated Knight, the Wounded Knight, the Crestfallen Knight Spurned in Love. "Anyone called Cordelia is bound to give him the jack. I love you according to my bond etcetera."

But this man isn't Godfrey. "Yes, he's bunging on an accent," says Weiner, peeping out from under the sheets. "But Godfrey doesn't know my surname, does he?" We are speaking in hoarse stage whispers. Launcelot and Guinivere caught in the act.

"Miss Barnett! Miss Barnett! Rhea! I know you're in there. I can hear you!" comes the stiff, Arthurian voice. And then I recognise him. "It's the Englishman," I say. "You mean there's only one?" Weiner comes back. "Thank God! I'll nip back and tell the natives it was all a mistake. Must have been someone else, etc. Sorry? Genocide? What?" And we're sniggering under the sheets again. But it's obvious he's not going to go away. And anyway, he might still be in trouble. So I finish dressing and answer the door. I'm still smiling, and trying not to, as two realities pull at each other, with me in the middle: Weiner, lovemaking, laughter and Godfrey's sad self-fulfilling prophecy of a life, and the drawn, spent, hassled disarray of dispossessed colonialism I see before me.

His story had continued in the same someone-opened-the-trap-door-on-my-life vein it was in when we left him in the lobby of the Janpath. The British embassy won't issue him another passport until he can prove in some way who he is, or at least that he's entered the country. Apparently they've had trouble in the past with dope freaks who sell their passports for a supply, then apply to be repatriated. So Wiseman goes to Immigration for some proof of entry, and they won't give it to him unless he can prove who he is. (Which, I gather, normally means a bribe. Which he can't offer because he has no money.) So he goes to Air India to see if he can get his ticket re-issued and a record of his inbound flight. But they want proof of identity too. He's spent the past fortnight trundling (literally, on foot) from one door to the next, trying to get some action.

He wanted me to accompany him to the Embassy, to identify him as at least the man who got off the plane, or had been with our inbound flight in some way. He reminded me of his role in rescuing our baggage, and in "garnering that buswaller into action". And it was true. He had. Nevertheless, I didn't want to go there and then. I asked if we could make a time to go tomorrow. Then came the obvious. "The trouble is, I'm a bit short of cash. I know it's a lot to ask, but if you have anything you can spare . . . " He must know we all do this on a shoestring. But then, I felt sorry for him, because he did appear to be genuinely in trouble. And we should all help each other, shouldn't we? So there I was, pulled between compassion and anger, when Weiner appears at the door behind me. "Don't youse reckon you're a bit old for this kind of caper," he said in his best 'Strine accent. I turned and looked, and he didn't have a stitch on! Poor old Ralph was visibly taken aback. "Er - I'm sorry," he mumbled. "Er, I didn't realise you had - company." Couldn't take his eyes of Weiner's handsome genitalia. More out of embarrassment than sexual preference, I suspect.

"How did yous find out the lady's name?" Weiner continued.

I couldn't catch his drift at first. Wiseman fumbled with a handful of attempts at forming words, but nothing came out. "How did yous find out her name?" Weiner repeated. And Wiseman had no answer.

"Perhaps I'll come back at some other time," the Englishman suggested weakly. I must admit that he didn't look as though he'd been starving. Stressed, yes. Starving, no. But I was still trying to help. Willing to believe. "Yes," I said uncertainly, "That would be fine." But Wiseman looked at Weiner, not me, before he turned to go. And the look in his eyes was one of defeat and fear, not hope.

"I think our Ralph Nestor Wiseman has just found his bow of burning gold too hot to handle," said Weiner as he closed the door.

"But how did he know my name?" I asked. I couldn't help it.

"Backpack labelling. Ticket. Boarding pass. Went through your effects while you were asleep on the plane. Asked Godfrey - he was on the same flight, wasn't he? Who knows. He's probably been doing it like this for years. Would've been round half the plane by now, I reckon. Sorry to bother you but, you were there, you saw what I did for you."

I explained about the bomb scare and the baggage collection delay, but Weiner just dismissed that as a "lucky break" for Ralph Nestor. "Or else, who put in the phone call to Air India?" he said. Made me shudder. To travel half way around the world to meet an English con man. My first time! Assuming Weiner's right.

"But what if I'd agreed to go with him," I said.

"Probably would've decided to try the Air India office first, cos it's on the way or whatever. Maybe he has a mate there, maybe he would've tried to get your ticket off you to copy it, or your passport. Who knows? Did you actually see him on the plane?"

I had to admit that I hadn't.

"Now then, how would you like to sample my arrows of desire?" Weiner said. He had an erection again. He called me "Callie" as he came. It came from so far away, so deep within him, I thought he was thinking of someone else. But no, he said, it was just a name that came to him. He said that perhaps it was his name for me. I didn't understand fully, but he explained that Aboriginal people 'back home' (he always talks about 'back home' - I doubt he's been there for more than thirty seconds in the last ten years) always give you a name when you join their community. It isn't necessarily an Aboriginal one, or particularly meaningful. But it's their way of accepting you, and giving you a place in their midst - usually an honorary relationship with one of them, like second brother or third sister. But the name itself is never explained. "It just comes," said Weiner, "In a special way."

I told him I'd always wanted to be called Zoe at school, after the girl in Dr Who. My first role model. He laughed. "Not the one that screams Doctor! DOCTOR! all the time and is forever falling down crevices and the like," he said. No, I said. That was Sarah Jane. And he laughed. "Fair enough,"he said, "Zoe it is."

*

Had dinner with Godfrey tonight. The predictable has happened. His unrequited love has "run a banker", as Weiner put it (inexplicably), and hot footed it off to Varanasi. Weiner is suggesting that we all follow. So, time for a move, perhaps.

Weiner and I had endless Sarah Jane and Zoe jokes all night long, of course. But at one point he said "I wrote a poem once." "Just the one?" I said. I thought he was joking. But no, he produced this crumpled piece of paper, that looked like it had been unfolded and refolded so many times it wasn't funny. It wasn't very good, actually. A fairly self-consciously pro-feminist piece in which patriarchy is the sky fucking womenkind on the mountain top while the newborn suckle on the nipple of love below - I think he means the clitoris. Some reference to the linga and the yoni, which are the objects of Shaivite Hindu worship.

He wouldn't explain it. I showed him some of this in return. Said he quite liked my 'flow', although he told me that my 'eagles' are in fact a local breed called the Kite. No less a scavenger than the vulture or the crow, apparently. So much for romanticism. And he said my 'cosmic kite' of them should have been a cosmic phallus slowly rising to "fuck the hell out of heaven". A way with words, our Weiner. Fear boys with bugs. What was that from? A film, I think.

*

10 November.

Godfrey has gone to Varanasi. Weiner warned him he would only be 'chasing himself around a gum tree', but perfection it seems is too strong an imperative for our Godfrey. Weiner wants to go with him, but has asked me to go too. I've said I'll go as far as Agra. I don't know that I can handle women throwing themselves onto funeral pyres and wizened, ascetic corpses floating down the Ganges just yet.

It seems a shame to be leaving Dehli just now. Apart from the fact that I've just started to feel settled, there are Diwali Melas everywhere. (I think Mela means 'fair' or 'fete'.) In odd little pockets of green or sudden clearings amid the squalor, up spring strings of coloured lights, stalls pop up as if from a kid's book, performers and music mysteriously appear as if from the wings, a puppet show reveals itself from nowhere as if by magic, fireworks shoot heavenward. It's lovely.

Admittedly it looks knocked up overnight and amateurs-ville, but so what? Our concept of art and performance depends so much on the fixing of meaning, the attempt to create permanence out of the centre, all windowless walls behind us and focussing in on or ahead at a controlled simulacrum. We fill it with artificial light and make our own dolls houses on its stages and canvasses. Working so hard to project ourselves as there, handleable, containable, knowable. Whereas the Indians just throw it up, walk on into it, it happens, and then it's gone.

Weiner and I went to one tonight. Quite a big one, in a large park. Parvati had told me about it - some of them were there. Madhu and Seema were bobbing around the place with giant puppet heads on. Couldn't work out what they were supposed to be, apart from a man and a woman. Perhaps that was all. The Hindu equivalent to Mickey Mouse and Goofey.

There is something very impressive about a large puppet entering a relatively small space. Must've been what it was like when we were kids. All of these giant adults looming around. But that's not how we remember it. The giants are always internalised. They say at that age the world is just an extension of us, as far as we are concerned. But then we throw them back out later, like balls to hoped-for friends. These larger-than-life, personified metaphors for an inner life we cannot know, because it occurs before knowing is possible. Or as knowing is becoming possible.

*

11 November - Diwali.

• Taj Express. We travel 2nd Class in fear and trepidation (well, I do. Weiner's done all this before, of course), but it is fine. 36 fans (I counted them) hang from the ceiling, each in its own little wire cage. It's as if we are carrying our weather with us.

• breakfast is served up and down the carriage from an old, ex-British Rail style trolley; coffee or tea in those now-familiar little white mugs, and vegetable cutlets and bread in silver foil trays. Weiner has no compunctions about eating it. I taste some too. Still squeamish about 'roadside' food.

• as dawn breaks, so does the chatter in the carriage. As if we have all suddenly become human again after a night as stone.

• We stop at Mathura Junction, and the train is suddenly transformed into a market place - as if someone's thrown out the table cloth at an English picnic, and the food's already there. Except for those ubiquitous cows, who move implacably through whatever is going on, following their own ineluctable, enigmatic paths of predestination, driven by another force, organised by a separate intelligence, proof positive that the cosmological argument for God (i.e. a unitary organising intelligence)(or is that the teleological argument?) is untenable. Unless God has more than one mind, of course. (They can bend their brains around anything, these lads!) Speaking of which - Agra!

[It's odd, I expected to see the Taj Mahal immediately. Of course it's nowhere in sight, not even on the horizon. Although, once you get

100

here, there's not much by way of horizon either. But Weiner assures me that it is here, somewhere. Last time he looked, anyway.]

*

I think Weiner and I are going through the re-entry shakes - those shudders and buffets that come as you descend once more from the safe, self-sustaining, independent orbits of orderly social discourse into the passionate, earthbound ecosystem of emotional bonding. When all of those facets of your personality you normally quite happily project are turned over, and find themselves falling into holes in the other, while their equivalents are being turned up elsewhere in the same emotional landscape. Or of course two emotional landscapes. Because we are, after all, attempting to bring our respective worlds together, swing one over the other and see if it fits.

Like when we arrived, Weiner wants to stay at the cheapest hotel possible. It's one that's in his Lonely Planet book but not in my Fodors, so I am already walking onto his map, as it were. But it's not presented as 'the cheapest' to begin with. It comes at me as "Look, I know this really great place to stay". It isn't until we've battled our way through clamouring porters and passengers and the battery of unmetered autorickshaws that I discover what "great" means. It's then that Weiner says, presumably seeing my heart sink, "Not exactly the Ashok Yatri Niwas, but it is the cheapest in town." Ah. But, says Weiner, we don't have to decide now. We could look around. He seems very bright and chirpy about it, but there's a rock in there somewhere. Something he's holding back.

Anyway, I want to look at the Grand. Fine, says Weiner, cheerily. So back in a metered autorickshaw, battling away through the moving forests of people and bicycles and unmetered autorickshaws to a far more palatial establishment (by comparison), slightly out-of-town, quiet, with a presentable courtyard. I breath an inner sigh of relief and relax. We look around, and I Ooh-look and isn't-that-lovely, as I would with anybody I wanted to share the experience with. I'm not really trying to sway him or anything. And he's nodding and beaming and agreeing, but there's still that rock in there.

So eventually I say I like it. So do I want to stay here? he asks. Yes, I think so. But - ah - it's not the sort of place he can afford on his budget. Ah. So we are to be divided. No, just independent, reasonable human beings, negotiating a communication opportunity. Of course. Well, I agree, it's not in mine either, but if I'm going to be in Agra I'd like to do it in style. Ease myself into things, etc.. No, says Weiner, best to start out the way you intend to go on. I've tried that, I tell him. It didn't work. It gets easier, he says. Especially if there's two of you. So here I am walking back onto his map again. The offer of companionship is there, but only if we go in this direction.

So I go. I'm not that fussed. He's both done this before and been here before, and there is a very strong part of me that is really grateful to have his guidance and support at the moment. So we go and look at a place called the Tourist Bungalow, which is pretty dire but very cheap. And it has a small garden. So I say I could cope with this. But, says Weiner, it's a bit far away from everything. For just 5Rs more there's another place in his book which is closer to everything, but especially the Taj. So we arrive here, at the Tourist Rest House, and it's not exactly luxury living but it's 100% better than the first place we looked at. And it's obvious he's been here before. He shows me around, making enthusiastic conversation about the room, its aesthetics, its colours. And I like that. But he still comes back to "Not bad for just 5Rs more!". Like a dog that just won't let go of it. No, that's belittling. I like him. But as the giant in my emotional vista at the moment, he strides amongst the mountains he creates and then suddenly ducks down behind one. Pops up again later and says "Here I am." Or else disappears entirely. I go and open up the mountain I last saw him near and there he is, crouching inside. As if he wants to be found. And yet doesn't.

So another example, we'd barely put our packs down in our room (we are sharing rooms now)(separate beds but sharing rooms) and suddenly Weiner's all keen to be off sight-seeing. Oh good, I say. I want to see the sights anyway. But with Weiner it's all chest-up stuff. I don't get the impression he's relaxed about it. All shoulders and head-chipper. And then, 'on the way', he just wants to leave a message for 'Godders' at the very first place we looked at, 'just in case he turns up'. And of course I realise that he's told Godfrey that's where we'd/he'd probably stay. It's the man in his life he's been hiding. That's an occasion where I open up the mountain and they're both in there, crouching, heads down and sniggering together. "She'll never find us here!" "Godders and I always stay at the best!" he jokes - there's an entire history here - but why couldn't he have simply said so in the first place?

Anyway, this went on most of the day. We're charging round the Red Fort like we're on some kind of Thomas Cook's Agra-in-30-seconds Tour, and I say I want a drink. Just see if you can last another half an hour, suggests Weiner. What? Head spins round - what's this one? I wait a bit, spot a stall and make for it. Just a bit longer, says Weiner. What? I get impatient. I just want a drink. It's hot, dusty, and back home it would be snowing where I come from. I want a drink! Just a bit longer. What's the reason? I should take my cue from the Indians. They go as long as they can between drinks. That way the body sweats less and you really appreciate hydration when it comes. And thus out steps the ascetic, the self-sufficient post-hippy-era let's-learn-from-the-locals Weiner. Which is fine. I like it. Am interested in it. But I just wanted a drink.

Then I spot the Taj Mahal for the first time. And it's wonderful. So unexpected. Magnificently framed in a strong, chunky hewn-stone window in a palace section of the Fort, there it is rising out of the shimmering surface of a river (the Yamuna) like a cumulus cloud, a pearl balloon of moisture issued from the earth by its own hot breath. Or the radomes of Southern Tasmania, says Weiner wryly. Pardon?

Next minute we are into a wonderfully informed and ideologically correct conversation about an American intelligence base you look out over in the middle of a plateau you have (evidently) spent a day climbing and two days bushwalking to reach, and is apparently the only reason the Tasmanian government gave the South-West its heritage listing i.e. they want as few people as possible near Black's Bluff.

Which I find very interesting - I am personally highly sympathetic to the issue, and back at Hie Die we'd choreograph a piece around the story, if we heard it - but I'm here looking at the Taj Mahal for the first time. So that when he suggests we move on I say no, I just want to sit for a few moments and look. I'm not at all unpleasant about it. I don't feel unpleasant in the moment. Just needing to enjoy my experience for a little way, having journeyed off into Weiner's particular knot of ideological intensity for a while. And Weiner's fine-fine, but even as he sits impatience beams out of him - very much like a radome, I suspect! Until eventually I say, jokingly, "Would you like to move on, Weiner?", thinking perhaps that playfulness is the best way of dealing with this. But even then his response is defensive. "No, no. It's fine." Smile. When it's obviously not.

And even though we move on, we're not actually moving on to the Taj. And why? Eventually a tourist-guide type of spiel starts to emerge. The Taj is a colonial imposition upon the Indian cultural landscape, only exploited by the locals for its tourist potential. It is a sexist institution, built by Shah Jahan as a monument to a wife of 17 years who died in childbirth, after delivering him 14 children.

"He was going to build a black one for himself across the river," condemns an affronted, pro-feminist Weiner, "Now if that isn't sexist oppositional iconography, I don't know what is. Not to mention the decadent exploitation of the subjugated native labour force." The Taj evidently took 21 years and 20,000 people to complete. Which I truly do find very interesting, although I think Mrs Jahan deserved a monument after bearing 14 kids in this climate!

Anyway, so it went on. Weiner was visibly relieved when an autorickshaw driver told us there was a bomb scare at the Taj, so we couldn't go there. Did we want to visit his brother's marble factory instead? Weiner looked at me nodding equivocally as if to say; now that's an interesting idea - yes? no? maybe? I leaned forward to the driver and shouted, over the traffic noise around us, "That sounds terrific! But could we just go by the Taj? I've never seen a bomb scare before!" (It was a lie, but still...) "Oh, barricades, police," the driver gesticulated. "Yes," I replied, "It would be very interesting. Go via the Taj."

So we went. And of course there was no bomb scare. Not a vaguely terroristy-looking person in sight. Let alone a police officer. So in we went.

I could live in the Taj Mahal. Just stepping onto that cool, clipped marble with water all around you, and the drip-clarity of sound, like a permanent inspiration of fresh, clean, moon-pure air - the full moon in the stillest of nights and clearest of skies. So luminescent, even the stars fade.

Even Weiner has to admit that he's impressed. And tries to comment casually that he's never been here before, because it's always seemed so touristy. And just when I think he might have stepped out from behind another mountain, he plunges into another intellectual rave - this time about religion as a culturo-political response to an actual biological condition - get this - de-oxygenation. I found it hard to swallow this one, I must admit. The Hindu god Vishnu is the same colour as de-oxygenated blood, right? (Blue.) The hierarchy of the Christian church also wear the same colour - purple. (De-oxygenated blood serves here as bluey-purple, I guess.) Yoga reduces one's breathing to the bare minimum, just as meditation focuses the breath to empty the mind of all non-transcendent thought. The metaphorical aim of religious practice is thus to reduce life to its transcendent form: absence.

In physical terms, says Weiner, this is equivalent to the expiration of oxygen-dependence: death. death in life. Life in death. So in a way it is fitting that I find Mumtaz Mahal's *tomb* a source of ascetic *inspiration*, concludes Weiner.

105

Like it? I think it's a work of intellectual genius, quite frankly. I did suggest to him that he might have somewhat lost the passion and romanticism that formed the basis of my original response, but he just nodded and thought about that too.

The not-quite-debate now is where to eat for dinner. I want to go somewhere nice because it's Diwali, but Weiner is back in asceticism mode. I've offered to treat him to the Clark Shiraz Hotel, which sounds really nice from the guide. And Weiner is nodding and agreeable at the invitation - no sexist I-have-to-pay-for-the-meal or even contribute-my-share from this man. But he just has to nip out and see if 'Godders' has turned up. Ah - the other-man mountain again! So he's out checking the other hotel.

I like Weiner, but I wish he'd relax a little. Reminds me why I stopped having relationships with men. I mean, compared to Aidan, Weiner is a veritable powerhouse of emotional coherence and personal stability. Even so, he's still now-you-see-me-now-you-don't. I don't know whether I want to cope with that *and* with India. I come back to wishing Belinda were here. You never seem to get this mercurial agenda gymnastics between women. Until they're walking amongst men.

But then there is my mother, I suppose - that was like walking through an ongoing shower of arrows, each one bearing a prescription, each one pointing to a future. Life and personality, Rhea? Find your own way? Ho-ho - no way! And what's this - anger, Rhea? Time for tea!

*

• Diwali in Agra. There are cows everywhere, daubed with blue paint. They roam the deserted streets. Little altars are set up in every shop - just a candle or oil lamp before an icon or photo of Lakshmi (Goddess of Wealth) and the year's books. No messing about with the Hindus. What they want for the new year is prosperity, and the old year's accounts closed. And perhaps a little joy and good judgement - hence the icons of Ganesha too, in some cases. Draped with bright-orange garlands of marigolds. Most of Agra is at home. Family celebrations tonight. But I find a cycle rickshaw driver willing to take me to the Clark Shiraz.

He's worth any auto-rickshaw or cab driver, this man. Every sinew, joint and bone in his body works to haul us through the dust-thin, viscous gloaming. The fading light is pearly, almost moon-white. We could be riding across the top of a cloud, with nothing between us and the night sky.

Except that who should come roaring (buzzing?) by in an autorickshaw but Weiner. "Come in," he yelled from the cab, "You'll catch cold!" I told him I'd meet him there, and sat back in my comfortable, leather-padded seat. I like the cold. (Although I suppose it was probably old vinyl. Same as they used to have in my Dad's old 50s cars.)

We actually had a lovely meal. Best Murgh Makhani I've ever tasted. And as the fireworks climbed heavenward across the city (our restaurant was on the top floor), Weiner and I had a bit of a talk.

He initiated it, which I'm glad of. He opened by saying that he had felt a little tension between us during the day and confessed (finally) that he had been uptight about Godfrey (who still hasn't eventuated). I said I thought it was more than that, and introduced the 'cheap' and 'asceticism' agendas I felt I'd been dealing with throughout the day. He immediately tried to defend himself against my phrasing of them as 'agendas', but I went on to talk about him hiding them from me, and/or hiding from me behind them. He then admitted that it had been a long term problem for him, and actually started talking about himself for a change.

His mother died when he was very young - before he could remember - and he spent the greater part of his formative years with one stepmother after another, none of whom were particularly memorable. Not so much that they were nice, horrible or indifferent - he just never bonded with them. Their focus was always the father,

107

who seemed to clamber from one generic relationship to another. First he had to have a properly 'Australian' wife. When that didn't pan out (she found him too 'German'!), he went for an 'ethnic' wife, and so on.

Weiner says he always saw them as projections of his father's needs, not as human beings. So instead of getting to know them, he spent most of his childhood dancing from role to role, pose to pose, stage to stage, like a kid in the sand dunes trying to attract his dad's attention (this is his imagery, not mine). Which, evidently, wasn't easy at the best of times, being the middle of three kids.

So, I find I have a lot more in common with Weiner than I had imagined. Except that his father seems to be a composite of my father post-mum's death, and my mother during my childhood. He remembers hating his father so much during puberty that he managed to convince himself his Dad wasn't a war refugee at all, but a Nazi War Criminal who had secretly evaded detection in the post-war confusion. He even went as far as contacting the police, but put the phone down when they asked for his name!

"I don't think I liked myself very much at the time," he said dryly. Masters of understatement, these Australians. I reassured him that I went through exactly the same experience with my Mum at that age. Although I didn't call the police.

Anyway, Weiner says the move into real dance was, in retrospect, an attempt to establish himself as emotionally self-sufficient. But he's always known there was something missing at the centre that he's never been able to quite put his finger on. "Or my big toe, I suppose the analogy should be," he said. Dancer's joke. (Pointing.) He also says he used to weep profusely as a child. Now he cannot pass a tear. The escape to India was an attempt to find himself. Ten years later, he escapes to Australia occasionally. But he's never really gone back. As in, home.

It's funny, as I settle into the impermanence of travel I fear the same could happen to me. I no longer feel that I belong to Britain. Home is there, I know, but it's not mine. I feel very transient. As if I could end up anywhere. Even here. But I   sure can cry. No doubt of that.

I told Weiner what actually happened to me when I first arrived here. I started to get the shakes again even as I recounted it. I still don't know whether I'm fully together or not. But Weiner was great. That's why it's good to travel in pairs, he said. Someone else is going crazy at the same time! But he said I was very together. When we met, he hadn't realised quite how bad a time I'd had of it. "It's just India," he says. "It has that effect on you." He described a similar experience of his own, about two months after he arrived. He was in Kathmandu, and had been dabbling in a bit of smack. Anyway, he decided to get off it. Had the shakes, hallucinations, the works. And was sick into the bargain. Then one evening he was sitting on the roof of his guest house watching the sunset reflected in the Himalayas, and something in him just fell into place.

"I know it sounds corny," he said cornily, "But it really was like a coin falling into the slot right at my very centre. And when it happened, it was like my whole skull just opened and the universe flowed in, and I flowed out at the same time. It really didn't matter, you know? The air was so cool and crisp off the mountain, it came in right over the turgid smells of squalor around us. It was like, the sun and the moon had come together in my centre as one, the two contra-rotating axes of the earth, moon around the earth, earth around the sun - I could have taken my own head off and carried it beside me and it wouldn't have been any different, you know?"
He seemed so clear, the experience so breathtakingly ordinary yet transcendent, and then the final image is a stolen head. I told him as much, and he said that was stunning. Because, of course, patriarchy so depended on the appropriation of rationality.

It was like he'd metaphorised that for himself in that moment of understanding. And we then went on into a more intellectual (and more usual, for Weiner) rave about feminism, patriarchy, and the transcendentalising nature of rational appropriation - which seems to be a theme of his. I don't quite follow it, frankly.

I was still thinking about the stolen head. And watching the fireworks, which were lovely. And remembering the time I told Aidan I was leaving. And that I want it to be a permanent parting for us. We'd dribbled on for so many bloody years, I just couldn't bear it any longer. This way, that way, to and fro. The odd affair in between. We'd always said we'd be friends, and Aidan couldn't really understand why that had to change. And neither did I really. It just did. I wanted a final break. Anyway, he found it hard to take. Came all the way up from London to 'talk it through'. We went all night. Ended up at Scarborough, of all places. Sitting on the waterfront, watching first light gradually lift the night from the sky. I seemed to go headfirst right into it. With this miserable, woolly clump of a man beside me, his fire-red hair hanging limply over his bowed head in lank, forlorn locks. And me just burning to be away. Not from him. Just away. Now that I thought about it, it didn't seem anything like Weiner's experience in Kathmandu.

He showed me the needle marks back in the room here. He's suggesting we travel together for a while. Says he's come to like me very much in a short period of time, and that's unusual for him. (Although he's very carefully avoiding anything vaguely 'love' or 'commitment' sounding. Which I'm glad of, at this stage.)

He's suggesting trekking in Nepal. It is cooler than Northern India at this time of year, and he says I cannot miss the Himalayas. I absently ask him why, and he says, "Well, they're very big." It was a terrible joke. I just had to laugh. Then he did a "No seriously". If I haven't seen them, I'll never know how comforting they are. "Once you've seen them, it's like having a permanent big brother, forever just over your shoulder." Which I thought was rather nice. Although I did venture to comment that a Big Sister might be just as comforting. And he was embarrassed again, poor sausage. "They really do make you feel at home in the world," he said. Which I thought was very brave of him. To keep trying.

I do like him. And it would be nice to feel at home in the world. But I also mentioned that I was interested in seeing more dance, and he said that the South was also good for that. There's Kathakali in Kerala and Bharatnatyam in Madras.

Tomorrow,
however, we've decided to do a day trip to Fatepur Sikri. And right
now, Weiner is asleep. (Didn't even have to check again for
Godfrey!) And so should I be.

*

12 November.
. Fatepur Sikri (1570-86) - an entire, fortified sandstone city,
superbly designed, once one of the great centres of cosmopolitanism
in the world. Built over a 20 year period by Akbar as his new capital,
with a (what must then have been, I presume, tasteful) blend of
Hindu, Armenian, Buddhist and Islamic architectures - each distinct,
and yet imperceptibly joined in the middle(s). Akbar was illiterate!
But gathered intelligentsia from across the globe about him; thought
that while we all have different beliefs, we all drink the same water
and are of the same flesh. Had four wives, two Hindu, one Christian
and one Islam. His main emblem, the six-pointed star, represented
the six (then) religions - Islam, Christian, Hindu, Buddhist, Jain and
Jew.
          Ironically, it was the 'same water' he created for his
cosmopolitan city that led to its premature abandonment after only
16 years of inhabitation. The massive artificial lake he had made to
supply the city with water dried up! But isn't it interesting how, from
time to time, these centres of inter-cultural exchange and
understanding seem to coalesce from history for a (relative) moment
from the oppositional chaos around them? Vis. Xuanzong's city of
Xian during the Tang Dynasty in China, and the grand days of the
Silk Road. (First contact between China and India.)
                                                    Mind   you,
despite his urbanity, Akbar still had one mighty (and prickly) phallus
of a tower built in honour of his most favoured warrior - who? (Wait
for it...) His elephant! On which the noble muslim used to trample
thousands of unbending Hindus on regular military interludes
throughout this refined exercise in global unity.

- I've found a book, <u>Hindu Mythology</u> by W.J. Wilkins. Quaintly Victorian in its phraseology. This Ramayana legend simply must be rewritten.

*

Ramayana II - The Movie

Lakshmi leant back against the cushion of cloud that gathered constantly now about the peaks of Mt Kalesa. She stared impassively at her husband. He was still young. From a distance. Divine. Athletic. Rectitude itself with his proud, straight back. And still the boy in him, as he played discus down there with young Ganesha and Kartikeya, or tried to outrun an arrow from Arjuna's bow, Gandiva. Yet beneath his skin at nights, Lakshmi could see the hardening ravines of age. His once-bright eyes sometimes simply fell away into a chasm deep within him, where his once-true self floundered weakly from the daily effort to be there, in control. The Preserver. One of the Supreme Three.

She was tired of staunching the unchecked outflow of his self-denial. She was weary of denying herself in the process. She wanted, more than anything, to be free of him, or the obligation he represented. She had had such hopes once.

Lakshmi had given her all to Vishnu. Just as Uma had thrown herself into the flames for Siva, so Lakshmi had committed herself to mortality. Born of the earth, she of the sea sacrificed her purity on the alter of the demon, Ravana, in the hope that it might bring her consort face to face with the darker half. But not his. It was Siva the women wanted to reconcile his alienated inner self, in the hope that these three male counterparts might cease their games of power and restore the cosmic balance that was their actual bequest.

But all Vishnu was aware of after the event was that, as the mortal, Rama, he had won. And that, as cosmic victor, he had license to indulge his rampant masculinity all the more. Banished his wife in her mortal incarnation, for having given herself to Ravana. And in his next incarnation whooped it up with the shepherd boys, vying with the Judaist Christ for pastoral sublimity (and silliness). And brought war to the Hindus in dynastic proportions, all in the name of preserving what Siva destroyed. They were senseless, the pair of them. And Brahma, in

113

whom wisdom and knowledge were supposed to be paramount, did nothing but pass the cosmic buck. Ah, men . . .

It was time for an end to it. Time she and Parvarti and Saraswati resumed control. The boys had had their turn. And this time, she would do the job herself . . .

*

Weiner has read this. He said it was interesting - very 'raw'. There are, apparently, writers in Australia attempting this sort of 'mythic rewriting'. So there are in the UK, but I didn't bother to go into it. I haven't read them anyway.

*

• On the train - Agra to Jaipur - a cattle truck. I thought there must be some mistake at first, but no, there is no third class. This is what it's *really* like, says Weiner. The Taj Express is for the tourists. Dark, dingey wooden compartments with bench seats and luggage racks which double as beds. Not so hard on the bum once we get going. The couple opposite offer to share food with us. We decline, Weiner I think out of respect for their apparent class/caste origins, me simply out of fear. They look like newly weds. Cannot let go of each other. All smiles and fragments of cuddles.

        The man next to me is fastidious. Keeps brushing flecks of soot from his cheap, light blue suit. The soot flies in through the window in gusts. (Steam Lives in India. Now I know why first class is at the rear of the train!) He tries to shut the window but other passengers object. So he sits back down and continues obsessively brushing his trousers, until he eventually leaves. Where to, I've no idea. He won't get away from the soot, unless he can afford first class.

        Weiner and I have a thermos of tea, thankfully. It's going to be a five and a half hour trip.

• At each station, the song of the chai-wallers under the dim, steely platform (or lack-of-platform) lights. As we go, the song of the train - roar, rattle and whistle. Small hamlets and houses we pass with yellow-lit forecourt/verandahs, in which turbaned old men settle down on those impossibly square, low, wooden-slat beds that also seem to double as day-beds and, in some cases, entire mezzanines! They sling their last beetle nut of the day round and around their tongues. And spit long, red, reptilian jets into the dust. While along the trackside: fires, around which people bed down for the night wherever they can find a place, silhouettes slipping between gaps in the economy, sung by the stars. With the roll of the train, it takes on a dream-like passing.

• The mother sleeping against the bars on the open window, head along her arms such that it looks like the latter is coming out of the former, a human-fleshed elephant. Her husband nodding off - onto my shoulder! Keeps waking up every time her realises what he's doing, but eventually gives in. And it's comforting to let him sleep there, a fellow traveller. The newly-weds opposite, falling asleep across each other, so sacred, so tentative, mutually protective. All of us, in and out of dream, except me. Or only me.

Jaipur:-

• The Royal Gehtare - a haven slung between two hills on the edge of Jaipur, where Jai Singh I and his six wives rest, along with the children, 35 wives and 200 girlfriends of Jai Singh II - who built the giant, Colosseum-like astrological compasses at Jantar Mantar, in Dehli, and here in Jaipur. His star-gazers certainly seem to have kept the younger Singh busy. A sort of three-dimensional Woman's Weekly! Today, monkeys sleep as they sit, tucked into curves and crannies of ornate marble. One mother suckles her young drowsily in the midday heat. Peahens stroll leisurely about the gardens.

• Ambar Palace - tired, whiskering elephants amble up the long, cobbled access road to the palace walls, and I wonder how such a large animal comes to concede servitude to so small a creature as a human being. But we ride one anyway. They seem so sagely, elephants. Like whales - small, intelligent eyes, encumbered by large, unwieldy, defenceless bodies. Can't imagine them charging into battle.

• From the Hawa Mahal we see two women drying a length of deep magenta cotton. They stretch it out lengthways between them and pass it rhythmically to and fro, as if across the air. This would look beautiful onstage, especially in a modern dance piece, yet here it is just a domestic business beside the road, amidst the traffic emissions and dust, people passing. And when they have finished drying one length, it is systematically (again rhythmically) folded up and then - down on the pavement with the rest! Jai Singh's courtesans may have watched the very same practice from these very windows, each looking down upon the Siredeori Bazaar from her own shuttered (and locked) embrasure, waiting her turn to be summoned by Jai.

Udaipur:-

• City Palace - built by Maharana Udai Singh around 1600, and augmented by successive Singhs; the most celebrated seems to be a Maharana called Pratap. He covers the walls and ceilings in various exploits of battle and love. So it seems the Hindus are not homogenously the ongoing passive victims of successive conquerors.

These Maharanas were the Hindu equivalent of the Moguls - waging war against not only the oppressors from the North but also each other. This is War Lord country. At one stage they lost this Palace to Shah Jahan (1623-4). Indeed, it seems to have been from here that Jahan rode out to overthrow his father, Jehangir. And was himself overthrown 30 years later by his son, Aurangzeb - who pulled the same stunt, it seems; nipped off out of town for a while, raised an army in Maharana territory, rode back into Agra and slapped his Daddy in the Red Fort, where he spent his last days gazing longingly down the Yamuna at the tomb of his wife (the Taj). But it was the Hindus who put an end to Aurangzeb - and the Mogul reign to boot.

The Marathas produced a Rajput hero named Shivaji (of Sudra caste - not quite Brahmin, but he was allowed to be a hero anyway), who led battle after battle against Aurangzeb.

Aurangzeb is described here as a 'penny-pinching religious zealot'. He captured and blinded Shivaji's son, but the Hindu warrior eventually won out and the Marathas went on to rule for a number of generations.

Make a great epic film. Just the magnitude of it, on the sort of plains you can get around here. Dry, dusty mega-battles waged with elephants and horses and infantry by the thousand. I don't know whether it's because I've slipped the orbit of my own culture and am an observer of another, but somehow the pervasiveness of patriarchy, and society's endless permeability to it, from smallest of personal gestures right up to the broadest of political sweeps (like a battle), becomes so clear in its vastness and comprehensiveness. It's not political, it's cultural. It's self-glorification is woven and re-woven into every inch of presentable space inside this Palace - including the very structuring of the palace itself - it's architecture, its fortifications, its inveterate attempt at permanence. This is way of life: it facilitates power as much as power facilitates it. Economy is what happens along the way.

• Lake Palace - built in 1754 by Maharana Jagat Singh II on Jagina Island. Converted into a hotel in 1971. (A James Bond movie was made here? Weiner.) It's beautiful. Because it occupies the entire island, it looks as if its walls simply rise from the lake.

• Jag Mandir - the other island on Lake Pichola; buildings by Karan Singh, but the Island takes its name from Jagat Singh. These Singhs do seem to have been a bit happier with each other than the Moguls - less inclined to tear each other's bellies out to get to the throne. In public, anyway.

Did the English introduce tea to the Indians or vice versa? I mean its cultivation, I suppose. I'm so used to drinking tea from Ceylon or India that I've always assumed it was a native product. (Weiner says

117

we got it from them, as did the Chinese about a millennium before.)

• Squat toilets - I can't get used to them. Weiner fell about laughing when he walked in on me at the Rang Niwas, sitting on the squat toilet. (It was a porcelain, flushing version of the hole in the ground you usually get; slightly raised with foot-rests moulded into the rim. So I just sat on it, as if it were an ordinary toilet.)(As in, an English toilet, I suppose.)(I can't even say European. I already know India better than I know my own geographical and cultural region!)

• Puppetry - Rajasthan is the home of Indian puppetry; a 5,000 year old tradition. At the Lake Palace, we watch an androgynous clown puppet which reverses - one head is that of a woman and the other, a man. In the show, a smaller man approaches a taller woman and proposes marriage. She transforms herself into a man and homosexually rapes her would-be fiance. Then she turns back into a woman and cries, so that the smaller man forgives her and they marry anyway.

I find this a deeply disturbing metaphor, but potentially very rewarding. Although on the surface it seems to be saying that there's a man in every woman, the act of sex indicates that it's the woman in every man, the woman as male projection. I don't think this is a misogynistic piece of theatre so much as homophobic and homosexual (male).

What's profound is that it's also (presented in this extremely upper crust tourist context as) folk culture. I wonder whether its dalliance with sexual libertarianism, then, is simply what the performers think we might like. Are like?

• Pathvary - Goddess of the road and protector of passers by. So the Pathvary is a small obelisk at the entrance to a village to show the path to those who have lost their way; provides solace to pilgrims and blessings for a successful journey. Good title for a novel about a central character who does the same, in a 'life's journey' sense: "The Pathvary"

• Kavad - miniature portable temple portraying various incarnations of Vishnu behind little doors - Rama, Krishna, etc..

118

Kavida-Bhats carry them from village to village and open one door after another, dancing and singing a story about each incarnation they reveal.

*

16 November - The Lake Palace

I have annointed my body with oils and unguents and bathed in scents and soothing salts. I have eased the turmoil of India out of my body with slow and languorous rituals. I have undressed meticulously and sat, or lain, naked, or wrapped in the fresh, clean towelling bathrobe provided, about the various luxurious planes, angles and folds of this truly fabulous hotel room. Then I have gently slipped into its capacious bath and watched, amid curlicues of steam, my womb release its monthly bed of life, and listened to the sporadic, hollow clopping of wet cloth on concrete across Lake Pichola as women on its shores beat the soilings of day and night out of their families' attire.

For I thought I was going to have a child. And now I know I am not. For I saw her, or him, this morning - red, membranous and already bruised, against white porcelain as I commenced my daily ablutions.

I have never missed a period before. But I miss not missing this one. I never thought I would want to have a child, but somehow Weiner has worked within me in a way that has brought 'child' to me. And I want it. I want him. I suppose the two are connected.

Weiner does not know. Weiner is not here. His ascetic, socialist principles will not allow him to waste such surplus as he might have on an industry that deepens the class division brought about by the exploitation of labour by feeding on the cultural colonialism and false consciousness of the tourist, or indeed the capitalist.

I put it to him that he simply wouldn't allow himself a little luxury, but he said that luxury was only a state of mind. Well, it's a state of mind he's

119

certainly not sharing with me right now.

I offered to treat him, but he prefers to wander the backstreets of Udaipur absorbing emanations of low life, by osmosis presumably. And I have left him to it. While I would dearly wish him to be here, for his body to share what my body both loses and gains, I am also happy to have this to myself. Just for one day, it will do me for a lifetime. Literally.

*

17 November - The Lake Palace (just before dawn)
Weiner came. Putted across on the motorised punt that is our only link with the shore. As he arrived, the colourful female giant who stands shoulders deep in the lake before the landing smiled and flourished water in welcome. And I smiled too as I saw him step off the boat, bolstered enough by the confirmation of events to say I knew he'd come, instead of just I'd hoped.

I treated him to tea in the garden restaurant (I've decided to put the whole stay on bankcard – the one that was to be only 'Break in case of emergency'!), and then we made love into the passing of our (my) child. Weiner brought the most amazing dope. Normally dope just makes me friendly and, after a while, drowsy, but this stuff! We seemed to last forever, in almost blissful stillness. Just the water lapping at the walls of the hotel below our window. And the cool, dust-free cleanliness of air conditioning and starch-white sheets. Weiner became so taut and sinewy to touch, but giving. His hair swayed gently to and fro in the moonlight. His face in shadow.

But
as I looked deeper into him, his forehead and nose began to merge, his brow grew and divided into two distinct mounds that rose through his forehead. Where proboscis and brow joined, lines of age deepened and replicated. The whole thrust of nose-brow streamed out into the space it entered, as his body moved gently to and fro above me - long, aquiline, infinite. Wisdom broke from it. Knowledge shone from his lidded eyes as he gradually moved into moonlight, or moonlight aligned itself with him.

120

We must have been together for a long time. His shoulders began to crease and float like wings. I could feel them sweep up his back into his generous, flapping hood of hair. I was making love to a man with the head of an elephant, and it was the most erotic experience of my life! We were flying. I was no longer on the bed. I was in the air, moving into and out of Weiner.

A wildness entered us. Entered Weiner. From behind. And we were leaping in great bounds across a moon-drenched, barren earth in wave after firm wave, sea, air and land as one. The stars seems to rush passed us, rush overhead. Strange, uncanny creatures and objects were hurled with them, propelled by the brush of Weiner's expansive wings of hair. We rode on and on until Weiner arched back his head and flipped the glistening trickle of light between my navel and breasts up over his head and into infinity beyond.

And trumpeted. Weiner trumpeted, I swear it, fit to fill the night, the universe, and whatever else there might be. As he crashed back down we were together, splashing in oceans of light, thrashing tightly on viscous darknesses no-one had ever known, afloat on its surfaces like little bursts of life, joined by Weiner's glorious length of sagely beneficence.

I held his seething back and soothed his clutching buttocks, and fell into a dream in which the head of an elephant came before me and spoke. It was Ganesha, the God of Joy and Sagacity. I could not hear what he was saying, but I knew that I had loved, and was loved. Was in love. Ah me. Perhaps just for a moment. Perhaps it will fade. But now first light ekes out its incremental claim upon the darkness and I feel nothing but happiness. It's so nice!

*

A Birth

121

The water is crystal clear. Lapping almost gently about the ears. With each successive wave, although the body is dipped and lifted, twisted and turned, rocked to and fro, although the mouth splutters momentary gobfulls of brine and, yes, the body struggles like a limp-limbed fish, the water itself is as clear as a bell.

> *Above is only the sun. Nothing in between but this sliver of flesh. The ultimate ball of cosmic fire beating out its unheeded message upon the planet below: that life is dependent on its end in the very act of its beginning.*

Light dances upon the surface of the water in yellow triangles which, as they leap from side to side, throw shafts of needlepoint thickness down into the depths beneath. These move with the aquatic body. Reflect its substance whilst themselves refracted by the membrane whereby it meets with the air above.

Michael is for the most part immersed in the water side of the membrane. Indeed, only his face basks in the full glory of God's golden orb above. And, while the occasional renegade wave sends him spluttering back into the grey compulsion of terror, he has for the most part emerged from black panic to the realisation that he is absolutely, completely and unalterably unable to make it back in. By his own efforts, anyway. So he can now lie back and enjoy the life-bequesting roundness around him. Beneath, baskets of light he knows but cannot see form and reform with each subtle movement in the surface about his head. It is as if the sea is a flower of water and light radiating from his face.

> *He knows that there is land beyond his head, and rocks not far off to his right, but he will never reach the latter because of his list to the left. He has never been aware of this lateral deficiency before, but as he wallows in semi-amniosis he can feel a definite apathy in his lefthand-side. As if he can't quite make the grade, so that his obviously stronger righthand-side is forever flapping him around in circles, like a drunken turtle rolled onto its back.*

> *With the sun approaching its zenith above him, its hand firmly on the handle of the world, an open sea to his left and right and beneath, and land above his skull, Michael is aware that he has*

five loci of awareness. Five faces. And from the depths around him come the voices of his past and present, picking their ways through the strands of light like fish that have just been given to life.

*

This doesn't work, does it? No matter how you try to begin something, you are still beginning it. It still comes to a point where it stumbles across that awkward, clumsy trigger of words that say: Hey, this is where the simulacrum begins, the myth of life as an apprehensible linear passage through time, with events conforming to a logic comprehensible in retrospect to the human mind. Everything falls into place because I can write it. Thought purchased from the bazaar of human imagination, mine because my pen happened to be the one to sign the invoice.

And why am I writing as a man anyway? Whoever Michael is, he isn't Weiner. And he certainly isn't me. They say (as in, I've heard) that women write men more accurately than men write women. But that's no reason to do it, i.e. for its own sake. I don't see myself as subjected by Weiner; objectified perhaps, but not in a way that positions me as a secondary element in his perceptual structuring of 'the world'.

In other words, I am not internalising him, and then projecting him here onto the page. I'm no more dependent on him than I want to be. And yet it comes. As if from nowhere. I am just drifting into sleep and I float into this. And now, I'm suddenly very tired. Daylight. Hotel staff padding around in the corridors outside. Yet we are in a corner room. So quiet. First boat of the day yet to arrive. Weiner angelic in sleep. Sleep. Dream. Wake. Where does the bazaar begin and end?

*

Lakshmi

123

Sri is the first to come to me. Her sharp features focus themselves with a beauty the timbre of her voice cannot quite replicate.

At first she seems to come from my right. Then from behind me. Then from my left, or above. Finally, words form, with touching irony.

"You have excellent hair," she says.

With that emphasis on the 'excellent' people use when the term does not actually mean what popular argot wants it to.

And I can feel it, too. My fine, brown fibres are filleted out by the water towards fingers of kelp and sea-grass that reach up from their ocean beds below me.

"Excellent hair," she intones again.

"Sounds a bit silly to me," I reply, placing my nose and forehead against hers.

It is a joke we share. Sri chose her name partly because it sounded nice, but mostly because it is also the name of a Hindu Goddess who is Mother of the World. Sri thought it was about time the mothers of the world had a go.

Not that she wanted to be a mother herself, but she was a third wave feminist. Apparently the Hindu Goddess was born from an ocean of milk churned up by her husband-to-be, who was disguised as a tortoise balancing a mountain on its nose whilst tied up with a snake. At least, that is how Sri revealed it to me in an intense conversation late one night after one or two too many bongs. My response was, in all seriousness and after several moments of thought, "Wasn't there an easier way?". That was the joke.

Now, however, that I am so ineluctably afloat upon the ocean itself, the notion begins to make sense. I can imagine turtles, for instance, if not a tortoise, weaving their ways through the submarine spears of sunlight behind/neath me with that wonderful cumbersome grace of theirs. They could indeed be hauling great slabs of submerged terrain along ocean, fashioning evolution with their scaled and flippery paws, just as the seascape itself might be modelled on their breast-plating.

But that is too much for Michael. Harmony. A sort of Darwinian pantheism. No, I am an elephant, sick of its whiskery existence in some dilapidated temple. Or, better still, under the querulous rump of a Mogul tyrant, trampling yet more unwilling Hindus into the ground. No more! I roll onto my back and crush the despot into a garland of frangipanis some fey embodiment of a God has just strewn in my path. Not that I had meant to squash the frangipanis. They are just there when I roll over. It was that bastard of a despot I was after.

Luckily the flowers grow again. From my navel. For I am, in fact, being born. My pale flesh is my mother's milk. Then her breast. I am sucking on brown mountains of aureoles for all they are worth, pulling on life to fill me out with white corpuscles and phospholipids, layering my body from the inside out. And 85% liquid. Well, what are bones anyway? Ugly things. Huge tusks that bludgeon their way through the subtleties of cellular society. Thrust their brutal shafts between the cuddlesome thighs of the corporeal.

And suddenly a boar breaks from the brush and turns on a fivepence with alarming if somewhat arbitrary accuracy. We thunder after it on horseback, our lances leveled, nets to hand, riding from our hips across the earth's drum as those persistent tusks deftly etch a pattern of survival from the once-still world. Then - a trick! He doubles back! And one of our number is speared; upended on a curving shaft of ivory and spun above the unearthly boar, which in an instant expands to four times its original size. I am the world, spinning on a boar's tusk. How will I fall out? Anybody's guess. I am ugliness. Ugliness is speared within me.

No, I will not have that. I am a man. A lion! Something in me roars out and I cuff the board with clumsy paws which nevertheless catch its fur with fatal claws.

Skin is stripped from its back to leave the flesh shredded, jelly red, heart still beating. Then the men run it through from anus to throat with an iron spike, heave it onto a celestial spit and roast it long into the night. I am the centre of the world. I am its strength. I embrace the sky wholly. My arms feel the full heat of the sun. I embrace the sun for the world.

*

God, I wish I'd been stoned when I wrote this. But I woke from a dream and just began writing. From all thought in the length of the bazaar, between dream and awake and dream again, could I make the purchase?

*

I told Weiner about my pregnancy today. Or my almost-pregnancy. He was sympathetic at first, but I could feel another of those mountains coming up just a little way down the track. All so reasonable. Very gently put. There are too many unwanted children in the world anyway. Being in India makes him constantly aware of the implications. He's never really felt happy about accepting responsibility for bringing another child into the world. Especially a world over which hangs the threat of nuclear destruction, be it through war or through waste.

But what if all of our generation thought like that? If I go childless, do we all go childless? What of the next generation? Anyway, I told him I had wanted to have it. Her. Him. He asked if I minded if he took precautions in future. I said I didn't, but it must have been so obvious I was unhappy. Then he told me that he loved me. "I love you, you know," he said. As if that made it okay. The promise of a future. The next step in the story. But I told him that I loved him too. Because I did. Do. I think. Feel. (Believe?) (Does my self come from the same bazaar as the thought?)

126

*

18 November.

• Our Deluxe Video Bus (everything that wants to be anything to the tourist seems to incorporate the terms Deluxe and Video) from Udaipur to Ahmedabad is devoid of videos (although it does have a monitor to display them on) and is about as deluxe as I imagine the early space capsules to have been i.e. body-moulded bucket seats of some artificial ribbed substance in which it is impossible to get comfortable, especially given a forward motion which feels something akin to an ongoing re-entry from space (which, of course, I've only seen depicted in movies, but still...).

Due mostly, I think, to roads that seem in constant states of disrepair. At one point we actually went off the road and launched out across country. It was supposed to be a short cut, I think. Our driver followed a pack of others trying to get around a traffic jam that seemed to snake on into the headlight-studded night forever. I think we got lost, but never found out for sure because I finally nodded off. My only personal concession to anything resembling comfort.

Not that I stood much of a chance of enjoying any there might of been. A congenial chap sitting behind us named Bahat pumped Weiner with questions about Australia all night. What sort of houses did they have, how much was land, what did people eat, what did they do, how did you set up a business, had he seen Sydney Harbour etc. He's been to the USA, he explains enthusiastically, and to England, Europe, Israel, Iraq and China, but never to Australia! (Well!) He seems to be in the rag trade: travels around Northern India with his boss (who does not travel by Deluxe Video bus) keeping the books. The company owns a chain of textile mills which turns out contract designer labels (and, presumably, imitation designer labels) for retail outlets around the world.

Bahat is ingenuously optimistic about his country. India may seem poor now, he says with confidence, but in twenty years it will

127

be the greatest nation on earth. It is logical, he says. Look how many people we have here who want to work? We all want to work. We all want to make money. He insists on giving Weiner his cards, and finds out where we are saying so that he can 'call around for a drink!'.

- The bus is so full. People squat in the aisles the night-long trip. At the last pick-up point in Udaipur, we watch the driver paying off a policeman while an offloaded passenger waves an obviously valid ticket angrily at them both.

- All night chai stalls along the way. Naked, thin yellow light - it's so common here. Everyone seems to awake. Large woks of large-leafed chai at the centre of a commotion from which travellers emerge with glasses or small china cups steaming away in the cool night. Everyone chatting. What about? Judging by Bahat, it could be anything from the state of the world to the price of rice. Weiner disappears amongst them. I nod off in the bus, clutching my passport pouch tightly under my arm. My passport is real. The rest merges into dream, like on the train. I am an extension of my passport.

- Arriving in Ahmedabad is like entering hell, at the end of our fragmented, vaguely surreal journey through the darkness. Huge bonfires burn everywhere, silhouettes flitting before them, as if the place is being looted and sacked. Bahat says it is nothing. Just building sites. Or the homeless trying to keep warm. They often stay up all night to do so. (I keep forgetting that it is winter here too.)

- Dawn over Ahmedabad. We go to the railway station to secure tickets out (to Bombay, en route to the Ellora and Ajanta Caves). On the footbridge across the flax of railway lines we are level with the skyline of flat factory rooves, broken by the scores of slim, black smoke stacks of the city's 100+ textile mills which rise and salute the uncomfortably grey hues of the morning. Each a tear from the eye of an aging elephant, a straight black streak against uncertain skin.

Or more phallic. The incongruous horns of the Brahmin Bull, through a fisheye lens - those bright, bleak corneas that betray no conscience. So Ahmedabad awakes to the sleepless song of the piston-driven loom and flywheel. Giant boilers yawn and stretch their black sides, adjust the red hot coals within, and belch their first for the day, but not their last for the night.

How ironic that this is what men have done with the art of weaving. There is a local legend that Ahmed Shah, after whom the city is named, keeps the goddess Lakshmi in the city, and thus the Wealth that is her cosmic mantle of responsibility. So here she is, captive and fucked blind around the clock by the mechanical shuttle and its fart. The Manchester of the East. Although the mills of my heritage are long dormant.

• The ticketing officer tells us to come back tomorrow at 11 a.m., for no apparent reason. We are dismissed out-of-hand. The tourist quota for today is full, he says. Yet we are first in the queue. Weiner says there is no point in fighting this. Cash under the table, if we had it, would get us further than any amount of logic and reason, let alone truth and honesty. Buy another thought from the bazaar!

• Hercules bicycles, Priya and Vespa scooters, Premiere cars. The models look exactly the same as those I noted in Dehli. Only the names have been changed to protect the innocent.

• Hotel Natraj - modern, quiet, en suite plus bath, and only 40Rs a double. (A Bahat recommendation, no less.)

• There have been riots here. A Hindu group wants to reclaim Ahmed Shah's mosque (1414), which they say was built on the site of a Hindu temple. All religious activity in (the predominantly Muslim) Ahmedabad has been banned. So the fires last night weren't just for the homeless. Bahat has warned us to keep off the streets after dusk. (True to form, Bahat fulfilled his own prophecy and called around for a drink. For which he paid. Indian hospitality, he says. Although of course there is another agenda. About which he is also quite open. eventually. We are his liquor licence. The sale of alcohol in Gujarat is prohibited, except to tourists. Mind you, Bahat obviously also wants genuine relationship with us. There is an intercultural door opening here the English in me finds so confronting. I keep wanting to close it!)

*

Bahat and Weiner went back to the station to have another crack at the ticketing officer this evening. The added 'weight' of a local seems to have been more of a drawback than an advantage i.e. they are more obtuse with their own than with foreigners - and we think we have a hard time of it! Anyway, the earliest we can get out is the day after tomorrow, so it looks like we spend a couple of days in the scenically spectacular, fun-filled, tourist centre of India, Ahmedabad. At least the train is overnight, so one hotel bill less. Plus we've (Weiner has)(all under his own steam, off his own bat, an independent initiative etc.) got sleepers! First class, no less!

Bahat took us to a 'safe' restaurant tonight, and genially unfolded his homespun philosophy of ergo-economics. People say, for instance, that Ahmedabad is the most polluted city in India. But isn't it better, Bahat reasons, that all the pollution happens in one place? (Picture this little cloudy smudge in the middle of an otherwise spiritually pure India, with the ozone layer yawning irrepressibly above it.) Another: India has successfully logged most of its accessible forest. We Westerners, posits Bahat, would see this as ecologically unsound, but isn't it better to leave just the smaller village stands, for local use (building and firewood), than deprive India of a valuable export resource? It encourages a sense of community and community enterprise. Whereas if the government and private enterprise did not farm the forests, local villagers would simply go in and selectively log themselves, doing far more damage to the ecosystem within the forests and at the same time neglecting their own ecosystems i.e. their villages. This way, everybody feels well used, including the trees! There is a magnificent logic to this, but I watch the conservationist in Weiner blanch at the prospect of it.

130

*

Weiner, I do not like condoms. It's like fucking a surgical glove. Even the name is rubbery - prophylactic. (Sounds like something you take to assist in bowel movement, doesn't it? "Have you had your prophylactic today, Mrs Jones?")

*

19 November - Ahmedabad (still)
• Sabarmati Ashram - Ghandi's home; v. peaceful, but having seen the film I didn't have the emotional reaction I'd expected. I kept thinking about his wife. The film presents them as being devoted to each other, forever in love, and being a willing filmgoer I happily suspended disbelief and believed. But how come he gets all the big ticks for spinning his own cotton and feeding the chickens while all she gets is to be devoted and, ultimately, obedient - as well as spinning the cotton and feeding the chickens all the time he is off trudging the lengths of India and Great Britain and non-violently protesting all over the place? Again, the purchase of thought is arbitrary here.

• Step Well of Dada Harit (1499) - one of Gujarat's distinctive baolis, it's like a palace sunken into the ground. Floor upon floor layered down towards the well so that on each tier the platform extends further, until the floor at water level forms a neat, natural octagon around the well. Lots of thin, stock stone pillars for exotically dressed women to disappear behind, or be found leaning against pensively. Great filming. Bahat rolled out lurid fantasies of Ahmed Shah's 'ladies' cavorting about the place with large breasts and substantial hips (he seems to be fond of substantial hips), but I see women of all castes, veiled in light Indian cotton, populating the various levels to escape the hot thrum of summer overhead. Private conversations flutter down to the surface of the water below, where it is dim, dark, dank, but so cool.

Words slip their meaning and sink down the deep, shaft of water through mute rock and into the

131

expansive underground lake at last. And there the words lie, a timeless store of them, while the women above dip delicate cups into the dense surface and pass them up to the women beyond. But no, this is not for Bahat. He is more interested in women bathing topless on Bondi beach, and wonders whether I do it. I try to explain that I am not Australian, have never been to Australia, and have certainly never sunbathed topless there or anywhere else. But this does not compute. I think he must've shown Weiner where to get the condoms!

*

A terrifying incident tonight, coming out of a restaurant with Bahat. It was a narrow street and a mob of rioters came around the corner as we emerged. We saw each other at the same moment and both stopped. They were all men, and all bore long staffs. You could feel their animosity - as if, when they stopped, it just kept right on coming. Bahat told us to walk away from them and pretend nothing was wrong. He told me to cover my head, the Muslim way. In fact, he'd been suggesting as much all day and I'd happily ignored him. Now I didn't.

The mob started to follow us. Without a sound. That was the eerie part. It was like being followed by a menacing scene in a silent movie. We turned into a wider street, and they followed. Fanned out to fill it easily. There were more of them than we had feared. Weiner told me to drop behind six paces. "It's the Muslim way," he said, and Bahat concurred tacitly. What amazes me is that I did it. I could feel the paws of the collective lion padding up to my back. I was just waiting for it to pounce. Then the first stones came.

I didn't look back, but Bahat did. He quickened his pace. So did Weiner and I. I continued to ignore the stones, even though one hit my ankle, followed by another at the back of my head. But as the first salvo of sticks clattered onto the pavement around us, Bahat said we had better run for it. He started to jog. So did we. But I knew I was closer to them than Weiner or Bahat. If they were going to reach any of us first, it would be me. I could feel them behind me,

132

breaking into a communal trot. Still no sound.

Then a cry went up, followed by another, and the whole mob roared in unison. "Run!" shouted Bahat, and broke into a mighty sprint. Weiner was a fraction of a second behind him, long legs leaping out into the space before them with balletic hunger. But me - short and lean, but nowhere near their gait. I knew I couldn't make it. I could feel the breath of the pounce at my back. I was running, not thinking, this was like a dream, unreal. So I suddenly stopped, spun around, threw my arms wide into the air and shouted at the advancing mob behind me for all I was worth. As if that would bring some reality back into the action.

I can't even remember what I said now - something like "Stand back!". The remarkable thing was that they did just that. More out of surprise than anything else, I think. Then I shouted at them something like, "Don't you think you've done enough damage for one night? What would your mothers think of you? Go home, before you get into even more trouble!" I could not believe the entrenched teacher-like conservatism of what was coming out of my mouth. I sounded like the British Raj personified. Do you find out what you really believe in these moments, or simply the parts of you that have been inherited (i.e. slipped in, through socialisation) without scrutiny? I was still unsure if this was real or not. If next second I would wake up. I felt so un-there.

Anyway, they wavered. Just for a moment. Enough for Bahat to get to my side and start gibbering to them in Hindi. I learnt later that he apologised for me; said that I was a tourist and did not understand local ways. That he was a muslim too, and had been trying to educate her. Then he thanked them for their help in showing me how important their Muslim customs were. And, thanking them still, he started bowing and backing away. So we bowed and backed too. Then bolted down the next alleyway for all we were worth. They didn't follow, but we ran anyway.

When we reached the safer ground of a street market we stopped to catch our breath. "I think we are safe," said Bahat. "Yes," I agreed, "Lucky I got us out of that one!"

I don't know what made me say it. I know I was joking, but from somewhere way off to the side. Like I threw the comment in from the wings of the event I had just been part of. Anyway, Weiner and Bahat looked at me, then they looked at each other, then they looked at me again, and we all burst out laughing. We laughed all the way back to the hotel. Laughing to make it real, safe again, our selves.

But it still makes me shake inside at the thought of it. I've never been so close to such ideologically directed hatred. I mean, the skinheads back home have always exhibited undirected manifestations of hostility and violence that sustain ready sociological analysis. With this mob, the hatred was not only far more intense but extremely well-informed. I was the focus of it, not a symptom or a scapegoat. And it wasn't that I was white. It was that I was a woman, and I wasn't doing it their way. It horrifies me to my very core. Even when I thanked Bahat later for 'rescuing' me, and I reproved him (jokingly) for his sexism in my defence, there was the same flicker behind the returning laugh: that reflection from a hard, hard stone of male resistance held so very tightly right at what he imagines to be his centre. But do we really have them; centres? When there are so many thoughts in the bazaar, who does the choosing? Why should it be self?

*

20 November - still Ahmedabad.

• Darpana Academy's (recommended by Parvati) puppet company are housed in an old temple. The doors come from Kerala - Siva and Parvati country. The puppets are cared for with an almost religious precision, and I wonder if the preparations for performance, and indeed the performance itself, have devotional significance. Preparing the lifeless to receive spirit.

- Andra Shadow Puppets - v. old, handcrafted and handpainted leather; the larger the puppet/shadow, the more important the character it represents. Not so different from the way we inscribe status in the media in the west.

*

I've just come back to the hotel room to find that Weiner has gone - out with Bahat, presumably. That was the plan. But he's left his diary on the occasional table. It's open, with the writing implement carelessly cast across it. As if he left in a hurry. Threw it down and rushed out with Bahat, enthused by some scheme Bahat had arrived with, some news that came to the door with him. This is a scene in a mystery novel, and I am to uncover the mystery.

I knew he'd been keeping a diary. It slips into and out of his backpack - not secretively, but not refereed to either. And suddenly here it is, like an open invitation. I know I should respect his privacy, and I do, but that is not what this is. Even the journalist in me tells me that. But here we are in the thought bazaar. He wants to sell me something from it. Something unexpected. Something unwelcome. I mean, I was expecting some tortuous, perhaps black self-analysis from Weiner - he seems like a very intelligent, reflective and (like the rest of us) fucked-over human being. But I was also overwhelmingly anticipating some delicious titbit of warmth and sensuality. A quiet libation of love left there for me to discover. These are, after all, the deepest, darkest secret sensibilities of my lover.

What I hadn't expected was the litany of paranoia I have just finished reading. I can't described how shocked, yet angry, yet deeply hurt, yet horrified I feel. I share a bed with this man. Yet suddenly I find I am demanding, unreasonable, defensive, too ideologically correct and thus culturally and personally insensitive, unbending - the list goes on and on. It's like he's constructing this court case against me. Although of course there is no court to hear this sort of stuff, except the pantheon of transcendent authority inside Weiner's brain.

First there is the general appeal for sympathy. He has tried to change, to meet the demands of feminism (who's demanding?), but what is the point when he's rejected (rejected? How can men be rejected by feminism? It's not about them) again and again. He then immediately jumps on me - in prose, of course. I am 'infested with so many defensive barbs of ideological perfection it's impossible to get anything right', he writes. He then systematically presents a case against me - it's like someone laying them down, one card after another. Then you did this. Then you did that. Then you did -

Why didn't I cover up, Weiner? I don't know, really. Didn't see the need. I'm not one of them. What can I say? But oh, Bahat had been hinting all day, hadn't he? Why didn't I listen? I was in India, for Christ's sake. Is it so hard for me to make just the slightest bit of an effort to accommodate to the local culture? No, I just blindly assert my position as a feminist . . . So, no arguing with that, is there?

Then there is my 'jibe' at Bahat over his sexism in 'defending' me. He probably saved my life! Couldn't I have offered him a moment's cultural concession? NO! I 'had to get stuck into him'. And of course Bahat 'pretended not to understand' but Weiner knows - he **knows** (his emphasis). Can't I see? Evidently not. Any more than I was, it seems, 'barely able to conceal' my 'disdain for Bahat's sexist innuendos' at the Dada Hari Well. Couldn't I for once have put my own 'prejudices' aside in the interests of a little inter-cultural exchange? I ask myself. Thanks for helping me through that one, Weiner.

And now I learn that Weiner has made *sacrifices* for me. He has given up close friends for me. Godfrey was abandoned, it seems, to cope with his arduous trials of love in Varanasi alone. And now Weiner is foregoing the opportunity of a real relationship with a real Indian because I'm not prepared to . . . he doesn't actually make it clear what I'm not prepared to do. I get the impression I'm generally just in the way. He feels responsible for me. Yet I won't 'participate' in Bahat with him. I won't entertain the idea of staying on here. (He's mentioned it, seemingly in passing. How was I to know it meant so much to him?).

Then we're back to his friends again. It's not that I actually say I don't want them around. Oh no, I'm much too politically correct for that. It's what I *don't* say that counts. (Of course it is! How could I have been oblivious to the fact for so long? It isn't what I say or do that represents me. It's what I **don't** say or do.) I 'openly deride them' in his presence, for instance - a dead giveaway, that one. The 'openly deriding' tactic. I am, apparently, 'so transparent it is painful'. (Now that I think about it, I remember back in Dehli joking about Godfrey's public schoolboy idolisation of "The Perfect Relationship". I remember Weiner sharing the joke too.)

And now Weiner becomes the victim, the oppressed. 'Frankly, if I want to assert anything of myself in this relationship, I have to fight for it. That's the truth of the matter. As if there has to be a battle of wills to test the value of anything that is of me.' And what is his example of this awesome state of personality subjugation? The condom! How can I refuse to let him wear one? Even as a feminist, apparently, I should be 'cognisant of the dangers of AIDS and other diseases transmitted by the physical and political dominance of men in the sexual act.'

So, I am not even a real feminist. I don't even understand my own ideology. That must just about wrap it up for Weiner, but no. Back to the sympathy trap again. Why can't I understand his commitment to a class-free, prejudice-free, exploitation-free, pollution-free world? Do I doubt that he genuinely does not want to contribute to the generation that will destroy the world by bringing a child into it? Yet he has spoken about it often enough. Don't I listen to him? Is everything he thinks and feels so valueless to me? Yet I 'lure' him into sex without the condom.

And he just knows that I disapproved of him riding the bull in Dehli. He just KNOWS! (So there we are, then, God and Man, Judge and Judged, become one in the universal intelligence of cosmic knowledge. I always knew it was the case.)

137

And here he is, heading South with me, when he wanted to go North to Nepal. And, if it really mattered, he could have been in Tasmania with his brother - who is, I learn (for the first time), sustaining a smack habit down there. Or rather, it is sustaining him. So, in the final analysis, I am simply keeping Weiner from his Good Works. How on earth can I even continue to exist?

So, he concludes, 'it is better to be a friend and keep myself to myself. But in order to maintain such separation, I must love myself and know myself. Otherwise I will continue to offer Rhea only my insecurities, and be scrabbling for ways to change in fear that she will go away, and I will be alone once more.' But if he knows this and understands it, where does the rest come from? God, there is so much here I don't know where to begin. It's like, the man is truly, deeply mad. Frighteningly innocuously crazy. Where is the person I met in Dehli and fell in love with? Why has he kept all of this from me?

Aidan was like this. Avoided speaking when it mattered. Kept emotions and sensibilities back. Rigid constraint of self-disclosure and expression. What is it about them that somehow expects that, because they've opened up one bit of themselves, the rest will somehow become magically known as well? 'She should know', Weiner writes. How? Now that's sexist - the myth that I should know him better than he does himself, or even as well as he does. Why doesn't he know himself better? Yet in the end, he does. Perhaps it's the process of writing, then, that gets him there. Perhaps that's what all this is for. On the other hand - and this is what frightens me the most - perhaps it's me. Yet I am here. I feel such tears of rage rising up from within me. I am self. I have self. Weiner flays thoughts from the bazaar - my thoughts - then pins them on me as prices, as my price. I feel so crucified. And I haven't even applied to join the club.

*

The bull silently enters the steely dust-mist of Connaught Place. A cycle-rickshaw hastens its exit from the roundabout. The couple making love among the flowers are oblivious to both exodus and arrival. They writhe together. Although this is not clear. They could also be wrestling. Both are fully clothed.

The bull moves suddenly. Darts forward. Before its movement has even registered in the space it traverses, it is at the couple. Deftly, almost gently, it inserts its horns into the moving knot of limbs and tosses them high into the air, parting the couple completely, and harmlessly.

There is a gun-shot. Or a shot. The discharge of a weapon of some sort. Surgical excision of life. As I land (for I am the woman), I know that the elephant has been killed. And that it will fall on top of me at the moment I hit the ground. So that even if I survive the fall, I will be crushed to death by the death of the mammoth. I awake with a start, as if hitting the ground.

*

Parasurama

"Don't sacrifice yourself for me!"

It is Sri, yelling at me from five sides at once.

I panic again. Clamber onto my chest and start paddling for the shore like a baby. I have drifted closer to the rocks, but am still a way off; certainly no closer than I am to the strand. I can see someone shadowing me along the beach. Surely somebody must be doing something out there.

The tide is stronger than ever. A hapless breast stroke brings me nothing but more dunkings from behind. Hope empties from me. Or rather, I hope once more, but less so. I am a small human being. I always have been. So I roll over onto my back again.

I remember a friend of Sri's. She talked once about an axe. When she left her

139

husband after years of oppression, and was feeling really low, she went to live on a commune with some other women, and learnt how to swing an axe.

It was the first task she was given upon arrival. After settling her things in. To chop up some wood. No-one made any big deal of this. It was just something she was asked to do, as other people were doing other routine chores in preparation for evening. So this woman went out and hacked at the seemingly immutable logs for hours, it seemed to her, desperate to have something to offer this inspiringly competent group of women. Eventually, of course, she massacred enough dead lignin to take inside.

It was a piecemeal effort, but the women were very kind to her, she thought. They told her what a great job she'd done, and made what she had provided last the entire evening, even though they could have had a bigger fire if there had been more wood. They simply accepted what she had achieved for what it was. A contribution.

So that her world, on that first day of liberation, was founded in the swinging of an axe, and the tenacity of concentric circles within a log of wood. As the days passed, she got better and better at chopping up wood, but from that very first day she could say to herself;

"I am a woman who can swing an axe."

And from then on, whenever she had to make a public appearance (for she went on to become a very famous writer) or enter an alien social environment, she always reminded herself: I am a woman who can swing an axe. And that made the ordeal easier.

*

This is a true story. She was a friend of B's. I miss B.

*

On The Train to Bombay.

Well, we've had tears. I must admit, I was preparing to leave when he arrived back. I still don't understand why I didn't want to hurt him, but I didn't. He seemed so pathetic. But by the same account, I didn't think I could take this on, or even deal with it. And he was leaving it so late. I hadn't eaten all day. But then in he walked, looking like a dog that had been well and truly kicked - although it turns out that he'd been stoned all day with Bahat, and was coming down off that.

He stood in the doorway with that stricken look of terror in his eyes, as if he knew what he'd done but didn't quite know what to do next. "I didn't think you'd still be here," he said, eventually, weakly. I asked him if that was what he had wanted. I was prepared to go, I said, there and then. I certainly had no desire to be where I wasn;t wanted. But he shook his head, and said "no".

So I asked him why he left his diary open on the table? Didn't he think I would want to read it? I tried not to sound angry or aggressive. But he looked so closed, suffused, like a dam about to break. But he started talking. As if forcing himself to. It was so strained at first. More so than in Agra. Like someone trying to claw their way out of a sticky web in which they had cocooned themselves. He admitted that he had half-deliberately left the diary open. He had wanted me to know how he felt, but couldn't find a way to tell me.

I commented that this was a pretty dramatic way of doing it. And he laughed a bit. But still so closed. I showed him my diary - what I wrote above. He started to cry. Just talk, Weiner, I said to him. Just talk to me. I was fairly calm by now. Had had my cry. Had even been down to the river and stood under a tree. Watched the world. Packed my bag. I even read back through this to see if there was any indication that I had provoked his projections. But now here was this sobbing, wracking bundle of masculine anguish before me. And part of me wondered how far back into childhood it goes, this pain of separation.

When words came again, they were like stones, he found it so painful yet

141

palliative to pass them through the emotional paroxysms that gripped his body. They spoke of the difficulty he had always had in explicating his emotional needs. Of how afraid he had been to make any demands upon me for fear I would be repelled by them, by him. They revealed how little Weiner thought of himself, and had always thought of himself, these words. They said that love and relationships had always cost him immense personal pain, and that it took a lot for him to say that he loved someone, but that he loved me very, very much, and that he would be desperate if I left him.

By now I was holding him. This man I had thought to be so together. The mountain collapsing into the corporeal. At last, I suppose. Its great shoulders heaving with the effort of the transformation. Coughing up giant boulders of meaning. Hands flexing and clenching in desperation for expressive form to match the magnitude of the movement within.

I told him that I loved him too, this mountain. I told him that taking risks and sharing needs was what relationships were all about, as far as I was concerned. Mutual vulnerability and emotional support were where they started, not where they got to. It was the land we stood upon, I said. Anything else was mere acquaintance.

I was speaking from a great distance within myself, yet it was also from a place in which I knew that I loved Weiner, and wanted to be with him. Yet so far from the self that dreams. The self that wakes. The self from which the writing comes.

He sobbed and said that he would try to change and be more open. He wanted to take more risks. He had only just found me. I told him I wasn't going anywhere. And it was the truth. Something like love bound me to him. I couldn't resist it. It just didn't bring me any joy.

So I nestled into the curve of his body in our little bunk in our very own sleeper on the train tonight, and we made love from behind - something he said he'd been holding out on. (Why? It's such a common position.) And

142

now he sleeps beside me while I write, under the blue night light of our compartment.

It's funny, one of the things I never thought I'd find in India (although I suppose I must have hoped for it) was that I was okay. But I think I am, compared to Weiner. The train rocks gently along the nightbound tracks somewhere between Ahmedabad and Bombay, this strange but darkly, oddly attractive man slumbers beside me, and I'm not so bad. Not really. At least somewhere very essential within me I know that I love and am loved. Weiner doesn't. And, despite my beration of her elsewhere in this, in that place I know it is my mother who loves me.

How did that come about? And how didn't it come about for Weiner, and men like him? (All men?) And yet that place is still not the place from which I write. It is not the self I am here. There is still that distance between where I am loved and where I am just okay. In two different places in the bazaar. Between two different vendors currently, Weiner and my mum.

*

We symbolically burned the offending pages of Weiner's diary before leaving the Natraj. It made him happier. I tucked my arm into his, but watched from afar. Do I 'get over' this?

*

21 November - Bombay.

• Arriving in Bombay, the morning squatters are out earning their namesake, relieving themselves of yesterday's sustenance beside the railway line - sometimes even on it - a few bare bottoms preferring to hide the face of shame, but for the most part facing the passing dirama, genitals dangling like elephants' trunks. So where do the women go?

143

- Makeshift shelters along the railway line, not even mud-walled, but rickety wooden constructions layered with sacking and cloth. To secure a new piece of cloth here must be like putting on a home extension, and polythene, like gold - something that really *does* keep the rain out.

We are 'splashing out', at Weiner's (somewhat ostentatious) insistence, at the Sea Green Hotel, overlooking Marine Drive, Back Bay and the famous Malabar Point. A calm. White-walled buildings, no autorickshaws, even the odd Mercedes in amongst the cabs. And a dense, grey thermal inversion layer hanging over the blue-ish ocean. Weiner says it reminds him of Bondi Beach (famous body surfing haunt of Prince Charles, I recall, 'before Diana') - even down to the turds floating off Chowpatty beach!

I have rung home. But Brook, this time. I've been worrying about these 'tests'. She's pregnant! And it sounded so ominous! Although all is not well, I fear. She couldn't talk on the phone, but I got the impression she was uncertain who the father was. She told me to talk to Belinda about it - which was weird. They don't really know each other that well. Anyway, when I rang B. I discovered that Brook has been having an affair with Aidan, of all people, *for years*! (At least ten, B. said. Brook has apparently been talking to her because she has been thinking of leaving Janaka, and wondered how I would feel about it. I told B. to tell her it was fine. Maybe I should tell her myself. I mean, it's a bit of a shock. The affair would've been going on while Aidan and I were still together. But in a way it's a relief too - I don't feel so guilty about Aidan - who never told me about it!) It does throw some light on Harry's red hair, doesn't it? I remember we all wondered at the time where he got it from - a child of an Indian father and North Country English brunette. I wonder if Harry's aware of the anomaly he represents? Brook said he was playing up at school a lot, fighting; especially with kids of other ethnic backgrounds. Most notably Indians, which makes it hard for Janaka. Unless, as I say, the lad's cottoning on somewhere deep inside there. Although Brook says the school counsellor puts it down to pre-pubescent angst. So - it's all conjecture, I suppose.

Meanwhile Devin (whose genetic heritage is too self-evidential to be in doubt) has decided he wants to be a reporter, "like his Aunty Rhea". He's such a sweety. How do they come so loving and caring and - I don't know. Normal is such a normative term, isn't it? I suppose I just like the fact that, at 14, he still calls me "Aunty".

The other thing that's been on my mind is whether I really should come home to be with Dad. Brook just laughed. Said he'd never been better, except that he had the guilts about how his children would feel about him 'living in sin' - yup, you guessed it: Stella's moved in!

I still fear, however, that my normally centred and balanced sister is suffering from deeply disturbed waters. B. confirms this. B., meanwhile, has left Hi DIE. She said that it was the only way she could get away from this guy who kept trying to 'mentorise' her, as she put it. Although the real reason, she says, is that there is so much writing on the wall re- arts funding for community-based and/or social action-based companies, there was no point in continuing. All the Arts Council are maintaining are the provincial theatre and dance companies, and of course the National, the Ballet and RSC. And the Opera, of course! (bo-o-o-oring!) She told me not to bother coming back.

She's talking about going to Australia. There's a women's action against the US intelligence base at - wait for it, Weiner - Black's Bluff, in Tasmania. Apparently it's a key site for collecting and distributing information on the nuclear arms network. B. has been protesting at Greenham Common, but reckons the action will be wound up soon, they have been moved on so many times by the police. I tried to persuade her to meet me in Madras, and we'd do India from South to North, but I don't think she was convinced.

Back at the Sea Green, Weiner and I 'broke in' our room, which was better than expected. Sex between us is still very good. Kind of helps put the rest behind me a bit. And Weiner has initiated a re-invigorated programme of 'communication' - I think what I'd call self-disclosure. He wants us to be more open about our sexual needs and desires. Which is fine with me. (Although I suppose part of the

145

joy, and the 'communication ', in making love for me is the process of 'finding out'. Why does everything have to be words?)

He's started to call me Melanie when we make love. It's not a former lover, but a (wait for it) pop-star of the late 60s/early 70s. I don't think I've heard of her, but she seems to have been very big in Australia. (She's American.)(As if that explains it.) Weiner says she was his first true love; by which he means his first object of sexual fantasy. I gather I look like her.

I don't care what he calls me really. Where did I get a name like Rhea from anyway? All of my sisters are so 'of nature' – Fleur, Verda, Brook. I don't even know what Rhea means, let alone why my parents chose it. Why have I never questioned this before now? Why have I never cared? Distance.

He asked me if there was anything I wanted of him. I found this hard to answer, but I did tell him about my experience at the Lake Palace. He said he sometimes likes to imagine me as a female warrior, dressed only in a skin belt around my waist and wielding a spear. Very Freudian. Says that he likes to be 'ridden'. I must admit I quite like that. I remember as a kid seeing Bo Derek riding on a lion. Or was it Ursula Andress? Someone with long, lion-coloured skin and hair, anyway. It looked so sensuous. Well, to an 8 year old. And Weiner actually does have leonine features, now that I come to look at him. That lovely, aquiline nose that slips up neatly into the broad sweep of his sloping forehead. Cat-like, almond eyes. Then all of that hair, springing out from the rim of his face like a mane. He'll do for now.

*

22 November

- Elephanta Island - a huge, monolithic cave, hand-hewn out of basalt around 600AD by monks as a temple to Siva. There is a huge,

146

three-sided bust of Siva at its heart. And before this, an altar is Siva's lingam - his phallus - which also represents the divine flame. If you meditate upon it, you can attain nirvana. The phallus is equated with the essence, with purity itself, as spiritual/cosmic transcendence i.e. deification of the phallocentric.

- the lingam always faces the east, so that the sun's rays strike it at certain times of day - presumably, times of worship. (ie. it 'cums'!)

- Siva = Nataraja
        Nat = dance
        raja = king.

He dances the tandava, a dance which shakes the earth and leads to creation, or re-creation, through destruction. Nataraja is the form in which Siva creates the world. The tandava can also lead to nirvana.

- also the God of Puppetry (and not Parvati?)
- His three 'faces' represent his three aspects:
        creator (ascetic)
        preserver (joyous)
        destroyer (angry)

(This is strange: I thought Vishnu was the Preserver. And Brahma the Creator.)

- Parvati (at last! the female aspect) always stands on Siva's left, except during marriage; during Hindu marriage ceremonies, the woman stands on the groom's right and then passes to the left as marriage takes place!

- 95% of marriages in India arranged by parents still. Dowry Deaths (brides killed by husband's family because dowry either or insufficient or all they wanted) still occur!

- Rivers of India = the three heads above Siva's head:
        Ganges
        Yamuna
        Sarasvati

\-> the Sarasvati now extinct; used to flow from the Himalayas.

- the Ganges is held in Siva's matted hair, then released onto the earth to give India its LIFE. If you are cremated beside the Ganges you do not have to be reborn. You have completed your cycle of reincarnation.

- Siva's snake = the symbol of reincarnation; as the snake sheds its skin, so we shed our bodies but live on.

- Parvati is the Shakti - the energy of Siva. Male and female aspects are thus equal. (As long as she remains the libido to his transcendent essence.)

- Bombay harbour - on the Arabian Sea; scores of rusting hulks - oil tankers, cargo vessels, tramps - dutifully turn in unison to the changes of wind and tide like a community of weather vanes pointing to the future. So this is where Western Capitalism comes to die. And between them the smaller, native sloops lean their white, bow-like sails into the breeze, fetching, carrying, fishing. India lives on, yet again!

- Weiner says India's numbers swells by the population of Australia every year. I can believe it!

*

I had to be Weiner's aboriginal lover tonight. (Apparently he used to have one.) So what happened to poor old Melanie? I rode him like a lion anyway!

*

23 November - on the road to Aurangabad

- There are 1200 excavated cave temples in India - 900 of them are in Maharastra.

- Daulatabad - the original Aurangabad. Like Fatepur Sikri, built as a new fortress capital of India - this time by Muhammed Tughlaq, the Sultan of Dehli, in the C14th., because Dehli was the first target

148

for any enemy attacking from the North. So he marched its entire population down here and built this elaborate maze of elephant and man traps. Well, these boys certainly knew how to defend themselves. Marauding hordes arrive at the front gate. Knock. No answer. Knock it down to throng into a courtyard surrounded by cannons at ground and battlement level. Luckily the gunners are all having tea, so we hurtle through there on our elephants to find there are another six walls to penetrate. Bang - barge through one. Bang - barge through another. Then, just as we are starting to feel real confident - bang! oops - uh-oh! An elephant-sized dog-leg ('scuse the mixed metaphor) which it is impossible for an elephant to actually negotiate. And there on the ramparts are the valiant defenders, armed with boiling oil, acid and other assorted goodies. So we get off our elephants, fire salvos of arrows and spears and somehow gain access to the dog-leg gateway. Through the narrow entrance we pour right into the face of a robust turret bearing a ruddy great cannon - boom! We all scatter like skittles, but struggle bravely on, committed to the conquest of our foe, to discover that - whoa! The turret defends a moat filled with crocodiles and venomous snakes. Access to the actual (boom! again)(strike two) castle is via a narrow footbridge. The last remnants of the marauding hordes skitter across this as (boom! strike three) the rear guard action is blown to smithereens.

The hole at the end of the footbridge is wide enough only for one person at a time to get through, so we're all standing around twiddling our spears as we are picked off, one by one and fall into the moat below - zip! flop - chomp, chomp, "Aaaargh!" etc.

By now, maybe a handful of us have made it. But as we wriggle through the hole, there is ample room on the other side for two defenders to stand and simply bop us on the conk as we emerge. And if by some miracle we manage to overcome them, there is the lightless passage rendered impassable by generous floor covering of glass marbles and multi-barbed nails. Defenders can also be secreted in the walls of this passageway to shoot at the thus-far immaculately successful attackers, driving them towards several fake exits which in fact deposited them in the moat.

Anyone who gets through that lot is gassed by chilli fumes in a spiral staircase which constitutes the only actual way out. And do you know how this astounding fortress was breached? The guy on the gate was bribed. As in, the Sultan's own Prime Minister, during an absence by Turghlaz, raised a revolt which led to the Sultan's overthrow, and a return to Dehli. And the flashpoint for the revolt? They ran out of water! (Ah, boys, it's always that water, isn't it?)

- It was also here that Shah Jahan's son, Aurangzeb, ensconced himself while Governor of Maharastra, plotting his father's demise. The Prime Minister he subsequently appointed to look after Daulatabad (which he renamed Aurangabad) then led a revolt against him! But then, is this so different from our own system of politics? Look at the Conservative Party, as they line up one after another to have a go at Maggie! But (unfortunately, in this case) the Iron Maiden is bigger than all of them!

• At some stage the Maharastra State Government must have found itself with a surplus of oil drums, for they line the entire road system. Painted white and filled with earth, they serve as roadside guideposts. These days some of them even support the revegetation efforts of the local weed population. So, even OPEC eventually returns (roughly) from whence it came. Or part of it.

• Hindu Temples - can be massive devotional institutions or small, Dravidian structures that you stumble into off the street as you round a corner. You can hear the little, handheld bells tinkling from them somewhere nearby as dusk approaches. An irratic but incessant incantation that passes for prayer dances through invisible passageways of falling night. At its source, always a few individuals seeking blessings for someone or something close. Then there are people at the mini roadside shrines, or the domestic shrines on the walls of dwellings, or set inside the home itself in a position of family focus - even hand-sized ones on the dashboards of taxis and buses. Religion is everywhere.

150

- It's like this at the Siva temple, Ellora. This is a medium sized effort, halfway between Big Tourist Venue and Roadside Stumble In. We reach the inner sanctum to be told 'ladies aren't allowed in'. Then a Hindu in glasses and a Nehru hat says to the saddhus on the door, in educated English, "Go in! Go in! I give them my permission." So here we are in the Hindu Holy-of-Holies, and is there that quiet, sanctimonious ceremony of the Christian church? Not on your life! The wild-haired old man in the centre chants inconsequentially (it seems) while people make offerings of fruit, flowers and coconut. He is obviously the senior saddhu, but you wouldn't know it. No-one is particularly looking at him. Nobody seeks anything personally from him. It's as if everybody has come along to make some sort of personal declaration to their personal god, and luckily everybody else's personal gods have come along too. As worshippers leave, the two saddhus at the door are chatting merrily away to each other, looking around as they do. They stop momentarily to deliver the appropriate words of blessing as they exchange devotional forehead blazes for money, then it's back to the conversation. It could be Friday afternoon at Tescos.

At one point, the senior saddhu looks thirsty. I offer him some water from my own cannister. He holds out his own metal cup gratefully - he could be a beggar. And for a moment, he catches my eye - or is it I who catch his eye. And the look is suddenly profound. As if I am staring into a bottomless well that is as full of void as it is of water. Then the moment is gone. On to the next thing. Mr Nehru-hat at the back of the throng, craning his neck, muttering a devotional song almost involuntarily, it seemed. A religion for millions. A religion for chaos. A bazaar full of spiritual relief. Thought as spirit.

- Ellora Caves - the Kailasa Temple, quarried and sculpted out of the hillside over 150 years; 200,000 tonnes of rock excavated. The whole temple represents Siva's Chariot, pulled by two enormous stone elephants. Access from the road is via the chariot's 'shaft', which as a bridge crosses a chasm where once a moat would have been. In the main pavilion, a low, squat mega-lingam - again so

151

aligned that at sunrise a single ray of light helps the great god seed the cosmos with transcendental enlightenment. (Weiner thought we should make love upon it between tour groups.)

Below, carved into one of the figurative 'wheels' of the chariot, is a bas relief of the demon, Ravana, shaking Mt Kailasha (the Himalayas) to cast Siva off. But Siva is unruffled. He calmly lounges, holding the mountain down with his big toe whilst playing chess and discussing matters of cosmic philosophy with Parvati. Ravana is thus trapped beneath the mountain for 1,000 years.

Weiner says this is one of his favourite Siva stories because it explains the nature of evil i.e. the demon we create within by repressing our natural urges. If the demon is not allowed out, it has only its own hatred to feed on - it's anti-selfness, its inner alterity. So, according to Weiner, it grows to immeasurable proportions - enough to match the potential it can perceive in the world known to the oppressing self. Eventually it will attempt to realise its own potential and, as the myth suggests, cast off the dominating self. Evil is the result of such inner struggles. Wars are the result of the same on a collective level.

I was interested in how this related to his evil-slips-through-the-void-within-us-all theory, but Weiner seems not to have thought that through yet. What was significant about the relief to me, given Weiner's line, was that Parvati is not part of this anthropomorphic conglomerate of highly volatile darknesses in opposition. She sits to one side and (literally) plays chess with it. The motif is thus to me more a metaphor for the mechanism of male domination. The organising (read 'dominating') masculine principle within men is seen to be not only suppressing but redefining in the process all other aspects of the self. Ravana didn't look evil, just in pain, and desperate to get out. Angry at his imprisonment. It was the smug, controlling, manipulative Siva above who seemed to be the cause of the problem. Why did Ravana want to throw him off the mountain in the first place? What had Siva done to Ravana? Or not done, as the case may be. Anyway, Weiner says we have to be Siva and Parvati tonight. Since we are staying at the Kailasa Hotel. I asked him who would play Ravana? He said he had a pretty good idea.

*

Weiner had the most extraordinary tension attack tonight. I've never seen it in a man before. I thought it was something I'd done at first. We were making love and Weiner was admittedly in fuller flight than usual, busily being Siva and hurling invective at me about the colour of my skin and my relative sexual status and other Parvati-oriented put-downs, and the guy just broke off and reeled away, clutching his head. I thought he was joking - bunging on a bit of the old Ravana etc. - but he was in real pain. As if all of the energy he had been focusing into his groin had suddenly decided to turn around and high-tail it out through the chakric escape hatch - only to bottleneck at the medulla. The muscles around the base of his skull were like bolts. I had to knead and knead at his neck to get even the beginnings of a relaxation. He says he's always carried too much tension in his shoulders - 'head tension' he calls it. Anyway, sleeping soundly enough now. Almost angelic.

*

25 November - Bombay.

Rex and Stiffles. I had the most unnerving freak out yesterday. Still coming down from it. We went to the Ajanta caves north of Aurangabad - some of the oldest in the country, dating back to 200 years BC. Weiner thought it would be enhanced by a bit of a number. So we got into this one, very deep cave, low ceiling, walls adorned with the most amazing Escher-like al fresco work - astoundingly advanced in form and style for 400AD. Anyway, Weiner thought this was the "go", as he calls it. And, quite frankly, after Udaipur I thought it would be too. But I only had a couple of tokes and just fell off the edge of my brain.

153

Maybe it was that the space itself was confusing. The roof was supported by lots of square pillars - all carved out of the rock, of course. But it was dark inside. The guides were showing groups around with little electric lamps. And the light from the entrance was very bright - almost surreal in its rectangularity, like a Speilberg effect. Suddenly the whole space became a wrap-around film screen. And I was inside it. Like plastic wrap. And beyond the screen, other forces were pulling at it, distorting it. My whole world was changing shape. People grew and shrank. I tried concentrating on the paintings but they began moving as well, like cartoons acting out the story they had been representing. But the story went wrong. They grew long dicks and breasts and started copulating lewdly, or they sprouted arms and legs and swords and axes and began swiping off each others heads. Heads going everywhere, dripping with blood. Video Games. I even started to hear the beeps and bloops.

I glanced sideways to see whether other people were seeing what I was seeing. But they were looking at me as if I was weird. (Weiner told me later that it was actually me who was making the video game noises!) And there was Weiner leering down at me with this maniacal grin. He kept looming up into my vision and shrinking away again, and I felt myself buckling under him at every advance, as if I were yielding to him.

I returned to the paintings. Don't fight it, Rhea. Go with the flow, float with the moat, etc.. But there was Siva dancing the Tandava. The ground shook beneath me as each giant foot came down. I was gripping the pathetic chain they'd strung between us for all my life was worth. If I wasn't careful, Siva would shake me to the edge of the world, and I would fall off into the cosmic abyss for ever.

I looked to Weiner for help. He was feeling it too. But he was dancing the tandava with Siva. Like a puppet, straight off 'Thunderbirds'. As if Siva were controlling him, swinging him towards me and away again, trying to taunt me. He was silhouetted at first against the Speilberg backlighting, but then one of the guides' spotlamps swung across his face and revealed the elephant's head. Ganesha, grinning stupidly, danced up towards me and over me, draping his long trunk up the length of my body with a kind of grotesque sensuality. I was horrified to my core. It was like being raped.

Suddenly he leapt to one side and became Weiner again, but with a foul face. Lit as if from my own vulva, his shadow flung upon the wall and ceiling behind him. He was huge. And I realised for the first time that we were in battle. I roared at him. The sound just came from deep, deep within me - from a centre I didn't know I had. I roared, and my voice was the most powerful source in the world. It came from a space before time. Before humanity. With it came dinosaurs and ancient trees and rocks and then lizards and rainforest plants and ferns and insects and birds and mammals and eventually people and people with weapons and clothes and horses and carts and grain and scythes and ploughs and machines and steam and trains and houses and buildings and skyscrapers and planes and they all howled from my unchartered depths, madly grabbing at words as they came - or rather, words flew from some other source and attached themselves to objects as they roared towards Weiner from my powerful throat. And Weiner reeled back in awe at the alternative to creation I was overwhelming him with.

I turned to make my escape, but now the giants were everywhere, dancing about the walls, jostling for position as they advanced, each most keen to seize his chance at me. I dodged and leapt and fought my way through the overbearing forest of menacing faces. I clawed my way towards the light. My hands became broad, flat blades. I cut off their hands, their arms, their heads, one after another. But as I defeated one, so another came. I was magnificent. Mad, but magnificent. This was no movie now. I was not fighting with fiction. What grew within me with each victory was intensely real. And immense. I became immense. From the darkness surrounding me, from the rock beyond it it seemed, I drew strength. I was big, and black, and bold, and beautiful. These men were paltry. I drank their blood. I brushed them aside. Swept

155

them away from the entrance to my birthing place to reveal and wide and wonderful full light of day.

I took in a deep, deep draft of fresh, cool air as if it was my first. But this sent my head reeling down and down into the ravine beyond. As I plunged, head over heels, someone was taking the river below and wrapping it around my head like a turban, turning me around and around. At any moment the rocks and friendly darkness that had made me would drown in the collapse of my watery carapace. So I shook my head, slapping that river against the sides of the recalcitrant earth that so sought to constrain it. Yet at the same time, it was the earth that was beating me about the head with the river. For the river was part of me. My product.

All of this seemed to occupy an eternity, but it could only have been in the moment of my emergence from the cave because the next minute I was back against the wall of the cliff, gripping it with outstretched arms. I could feel the firm striations of the rock beneath my fingers, and knew the wall reached out from either side of my body like great geomorphic wings. I understood at last that I was part of the earth. I would beat my massive basalt wings across the firm shifts of air and rise from the surface of the planet. But here was Weiner, his foul face contorting in burlesques of concern and care. The charlatan! But I would love him too. I would wrap my earthly arms around him and consume him in a life-exchanging kiss. My tongue sought his and beyond, searched deep into his body. I secured my prise and sucked. We would merge, this god and I. His arms flailed as if they numbered thousands, but I knew he could not resist.

When we disengaged, however, there were two of him. I could not understand how this had happened. I had been so sure. He was jumping from foot to foot like a man on hot coals, running towards me and retreating again. He was a film loop. I had to repel this factition. I had to repel him. But had no idea how. I gripped two arms, but two more appeared. I gripped those too, and two more appeared. Each arm I grasped disappeared, and reappeared beyond my grip.

156

I grasped his head, but this just detached itself from his body and another grew in its place. I was forever throwing blood-dripping heads into the ravine below. This left the blood on my hands. I was compulsively licking it off between blows, trying to keep myself clean. Yet I knew I also needed the sustenance to survive. Nothing was simple. Weiner started grabbing my hands again and again, like a dancer. He wanted me to become his puppet. But I would not. I repelled him. Through dance. Repelled him with his own ploy, hand by hand, step by step. He pawed. I danced horribly. I stuck out my tongue to shame him. I deployed my voice again, uttering bellyfuls of sound that would repulse him utterly.

But it was okay, he kept saying. He understood. As if my repulsive tongue was a weakness, my guttural cries a symbol of submission. Calm down, he said, and smothered me in his arms. Engulfed me - it's okay. Until I had no strength left. Was consumed. By him. And ferried through a traffic of leering eyes back to the bus, along the precarious edge of this gulf, this rent in the earth from which I knew both water and rock flowed back deep into the bowels of the planet, our hair. We trailed our hair.

I was as sick as a dog afterwards. All the way home, all last night. I'm still shaky. But the black lady has remained. Within me. Part of me. Huge, and beautiful, and powerful. Created by the aggression of men, but yet not so. A function of the transcendent authority of patriarchy, and yet independent of the same. Her own dogged and determined self. And I never knew she was there. This is no purchased thought. No product of the bazaar. This woman lives within me. Is from me.

*

Met a really weird guy on the way back to the hotel this evening. Well, not so much 'met' him as tacked into him. Or he tacked into us, like a yacht breaking away from the pack. Obviously a backpacker. Tall, blonde, Nordic. But filthy. No pack. A beggar. Holding out his hand for money, bearing down upon us, speaking in thickly accented English. And for a moment I thought: this could be me. If I run out of funds or get into trouble and cannot repatriate myself back or - panic, etc. But luckily my black lady came to warm me from within, and showed me a picture of Weiner selling flutes in Kathmandu instead, to fund the purchase of heroin.

One brief irony: Weiner pointed out today, after we went back over the experience, that there are no Hindu caves at Ajanta. They are all Buddhist. i.e. no Siva!

*

26 November

Kovalam: - the heart of Siva country! We decided to fly south, just like that! No hassles with travel agents or train stations or bus operators. Just went straight to Bombay domestic and bought two tickets with travellers cheques! Simple. Indian Airlines, fall out of the sky if you dare! (They didn't.)

Weiner reckons we can hole up here for quite a while. Save some money etc. It's quiet, the weather's fine. In fact, it's fabulous - better than an English summer, and this is winter!

You certainly notice the difference between north and south doing it this way. As soon as we stepped off the plane in Trivandrum, we were met by a moving bank of black, black faces. And the features, so much broader. More identifiably 'indian' than the paler, Moghul and Eurasian nuances up north.

Then we emerge from the airport and it's - palm trees! From horizon to horizon. We drive through whole forests of them to get down to Kovalam Beach - and are driven by a card-carrying member of the Communist Party, who gives us a lecture on Kerala's agricultural economy of scale i.e. they export - rubber, coconuts and bananas. And that 24% of the population are Christians (although he is not) due to the Portuguese influence. (Cochin, a fishing port to the north of here.)

His English is very good. In fact, English seems to be more readily used here - none of the post-colonialist snobbery of the north. And architecturally very different as well - high-pitched thatch or tiled roofing (again, the Portuguese influence?). And a sense of social equality. Men and women working side by side on the roads as we pass. Although admittedly the men are doing the 'big' work - the quarrying and carting and laying of the new road - while the women are confined to the middle of the chain of production, breaking up rocks or carting smaller loads on their heads.

I don't know quite what it is but somehow the greenness, the lushness, the sense of labour and construction as well as destruction in order to re-construct, everybody working together, the dust in the stronger sunshine, it has very much the sense of Siva country - Siva being the main God of worship down here. You could imagine a God who could stamp upon the earth hard enough to make it shake, to destroy in order to re-create.

We're staying at a beachfront guest house - a cane and thatch affair, but very comfortable. We've got the whole place to ourselves, almost. Very quiet, for India. We simply walk out of our room onto the beach. Traipse the sand in and out as we please. Saltwater shower. Plenty of little beachfront cafes (the same, cane-and-thatch) to choose from. And the food looks terrific i.e. seafood you can actually eat!

Mind you, the beach also seems to abound with freaks. As in, Western freaks, of the dope-consuming kinds. Post-70s hippies playing with frisbies, portable tape recorders blaring out psychedelic antiques from the 60s. Either that or Deep Purple! There's a vaguely alternative lifestylish handwritten advert for a full moon party down at the (wait for it) Woodstock Cafe. If this is the Goa of the South, Goa must be dreadful. (Weiner assures me the backpackers haven't actually discovered Kovalam yet. I pointed out that he had, but this seemed not to compute. Weiner is, apparently, special.)

I am still unable to escape the ever-present economic objectification of the Westerner. The lungi and fruit sellers start working the beach from around 10 a.m. and don't stop until sunset. A steady traffic in wares. But basically it is . . . relaxing.

I've been doing some reading about Siva's consort, Parvarti. Much more my cup of tea. Far more identified with dance, for a start. And also, more interestingly, in one of her forms becomes the massive earth mother Kali - the god who is responsible for crops as much as she is for earthquakes. And another form, Durga, battles demons and entire armies of giants, rips off their heads and devours them, etc. This is my black lady! Or a combination of her and Kali. Yes!

*

28 November

A woman named Savithry has become my regular fruit seller. She is visibly older than the rest: there are any number of lithe or fullsome young beauties who sway their way along the foreshore each day, baskets of fruit upon their heads. A smile and a 'You buy? You like? You lookey?' A sale, or no sale, and they pass on. But Savithry spends time with you. Squats beside you, not necessarily speaking, but present. Services. Again visibly. Methodically prepares the pineapple as you wish it. Cuts the top off the coconut and waits for you to drink the milk before deftly slicing the fresh, white fruit itself from its chocolate brown husk. Chats. Takes an order for tomorrow, securing exclusivity of custom. If she makes a good sale she might eat of her wares herself. Or produce an old tobacco tin the keeps wrapped in the cloth of her skirt and shows you letters, references from satisfied customers, developing her story a little more each day.

She has two daughters. One is in fourth year at Management School, the other is 22 and still single. This seems to be Savithry's central narrative. She needs a dowry of 5000 Rs to secure a good husband for her daughter. Savithry's husband only cost 100 Rs, and he drank -

'too much arrack' - and used to beat her. He died seven years ago, leaving her nothing. So now she sells fruit to tourists on Kovalam Beach.

She catches the bus (1 Rs) from Muhoor each day, goes to the Market to buy her fruit, then spends the day working from customer to customer. Indicates the towel about her head - her characteristic headdress - and explains that sometimes people give her presents or send her money. Letters must be registered in India otherwise they are often stolen. Reminds you that only three months remain before winter sets in - six months during which she has no business because there are no tourists. She makes enough during the tourist season to eat and put a little aside for her daughter's dowry. But only a little. A kilo of tapioca costs 5 Rs. Rice is 3 Rs a pound. And her daughter is passing marrying age.

If her daughter marries, Savithry can live off her husband into old age. But if her daughters have no husbands, how can they live with respect, this family of women?

Then Savithry leaves her basket with you while she goes off to a prospective client or regular customer nearby. Returns after a while to collect her basket for the next sale. Before she launches out towards the next group she lifts the basket onto her head, carries a pineapple in each hand, smiles and reminds you: "Savithry. I will come tomorrow, yes? Mango, pineapple and coconut? No coconut. Mango and Pineapple. Good. See you." She leaves with statement and affirmation, and a smile. Not questions.

So I am eating well! Of course I don't know how much of her story to believe, but why should I disbelieve? I want to know what happens to a woman like her. I want to know more about her. Whatever I pay, surely I pay for what I get? We should, none of us, ever be so dependent. Not on a man who isn't there, anyway.

*

Weiner has taken to calling me Matilda. I gather it is an endearment, being the name men gave to the swag they used to carry with them during the Great Depression when they went 'on the wallaby' looking for work i.e. the surrogate 'woman' to sleep with under the stars. Not so sure I appreciate being compared to a blanket, however.

Weiner has also been badgering me to have anal sex with him. He argues that it will be 'safer' for both of us. I don't really want to. Anal stimulation during lovemaking can be very erotic but the idea of the entire act being focussed upon entry through my rectal passage doesn't exactly present as a major turn on for me. I don't know. Maybe it's simply because I've never tried it. I can't help fearing there's just some new form of objectification going down here. The next power play, as it were. I don't want to think like this about Weiner. I want to support him, and to believe he is trying. But here I am, waiting again.

*

29 November

There seems to be an extraordinary assumption on the part of Indian males that, because you are both a woman and of a visibly different ethnic group, you virtually cease to exist as a human being. They simply stare at you. At your body. You stare back - I stare back, and they just return my gaze, at my face, at my breasts, at my loins, and any other part of my body that takes their interest. Are they so blatantly appropriative with their discreetly sari'd wives, I wonder?

Last evening on the beach a young adolescent came up (I was alone) and tried to foist off some lungis on me. When I refused, he offered me some dope. When I rejected that as well, he started playing with the hair under my arms and said, "You like me?" What sort of mythology is this? White ladies like it with young black studs? Do these guys actually score sometimes?

162

Today Weiner and I were looking round an Arts Emporium in Trivandrum. A salesman came across to show me a decorative sword. I looked past him to Weiner because I wanted to show him the letter-holder beside it. The salesman looked too, and for a moment I thought he was going to motion Weiner across to join us. Instead, however, he smiled blithely at me, reached across and handled the object. "It is for Krishna," he said, then withdrew his hand, deliberately brushing my breasts as he did so. He looked at me as he did it, still smiling. Both breasts, quite firmly. I glared at him, and he stared equably back. I looked to Weiner, and the salesman half-followed with his eyes, but then returned to me as if to say: So what are you going to do about it? Is it him or me?

If I had been back home, I wouldn't have stood there another second. It would've been straight to his supervisor and him out of his job and into court. But because I was in another country, some mythical 'other's' culture, I just turned and left. Stood in the stairwell without looking back until Weiner approached.

Weiner, unfortunately, only made it worse. Not only had he been completely unaware of the exchange but was, whilst sympathetic, once more unable to provide the support I needed. The worst time to ask me to 'see the other person's point of view' i.e. it *was* their country and they are used to women dressing in a certain way whether we like it or not and etc. etc.. I mean, this wasn't happening in my brain. And I told him as much. I'm not sure whether he understood really.

Once again, perhaps it's having the benefit of being an alien in another culture, but I become less and less convinced facts have much to do with anything when it comes to the construction of (so-called) realities. I still remember my dreams in Dehli with such cogency, as if they were yesterday, as if they were still with me. I still think of the distance in the thought bazaar between myself and my mother. And here are these men…

*

Kathakali, at the Margi Theatre, West Fort, Trivandrum.

• A courtyard, and performance in the open air once more. The performance space is defined by a slack canopy supported by four poles. A low, rostra-styled stage with an alter before it which burns incense oil throughout. The performance usually lasts 8 hours, but these days (this is an amateur group) they spread it over two nights - 6 pm to 10 pm.

• curtain - each new character enters behind a curtain, which is carried on in front of them. First the hands appear - one with long metal nails, the other not - and shake the curtain. These disappear suddenly, then reappear and shake the curtain down enough to reveal the helmet. This is the first indication of the identity of the character behind. Then the face appears for an instant before the curtain is snapped back up. The next shakedown reveals the torso, or else the character dances with the curtain, exposing an arm or a leg until, after one last return of the curtain, the cloth is dropped to reveal the full character in all its elaborately costumed splendour. Music builds the suspense throughout. This is high theatre. The egg-white neckpieces take the men all afternoon to prepare. It is a devotional activity.

// the suspense technique in films: first we see the hands of the walking person, then their feet against the street; the back of the head; pan back to reveal the back of the body. The accidental collision with the oncoming victim, whose face we can see. The close up of the knife in the hand. The victim's face as she realises she has been stabbed. Her visage empties of life. She collapses as the murderer walks on. We stay with her. From her perspective, watch his back disappearing down the dimly lit street. Close up of him wiping the knife and concealing it about his person. All in black and white, of course. Although the Kathakali is far removed from this in scale of meaning. The shaking of the curtain is cosmic - like a shimmering veil of illusion through which the gods burst, become manifest. And the dismemberment again: each part of the body having an initial existence independent of the whole, a significance of origin. Then the whole emerges with a rush. Pre-emptive glimpses of a unitary immanence? I don't think so. I think in Hindu mythology different parts of the body have different origins, different meanings; or rather, perhaps, *are* different origins.

• Narrative - first character speaks and seems to present an entire case. Is heard whole. Heard out. Musicians play and sing the story behind. Second character presents their reply, again in its entirety, again sung behind by musicians. Then the drums and cymbals ring out, the singing stops and a cacophony of drums and cymbals accompanies the action e.g. Ravana grabs Sita and carts her off, or Ravana and Laxman fight with bows and arrows, or Hanuman bops Ravana on the head. This sequence represents one unit in the narrative. Another in the same pattern takes us on to the next step. I like this. It seems to allow us to look at a usually linear time continuum from component parts. We aren't prevented from empathising, but we are permitted to observe and consider at both the intellectual and sensible levels.

• Communication is as much through hand and eye gestures as through words and music. Each gesture has its own specific meaning, usually of an abstract, symbolic/conceptual nature. The eyes literally dance. Ravana in particular has a rapid-eye-movement which is quite dazzling. Others use left-right movements, up-down and an almost comic eye-rolling, clockwise or anti-clockwise. Interestingly, the characters never look at each other during speeches. They either look away (as in Sita's case) or across each other's fields of vision. Even blinking is highly controlled and communicative. As are the eyebrows.

• Ritual repetition of body movement - advancing and retreating between sentences, for instance - reminds me of Bower birds courting.

• Point of View - the narrative seems at times to present one point of view, and then presents the same action again from another

165

character's point of view. The idea, for instance, of telling the whole of the Ramayana from Ravana's point of view in tonight's performance allows one to concentrate wholly on one coherent, developed and argued set of ideas. My experience of narrative is, increasingly in the twentieth century, that we cut and splice it more and more to both present and conceal our (the author's) point of view in the same act. Kathakali - or my interpretation of it here - allows the narrative to speak for itself, as narrative. I like this.

• Suicide - at one point it seemed to me one of the methods deployed by Ravana to seduce Sita was to threaten her with his own death if she continued to disdain his ardour. How wonderfully perverse. I'll kill myself if you don't let me rape you. And quite overtly presented, it seemed to me, by Ravana as cynical i.e. he knows that Sita, as a virtuous woman, cannot allow him to take his own life even if she does not believe he will actually do so. Truth is not at stake here; it is in virtue that value is invested.

*

I disagree with Weiner. If there is a 'shadow' demon within us, it is one we have internalised on behalf of the men, or their masculine principle, which we are socially structured to service. Whereas it appears that in Hindu mythology, once, there was a female demon equal and not opposite to so much as complementary to the male; a Durga or Kali to the destructive Ravana. But somewhere along the line Ravana and Siva became separated. As in, Siva put the big toe on Ravana and buried him in the Himalayas. Whereas Parvarti, Durga and Kali have remained aspects of the one deity. Or aspects of the female aspect of the one deity. The mystery for me is how, in the process of internally alienating the masculine deity, creating two from one, patriarchy created the still unified female aspect as negative i.e. all demon.

Although why either men or women would want a deity at all seems to me an artefact amongst ideas. To discover how it became so might tell us a lot about transcendence, and the way in which power and authority are constituted within patriarchy. But this could, of course, be just another story. Another component of narrative. Another book in the bazaar. Just one I happen to be looking for. And in the meantime, along come Rama and Sita to separate male from female, mega-good from mega-bad, forever.

*

I acceded to Weiner's particular desires tonight. He tried to make it sensitive, and tender, and sensual, but in the end (pun not intended) it just felt sticky and difficult and I felt embarrassed. And I didn't know what to say because I didn't want to embarrass him. I think he felt guilty anyway, even though he tried to have his usual frank how-was-it-for-you discussion afterwards. I told him it was uncomfortable. He said he was sorry. But he's asleep now, and I'm not. Why am I trying so hard at this? Why do I want to love this guy? I am starting to feel very lost again.

*

A Petition To The Gods

Back on his back, Michael was wondering what had happened to his brother. Survival was such a remarkable event. He could not believe how little he had tried to help when he heard Lachy screaming out in horror not metres away. Just lay serenely on his back, confident that at any moment he would roll over and put on one of his famous "bursts". But he must have known. For as he lay there, listening to his brother's cries, part of him acknowledged: I can't do anything. I haven't the strength. Hardly enough to help myself.

And then the cries stopped. And Michael hoped like mad that Lachy was safely ashore. And as he turned over to crawl in he thought he saw his brother, torso above the surf, striding out. Then to his "burst". Then tiring. Slowing to a breast stroke and surprised to find himself no nearer to the shore. Thinking he must have misjudged the distance and trying again, head down, tiring sooner. Kicking and hacking, at the sea bed almost, willing it to pass beneath him. Without success. For when he looked again, he might have even been further out.

The horror, then, of realising that your belly just hasn't got what it takes. That your frail frame has spent itself, given its best, and simply isn't there any more. Bears no comparison to - "Help!" - you tell your friends on the shore - "I can't get in!" - if you have any - "Help!" - before you are even aware - "H-e-e-e-lp!" - that this is the truth of it -

"H-E-E-E-E-E-E-L-P!"

Your cries take on frantic proportions. They issue from your very being in mad convulsions, hollering their terror to anything in the universe vaguely capable of responding. They are your lifeline, thrown wholly out, mostly to the shore. As if you would already be there, rising manfully from the foam to step onto dry sand. Or fly. Fly NOW! (If there was a God . . .)

Then the whole event halts. Something else takes over. Your mind assumes that it simply needs the rest. Tells you there will be help. Finds reasons. But your heart

168

harbours no such hope. Has no ready salve for the burnt and throbbing neurones. Has another agenda altogether. Has the limbs rotating limply, keeping the body loosely afloat. Has the head lifted slightly, calculating the force and height of oncoming waves, accommodating their rhythm. Has the mouth accustom itself to breathing despite the odd clamourings of sea water about its strangely distant opening. And, at last, has the body laying back, accepting the water beneath, buoying it up.

Hope thus has us halfway, a human splice in the membrane of surface.

*

I'm actually *writing* this now. Like, the brother, Lachy, is Lachman. I know I'm lifting that directly from the Ramayana. And the imagery from the Wilkins. But not all of it. A lot of it just comes. Once I start writing, it's just there on the page. And the whole ocean metaphor - I mean, obviously it's me. And I'm happy to let it *be* me. I stated at the outset that I want this journal to serve that function, of writing me *out*. But I know I am also now consciously constructing a story. Or rather, I am looking for it. Writing to find it. The younger brother, for instance, is clearly *my* **older** sister. Why the contra-placement? Well, that's my task to find out. As a writer. But now it's time for me to sleep, as each little 'burst' of literary self-disclosure satisfies whatever is osmotically making itself manifest from my mind's deeper impulses. I am walking through the bazaar by myself now. I am making the choice of purchases. Finding my own path.

*

Michael was worried about the rocks to his right. He was not sure he wanted to reach them. He could already imagine their sharp and jagged edges tearing the flesh from his right side like serpent's teeth. The land above his head, on the other hand, was just a problem. Too far away to be of use, but still a pain. As if some malicious band of

169

natives bent on revenge were bashing his skull with it. But softly. Black bastards! (But quickly - I'm no racist.) *I never asked to come here!*

It was then that his family started to come to him. Or rather, he went to them. Because he wondered what his father would say if he died. (My father? My mother.) *The thought was untenable. How often he had toyed with the idea of suicide in his youth, wringing himself out over unrequited loves or betrayals, locked in his room, stuffing his bursting face with pillows and writhing on his bed, or smashing his head against a wall until it hurt.* (This is Weiner, not me.) *As if that would release the unfairness of it all from his brain like yoke from an egg.*

Yet if he ever had the chance, it was now. And here was his body, in spite of himself, working away at the water below. He almost laughed. Smiled, anyway. Into the sun. And listened to his brothers talking.

Barney was the closest to him in age. A mother's son. With his thick-lensed glasses and clumsiness. Intelligent, but mostly a hard worker. Always wanted to do the things Michael did. Now secretly kept a pair of Michael's slippers under his bed. To remember.

"They're yours, Michael. Whenever you want them. Please return."

He offers Michael the slippers, his glasses misting up.

Then there was Lachman. Another hard worker. But such life! Lachy always went for it, whatever it was. Hunted it out. Vitality in everything. Yet conscientious. Responsible. But with a sense of humour. Always did the right thing by the people who mattered to him. Got through University. Got into Law. Took after his father. But as soon as the draft got him, he was up and off down South like a shot, so to speak.

"You have to stop doing this," Lachy was saying.

But Michael does not understand what he means. He just thinks how

170

ironic it will be if he survives and Lachy has drowned. How will he tell his father?

*

30 November

I've been thinking of my mother a lot lately, without realising it. I have the feeling, for instance, that I've been having this ongoing internal dialogue with her somewhere 'down there', the meaningful results of which are only now rising to the surface. Of the murky pond of my subconscious? (An unpretentious little metaphor...) I am sitting here, for instance, watching Weiner stroll off along the beach towards the shade of his now-favourite palm, already stoned for the day, waving as he passes to the German couple who share the cabin adjacent to ours, and I catch myself wondering (here's a 'for instance', as our American friends would say) whether she was conscious of the extent to which she created me, as a personality, as a social entity, as a set of motivations. And there she is. My mother.

She was certainly the voice of my major internal prescriptions. I must have the education she never had. No point in sitting around when there are things to be done. Why do it later if you can do it now? Never believe a man when he says he'll give you the world. He just wants you to give yours away. They float around in my brain, competing with my intellect for some sort of currency, already weighted by the trade index of their inscription against all of the knowledge I myself might have acquired.

Oh God, fuck these economic metaphors. Got to get off this. The rational-empirical world I inherent from the corpus of my education, and the very processes by which it inheres, forever force me back into the rational, the intellectual. It's like forever stepping out into the traffic. Why did you do this to me, Mum? HOW did you do this to me? Traditionally the daughter is supposed to be the child the mother keeps close to her, does not

171

objectify, maintains within the ambit of her own subjectivity. You seem to have done the reverse. Pushed me if not towards my father (perhaps I pursued my own gay and inescapable Oedipal dance there myself) then away from you. Perhaps it's because you didn't want me to become the woman you were: to have to devote all of your energies to the maintenance and construction of another's world, and be his life-cushion at the same time. But that's a projection on my part, Mum. You never told me what was in your mind. I wasn't invited in. And Dad moved in anyway, "snaffled me up" as Weiner puts it.

So don't you lose twice? Don't you both lose me, and lose me *to my father?* Yet you kept Brook. Jealous? Of course! Yes, Brook has married, services the needs of a husband and a father at the expense of her own self-expression and self-possession and self-determination and self-fuck-self-fuck-self-fucking-lessness, but at least she had you. Don't you understand what that means? To live within the comfort of another's love? Brook's only deviation from the model path was Aidan, and that's a mystery. Or was. Or still is. Who is jealous of who, here? And so I wonder if you ever had a lover? Did you know the type of man my father was all along? Maybe you withheld your love from me so that I would withhold mine from him now?

But this is foolish. I have become the thought seller. How could my mother have known? How could I have known? What is possible is that my mother didn't actually like me, but I never thought she was a murderer or an escaped Nazi war criminal, as Weiner did his father. She was always an eminently sensibly dimensioned woman. I never doubted that she was there for us. Even in death she was trying to salvage my father from the career he was so willing to relinquish. I only wish . . .

I wish to know the woman that I might have been, might be yet, had I shared the same umbrella of subjective identification as Brook. I want that woman to come out and stretch a little, lie in the sun, take off her t-shirt and let the sun get to her breasts (as Weiner is always encouraging me to do, but not because of it) - and there is Weiner again. The man I wanted to have

172

a child with for a microsecond. Yearned. But of course he did not. Was frightened. So easy to see in retrospect. So easy to see at the time. What would make Weiner truly fertile, genuinely so, in the way I briefly felt as a woman? No, I'm not male-identified in the sense that I see myself as dependent on men and on an advocacy of patriarchal values and constructs. But I am male-identified by virtue, it seems, of my very education, socialisation, and the means by which I was constituted as a social, sentient being. I just want to get away from all of that for a while. Get out of the bazaar, out in the sun and dance with my black lady. Be myself. And hope that there I also find my mum. Or she in me. Somewhere comfortable. Where we can both be my black lady together.

*

Michael hates Daniel. Can't help it. When Michael was born, his father was approaching the height of his career, a Queen's Counsel, starting to sit on the bench. But never had a child. Could not have a child. Until they brought out the fertility drug.

They had received such a hammering in the press, these drugs. Funny, when they had developed them for women no-one batted an eyelid, but when it was for men . . . Somehow they had become entangled in the public imagination with genetic engineering. The drug companies were already pretty desperate for credibility, if not some success. Fortunately for them, Daniel was also getting desperate, for that final step in his career. For in post-Thatcherite Britain, regardless of political affiliation or ideological persuasion, no-one could avoid the pervasive, quietly hegemonic brokerage of capital at the very top. And one particular firm had handed Daniel a Toxic Shock Syndrome case early on in his career . . .

Michael was thus the pay off, all round. The first son was born into a blaze of quartz-halogens and camera lenses from which he had no relief for the first year of his life. Daniel was Mr Virile. And the publicity lifted him out of the

173

realm of government contracts, in which he'd made a name for busting tax avoidance schemes, into the arcane suzerainty of Corporate Enterprise, where he acquired a reputation for creating them again. Not that he ever got his own hands dirty. (Not even in bringing up his own progeny, Michael mutters bitterly into his brain.) Oh, he drove the car, donned the clothes, did the interviews, phone ins and chat shows - for a whole year his reputation and sexual prowess (or lack of it) were trotted around the media arena like some prize stallion. In an age that needed New Age men, Daniel was the softest touch. But no-one touched on what was lost in the process. A small price to pay for progress, really. Died in childbirth, poor love. A rare and unforeseen occurrence. Too old for it, really. And no-one had a drug for that at the time. Michael had not known what made him so angry until he discovered the file of faded clippings in the top of his father's wardrobe.

And that was not the worst of it. Barney's mother, Daniel's next wife, turned out to have been his lover all along. The woman who had hounded him from contract to contract, harried him along when his ambition floundered (as, evidently, it often did). So that Daniel could go home to the harbour of Michael's mother and play host to the gathered multitudes on lay days; entertain the fleet and generally be seen to be in command; always one for a laugh and such a good couple.

No wonder Barney's mother had wanted her son to be Number One. He deserved it.. She deserved it. (Michael didn't dispute that.) Trotting Barney out at parties with his lap-top desk and state-of-the-art computer. It was the father Michael hated. For his gutlessness in letting it happen. Letting everybody do it for him, around him, underneath him, behind him, shore him up so that all he had to do was step off the platform and twiddle the knobs, press the buttons, cut the ribbon, make the faces, tell the jokes, be clever. A Man.

Even that wasn't enough for Daniel. Left Kelly for an actress who was also a leftist feminist. Which might not have been a bad thing, except Kathe was not of Kelly's mould: the femocrats in their smart suits who deftly sliced subjectivity from their gullets as men gut fish

174

so that they too could have the inner emptiness required for business and politics. No, Kathe was one of the next wave, who said motherhood was fine, femininity a woman's prerogative to be reclaimed from the cultural hegemony of patriarchy, and sexual equity a prophylactic to preserve the inherent conservatism of masculinity. If men wanted to change, let them change themselves. Why should women perpetuate their traditional support role and do it for them? Jettison the second stage. Let the old boat go. Down, if necessary. And them with it.

This was not done unkindly. Indeed, Daniel was very much loved. It was, therefore, understandable that, at the time of Kelly's settlement, Barney replaced Michael on the steps of whatever castle Daniel might leave behind. For Michael had no-one to lobby on his behalf.

Not that Michael cared particularly. He secretly loved Kathe, and resented what he had inherited from his father anyway: the belief that everything would come to him if he waited. Michael felt like a chicken stuffed with intellectual artefacts for ideas, plucked and basted and rolled out into the world - "Alright, off you go now." Where? With what? Nobody was picking us up anymore, father. Hadn't you noticed? So don't sit there in your zillionth-floor office and tell me to hang on. For somebody was. I could hear them through the water as clearly as my own voice. "Hang on!" Like a tolling bell. But it wasn't me. It wasn't in my head. It was my father.

"Hang on, Michael! Nearly there!"

Nearly where?

I laugh. But the voice persists. I cannot banish my father from my brain. He leaps out and unanimously claps himself about my shoulders with a resounding -

"Hang on!"

But from afar. So far . . .

175

Michael had never understood the nature of reality before. It was like being born. But in reverse. For reality penetrated his profound inner space like an arrow. Entered his right ear and then, like a grappling iron, clung to his consciousness, pulled the body of reality towards him.

"Hang on! Almost there!"

It was not his father's voice, of course. Michael did not want to believe it at first. Could not entertain the possibility. His limbs had been tiring and he had thought he might need to rest soon. Perhaps forever. And then came this voice. Lachy's voice.

"Michael!" it called again.

Too much to hope for, as it were. But Michael lifted his head anyway. And sure enough, there was Lachy.

"Hang on!"

In some sort of kayak. Just a few waves away

So Michael hung on.

"I thought you were a gonner there for a moment. Can you hang on to the stern? Don't want to lose you now. There wasn't a paddle on the beach so I had to run all the way up to the shack. All those hours in the gym paid off, eh? I couldn't see you at first, but someone on the beach kept pointing, and there you were. Each wave, I thought you'd go. You did the right thing, floating. No use struggling. I only just found my footing. That's how I got in. Never run so fast in my life, Michael. Shit, I was scared. Never had to handle one of these things before. You alright back there? Lucky there were a couple of canoes in the bay there. God knows whose they are. I just grabbed one that wasn't chained up. Hope they don't mind. Funny, I couldn't help wondering how I'd tell Dad. Each wave, I thought . . ."

Michael felt the sandy bottom rub against his feet, but still he hung on. Just for a little longer. This was something new. Like being human again. Or simply being human.

*

The German girl next door has lost her partner. They were standing on the rocks near the lighthouse and a freak wave washed him off. Just like that. Reached out and plucked him. Left her standing there, bereft. She is in a terrible state. Understandably. I spent most of the afternoon with her, but there seems so little I can do. I sit. She cries. We hug. She is silent for a while. She cries again. I touch. She does not want to hug. Then she does. That is all I can do. Her English is not very good. My German is non-existent. And there is the vast emotional gulf of just one instant between us. It could have been me there with Weiner.

The Rockholm Hotel up on the point have agreed to take her in while she does the necessaries. They are Christians, and have been very supportive. We have been able to use their phone to notify the German consul in Dehli and they have arranged for the police to document the incident and so forth. It's been such a shock to all of us here, that something so dreadful can happen so arbitrarily and so suddenly.

*

1 December

Pinch, punch, and Godfrey has turned up, licking his wounds after 'rescuing' Cordelia from her Sri Lankan lover in Varanasi. Oh he rescued her alright, but two weeks later she discovered she was pregnant and 'Godders' made the mistake of asking whose it was. Needless to say she left him.

177

He and Weiner are already stoned out of their brains, out on the beach dancing to a tinny portable tape recorder Godfrey picked up somewhere along the way. They've only got the one tape, however - India's latest rock sensation, Siva, whose big hit is, naturally enough, "The Tandava". The youth of India are evidently dancing the dance that will shake the earth - well, the nation, anyway. And if their efforts are anything like Weiner's and Godfrey's, there ain't gonna be a whole lotta shakin' goin' on. Think I'll just wait until the batteries run out.

*

3 December

I've lost contact with Weiner somehow. It took me a while to notice because I've been spending some time with Pratyangira, going up to Trivandrum with her to sort out her partner's documents, notify his family, arrange her journey back etc.. This was their summer holiday. They had come across to spend time at an ashram near Poona, and flew on here for some quiet sun, as I can best understand. She's handling it amazingly well. I just wouldn't be coping if I were her, I know it. She flies out tomorrow.

Anyway, it's taken me this long to realise that Weiner virtually isn't there for me at the moment. He's either off on the beach with Godfrey, or in Godfrey's cabin. He comes back to invite me for a meal, and returns at night to sleep. But when I approach them, I just get the silent treatment. Very polite and assiduous, but no Weiner. As in, hallo, anybody home? It's Rhea here, remember? At first I thought it was because he was stoned, or still subdued like the rest of us after Pratyangira's boyfriend. But there's just no contact. Even when he touches me, it's as if there's a layer of air between his hand and my skin. The return of the ascetic. But only in relation to me. He's all over Godfrey - back-slapping and hugging and wrestling over the frisbee. Beef-hearty boys' stuff. And of course I've long since forgotten the last time we had sex. It was sort of driven out of my mind by the drowning. But now I look back on it, I wonder if he isn't carrying something from then. Although if he is, he isn't telling me. So where did Mr Communication go?

*

Red embers of the day, dancing in the waves as the sun sinks. The colours of extinguishment so transient compared to the surf in which they appear. The surf itself, so powerful and unrelenting, and oblivious to the departing power behind it. I want to remember the sunsets at Kovalam. They have been marvellous, every one of them.

*

4 December

2 am. Or thereabouts. Weiner hasn't come back from Godfrey's. I've been waiting. I wanted to talk to him. We went down to the Woodstock to eat but then he and Godders just wandered off together. So I've been reading the Wilkins. And waiting. And now I'm nervous. I mean, they could have just fallen into a stoned slumber together - I know Godfrey brought a fresh supply with him - but somehow I've just got that feeling . . .

I've never had a man turn gay on me before. Not that it's a problem as such, and not that I'm worried about gay men as such. I mean, heavens, I worked in a dance company for three years. Some of my best friends arc blah blah. It's just the turning bit; the element of transformation. Not the process in itself, but what it does to the parts of me that identified with what was there before. What happens to the man I thought I was in a relationship with? The man I thought was pro-feminist and, despite subsequent revelations, still seemed to have a lot together, and then despite further revelations ... the man I had 'been through things with'. Where is he now? Which reads, of course, where am I now? Why do I feel betrayed? I know I don't love him. I doubt my own feelings for him. And yet there is something there of mine that he   didn't purchase for me...

179

It's funny, part of me simply wants to slip across to Godfrey's cabin, enter silently, take of my clothes and get into bed with them. Then at least we could all do something together, no matter what it was.

But all of this is conjecture. He might just stumble through the door at any second. It just gives me the heebies again. I don't want this. Not on top of Pratyangira's situation. She goes today. I'd like to be there for her.

*

I've been reading Weiner's diary, which I found had been once again conveniently left out, although this time not open to any page. This man is mad, truly mad. From the moment we arrived here he was, he says, 'totally separated out' from me. His 'true self is totally suppressed'. Nothing he can do is right for me, he says. Writes. If he remained 'present' in the relationship he believes I would 'suck out his very soul and feed upon it'. 'She tears me inside out and the dances on what she's exposed.' I leave nothing of him untouched, for himself. (Is nothing sacred?). He says he just agrees with me and sees my point of view now. That's the only way he can "get by". (So why are you still here, Weiner? What do you think will happen? Why aren't you addressing this situation with me? Even if it means some sort of parting, isn't that better than this? Are these considerations just too pragmatic for you? Too centred in human relationships? But here I am, taking on the barbs.)

Then he gets on to our lovemaking. I use my tongue too much for him. 'Sometimes I almost choke!' he wails to the page. He might as well be saying I have bad breath in the morning. But, so sad, it totally ruins his lion fantasy for him. Now it seems I actually have to get off the lion and masturbate on the axe handle before he can cum at all! (If only I'd known!) I can be so dominating, it seems, it is humiliating. His only chance is if he can 'hang in there' long enough to allow his 'real self' a chance to 'breathe' and gather enough 'strength' to 'cope'. (God, am I such an ordeal?)

180

Next comes Pratyangira. He starts talking to them on the beach, about the ashram and their sect. He is turned on by the fact that Pratyangira sunbathes topless, and wishes I was the same. The Germans, he claims, always were more open to 'alternative approaches' than the British. Complains that I am too limited in my range of sexual options, and that we should be able to experiment more, or that *he* needs to experiment more. Then we get to the anal entry episode. There's quite a jeremiad about that. 'All I wanted to do was *try* it, for fuck's sake. Was that *so much* to ask? But I had to do *all* the work, and even then she wouldn't talk about it afterwards. It's like, I can't do *anything*.' Lots of emphases. Weiner on the offensive. Rhea as a 'tightarsed little Pom'. And here: 'I can't bear to look at her body anymore. The sight of Rhea repulses me.' That's me he's writing about. I'm reading about.

Then comes the death of Pratyangira's partner (whose named I never learnt)(and neither, it seems, did Weiner). And there I commit even greater sins. 'I just want to be in there, holding her and comforting her. I know how she feels. If nothing else, I can speak some of her language. But instead Rhea's in there with her stick up her bum, cold little arms offering nothing but British reserve. Cold comfort indeed. But that's okay. She's a *girl*. That's what seems to be important here. To the dickhead Christians at the Rockholm, anyway.'

Nothing about Godfrey. So perhaps I'm wrong. Perhaps he is with Pratyangira. Perhaps that's where he's been going these last few nights. Up to the Rockholm to sexually experiment with her. Perhaps I should be jealous. Perhaps I should want to tear the night apart so that only the darkness is real, and there flay Pratyangira's flesh from her body with my own nails, my own teeth, my own frail 'Pommie' arms, so that her limbs are torn from her and flung into the endless blackness beyond, her innards disgorged and fed upon by my various uglinesses, my blacknesses, my ink-dark absorbent many-forms, to punish her for accepting my ministrations by day and taking my lover from me by night! Yes, perhaps I should be so angry. But I don't believe you, Weiner. I don't believe this diary. It has the ring of something that was written for others to read, not you. Something written out of jealousy, out of a desire to appropriate something not understood, rather than a quest for personal development. A big purchase, Weiner. So uncharacteristic of the fiscally prudent you.

So what can I do for you? You make me feel so tired. And, oddly enough, so old. You seem so keen to bleed at my expense. Yet whenever I come to patch your wounds, you spring anew from the droplets, always more awesomely self-alienated than before. Are all men like this? I guess they'd have to be deeply sick inside to get away with the things they do in the world. And let us get away with in their name.

In the end I don't really care how fucked you are. It's simply that I cannot do for you what you want or need me to, whatever that is. And perhaps it is you who is the insatiable problem, not me. I still have so much to do for myself. The holes our parents leave in us are like bottomless wells. And I think it's time Weiner disappeared down one of them.

And there, even as I write, a false dawn. Someone has lit a bonfire on the rocks beneath the lighthouse, just as the sun begins its slow ascent way behind hill, trees and entire land mass of Southern India that keeps shadow between it and us down here on the beach at Kovalam. A beacon, for me.

Especially as I thought at first it might be Pratyangira, lighting a farewell votive for her partner before she leaves. But now I can see two lankey, eminently European figures leaping around it in bizarre silhouette. And now more commotion. Indian voices. People remonstrating. Weiner and Godfrey have obviously pissed off the locals, waking them up at this time in the morning.

*

5 December - Kanyakumari

I have just spent a whole night and a whole day watching a crescent moon arc its way across the sky, followed by the sun. From sunrise

182

to sunset. An unimpeded panorama which encompassed the whole of my verandah. And me. The night was as clear and dark as it has ever been, frost-sprinkled with stars. The day has been hazy and blue, broken by clouds. Oddly enough the moon, despite its scimitar-like aspect, was friendlier than the sun. The sun was remote today.

I am alone. In a nice, comfortable hotel on the southern tip of India. I can see ocean for 270° around me. Where the Bay of Bengal becomes the Indian Ocean it is absolutely impossible to tell, but it's out there somewhere! And I feel fine. Even a little bit wonderful. Although not entirely. For the bonfire yesterday morning was Pratyangira. As in, she dowsed herself in petrol and set alight to herself. And the figures dancing around her, attracted by the blaze, were Weiner and Godfrey. And they weren't there to help. By the time the Rockholm people got to her, she was already dead.

So I feel guilty. Had I been more attentive, I would have seen the signs. Coping too well. Overcompensating. A stillness which indicated a premature suppression of the grieving process. Tying up all the loose ends, including her own flight home (and attendant travel insurance, which included life cover, so that no-one would have to pay for her burial). I should have stayed with her that night, instead of returning to myself (and, I had thought, Weiner). But strangely, I don't find myself disturbed by Pratyangira's death. Sad perhaps, but no recriminations. Somehow there is a tremendously powerful sense of self-determination in it. She wanted to be with him, and that's all there was to it. The consul wanted her to take him (or what was left of him - clothes, belongings, personal effects) back to Germany. The family wanted those same effects back - to identify? To confirm? To focus their grief? And Pratyangira's family wanted her back. But for her, home was just out there, in the water somewhere just off the rocks at Kovalam. I don't know whether I could've let her burn, had I known, but now that she has I accept her decision. And only wish, in a way, she had been allowed to see it through. Without Weiner and Godfrey whooping about her funeral pyre, drawing attention and, thus, prevention to it.

183

Her body was so sticky and black when I got to it. (I had to identify her. Godfrey and Weiner were too stoned.) Yet she could have gone so well. Notwithstanding the pain. And if she cried out, it was only to the waves, and her lover. So I guess I feel angry, amongst other things, that she wasn't allowed to go as she had determined. Those silly boys again.

I left Weiner playing frisbees on the beach with Godfrey. I don't think he was even aware I was leaving. I tried to tell him after I came back from the Rockholm. The staff there wanted me to accompany her body back to Germany and talk to the police and phone her parents but - I don't know. She was already gone for me. Let her parents come and get her if they want what remains of her. (And of course they will want to see the body. And should. So of course I should. But, hell, I'm not everything.) And anyway, there were Weiner and Godfrey. I told them I wasn't going back that way, but that Godfrey probably was. Offer him the free ride.

Funny, in the Nineteenth Century it used to be novels. In this century it's been radio, film, t.v.. But in reality, there is no slamming of doors or final departure. No last words or stopping at the door for that contemplative look back. Just me giving 1000Rs to a surprised Savithry, picking up my sausage bag which is easy to throw on and off trains, and walking up the beach towards the Rockholm and the bus to Trivandram beyond. (I gave Savithry my sister's address in Northampton, and made her promise to send me an invitation to her daughter's wedding.) (She was opening the envelop discreetly as I left. I don't think she'd have hung around Kovalam Beach for long that day, fruit or no fruit!)

*

It's comforting to be in Parvarti country. This town is dedicated to her, as are a couple of others further up the coast in Tamil Nadu. I might pay them a call before I leave, with my black lady, who still lives large within me. I touch her from time to time, just to make sure, and find she is not slaying or devouring anyone. Especially not

184

men. They don't seem to know how to enjoy it. (Being devoured.)

Basically, however, I'm close to the end of my funds. This will have to be my last 'treat' before I head home. I might eke out another week or so if I watch the pennies, but Madras will have to be my point of departure. Time to face the music. Dad, the universe, and everything. Although I find I'm not thinking about him so much now. I'm more concerned to get to Brook. She'll be feeling so awful about Aidan, and she needs to know she needn't. I'd also like to join Belinda at Greenham, if it's still on. Time seems such a magnitudinous entity here, but back home it hasn't even been two months. So much for my year away.

And I miss my Mum. Big tears drop onto the page as I write. For someone I never really knew. But wish now that I did. Even though, of course, part of me still doesn't. Such a waste. Such a lost relationship. A closing of an opening in whatever spiritual dimension of possibilities we might understand as the cosmos.

Meanwhile, of course, what I'll really need to do is earn some money. I've had the luxury of not having to think about that for a good few weeks, and it's been nice. Although I'd like to write Michael's story. I've become fascinated with the idea of focusing narrative around a character whose story has already happened, but who thinks he is in another, new story, while the real story is happening around him unbeknown.

It sounds weird, I know, but it's this dogmatic control over narrative that has come to characterise patriarchy for me over the last few weeks. The fact that I have, more than anything else, increasingly come to feel myself as being written, living within a narrative beyond my control. Not just on the personal level i.e. by Weiner, but on the institutional, global, nay - life-forming level i.e. by my entire and ongoing socialisation. If I'm going to find a way out of the bazaar, I have to write it myself. And that means not only rewriting the men in my life, but rewriting the myths upon which they depend to legitimise their personal journeys of fiction/factition. I mean,

185

maybe that's been done, but I think the Mary Dalys of the world focussed on the language of myth, and the myth in language, in an attempt to rewrite both. I suppose I want the subject to remain central, and therefore want narrative to serve the subject, because I want to keep myself whole throughout. I want to be the author, exercise that control, even though I know the literary journey I seek is one that will dismember most of the masculine or male aspects of myself in order to let me and my black lady step out. It's time to stop skirting round the holes in my life-self and jump in, write myself out. It's time for me to revoke the correlation between language and meaning as the permanent property of those in power. Time to take power, as it were, even if only for myself.

*

11 December - Madras

- Imperial Hotel. It's so nice to be able to sit on the white, porcelain throne of a Western-style toilet. One thing I will not miss about India is those shadowy pits of cess over which you have to squat, the combination of miscellaneous turds and mixed urines swashing up in a stench so high even the flies won't go near it.

In Kundalini yoga, they use the image of a snake coiled at the base of the spine which rises up through the chakras, awakening each centre of energy as it goes to finally emerge through the top of the skull, leaving a sort-of atom-blast residue of enlightenment in the third eye. Well, perhaps it's not quite like that, but I've decided that Weiner is the turd coiled up just in front of the snake. One of those long, thin, sausage-like turds you pass after a couple of days bound up by the tension of travel and constant change.

It's not an unfair comparison. He's long and lithe and a sort of characteristic, vegetarian-dun colour. Sometimes he even smells like a turd, when he hasn't washed for a couple of days and the sweat has dried upon his taut, lean skin. So now I am 'passing' Weiner. It's a meditation. My pathvary. And after that I am going to bathe in a deep colonial bath in my white-tiled en-suite bathroom and wash him all away. It's not quite the Lake Palace, but it'll do for my last day in India.

I've had such a hard time these last few days. I suppose the full force of leaving Weiner has come home to me. Which is another way, I suppose, of saying that I've come home to myself. I didn't ask for that relationship. I didn't particularly want it. But once it began - I don't know, it inspired 'hope' in me. I wanted there to be an 'us' to work; which means, for him to be as he had promised. But the signs were there from so early on really. No, I'm not angry. But bitter. Wonder why or how I put up with him for so long. Wasted myself, wanted to have a baby with him. For being so stupidly, stupidly hopeful. And I thought I'd become such a cynic! (And of course, no I didn't really.)

I ended up travelling in a sari and veil for the last leg of the trip, I got so sick of being stared at by men. Even so, on the journey from Kanchipuram I was sitting by the window in the corner of a crowded carriage compartment (2nd and 3rd. class became too much in the end, for a woman alone) and a man came to the doorway, had a good long look, then took out his penis and started masturbating. Nobody lifted a finger to stop him. I wasn't frightened, but there was something so deeply pathetic about the act. In the end, tears were just streaming down my face beneath the veil as the yellowish globules of this man's thwarted manhood fell sadly short of my feet. I was so intensely angry, and yet so deeply miserable at the same time - not for myself, but for them. How is it we carry this capacity to empathise, even in the face of complete and utter objectification, while they remain immune - nay, pathologically resistant - to the mildest identification?

Despite this, Kanchipuram was worth it. The whole town is dedicated to the worship of Parvati, and temples to the Goddesses of every shape and size abound, but most notably in the wonderful, tiered Dravidian steeple that almost characterises India for me. The irony of it is that, despite my own deeply empowering identification with the Goddess and her various aspects, here she is supposed to stand in the flames forever, on one leg and under a mango tree, as an eternal act of contrition because she snuck up on Siva while he was meditating and playfully put her hands over his third eye. It caused the cosmos to collapse, you see. Small detail. I think that's how I felt with Weiner - punished with the collapse of the cosmos because I wanted to play, but not his way. Well, I trust Belinda and I will devour lots of mangos when we get to Australia.

I phoned her from Kanchipuram, and lucky I did. Greenham has wound up, so she is off to join the Blacks Bluff protest in Tasmania. She gave me an address in Sydney, so I've arranged to meet her there. Can't get much further away from home than the opposite side of the world, can you? Why am I going back to do things for other people anyway? This is my time.

So, I fly out tomorrow. As simple as that. And in the meantime, just 24 hours of colonial incubation, dining outside in the warm, moist, evening air at white linen tablecloths with silver service and attentive waiters, surrounded by high walls and a European garden which, nevertheless, cannot keep the tropics at bay. Eating slightly-too-red tandoori chicken and ice cream that tastes like those bricks of Walls Neapolitan we used to get as kids. Fruit salad out of a can. (Yup, I'm off the toilet now.) Watching a wedding reception nearby, saris intermingling like columns of the pantheon come to life. So many rich and differing colours, some with gold and silver embroidery, but also much religiously observant saffron. And frangipanis at every natural place of adornment.

And yet this is the Madrasi rich, still exquisitely oblivious to the poor at the gates. The bequest of caste one no longer available to me. You cannot become Hindu. You have to be born one.

*   *   *

BOOK 2 – BOYS WITH BUGS

Rama

Michael walks along the lamplit street. It's orange glow is comforting, like a cigarette in the dark, burning and dulling with addictive familiarity as he passes from pull to pull, pool to pool.

The first trains are beginning to clatter across Sydney, but they could just as easily be the first-light volleys of machine gun fire across Beirut, or San Salvador, or wherever else is next. And the lone motorcyclist wending her way through the deserted streets, the first dispatches for the day.

Across the city, silent shadows move towards sound in a bid to intercept the day before it happens. Rough hands clasp open mouths from behind. Steel blades slip between ribs and short jets of blood spray assailant hands. It could happening anywhere, somewhere, right now in this city.

It was all bullshit, of course.

Well, to Michael.

What Michael is aware of is that his jacket flaps uselessly over his hands, which are bunched into his pockets like hoarded grapes. Michael likes to think of himself as a poet sometimes. He walks with a kind of aimless shuffle. He doesn't really know where he is going. He doesn't really care. He thinks he might have seen a murder once. He might even have committed it. Or seen it on t.v.. Or it might have been a dream. Michael can't be sure. But it keeps him off the streets from time to time - the idea that he might have been party to something like that. And at others, it puts him on them.

189

Tonight, however, he had wanted to smoke. Not that anyone where he lived was going to stop him, or even worry about it. But guilt is a tenacious beast, and Michael can't afford it anyway. Smoking. So now that Michael has gone out and made himself feel worse about himself, he can look towards the dawn with optimism.

Michael always looks towards the dawn with optimism. You never knew after all, did you, what each day would bring. Although in Michael's experience it never usually brought very much. The next day was, more or less, pretty much an ongoing symptom of all that had gone on the day before, and the day before that. Life, as it were. But the day itself, each one as it marked itself off from the one before, usually found a way of kicking off in grand style.

Even if only as first light, making its way bleary-eyed through the clouds that had hammered the ground mercilessly all night, stumbling into the covert puddles which now lay listlessly about the street. And suddenly there, in abrupt brilliance, declaring insolently, "Here we are, folks! The Day!", first light surprises even itself.

That was what made the day such a cracking good marketer. It knew how to present itself. It was when people trickled onto the scene that the day generally started to fuck up. From there on in, best to sleep. Unless you wanted to catch the sunset. Which Michael sometimes did.

For the moment, however, he turns disconsolately homeward, for no particular reason. It is not that he has just arrived in Sydney, or that anything astounding has just happened to him. Or that he is in the throes of making some monumental decision that will profoundly affect his future, or experiencing some emotionally immaculate crisis. If anything, Michael's story has already happened. He is simply here. And he doesn't like it.

*

Ravana and Sita

190

When Michael got home, Bozzo and Sheena were down in the kitchen. Bozzo's hands were covered with yellow spray paint. Sheena had similarly soiled clothes. They had obviously had a good night out.

The ash tray was flowing over onto the laminex table with residue from the previous evening. An empty flagon stood by the sink, more butts rotting in the dregs of cheap red.

Bozzo was a Punk. Of sorts. He wore a black top ripped off at the arms so that his biceps bulged out like chicken legs. His head was shaved on either side. His curly, matted crown fell in a failed mohawk. (Bozzo didn't use gel because it was trendy and thus supported the fascist capitalist system that took whatever manifestation of individuality it could and turned it into a "market" it could then exploit with its amazing business acumen. Bozzo thought businesses were fucked. He thought the whole system was fucked, and told it so regularly from every available surface in the city. In fact, if Bozzo saw himself as having anything remotely resembling a 'job', it was that. "Keeping the bastards honest," Michael had once offered in supportive validation. "Get fucked!" had been Bozzo's reply.)

Sheena was into needles. But only sometimes. It wasn't a habit. She just liked the buzz from time to time. She'd never get hooked, she said.

"Just another fucking capitalist enterprise," was Bozzo's non-committal response. "They're all fucked. At least the dopies are honest about it."

Which, considering the fact that most of the dopies round the Cross robbed their friends, parents, lovers and just about anybody else of vaguely robbable disposition in order to support their habits, led Michael to seriously question whether or not Bozzo had an entirely normative understanding of honesty.

Bozzo's current theme was that Sheena should become a radicalesbian. Which Michael thought somewhat contradictory. As he understood it, the

191

whole point of being a radicalesbian was that you lived in an exclusively female-identified way. Bozzo was hardly female-identified, and did very little to redefine anything much, let alone in terms of women's experience. Which led Michael to suspect that, basically, Bozzo just liked the idea of fucking a lesbian.

Bozzo and Sheena weren't arguing this morning. They were tired. Spaced out. Sheena's lank hair hung down in greasy strands and her face sagged likewise. The rims of her frail eyes were red, and Michael thought she might have been crying.

"I made her write LESBIANS ARE EVERYWHERE - FUCK LESBIANS! on the wall of the nurses' hostel," Bozzo explained with a peculiarly boyish combination of glee and pride. "Nurses are fucked," he said, and smashed a cockroach a few feet away without even looking. A length of wood always sat on the table for such purposes, and Bozzo was always the first to reach it. When the bomb dropped, Bozzo and the cockies would be fighting it out together.

The dim 40 watt globe was becoming paler as daylight banked up against the basement kitchen's sunken window and peered in. It leapt down from the roof of the hospital opposite and moved testily about the yard Bozzo and Sheena shared with the other four terraced houses on the block. It stumbled over rusting car parts, body work, old iron, mattresses disgorging their innards onto the long, grey grass, to finally fall against the window, panting but vaguely curious about the occupants within.

Soon the waning tenants would give the bulb away, and the damp yellow walls of their nocturnal habitat would surrender their nightly gloss to the inert dullness of the day.

"Watcha got on?" Bozzo asked Michael.

"Nothin' much," Michael replied. "Have to see my agent sometime."

Not that Michael wanted to be a film star. But he'd done a bit of t.v. as a kid, with his father, and it was useful to have an agent to keep the dole office at bay. There was never any work around anyway.

192

Although there was a big war movie coming up Michael wouldn't mind being in. But then, there was always a big something coming up. That was how they kept you on their books.

"Well, we're gonna hit it," said Bozzo for both of them, before Michael could come any closer to a determination. He had only been in Sydney for a month and nothing made much sense yet.

*

Vedavati

Michael didn't go and see his agent that day. The sound of Bozzo and Sheena fucking upstairs was too much for him. He went to bed and masturbated.

It wasn't that he objectified women. On the contrary, the reason he fantasised about them in private was to avoid making them the objects of his sexual construal in public. But still those neo-Freudian snails of guilt emerged from the darker recesses of his conditioning, so that something in Michael believed he was objectifying them anyway and was thus betraying himself.

At least this way he was doing it with other people. Almost. As Bozzo and Sheena vaulted away on their Valkerie Ride to united bliss, Bozzo yelling "Fuck you! Fuck you!" while Sheena yelped to orgasm, Michael propelled himself to corporeal nirvana. While Bozzo and Sheena fell out throbbing on the stuffed mattress and sweaty sheet mountainside of Valhalla, Michael floated amongst bodies, flesh, and an idea of love that he could hardly bear.

Michael wanted a woman.

Not that he hadn't known plenty, but women had become a difficult area for Michael. "And anyway," he rationalised, "We could all be blown up tomorrow." So Michael worked himself into oblivion and then slept.

And as he slept, Michael had his dream.

He is returning home one night. Not to his present house, but to another. One he doesn't know, but might have lived in once. In another State, maybe.

The entrance to this house - it is a basement flat - is below the level of the roadway. The roadway itself is going uphill and around a corner, so that from street level a concrete slab connects the pavement to the upstairs flats. The entrance to the downstairs flats is thus in shadow and darkness.

In this darkness, Michael has forgotten his key. He searches his pockets. He searches under the mat. But he cannot find the key. Which is a bastard because the woman he shares the flat with is not home yet. Even though it is late at night. Or perhaps she is inside asleep, and Michael doesn't want to wake her up. So he squats down in a corner and waits for something to happen.

He must have nodded off then because the next thing he is aware of is movement in the darkness opposite. And the sounds of somebody fucking, not feet away from him. Panting. A man's half-voice. A woman's punished gasps. The heaving of heavy clothing, for it is winter. They are definitely fucking in her doorway.

Michael doesn't know the girl very well but he doesn't want to interrupt her. He thinks of slipping away quietly, but isn't sure he can without making some sort of noise. And even if he did, they might see him as soon as he entered the orange street light. So he decides to stay where he is in the hope that they will not notice him. But it is very embarrassing.

While he is thinking how embarrassing it is, Michael notices a new note enter the girls gasps. It is almost a word - "No!" - uttered with muted desperation. As if she is coming to the end of a long struggle. And as he listens more closely, it becomes clearer and clearer to Michael that the woman doesn't want to be fucked at all. She is being raped.

Michael then realises that the girl is Sheena. And the man is Bozzo. His grunts certainly sound like Bozzo's - insistent, alien, nothing to do with the object of his lust. He is pounding away in the

194

darkness as if merely to exercise his dick: gripping her, pinning her down, having his way.

Then it is not Sheena Bozzo is rooting anymore. It is Sri. Bozzo is raping Sri, and Sri no longer has the strength to fight back. Her cries become clearer and mingled with pathetic pants of "please". But Bozzo is not listening. He is just fucking her on and on.

Michael knows he ought to do something but is paralysed with fear. For he knows Sri. He and Sri used to be lovers.

But what if he is wrong? What if Sri really is enjoying, wants this man? She will be angry with Michael. And even if he does disturb the rapist, what can he do against a man capable of doing this to Sri? For he is not sure that it is Bozzo anymore, and even if it is, he could overpower Michael in seconds and calmly turn back to finish Sri off.

Michael is scared. He is sweating. He can feel moisture cold upon his forehead. He attempts to control his breathing so that he is not discovered. He can hear Bozzo's grunts (if they are Bozzo's) becoming uglier, and Sri starting to struggle in panic. Michael wishes he were somewhere else. Wishes his brother would wake up and open the door. For it is, after all, his brother he shares the flat with.

And what when this guy is finished? Won't he then see Michael as he turns in the half-light, heavy with his exertions, doing up his fly? Won't he seize Michael by the lapels and fling against the dark retaining walls around which the climbing hill wraps itself? Won't Michael be flattened into the recesses of his cavernous entranceway by the relentless blows of this crazed monster of a man?

Suddenly the girls cries break out into wild yelps, and Michael realises it is not Sri at all. Probably never was. But she hollers for help anyway. Uncontrollably. And the man isn't stopping. He is driving on. And Michael hasn't a sound in his throat. Any minute someone must come. Any minute this guy could kill the girl. Any minute Michael could be discovered. Any minute -

Michael rushes forward, almost involuntarily. He grabs the guy from behind. "Get off!" he says. "Leave her alone," he says. But nothing changes. The guy keeps fucking and the girl keeps screaming.

Michael starts to pummel the guy's back. "Get off her!" he yells. "Get off her you bastard. You fucking bastard! Leave her alone! Leave her alone! You bastard! You fucking bastard!"

But still the man does not stop. Does not even falter in his onward ride to self-exultation. Looks vaguely around to see what's bothering, but more as if it were a bee than a boar, a monkey than a man, a wimp than a warrior. Michael is ineffectual. And suddenly the girl's face catches the light in all its gruesome horror.

"Fuck off, you moron! Fuck off!"

She is talking to him. The girl is telling Michael to fuck off.

So Michael bolts from the darkened porch.

Bolts from the shadows into the orange light.

Bolts from the steep driveway out across the tarmac'd street, his own feet smacking into the night.

Lights go on in the houses around him. The girl's screams echo off anonymous facades. And Michael feels a sudden heat behind him. He knows that a red tongue of fire has engulfed the doorway from which he has just fled. Michael is running into silence and the raped girl has been consumed by flames. Only the sound of slapping feet suggest a reality nearby, as the lights continue to go on, curtains are pulled back, and shadowy faces peer out. To see a red glow retreating into the night beneath the porch.

And in that instant, Michael knows that he is the man the public will see running from the scene. That the girl has been burnt to death while her rapist murderer slipped quietly away through the shadows.

196

It is Michael's description that will be circulated by the police. And it is he, Michael, who will have to live the life of a fugitive forever, running from something he did not do. Michael *is* The Fugitive!!!

And so Michael takes to the night. A night in which he alone must find the rapist, the murderer, and pursue him to his death if he, Michael, is to have a future of his own.

This is Michael's dream. He always wakes up from it at this point, feeling uncertain, uncomfortable, and unsure what time of day it is. But he has the sneaking feeling that its construction is drawn, at least in part, from a popular television programme made in the 60s, which is still screened late at night.

Michael fears his subconscious is sending him up.

*

The Origins of The Rayamana, Part I

Michael went to India once.
He didn't like it.

*

The Giant Suparnaka

Whenever Michael awoke from his dream, consciousness set about him like a band of unknown assailants. He gripped the bed and stared blankly at the ceiling, straining his ears in panic. How could it be dark already? The clap of a warning detonator on a railway line nearby told him it was either late evening or early morning, but he did not know which.

Music was coming from somewhere. Not many cars. And someone crying. Upstairs. It was Sheena. And Michael wondered why Sheena cried so much. Why she let herself cry so much. Why she let Bozzo

197

make her cry so much. Surely it couldn't all be him.

Upstairs Bozzo had in fact gone out. He'd beaten Sheena up because she had refused to go out spray painting with him. She couldn't stand the thought of the "FUCK LESBIANS" again.

"Why do you stay with him?" Michael sympathised as Sheena's mascara ran liberally.

And Sheena told him how she used to be a lesbian. Not just on a personal level, but politically. She was a member of a radical collective that had been organising a network of refuges, graffiti campaigns and a gay child-rearing lobby when the DSS mounted their first blitz on all-male and all-female households. This was after the State Labor Government's pro-homosexual parenting legislation backfired.

"The bastards went for a conscience vote," Sheena explained, "Just because there was an election coming up and Alsoran didn't want any trouble. Not with the Libs blah-blahing about the cornerstone of democracy all over again.

"Course they used it against him anyway. And the Catholic Right dumped him, the McCloud press changed horses midstream and before you know it, Alsoran was run out. And the whole bloody Labor machine went with him.

"Well, once The Grinder got his clammy little hands on the joystick, he had a field day."

Michael knew from his own experiences what this would have entailed. Social Security were usually okay with the more marginalised recipients of welfare benefits. They liked their clean-cut, university-educated public image too much. But then again, the Feds had legislated them extraordinary powers. They could enter any house at seven days notice on no other pretext than an enquiry into benefit eligibility. They could summon any member of the public to an interview on the basis of someone else's benefit application, and impose a fine of $2000 for failure to attend. They had the power to sign anyone on or off their allotted form of subsistence at the whim (read 'discretion') of the 'interviewing officer', and could ask details of your private life that would shame most people even to imagine. And once you obtain paid employment, they could construct an 'overpayment' on almost any retrospective obfuscation of mathematical accounting, walk into your bank account or your employer and literally take the money out of your hands. So they could afford to smile.

And they did. They smiled as they knocked on your door at six o'clock in the morning. They smiled as you refused them entry, or demanded an interview at their office at a later date. They even smiled if you slammed the door in their faces, because they knew they would get you in the end.

And if you weren't in, they went and smiled at your neighbours, and asked them who you slept with, how often, whether you went out with them, who you came back with, when . . . and, thanks to one of the Feds' periodic guilt-driven job splurges, there were thousands of them, right across the country. All of them linked by the same, huge computer. So that wherever you went, under whatever name, in whatever circumstances, the minute you applied for any form of social assistance you were instant Commonwealth Knowledge.

As soon as The Grinder got in in New South Wales he did a deal with the Feds. Traded a modest "poofter hunt" for a commitment to the National Manufacturing and Service Industries Compact. The jobs would not roll, so the lesos and poofters could. And the Moral Majority had waited a long time . . .

Sheena had been living in one of the Glebe squats when the first assaults came. They'd had the power put on and a juicy bundle of telephone lines serviced their Crisis Care, Women's Refuge and Rape Crisis services. They may have been illegally in occupation but Telecos weren't slow to make a buck out of them, and Council freely admitted development was years off yet.

Nevertheless, the bailiffs came. Early one morning. Sheena was still in bed at the time. Just woke up and they were there.

199

Phone lines cut. Straight in through the front door with a Council authority and a large axe.

They didn't beat her up that time. Or her lover. The Police stayed outside.

So the collective tried going public. Registered themselves as an incorporated collective and rented a huge house in Annandale. Sympathetic Council. Federal funding. Established areas of need. Credible personnel. Tentative State support. More funding. Then . . . a knock on the door, and the Smiling Men were back again.

"Do you have so-and-so and so-and-so in residence here? Could I speak with them please? Do you mind if I come in and verify these living arrangements? Could you sign this record of our interview?"

They had lists and lists of them, every client, every service agent, and every activist. Only a court injunction kept the bailiffs at bay. The Grinder didn't want to seem openly prejudiced against the lesos. He got them in the end under the new Family Law Reform Act, on the grounds that the refuge and child care services actively promulgated the breakdown of marriage. Again the Police stood outside while the bailiffs marched in. And this time, no-one was taking notes.

"We tried to rent houses in small clusters after that, three or four to a house. But the DSS smiled all the more, and the bailiffs needed no excuse. Clauses against 'illegal practices' in rental contracts, early morning 'poofter busts', it all became more common than the Western Freeway.

"Effectively we forced underground. I got so badly beaten during one eviction I just couldn't take it anymore. They'd already pounded my partner into a screaming heap, and then it was my turn. I know we're all meant to stick together, but you can only take your bed being violated so many times . . . it's worse than being raped because it's liked the whole system is fucking you. Always early morning, just when you are waking up into the arms of someone you love, and the great dick of Patriarchal Justice comes in,

200

rams you up against the wall and fucks you from behind.

"I wanted to be safe. I wanted to be held. I wanted to be where some bastard'd never think to look. That was when I met Bozzo . . . "

*

The Origins of the Ramayana, Part II.

Once, Michael went to India. He went to India because some of his friends had gone to India before him. He went to India to find what they had found. He went to find himself. But when he got to India, with his sausage bag that was easy to throw on and off trains, his water purification tabs to ensure he did not get sick, his injections, salt tablets, and the smallest reduction of personal belongings he could live with, all Michael found was that he was afraid. So he went home again.

*

Ravana

"They'll never get me," sneered Bozzo belligerently.

His lone nightly rampage had ended up in the hospital. At four o'clock in the morning he had broken into the dispensary and sprayed "IF IT WERE LEGAL, YOU'D BE UNEMPLOYED TOO" in red and "DRUGS ARE FUCKED - THEY GIVE ME THE NEEDLE" in yellow on the sterile walls. Red and yellow were two of the colours of the Aboriginal Land Rights movement.

He then beat up two orderlies who tried to stop him raping a young asian nurse, and ran through the ward for the terminally ill turning off their life support systems yelling, "Society's fucked! Get ahead while you can!"

201

He spent the final hours of darkness eluding the police. Bozzo always eluded the police.

"I mean, what the fuck are they gonna do, put me in prison? I'd take the place apart. They know that. And I'd kill anybody who tried to stop me. They know that too."

"Do they?" Michael enquired of Sheena.

"Too fucking right they do!" Bozzo replied for her.

Sheena nodded with blood in her eyes where the tears once were.

"Who am I an example to in there? Much more useful out here, convincing the public that there are real villains about; rapists who steal into their beds at night with thick, shining knives to force them into illicit sex; hoons who will elbow them off the road, strip them naked and set about them with chains before driving off into the dusk; drug addicts who pull them roughly into desperate alleys and paw money from them at gunpoint; mobs of drunken men who roam the streets at night just spoiling for trouble. People like me prove to the public that the police have a real job to do, while Corporate Enterprise and Government Bureaucracies roll them over and fuck them blind without so much as a howdo.

"Of course the fucking police will never catch me!"

And Michael could believe it, as Bozzo stood there reeking of dope and alcohol, his hair matted with dirt and bits of rubbish collected along the way, his neck blue with a self-egrandizing rage that made him seem a mountain in height. Turned out in honour of the full moon, best leathers ripped off a poofter, strips of genuine tiger skin stuck on with Araldite, a prized necklace of plastic shrunken heads he'd stolen from a kid in a joke shop - Michael could believe anything of him.

He could even believe that Bozzo didn't notice that Sheena had been crying. Or that Michael and Sheena had spent the night together.

*

Rama Doubts Sita's Purity

Neither Michael nor Sheena had intended to make love. Michael had simply wanted to hold Sheena and comfort her. Sheena hadn't cared. She had merely wanted something. And wasn't sure she got it.

In fact, the entire experience had surprised Michael. Not because he entered into it. He had fucked spontaneously before. Fallen into bed with somebody who just happened to be there. Or a night of closeness ended up in the almost painfully inevitable friendship-ending lovemaking. What surprised Michael about this occasion was Sheena.

Normally (that is to say, in Michael's experience), first night action was quick, embarrassed, unsatisfactory. But not with Sheena. She seemed to know where she was going from the start, and took Michael there with her. Talked him through it, almost. Not with words, but with soft touches and gentle reminders, where he was and who he was with, which generated responses Michael simply hadn't known he had in him.

As Sheena headed for her orgasm, there wasn't the violent, powerful extinction of self she rode out with Bozzo but something erotic, quietly consuming. Even joyful. Sheena was steering a boat into the centre of herself and discovering once more with wonder the gentle coruscations of ecstasy embedded there.

And as she went, she took Michael with her, like a child by the hand between two young friends. And as he went, love grew inside Michael like a flower. He couldn't help it. Petal after petal just came and came, each one more revealing than those before. There must have been thousands of them.

But Michael wasn't counting. He was approaching his own orgasm, so full of love he thought he would burst. Then, as Sheena's exaltation swam in through the openings of Michael's aural canals, so it gently cupped its hands about him from behind and let his accumulation of pituitary warmth flow blissfully into his lover. It was as if a third eye opened somewhere in the region of Michael's mind, and he could see through a sea of hormonal beatitude forever. Michael was in heaven.

*

Rama Takes Up The Fight On Behalf Of Sugriva, The Monkey King

Michael did go and see his agent the following day, and luckily scored a job right away. Not in the war movie he'd heard about, although another one in the same vein. Nor in a major role. Or even an actor as such. More of an extra, really. Well, solely an extra. He gave a false name so as not to lose his dole, or his hoped-for professional credibility, and signed on for the day with the union.

It was a huge warehouse down on the harbour. Lots of corrugated iron and disused machinery orange with rust. Out on the water, colonies of seagulls gathered on the concrete pontoons beside which the hulls of international cargo vessels waited for a berth in port.

Michael secretly liked being an extra. Nobody knew him, and they fed him really well. All he had to do was dress up in whatever costume they gave him and hang around waiting for his bit. Which was often a very long time.

Occasionally the floor managers would come and tell Michael and all the other extras how unavoidable the delay was, but how each member of the team had their job to do and what a testament to cooperative effort it was when the whole thing came together, as it sometimes did, and how important it was that they, the extras, played their part. (Michael always suspected this last comment was some sort of industry joke, but he wasn't quite sure. Nobody laughed.)

If things took unusually long and the director wasn't an elitist shit, he or she would also come and tell the extras what a terrific contribution they were making, sitting around doing nothing.

What both floor managers and director failed to realise was that most of the extras didn't give a shit how long they sat around doing nothing as long as they got paid for it, and got paid well. It was only a very small number of them who actually wanted to be actors.

You could spot them a mile off, the would-be actors. They sat in silence, their knuckles whitening with the strain of their desire to be part of "the team". Or else they laughed louder than everybody else, glancing out of the corners of their eyes in the hope that the floor managers or assistant directors might spot them.

Then there were the veterans who'd been at it so long they were dying inside, and sat around in groups hissing criticism and gossip under the painfully thin veneer of fraternal conversation.

The one thing that bound them all was a myth someone had created somewhere once called "the profession". And all of them, without fail, would rape, murder, pillage and generally tear themselves limb from limb to get into it.

Michael often wondered if it ever occurred to these people that they were like moths to a flame, all so gloriously inspired by its luminosity that they were quite unable to see Michael, and others like him, standing quietly beyond its rim. They were just part of a recurrent curtain of moths forever burning their wings and falling away again. And, quite possibly, they were all "the team" ever made movies about - dying moths, and themselves - because that was the only world they knew. Talent, Michael believed, like vision, was a figment of the imagination.

The process today was a good example. The extras had to wait longer than usual because the lead actor, who was a man, had a problem.

The film was about this pacifist who has been drafted into the army but refuses to handle a gun. He works as a medical orderly rather than go to gaol. But, during the battle, he sees his mates dying around him, thinks of their wives and children back home and, inflamed with patriotism, picks up the gun and fights his way to glory.

The problem was that the actor playing this part really was a pacifist, and he wouldn't pick up the gun. So there they all were in the studio, fake smoke smelling like chalk dust all over the set, dead bodies and artificial blood everywhere, lights blazing, speed, action and the lot, and this actor staggers out of the arc light, looks at the devastation around him, clasps his wounded head in seeming anguish and says;

"Look, I'm sorry Bill, but I really don't think this works."

The camera crew all look at each other. The sound operator reels in the boom swiftly. The production assistant looks at the script, and the dead extras sense a hiatus but dare not open their eyes.

"Why not?" says the director flatly.

"I just don't think it's what he'd do."

"But I thought we discussed this."

There is a pause.

"Alright, cut! Hold your positions, everyone. We'll go again in a second. Now what's the problem, Graham?"

"It's the gun. I don't think he'd take it up."

"Not even when he sees his best friends, his buddies, lying all around him, slaughtered by the senseless plunder of war? Wouldn't you be angry?"

"Well, yes, but if you're asking me personally, I think I would also be aware that the soldiers on the battlefield I might wish to

206

construe as in some way my natural antagonists, as 'other', aren't actually 'the enemy', as such. I would know that, in effect, they are just another form of worker exploited by the capitalist system, like the rest of us. It's the employers I'd want to take it up with."

"Okay, but supposing you're not a commie - "

"Socialist."

"Socialist."

"Well, just Left, really. There's no such thing as meaningful socialism any more."

"Yes, but your character - is there anything in the script to suggest that your character is a socialist."

The boom operator lights up a cigarette.

"Well, the mere fact that he is a pacifist surely indicates -"

"Indicates. But there's nothing that actually says it, is there?"

"Except subtextually, no."

The key grip sits down. The best boy risks ducking out for a leak.

"So couldn't you want to avenge the death of your mates? Your character. If not for his own sake, then for the wives and children back home?"

"But surely that's the point, Bill. The wives and children wouldn't want it this way. It's the women who always lead the fight against war. They are the first to call for peace. They call for an end before it's even begun. They consistently repudiate the power structure it represents, Bill. They don't want revenge. They want the killing to stop."

"But isn't the quickest way to stop it by taking up the gun? Might not your character see it that way in the moment?"

"In the moment, yes, but in the next -"

"But it's this moment that counts, Graham, because apart from the fact that the employers aren't exactly hanging around the battlefield for you to have it out with right now, if you don't pick up the fucking gun you could be shot at any second!"

"There's no need to shout, Bill. I can see your point. I'm just asking you to see mine."

One of the extras sneezes. A few start to fidget restlessly.

"Keep your heads down, corpses!" yells the ever-vigilant first assistant director.

"Look, could we just try it again, Graham?"

"Sure, sure. I mean, I just want it to be right, you know?"

"Of course you do. Can we have some more smoke please?"

The extras splutter as more chalky dust is puffed out over the set. The best boy trips over a lighting stand as he hurries back to his post.

"Okay, roll cameras - "

"Look, what if I pick up the gun in anguish and rage and then throw it down again, like the ape in '2001'?"

"Cut. Take five, everybody."

"I'm sorry, Bill, but it's not anger I feel. It's pity. I'd rather direct the gun at myself and ask them to pull the trigger if they are so bent upon destruction."

"Suicide's not in the script, Graham."

The discussion lasted most of the afternoon. Eventually it was agreed that the gun itself was the problem. As a phallus, it was symbolic of the violence inherent in the patriarchal power structure that generated war as a means of economic regulation. If the symbol itself was neutralised through a symbolic castration, then picking up the rifle became a gesture of defiance; an empty, hollow weapon firing nothing at the victims of patriarchy.

So the lead actor agreed to do the sequence with the bolt removed from the breech of the rifle, and the director quietly angled the shot so that it didn't include the breech anyway. By then, however, the next shift of extras were coming on, so Michael never got to appear in the film after all. But that was okay. He was only playing one of the victims of patriarchy, so nobody would have noticed him anyway.

*

No Man Of Woman Born . . .

On the way home the train, as it plunged into the roaring darkness of the underground railway that encircled the city, sounded to Michael like a bullet travelling the barrel of a gun, but in reverse. As if the act of firing had been introverted.

So that, with each station the train came to, the shot volleyed out across the cavernous platforms backwards and day-weary commuters were sucked into the breech, to be imploded once more.

It was a complex model, but it made Michael think about humanity. He gazed at the drained faces, waxen with the effort of maintaining the daily commitment to employment, trying to hide the gradual accumulation of disinterest behind a tabloid or two. Sport on the back page, war on the front. Michael wanted to ask how many of them were aware that, at that very moment, thousands of human beings were perishing in a World War that was reputedly underway for their benefit. Who among them was aware that hundreds of unemployed workers, whom their taxes presumably supported, were assuming false identities in active resistance to the draft? Urban terrorism, even. Here, in Australia.

Here the metaphysical bullet hole in Michael's intellectual sensibility, compounded by the ongoing implosion of the train, hardened at its edges. There were some atrocities with which Michael was not yet ready to deal. Things that were concealed, like the electronic micro-sensors inside the rim of a camera lens.

Things like an image of Conan, Michael's longtime friend and compatriot, being manhandled from a shack on the East Coast of Tasmania. Or Samson and Jamie and the others, bounding across the paddocks nearby, hounded by the police. Or Sarama, the love he had faintly hoped would be 'the one', at the hands of idle hoons in the back of a beat-up panel van. Or Sri being dragged by her hair from the top of Mt Kalesa by a man in a business suit oblivious to her screams. And now Sheena, being torn from her lover with violence and rape.

Things he'd never seen but which were nevertheless alive in his memory like fire. Things the powers of law and enforcement had stood idly by and watched.

With logic like that, part of Michael's protective mechanisms reasoned, what did it matter if we were at war or not? It wasn't as if things were any different from before. Politics were still the same. Capitalism slaughtered just as many people in the Developing World now as then, either through culpable neglect or material legitimation. Who was it, after all, resourced the imperialist interventions in South America, Africa and Asia? In whose interests were the sudden eruptions of localised, trans-border conflicts which had become known as the 'sandwich wars'? Surely only corporate enterprises large enough to have interests diversified across the nations of the world would truly benefit from the international bet each way?

The irony that came into Michael's consciousness as he sat was that, now it was all out in the open, the Third World War public knowledge, those who had created the conflict didn't want it. It was the threat of escalation, Michael argued with himself, that had been productive. Once the monsters of government Enterprise had created to keep its microeconomies apart had waded into the battle, the whole system caved in. Serious material concerns gave way to a sort of insubstantial whirligig of rhetorical platforms, none of which

210

seemed properly connected with the rest.

And who could blame the politicians? When they were told on one hand that government safeguards the will of the people but, on the other hand, keeps hands off to allow Enterprise free reign to exploit the same. When they are charged to protect the rights of the majority but preserve the autonomy of the individual, so that select individuals can strip the majority of their autonomy in order to preserve rights for a few. With that kind of oppositional, binary confusion, what price humanity?

And so Michael leaves reason to the blackened walls of the tunnel through which he passes, and the hardened grooves of vicarious experience inscribing the hole in his soul become the lens of a camera, shooting the dead and dying of the world into the void of the complacent millions. And a train hurtles homeward, aiming Michael, and the oddly balanced world he carries inside him, firmly and indisputably at Sheena.

*

Rama Slays Two Demons Set upon Visvamitra By Ravana

That night, Michael wanted to sleep with Sheena again. But he didn't. Not to begin with, anyway. To begin with, he went out with Bozzo and Sheena on one of their nightly escapades. A casual invitation. If he had nothing better to do. Which he hadn't.

They began by getting pissed on some Tequila and Scotch Bozzo had lifted from a Discount Liquor Mart. Down in the cool of Rushcutters Bay, they sat in the growing dimness drinking in silence to the applause of the yachts nodding at their moorings off the Yacht Club's many jetties. Rigging clinked against alloy masts in a stiff evening breeze as tiny, frigid waves slapped against million dollar hulls. On board, you could hear the partying of rich people in roll neck sweaters and the latest fashion from Double Bay, laughing and carefree as adverts.

Bozzo remarked out of the blue that the oak which currently supported their backs most probably shaded the very spot on which the legendary Les Darcy had fought. Not that he fought for long. He could have been Australia's first World Champion, Bozzo extolled, had not the First World War come along. They called him a coward because he wouldn't join up, but he only wanted to see his mum right. Just that one, vital fight.

You could make a few quid in boxing then, Bozzo assured no-one in particular. It was like the Music industry today. Big Entertainment. Megastars. (Or the movies, he qualified.) So when they banned boxing at home, along with other pastimes that apparently detracted from the war effort, the old Les jumped ship for America . Sucked in by the burgeoning Mecca of Private Enterprise. Then the Yanks entered the war as well, and Les was left up the creek without a paddle. Died of a broken heart, they reckon. Queues the length of George Street, the day they brought his body back. Grown men wept.

"Broken heart be buggered," Bozzo interrupted himself and rose. "Whose fucking war was it anyway?"

And he headed off towards the Cross, Michael and Sheena a step or so behind.

The prostitutes were lined up along the chocolate brown balustrade on the first floor of the double-fronted terrace which boasted:

THE BIGGEST BED IN THE WORLD

So that you could see, presumably, just how many sheilas you could fit into this one huge bed.

They called down intimacies to Bozzo, Sheena and Michael, but only Michael looked up and smiled as they passed beneath.

In the back streets and alleys, hookers and junkies alike were scoring deals, being raped, fucked, beaten up, or all four. Derros were keeling over in their own piss and vomit, and homeless youths were spying on guys with big cars making fast bucks in back rooms.

Meanwhile, in the underground car park of the Hyatt, where rich people had their cars parked for them, Bozzo and Sheena set to work. They picked out the most expensive specimens, sprayed them with red swastikas, and then daubed them with slogans in white and blue such as "WE CAN MAKE IT, BABY" and "LET'S DO IT FOR MONEY". At this stage, Michael was somewhat uncertain of the extent to which he was prepared to commit himself to this kind of activity. He was not, at heart, a petty lawbreaker.

The three of them nicked off as soon as the first guard-type person appeared. It was too early in the evening, Bozzo reckoned, for any major confrontation with authority. Michael was not to be sure what he meant by this for another hour.

They went to a Lebanese street cafe and watched the prostitute on the corner go through five men in half an hour. Michael thought it must be some kind of record. She was gone with one guy for less than a minute.

"Must've changed his mind," mused Michael.

"Nah, just lonely," Bozzo replied.

Sheena said nothing.

After that, Bozzo shouted them a strip show. He knew the guys on the door. It wasn't much. Just a girl with tassels on the tips of her breasts, which she twirled in the faces of the guys at the tables nearest her. Then she bent over and looked back through her legs, so that her crutch and anus were bathed in red light. Michael thought Bozzo was only doing it to upset Sheena, but Sheena's faced remained impassive throughout.

A few Tequilas later, Bozzo led them into the back streets, where more rich people parked their cars in the darkness to attend expensive bistros and brasseries nearby. Here Bozzo and Sheena started to spray-paint again. They kept handing cans to Michael, and he continued to be in several minds about using them. Occasionally he would take the cap off one and make jabbing movements with the nozzle, but on the whole he never quite got there.

Bozzo and Sheena seemed unaware of his indecision. On the contrary, they evinced the impression he was having a good time. And Bozzo soon lost interest in the activity anyway. After two streets a couple of the cans ran out, another jammed, and Bozzo got pissed of with the poor light. So he started slamming into bodywork with a jemmy he appeared to have had all along.

Back down the street he went, delivering precision dents to every vehicle he'd previously marked with a swastika.

As was to be expected, the audibility of his progress was matched by a series of lights appearing in the urban dwellings accompanying it, and it wasn't long before Bozzo was being shadowed by two conspicuously anonymous headlights.

Bozzo ducked into a garden and let the vehicle pass the first time. Then he snuck down an alleyway into the street the trio had already completed.

The cops were waiting. They'd spotted the graffiti. But Bozzo had also anticipated them. He broke into a dormant house off the alleyway and phoned the police. Michael heard him mimic a woman's voice to complain about the damage currently being administered to her vehicle in the street they had all just vacated. And sure enough, the cop car crept back around the block, allowing Bozzo to complete a flying strafe run along the second marked street.

Michael was beginning to feel that he no longer wished to be part of this activity, but Sheena was dragging him into the house from which Bozzo had just phoned.

"We'll be safe in here," she whispered.

But Michael was not reassured. Especially when Sheena turned on the front room light and repeated Bozzo's phone call, this time complaining of a disturbance out front.

The car was there in seconds, blue lights flashing, sensing the chase. A uniformed policeman athletically mounted the steps to the terraced house and Sheena answered the door. Michael was wishing a hole in the floor would rapidly open. He was scared the owner of the house would come down the stairs any second and expose them both.

No-one did, though. Instead, Sheena started pointing in the direction she 'thought she'd seen the man go' before the policeman even had time to verify that she was the caller. He was a young chap.

And so was his mate, who was already half out of the car as Sheena pointed. The two officers exchanged looks and the mate was off down the road to investigate.

Then Bozzo emerged, hooked the blue lights from their mount and smashed them onto the pavement. A second blow was well on its way to removing the computer-communications unit from its housing under the dash before the officer at the door, who had turned back to ask Sheena a few questions, could look around. When he did, however, Sheena slammed the door and switched off the lights, which must have conveniently confused the young policeman as Bozzo took out the windscreen, headlights and front, off-side tyre in pretty much the same action. Michael had never seen anyone move so rhythmically fast.

From the lightless front room he and Sheena watched the policeman who had gone after Sheena's red herring cop it in the abdomen as he ran back to his besieged vehicle. The officer at the front door, seeing his mate making after an apparently fleeing Bozzo, made for the car to radio for back-up, or whatever it was cops radioed for in such situations.

By the time he realised the radio was out, his mate had been grounded. By the time he was set to spring to his mate's aid, he had been grounded. By the time both were up and ready to run again, Bozzo was   well away.

215

"Quick," said Sheena, "They'll be trying the house next."

And sure enough, as Sheena and Michael slipped over the side fence into the alley, they could hear a frantic banging on the front door. As they turned from the alley into a parallel street, one of the flat-capped forms appeared in the light at its other end.

"What about Bozzo?" Michael puffed as he and Sheena ran through a maze of back streets guaranteed to confuse the most ardent pursuer.

"He'll be alright. He'll get back to the Hyatt if he can," Sheena yelled over her shoulder. "Or just keep the cops busy for the rest of the night."

Which was, it seemed, something Bozzo did rather well.

For his own part, Michael was not at all sure he wanted to go out with Bozzo and Sheena again. Although he would, eventually. For this night, however, he was content to compensate for Bozzo's heroic absence in the unbelievably sublime arms of Sheena. For just once more.

*

Daksha Refuses To Invite Siva To A Sacrifice

Michael had a friend once who had been a member of one of those religious sects that bundled out of India after the Beatles gave them international credibility during the 1960s. Michael conducted a historical search once and estimated it was about the 54th to achieve international recognition. It was definitely the 54th. to have its funds ripped off by a the-money's-in-a-Swiss-bank-account guru in the tax-shelf-rort manner so admirably pioneered during the 1980s. Claim the individual can attain world peace just by thinking about it (or not, as the case may be), get one of the staff to run off with the money, declare the organisation bankrupt, dissolve the religion around its thronging mind-insolvent followers, and mysteriously reappear months later in an expensive hotel, wearing expensive clothes, eating expensive food, driving expensive cars, and generally whooping it

216

up for the remainder of one's eminently corporeal existence.

The money, of course, is untouchable because it has been donated to a religious charity. It is also untaxable for the same reason. Before you know it, multinational corporations are sponsoring new religions like they are going out of style.

Which they probably were. Nevertheless, Michael's friend went on believing. Although what could you expect from someone who rose at three o'clock every morning to meditate? It was the sort of technique employed by torture squads in military dictatorships to pulp their victims' minds into the numinous jelly of submission. You'd believe just about anything the living God Baba was even vicariously reputed to have vaguely murmured in his vast, immeasurable, cosmological sleep after a couple of months of that kind of treatment.

Even when her Spiritual University was blown up during the bombing of Dehli, Michael's friend had gone on believing. [The Indian Prime Minister, it seemed, had decided that despite oceans of world aid from all sides, and a substantial lead in the Asian techno-industrialisation race, India was not making Developed Country status fast enough.

India and Pakistan had been playing at World Powers as long as they had had independence, jostling each other with nuclear deterrence, waving metaphorical fists of political disapprobation and religious hectoring across their mutual border. It was logical for India to take its near-war economy to its logical conclusion, in the form of a limited tactical nuclear strike.

Not on its enemy, of course. Although no-one would ever admit that Pakistan's opening act of aggression was actually solicited by India, many conceded that India needed a dose of world sympathy, in the form of a swift economic shot in the arm. And that India had been the more successful dissembler of the two on the world stage, grandstanding as Universal Peacemaker whilst covertly throttling the identity out of its muslim minority. It was fairly predictable that

217

Pakistan would not only refuse to come to the sacrifice but would lob a votive of its own onto the negotiating table. But conspiracy theorists maintain to this day that the Police Powers had satellite evidence that, though the nuclear strike originated in Pakistan, it was not of Pakistani origin.

As for the Police Powers themselves, it was just what they needed - that one extra sandwich war in the Middle(ish) East to nudge their global micro-escalations into the economically much-needed World War Nobody Wanted.

In the event, no-one was satisfied. As far as Michael could tell, all that resulted from the carefully engineered spectacle was several million Indians dead and the disappearance of an entire range of medium level goods from Western supermarkets and boutiques. Developed and Developing countries alike were far too busy worrying about their own economies, as third stage capitalism creaked and shuddered under the strain of global equalibration.

Despite the deaths, and the loss of Dehli (which was, after all, no more to Indians than Canberra was to the Australians), Indians went on being Indians but with a radically higher mutation rate, and Islam became more powerlessly entrenched than ever in its pathological mistrust of what it called "The West".

The Police Powers went ahead with the World War anyway. It looked good on paper. And Michael's friend still maintained her faith in the healing power of thought, or non-thought (Michael was never quite able to work out which). "You can't believe everything you read in the papers," she had reasoned wisely. And was probably right.

[It must be great, thought Michael satirically in the darker moments of non-sleep, to have a God who did so much for you personally.]

*

218

Rama Spends Sixteen Years In Exile

For himself, faith was no easier than belief.

Not that he had never had belief. Nor something which may have amounted to faith. But Michael had experienced such changes since the War began that, when he took away the things his parents told him about himself, the things they intimated he should be, the things his brothers obviously admired in him, when he removed the layers overlaid by culture and the painstaking years of role modeling, all Michael found at the centre of himself was an astounding void.

This void could have been a great thing for Michael to have discovered. If he were a kundalini yogi, for instance, he could have focused through it the metaphorical snake coiled at the base of his spine and caused it to rise through the seven chakras to burst through his skull into the pure light of ultimate consciousness.

Or he could have meditated within it upon the seven-fold path and, through contemplation of the mahayana, attained nirvana.

Alternatively, he could have found the sacred flame of purity there, from which Brahma, Vishnu and Siva emanate, and thus achieved unity with the cosmos.

But all Michael did with this centre of his was to mourn the huge, engulfing emptiness of it, in which nothing really mattered. Someone could have fired a fairly sizeable thermo-nuclear device through its middle and Michael couldn't have cared less.

Given such universally reductive apathy, Michael had often wondered why he hadn't simply accepted the draft. Perhaps it was because there was still an angry young man down there somewhere, struggling to get out from behind the void: a man who resented the tendentious layerings of parents, friends and culture, who reviled the prospect of living out the dreams, expectations and desires of others, who challenged the self-fulfilling prophecy others so blithely accepted as life.

But if that man was there, Michael wasn't aware of him. There was, however, one emotional tug capable of enticing Michael's alienated inner-self out from its self-imposed exile, one human condition that unmasked that masked man completely, one tragic flaw . . .

*

The Golden Deer I

After they had made love for the second time, Michael wanted Sheena to run away with him.

"Oh what?" said Sheena with more than just a trace of annoyance. "It was just a fuck, okay?"

"But I love you!"

"Sweet Jesus where do you guys get these ideas from?"

Michael was somewhat affronted, not to mention embarrassed. Something in him believed that when emotions were aroused with such vigorous ineluctability, they should at least be destined to some form of actualisation. And he would have pushed for a more material manifestation of his desired romantic apotheosis had not Sheena offered such pragmatic disincentives as:

"Bozzo'll kill you if he finds out. And me."

Whereupon Michael restrained himself from the immediate pursuit of gratification - for Sheena's sake of course.

"Perhaps you really do love me but you don't know it," he suggested instead.

For it had occurred to Michael that perhaps Sheena was afraid of her seminal love for him because its object was a representation of the patriarchal system that so oppressed her. But, thought Michael nobly, with caring love and patience she would see that he was not like that.

220

"Jeezus Christ!" said Sheena with a disturbing lack of reciprocity.

"You don't have to give me anything back," Michael offered by way of qualification.

"What do you think love is, Michael? Some sort of neatly packaged commodity for you to dole out and receive, turn on and off at your convenience? I don't love you, alright? Now keep it quiet when Bozzo's around. He's not stupid, you know."

The door banged bad-temperedly as Sheena left the room.

"Alright," Michael replied to nobody. But secretly committed himself to loving her anyway.

He began following her when she left the house - at first, just to be near her; but when he found out where she went, to look after her. Not that he could have done anything particularly. He was not the most physically accomplished of men. But perhaps the mere presence of another body might be of help, should an affray occur. A deterrent. Or even just a witness. because during the daytime, Sheena frequented not only the Cross but its most notorious brothels and drug freak crash pads.

To begin with, Michael feared she was working as a prostitute to support a habit, but after a while he realised she couldn't possibly be working that many clients. Or indeed consuming that much heroin. (Michael was at this stage in his life sadly ignorant of the human body's capacity to accommodate both heroin and sex.) Which left him confused for a while. Until his agile mind came up with the understanding that Sheena was some kind of undercover social worker who secretly took care of the drug-addled prostitutes of the Cross for no reward other than the knowledge that she was saving one more deflowered madonna of womanhood from the flaming pit of patriarchal sublimation, and crucifixion in perpetuity on threefold cross of sex, smack and capitalism - well, just capitalism, really - albeit against the steamy odds of almost inevitable recidivism and thus continued oppression. It made sense to Michael that Sheena's feminist

221

commitment would find its focus here.

"We just help each other, Michael," Sheena explained impatiently, revealing the needle marks in her thin, pale arms.

Michael had followed her to a basement in the Cross where, unfortunately, she had spotted him. Couldn't have avoided him really, he stood so haplessly in the doorway oozing his quiet confidence in the transcendent synchronicity of love.

It was neither a brothel nor a dive. Although it was true that the low-ceilinged bar-cum-cafe was bathed in red light, and short-skirted shoulder-bagged hookers littered the joint. They were, however, for the most part engaged in no activity more meretricious than drinking coffee. And perhaps talking.

Sheena was sitting on a high stool at a laminex bar, engrossed in the latter act. Probably discussing some vital detail of the depersonalisation of drug addicts by patriarchal welfare services bureaucracies with a colleague, Michael guessed. Although he interlocutor was somewhat incriminated by the tell-tale shoulder bag on the table beside her.

Which gave Michael some remedial comfort, for no sooner had he spotted the two than he noticed that they were holding hands across the table. It was a casual contact, but also a familiar one. There seemed an insouciant reassurance about it. It let Michael's eyes not to the intellectual frowns and intently nodding heads, but to the moist lips moving around words that obviously did not matter.

Trying to belie the obvious, Michael resolved to leave on the assumption that this was just a very very meaningful professional discussion. But then Sheena glanced up and saw him, and the love in her eyes was unmistakable. And unmistakably not for him. For like a dart the instant engagement of fear shot into them. Michael. Bozzo. Men.

He found it difficult to leave then, for he did not want to intimate any residue of betrayal. He, the spy. She, the victim. He to return to Bozzo with the fruits of his forbidden foray into Paradise. But he didn't want to join her anyway, because he himself also felt betrayed. He knew he shouldn't. He knew he had no cause. And he could see that he clearly wasn't welcome. But, in order to preserve what future he and his sex might have with the likes of Sheena, join her he did. In a shuffling, crab-like, arm-flapping kind of way.

"This is Sri," said Sheena, a curtness enveloping the tenderness in her voice.

"What are you doing here?" Michael replied, unable to keep the petulance out of his. And the gaps of warm and dreamy infinity that had opened up beneath Sheena's eyes at the mention of her partner's name snapped shut.

"Hallo Michael," said the other woman. "Long time no see."

A set of signals somewhere on the train tracks of Michael's mind changed, so that the name from the past could connect with the woman now before him. Even though Michael himself remained on the opposite platform, and so had to wait for an intervening train to pass. She had cut her hair. Her face was thinner, more tanned. Yet pale. Pock-marked. But the woman with whom Sheena was in love was irrefutably Sri, a woman with whom he himself was once in love. Indeed, he had cohabited with her. For quite some time.

"Is this your lover?" asked Michael, somewhat unnecessarily.

"I'll see you later," said Sri, and Sheena for a moment dropped her sub-ocular shutters as she and her lover clasped forearms in parting and allowed their lips to meet for one, brief exchange.

Michael looked away uncomfortably.

"I've been following you," was all he could blurt out as Sheena bustled out of the basement.

"I have to go back to work," she said, irreverently. And Michael noticed she was now carrying the shoulder bag Sri had brought.

"It's alright. I won't tell him."

"It wouldn't matter if you did. He can't do anything."

Michael began to suspect they were talking at cross-purposes.

223

"Where is work, exactly?" he ventured.

"I thought you said you'd been following me," she replied, stopping outside one of the many brothels Michael had seen her frequent during the day.

"Look, we do six of them, right? Three each. And cover for each other at the same time. You can earn more that way, as long as the pimps don't catch on too often."

"We?"

"Me and Sri."

"So you aren't . . "

"Of course we are."

"I mean, yes, you are."

"Are what?"

"Well, exactly."

Michael still wasn't sure what it was wouldn't matter if Bozzo found out about it.

"So what do you do with the money?" he asked eventually, for want of a better question.

And the exasperated sigh that followed gave Michael long enough to notice how protectively Sheena's hand clasped the top of her shoulder bag. As if she were trying to prevent it from taking off. Or else nurturing her forearm.

"I thought you said you'd been following me," she almost whined, for she was following his gaze as she spoke, realising as she did that he hadn't realised what she thought he had.

"I thought you were helping them," Michael said weakly.

"We help each other," Sheena replied with resignation. It was then that she showed him her arms.

Now Michael knew that he could pity Sheena for her addiction. That would make him feel superior, and he could continue to love her blindly. He also knew he could admire her for having the courage to live right on the twin nexi of patriarchal oppression, Bozzo and prostitution. Perhaps he could even envy her her lover - although at the moment Michael basically felt irritated that Sri had popped up in his life again so irksomely.

Unfortunately, what Michael fundamentally felt was revulsion.

*

Dandaka

Try as he might to deny it, the discovery of Sheena's habit, her method of supporting it, and her relationship with his former lover, all presented severe impediments to Michael's determination to love Sheena. Especially given Sheena's not inconsequential lack of encouragement in this regard.

His brain was, however, locked into one of those impossible circuits that so thwart unrequited lovers that it seemed easier to find another object upon which to unload his frustration than to confront the fact that Sheena was in love with a former lover of his and had needle marks in her arm which disgusted him. And that object was Bozzo.

How could she stand his body anywhere near her, let alone inside her, loving Sri as she so obviously did, Michael asked himself rhetorically as he wandered aimlessly down the hill from the Cross after Sheena had left him with an image of pitted milk floating before his eyes.

It was clear Bozzo was responsible for her addiction. Why did she so blatantly rush to his defence, claiming upon interrogation that it was she who supplied him, rather than the other way around. She was protecting him, in fear of reprisals. Michael had read in newspapers how the drug lords did it - rule by terror. Bozzo had probably known about Sheena and Sri all along, forced them into the habit out of sheer patriarchal bloodymindedness.

By the time he reached Rushcutters Bay, Michael had realised it must have been Sri with whom Sheena had been living when she first met Bozzo. Sri was the lover with whom Sheena had been fighting over the little golden faun the latter had treasured since childhood. It was Sri who had, in a flash of

225

ideologically informed irritation, snatched the idolised ornament from its owner and thrown it out of the window, yelling:

"It was given to you by the man who tried to rape me!"

And it was Bozzo, one of the punks next door, at whose feet the faun had fallen as he was arriving home, and who returned it to Sri and Sheena just as they were enjoying a tender reconciliation. Of course he knew!

And it was Sri who had the shit beaten out of her by bailiffs in a dawn raid upon their squat; Sri whom Sheena had watched dragged away, herself restrained by the helpful neighbour, Bozzo, screaming her horror to unheeding walls for the rest of that day and into the oblivion of the next.

And how was it Bozzo came so conveniently to be there? Who let him in when the bailiffs broke the door down?

By the time he reached the easternmost ambit of Rushcutters Bay, Michael felt quite sick with the intensity of his indictment of Bozzo. At that moment, the Manly Ferry was making its way up the harbour. In his short time in Sydney, the Manly Ferry had become the one cheap refuge that had never failed Michael. For a modest percentage of his dole money, Michael could join the almost sea-going thump thump of this near-mighty vessel and journey toward the swell of the ocean just beyond the Sydney Heads. It was the one event he could afford that took him out onto a terrain that was substantially other than the city, the war, and his life-enmeshment in both. The Manly Ferry was, as it had been for so many Sydneysiders, Michael's escape.

Now he mentally zoomed out to join it as it luffed its way across the stiff, choppy waters. But today the ferry seemed surrounded. The city was watching, anxious to observe its bid for freedom. Buildings threw their occupants around sumo-style, as one concrete-verandahed, glass-and-sun-visored apartment squatted on top of the next and another for a better view of the harbour. Or snuck

226

a foot between waterfront mansions to wedge a toe into the oily brine.

The mansions themselves poked out pink, forbidding boat ramp tongues at passing water traffic. Close to the harbour's edge, denizens of citydom bobbed about in fibre glass water birds whose white wings unfurled only at weekends, looking back awkwardly over their shoulders in case the Manly Ferry were to succeed.

A helicopter dragon-flies menacingly across the water, its rotors battering the belly out of a cloud base, buzzing the departing vessel. Back inland, an electric train rollicks out of Edgecliff station with message of the escape like a chain of silver elephants, trunk to tail, and slams into the root system of the city to writhe there like a snake - nay, a hi-tech worm, digesting and egesting nutrients out of which grow the canopies of the Central Business District.

In those tall trunks of the CBD, colonies are at work, clambering from their underground nests to feverishly chew up paper and feed it into the xylem and phloem of fibre-optic wires that maintain this vital econosystem, soaking up electric light like leaves and issuing the result back onto the streets, where they are snapped up or lost by the incessant rush of tyre on bitumen, orange tongues of left or right indicators, lizard heads on starched human necks sparring in the quest for another so-called lane.

Cars stack up on each other and mate at every opportunity. Whenever you look, there are more of them. Furry cyclists are lost in the frenzy of vehicular copulation. The entire city teems with the life of it, weaving in and out and back upon itself. It is an ecosystem. And Bozzo is but a bug within it. An ugly, black bug, who turns the soil rancid around him and feeds on humus. A bug other insects avoid because of his unpleasant discharges. But only a bug, nevertheless.

Well, logic tells Michael this, but in his heart and mind, Bozzo is bigger. He is huge. He has horns, and towers over Michael. He is a bull, loosed and on

227

the rampage, gouging great chunks out of buildings, trampling cars like toys and battling with the giants of capitalism that walk invisibly between the towers there.

Bozzo is a bug on the back of a bull. And Michael is no matador. He cannot ride into the ring with his blood red cape and fire fatal darts of masculine superiority into Bozzo's coarse neck. He cannot even ride. All he can do is cast his eye out across the gentle light criss-crossing the water like a net and think how beautiful it is, even on an overcast day like today. And the Manly Ferry disappears from view, and Michael finds himself inexorably in the present tense, despite all of his best intentions to the contrary.

And Michael suddenly feels terribly, terribly alone.

*

Siva's Fever

"Do you want to come on the blood run?" Bozzo asked one morning as Michael was pondering on what to do about Sheena.

Caught off guard, the erstwhile rescuer thought he heard Bozzo say "drug run" and had to ask for the question to be repeated.

"For the Red Cross. I do it once in a while," Bozzo explained.

Michael was so surprised at this sudden emergence of humanity in Bozzo that he involuntarily agreed.

As they honked their way through the lunchtime traffic with a batch fresh from the city's donor centre, Bozzo told Michael a story.

"In Bangladesh - you know Bangladesh? It used to be part of India. Then they had this war of independence, which they won. And suddenly found themselves with all these people they couldn't feed. Socially irresponsible, if you ask my opinion. Grabbed for power before they knew what it entailed, you see. So do you know what they did?"

Michael didn't.

"They called in all the young blokes to give blood. This was towards the end of the war, see? Sort of like, give generously because you're probably gonna die of starvation or disease anyway. Oh, and here's your gun. They were kids mostly. Anyway, they stick the old needles in and whack on the old bag, and when it fills up they just take it off. Put another one on. And then another. And then another . . . "

"But they'd bleed to death!"

"Painless way to go, but. Gently pass out thinking you were doin' the world a great favour. You just didn't realise how great. And boy-o'-boy, there was plenty of blood in the Bangladesh blood bank. They were selling it to India!"

"But . . . weren't there authorities to intervene?"

"Who, the United Nations? Everybody knows they're just a front for the global powers."

Bozzo did not use the term 'Police Powers' as others did these days. Michael wasn't sure whether he therefore meant the new transnational feudalism or what remained of the pretence of nations. But he didn't like to ask for clarification just now. Bozzo was in full narrative stride.

"But yeh, they were there alright. You can't cover every crisis-threatening event, can you? This was only every second or third donor maybe. Enough to curtail population production, as it were. They started on the patients too, it was such an effective method of hospital bed reduction. 'I'm sorry, madam, but we just have to take a small sample of your blood.' Who's going to say otherwise? Accidents will happen. 'Oh, we just left it on too long.'"

And Bozzo leaned over to pat the jelly-like plasma bags behind him, the bags wobbling redly in reply.

"Of course, it wouldn't happen here," he went on to reassure the obviously disturbed Michael. "Although it'd be a clever solution to the AIDS problem, wouldn't it? 'Er, excuse me, but my friend came in for an AIDS test recently and I haven't seen him/her since.' 'That's alright sir/madam. Just sit down and roll your sleeve up, will you?'"

"That's incredible," said Michael needlessly.

And Bozzo laughed. Michael glance sidelong at him. It was true that you didn't see so many gays any more. Not on the street. But Michael had always thought that was because the AIDS legislation had effectively driven them underground. Just as they were gaining legitimation and public acceptance etc. etc.. But now that Michael came to think about it, that was only the media's version of the story. And AIDS testing was still compulsory for blood donors, and a blood test was a necessary prophylaxis amongst gays. So it would be possible . . .

"The irony of it all," said Bozzo out of the blue, "Was when they discovered Frank Amazon had AIDS."

"Yes," Michael agreed with a faint laugh, because he hadn't the faintest idea who Frank Amazon was; let alone that he had been the leading light of a Fundamentalist Christian Movement before his sad and untimely death.

"I'm just joking, Michael," Bozzo said, as if he were stating the obvious. Then he laughed at a joke known only to himself. "You'd believe anything, wouldn't yuh."

The thought had never occurred to Michael before.

*

Sugriva Renegs on His Promise

That evening, while Michael and Sheena were watching the news, Michael saw a man he thought he recognised. This did not often happen to Michael. People he knew did not often get into the news. Especially not footage filed from the front, of Australian 'advisers' helping PNG beat back the Indonesians - just one of the many 'Vietnams' in which our overstretched forces were being further stretched these days. Although the Government continued to deny any commitment of troops to global 'police actions', embarrassed as they had been by Australia's singular lack of response to the Third World War, they weren't doing much to disguise the fact that they were in there boots an' all.

In this particular footage, a soldier carrying an ill-matched rifle emerged from the body-strewn battlefield looking uncomfortably victorious. Michael looked closer.

"Is there a bolt in that breech?" he asked aloud, as the soldier trudged past the camera, gun hanging loosely at the lowest extension of his ape-like arm. But you couldn't see.

"What?" Sheena asked, munching on popcorn they got out of the ecologically friendly packaging for their mail order supply of naturopathic medicines (purchased on someone else's bankcard, of course).

"That guy. He was the hero in that movie I was in the other day. Or wasn't in, as the case may be," Michael explained.

"Must've been called up," suggested Sheena with little interest.

"But this is supposed to be recent footage," Michael persisted.

"They train 'em quick these days," rejoined Sheena with laconic irony. "'S all done with computers."

But Michael was certain now he recognised some of the set as well. Even a few of the bodies. The one rolled over by the victorious soldier's boot, for instance, was the guy who gave him a swig of beer as he finished his shift. He was just going on as Michael's replacement. He had his blood made up in exactly that same spot. Michael remembered it.

Mind you, supposed Michael, people did tend to get shot in roughly the same places. Not that he'd ever seen anyone shot, but nevertheless . . .

In the end, Michael dismissed the idea. He knew the war wasn't going too well. People still weren't signing up, even for the so-called 'police actions'. Nor were they particularly following it on t.v., or even buying the newspapers for the photos anymore. As a means of exhorting a nationalism that could be exploited to regain control of a flagging economy, the war was giving the Government little joy. Michael was himself a case in point. But surely they couldn't be so desperate as to actually fabricate the whole event.

*

Vishnu and Lakshmi

Michael had been in India being frightened of himself when the Third World War started. As soon as the Bomb dropped on Dehli, he had found a sudden and dramatic external focus on which to concentrate his internal pandemonium. He was amongst the first in a mass exodus of worried Westerners lucky enough to be far enough South to escape the worst of the fall-out.

Singapore airport had been like a cross between an international share market and a geiger counter fair, with Southeast Asia struggling to keep radioactive Indians and Westerners out while those who got in were frantically bargaining for the fastest ticket home. Or to relatives - whichever was safer.

For Michael, however, the melee was like a holiday. Lost in chaos. Without any hope of reprieve that mattered. As in, home might not exist by the time he got there. Michael had gone to India to recover from his relationship with Sri. He had been living alone on a plot of land he had bought to practice permaculture on, in a house he had built himself with the aid of only a few essential tools and his van to erect the uprights. It was a homey sort of place. Lots of long lonely nights watching the gloom grow and animals move, comforted by the gentle warmth of his Hot Prospect combustion stove and, occasionally, a radio programme - the only luxury from the old life he allowed himself there, apart from his books.

Then Sri had entered his life. She too had been in alternative lifestyles.

She was living on a farm run by a collective of feminists just up the road. Set in the north-western foothills of the Tasmanian Wilderness, such rural outposts as these tended to attract the leftist, feminist and conservationist fall-out of the 80s and 90s.

It had been Sri's turn to be the collective's milking person. Because their farm was not yet supporting itself, it was collective policy to integrate with other marginalised activists in the area. So in rotation they solicited contracts of exchange with sympathetic neighbours. It was in search of such a contract, a contra-deal on the milk, that Sri negotiated the muddy track into the rain forest that concealed Michael's hideaway.

He remembered seeing her for the first time, standing on the edge of the clearing, her long hair slightly frizzed out by the Valley mist so that it formed a triangle in perfect counterpoint to her aquiline nose and chin. She looked like an urban hippy in her Indian cotton clothes and St Vinnies cardigans, old leather sandals still in autumn. But there was something duskier, earthier in her demeanour. The way she stood on the edge and stared, sized up the situation with those cool, ocean-blue eyes - which Michael was sure he could see, even at that distance.

She couldn't have arrived at a better time for Michael. Not only had he just about convinced himself that he didn't have to lead an absolutely autonomous existence in order to avoid the all-pervasive conditioning of Western Capitalism, but he was also desperate for milk and cheese, of which he had had neither for three thoroughly vegan months.

So Sri and he entered into a symbiotic relationship. He exchanged her milk and company for his home-made preserves and some vegies. And they both exchanged their respective states of self-imposed celibacy with a little well-negotiated sex.

This negotiation was not, however, without its shortcomings. Both Michael and Sri had grown up at the end of an era which believed that, if something could be understood, then it

233

could be conceptually controlled. An idea enunciated was an idea owned. Before the Bomb came along and completely confounded the efficacy of human rationality, this type of intellectual appropriation has perpetuated several centuries of spiritual and emotional alienation; of which, in their bid to reclaim some autonomy for themselves, the feminists had been no less guilty. Five thousand-odd years of recorded patriarchal oppression did, after all, require no small measure of mental de- and reconstruction. Intellect was thus the natural medium by which Sri placed relationship between herself and her new lover.

For Michael, on the other hand, alienation was inherent and intellect simply native currency.

Between them, then, the young(ish) couple were able to, in their own terms, exploit a rational objectification of sex which enabled them to retain their mutual emotional independence. This arrangement endured for some time, even after Sri moved in with Michael (after a suitable period of intellectual concurrence). The problems began when, despite a personal commitment to the primacy of intellect, Michael fell in love with Sri.

Sri had always accepted her love for Michael. But she had also accepted that it need not necessitate a total surrender to emotional dependence. Indeed, the kind of confluence of emotional bonding and identity loss/appropriation that seemed so to characterise men in love was not an issue with Sri. Michael understood the differentiation. He just could not do it. So he became defensive, jealous, embittered, angry, argumentative and all of those other ugly traits that can emerge in men when they finally release the clamps of rationality they keep so firmly fast upon the pressure cookers of their emotion.

In the end, the intellectual sting in Michael's tail got the better of him. His sex became brutish, his sarcasm vicious, his logic belligerent, and counter-analysis like a weapon in his hands. Sri, whilst fighting back, did so through a waterfall of unfettered tears, which only spurred Michael on to further aggression. Eventually Sri declared she could no longer take

Michael's self-hatred, and left to join a separatist group down south.

Michael struggled to regain control of himself for a while. Read some new books. Re-read some old ones. Listened avidly to public broadcasting. Argued endlessly with himself out among the vegetables. But even they could sense that his heart was no longer in it. Even his van failed to hang in there, no matter how many times he lovingly took it apart, cherished each lubricant piece, and reassembled the parts into mechanical perfection again.

So he chucked it in. Sold the lot and trudged off to India, a broken man; nurturing a vague hope that he might find some universal solvent for his inveterately linear 'straight six' of a mind. The possibility of logical duality, for instance, would help. Or a plurality of culture. Even something remotely resembling spirituality: an essence beyond the corporeal. That would be nice.

Of course all he discovered was that the disintegration of his relationship both with Sri and the land opened like a can of worms inside him. These mushroomed into his mind in Medusa-like snakes which slashed and thrashed around the innards of his emotional self, wherever that was.

It did not occur to Michael that these snakes might have the power of healing and regeneration. That if he returned each of them with love, he might find in that Medusa's head the kernel of a self he might, in turn, also learn to love. For Michael had long exhausted his reserves of mental energy. He limped from thought to half-baked thought like a cripple in a viper's nest, trying to avoid the soaring fangs of unleashed feeling as a strange and alien culture collided with him from all sides. Just as he had had it all worked out too . . .

Thank God for the Bomb. Although Michael had never thought to hear himself say it. And never would again.

*

235

A Drop of Siva's Sweat

The anomie of Singapore airport engendered a false sense of security in Michael. Unable to get out, he stayed in. In the rush to leave Madras he'd failed to secure a connecting flight to Australia and was thus marooned, like so many others fleeing the devastation India had presaged.

For himself, he could have stayed in that incubatory maze of transit concourses forever, stepping from one subdued strip of moving rubber walkway to another, allowing other travellers, with their armouries of suitcases, worldly belongings and, ironically (considering the circumstances), Duty Free, to shoulder the inner turmoil he might otherwise have to bear himself.

Poking his face into the perspex ambience of the seemingly endless passing parade of shops, Michael had absolutely no intent (nor inclination) to buy. But a surfeit of idle interest caused him to reflect upon the material excesses of the human race, and the folly of their creation in the face of such imminent vaporisation.

For Michael was convinced that, now that one Bomb had actually been used in armed conflict, it was only a matter of time before the rest of the world's considerable nuclear arsenal joined in with admirably normative zeal. Global conflagration was, in Michael's mind, definitely on the cards.

So, having secured an ongoing flight, he blew what money he had on a couple of nights at the famous Raffles hotel. Once the epitome of British Imperial aplomb, Raffles was now dwarfed by multimillion dollar convention centres and ever-mushrooming shopping precincts. While mad scooters, buses, taxis and cycles honked, buzzed and tinged their white-shirted ways around the intersection outside, Michael sipped Gin Slings and ambled through the tropical flora where Somerset Maugham once composed his ponderous tales of colonial perversity. While he felt almost at rest, a contusion of events unravelled in a world beyond like blood vessels bursting from an opened wound. Or at least, so an understanding of them formed in Michael's mind.

It came as no surprise to Michael, for instance, once he had the chance to reflect upon it, that the Police Powers had used the bombing of Dehli to initiate World War Three. It was long overdue. How could any self-respecting developed nation compete when the depression of a computer key in the office of some obscure Multinational subsidiary could undercut a local economy with Third World products. The governments of the European Union, the East and the West had absorbed offshore macro-economics for as long as they could. It was by now abundantly clear that national currencies were like Monopoly Money to the transnational corporations. The only weapon the Developed Countries had left was their national debt, and that was rising at such a rate not only would they never repay the interest themselves but their less developed debtors would not even begin to scratch the surface, as it were.

The nations of the world were, in effect, bankrupt. To each other. They limped from one mini-Wall Street Crash to another. It was only a matter of time before the Multinationals stepped in, picking up national mortgages like disused beer tickets. If government was to have any chance at all, it had to be war. Although the Multinationals would still benefit, at least the politicians would be running the show. They all had their nuclear bunkers, after all, if things got out of hand.

Michael was still grappling with the magnitude of it all as his 747 lumbered into Tullamarine. He drank Australian beer all the way across the Indian Ocean without even noticing. The Great Australian Bight swung beneath his aerially suspended body with barely a moment of recognition. He only registered the lights of Adelaide because the First Officer announced they were there, and he took the opportunity to curse his father not far beneath him.

At Tullamarine it was dawn. Dawn in Australia. And the smell of home soil. But in that insulated environment of airport terminals, in which escalators carried individuals from the verge of emotional collapse to magical cigar tubes which lifted them up to the heavens, so thoughts rose and fell in Michael's mind. How, he wondered as he sat in the International lounge watching early morning commuter flights depart and dock, could these people continue their daily existences when the world was on the brink of extinction? Even high over Bass Strait, as the sun shone and the holocaust floated down amongst the clouds for a last respite, Michael was oblivious to the full implications of the enormous gulf between the reality of World War and the apparent absence of public concern over it.

It was not until he stood upon the firm (if somewhat remote) ground of Tasmania that he fully comprehended what was already transpiring in public consciousness around the world. As he sat in a coffee shop in the northern Tasmanian town of Launceston, sipping a bad cappuccino he couldn't afford, Michael found himself pouring over paper after paper for some news of the war. But not only was this absent from their pages, so was any information of global significance whatsoever. Pokey little reports on escalating sandwich wars were tucked between the Classifieds and Sports. An Armed Forces recruitment drive appeared to be dying in the bum.

Michael went to the Library to confirm his suspicions in the Reading Room. He talked to friends. He observed people in the streets. And gradually it dawned on him what a couple of decades of structural unemployment, coupled with a growing public insouciance in relation to the information overload of the microchip 80s, had produced. An acute case of chronic, mass apathy gripped the nation. The employed, internally besieged by a compulsive fear of unemployment, clung to their jobs like climbers strung out along the lip of a glacier, hanging on with all their ice-pick-might to the old adage "Don't look down" in the impossible hope that the ice age would end before they did. The unemployed, meanwhile, had for so long been denied membership of the hieratic and material structurings of developed society that they no longer seriously considered themselves to be part of it. When the government gamely offered them an entree in the form of a national recruitment drive, they simply weren't interested. Terms like 'manliness', 'courage', and 'your country' didn't compute. Especially not with women.

What politicians around the world had, it seemed, been unable to foresee was a collective self-esteem so low that it no longer connected anger with anything of immediate social relevance. It had worked with Hitler, governments thought. It had worked in the Third World. Exhort the structurally oppressed with National Pride, offer the thus-created 'hero' class as a model for national sacrifice and immediately implement wage freezes and rationing. Surefire.

Unfortunately, all they had succeeded in doing was exhausting the concept of nationalism. Across the world, attempts by Developed Countries to get World War Three underway were being frustrated by an overwhelming non-participation on the part of their respective populations. By the time the draft was introduced, people were so apathetic they, on the whole, ignored it, treating their call up notices rather like parking fines: putting them on the bottom of the pile and waiting for the next amnesty.

*

Viradha

In Australia this global apathy was complicated by the nation's multicultural composition. Migrants and refugees from so many racial and ethnic origins had thrown their cultural lot in with the antipodean continent that there was no one nation in the world against which Australia could aim its national ire - not without offending some portion of its population. And the young country could not afford to take on the entire world.

Moreover, government made the mistake of drafting the unemployed first, in the hoping of enlisting "taxpayers' money" support from those still with jobs. The move succeeded only, however, in uniting the country's disparate reserves of marginalised activists who, disaffected with the Left, had elected unemployment in their attempts to redefine work, the patriarchy, consumerist lifestyles or whatever their particular ideological beef was with the dominant hegemony. Unfortunately for the Government, enough of the employed agreed with this emergent resistance to make the policy exceedingly unpopular.

The result was that the Government had to soft pedal - even back-pedal - and the draft became a covert operation conducted through DSS offices something akin to the neutralisation of dissidents in Third World dictatorships. People just 'disappeared' after their fortnightly or monthly visit to their 'case manager'. Family or relatives were told, upon enquiry, that recipients had elected to travel interstate for a job interview, or had failed to present for their interview that day. Friends and lovers were, of course, told nothing, although their interest was recorded - on internal video surveillance systems, naturally. Basically, the Department of Social Security had long had the power to freeze assets, raid bank accounts and incarcerate individuals in the name of debt recovery. The extension of these strategies to human life was a mere formality, the meritocracy of bureaucratic protocols unable as it was to respond to such conceptual defibrillations.

It was in resistance to this covert operation that Michael found an outlet for his now considerable numinosity; for he had, in reality, returned to Tasmania in pretty much the same state of psychological panic in which he left, albeit repressed. Being amongst the first wave of unemployed in the country to receive his call up notice, he was also amongst the first clients of an elaborate escape route designed to get draftees out of the public system. False names and double identities were such an essential feature of sustainable long term unemployment that it was easy to 'lose' someone by ferrying them through a network of 'safe houses'.

Thus it was that Michael became Rama Chandra, a refugee from New Dehli stranded in Asia when the Bomb dropped. He even (fortuitously) had an air ticket which, suitably doctored, proved the fact. And by the time the DSS could check him out, he had his 'emergency relief' cheque and moved on. And soon he disappeared altogether, becoming a key organiser in The Chain, escorting draftees from one safe house to the next, distributing new identities like lottery tickets, and entrepreneuring the public profile of The Movement with a hitherto undiscovered talent for the histrionic. Although it was not until the arrival of his brother, Lachy, that Michael began exploring this newfound flair for publicity.

*

Michael's brother Lachman was also amongst the first young men in Australia to be drafted, and Michael found it interesting that their father had been 'owed one' by the Federal Government since his defection to the private sector.

Although Lachy had tried to model himself on his father, the youngest brother's heart has always been with Michael. As kids they had bushwalked together in the Flinders Ranges, and it was Michael's taste in music and politics that Lachy had adopted when he went to Uni. He had been neither keen on Law nor suited to it, and as soon as his draft came through he was off down to Tas. to join his brother.

Now there was nothing Michael loved more than the ice-fresh frost-gasp of dawn over the Tasmanian Highlands. Even in summer (especially in summer) the dew simply broke under your feet like a thousand globes at a time, and all of the green joys of the universe were release at every step. So it was logical that the two brothers would bring their 'safe house' charges up here for a couple of weeks when the stags from the DSS started to get close.

Near the centre of Tasmania, on the northern edge of the central highlands not far from where Michael had once hibernated from Western society, was a geologically stable dolorite formation in which the State Government had agreed to store radioactive waste for a number of clients to whom they sold uranium. These were countries of dubious commitment to any global

241

agreements on nuclear arms control, and the Tasmanian government had incurred considerable public wrath when the sale of the raw resource fuel for nuclear production had first been mooted, and near insurrection when they also agreed to take the rubbish back afterwards. The value-added fact that the raw material would first be processed in Tasmania at either end of its industrially active life was not, to say the least, seen by many as much of a flow-on benefit.

The particular mountain chosen to house the downprocessed waste for its not inconsiderable radioactive life contained a number of rare natural dry caves ideally suited to longterm storage. The granite was billions of years old, hadn't moved more than a centimetre or two in as long, and was relatively unfrequented, lying as it did in the heart of a national park.

The government had promised no end of security measures to prevent the possibility of nuclear terrorism at the time, but when Michael and Lachy stumbled across it, it was at the end of what looked like just another logging track, unmonitored, unstaffed, and looking for all the world like the entrance to a disused mine. It wasn't until Lachy and the party took a peek inside the first cave that they discovered the hundreds of metres of uncovered oil drums stretching off into the dimness like pockmarks in some Sheik's muddy treasure trove. The stench was as overpowering as the eerie stillness, and something definitely wasn't working in there. Whatever was happening inside those drums was blackening even the supposedly indestructible yellow and red radioactive warning flash.

It hadn't been the party's intention to leave their entire stash of real-life identity papers there. It was simply that in their haste to retreat, having realised they were in danger of radioactive exposure, Lachy had simply dropped the pouch containing the real ID. He kept it in a passport pouch tucked under his arm and inside his clothing, as advised by Michael, for safe keeping. But somehow a strap had broken or had worked its way loose, and as Lachy turned and led the charge out in what he had to admit later was blind panic, it simply slipped out through his cumbersome winter layers of oil skin and wool and was trampled into the grimy floor of the entranceway by a dozen or so similarly fleeing pairs of escapee boots. The pouch must have split open in the stampede.

It was actually due to the action of an entirely different group of Australia's many politically marginalised that led the press up there some weeks later, on a good will invitation by the Tasmanian government. By that time, the passport pouch seemed to have disappeared altogether. What the foraging eye of the journalist noticed was the ID notices themselves, grubbing around in the mud on the granite floor. He picked them up, said "What are these?", and made sure he kept hold of them when the government official accompanying the party showed the first trace of confusion and alarm.

The resulting banner headlines accused the Federal Government of consigning renegade draftees to all manner of hideously radioactive ends, from live incarceration in radioactive containers to imprisonment in the storage caves until they mutated beyond human recognition, whereupon they were released into the Tasmanian Wilderness to speed the extermination of the dreaded conservationist!

After that, it became an easy matter for Michael and Lachy to make periodic trips up to Mt Kalesa at will with their bagfulls of now defunct ID. Even though the guard on the nuclear dump itself was reimposed, experienced bushies like Michael and Lachy found it easy to slip in to Wisdom Creek, where the heavy duty vehicles invariably got bogged in winter or stopped for a smoko in summer. One of them might even engage the truckies in conversation while the other darted up onto the truck under the camouflage netting to stick the draft notices onto the cave-bound cannisters.

Once done, The Movement would then release all of the names of the 'disappeared' and repeat their claim that the Government was abducting draft resisters and burying them alive at Mt Kalesa. And the press, always glad to rekindle the Mt Kalesa controversy, invariably carried the story. And the Government,

243

always equally anxious not to have it rekindled, always opened up the storage facility to chopper loads of reporters. And the reporters gleefully spent the day harrying government officials about why draftees were being buried alive in cannisters marked for radioactive disposal and, incidentally, noting that the number of cannisters in this particular holding bay seemed far in excess of the permissible quota. The press loved having the Government over a barrel, so to speak.

It was about this time that it began to dawn on Michael that he was no longer the author of his own story.

*

Kali

It was on one Mt Kalesa operation that Michael ran into Sri again. On one occasion when Michael and Lachy arrived to find the area not exactly as ill-attended as it usually was. For Sri was a member of a radicalesbian collective which had decided to mount a vigil over the nuclear dump.

This was not in itself unusual. Mt Kalesa had a history of women's activism. It was on top of Mt Kalesa that the remaining female descendants of Tasmania's Aboriginal peoples self-immolated after the State Government reneged on both Land Rights and World Heritage declarations for the area.

The State Government of the time had a perverse attitude to its aboriginal population. But then, governments in Tasmania always had. As early as 1824 Lieutenant Governor Arthur extended the dubious protection of British law to the island's natives only to authorise a massive sweep of their country six years later in order to deny them the same rights on a permanent basis.

One hundred and forty years later, as if to rid themselves of the stigma, another Tasmanian government claimed that Arthur had succeeded - there were none left. An interesting proposition for those remaining descendants of the state's indigenous peoples, and a problematic expiation of state guilt if ever there was one. Nevertheless, after the canning of Land Rights legislation for Mt Kalesa and the deregistration of its World Heritage listing, followed by the self-immolation of these same claimants to aboriginal identity upon Kalesa's summit, it was a proposition which became pretty much substantiated by fact.

*

Lakshmi Is Ravaged By Ravana

It was not surprising, then, that the sacred site with its naturally hollow centre should also attract the next victims of State de-legitimation; the feminists. Or radicalesbian feminists, to be precise.

Although the Tasmanian Government had not the same need as their New South Wales counterparts for a political scapegoat, they did sustain an ongoing demand for means of discrediting the conservation movement - a movement which the government saw as perverting its valiant attempts to bring the Island State into the Twentieth Century - or the end of it, at least. Unfortunately conservationists did this by regular resource to an unfailing and seemingly inexhaustible capacity for sound, logical argument - a tactic which frustrated the government's position again and again.

The fact of the matter was that the government was desperate for success, no matter how marginal, and the appearance of radicalesbians on the slopes of Mt Kalesa provided as handy a target as any. Not only did they advocate abortion, women's rights, equality of opportunity, affirmative action in the workplace and ecofeminism but, as such, posed a threat to the family, the economy, the state and just about anything else the government could plausibly claim to stand for. They were also, it was rumoured, responsible for the consensus model of decision-making adopted by the conservationists; a fact for which the government could not decide whether it was grateful or worried.

It is not well recorded elsewhere that the government campaign against Sri's collective began while the radicalesbian action was in fact still in its planning stage. Which indicates that government sources had access to inside information.

It is also not well documented that the Transnational Corporation of America was finalising its dumping rights at Kalesa at around the same time. Yet, while political hectoring about radical women's refuges, value-challenged collectives and lesbian mothers received substantial media exposure, the deal with Transnational received none. Until the collective actually commenced their blockade.

The action took on a national profile, with red-faced drivers declaring before cameras that they'd "job 'em, women or not", and proceeding to doze down trees with protesters still in them. Eventually the Big Boss from the North flew down in his private jet and said he'd go up there and bring them down himself if the police wouldn't do anything. And he did.

The police did not do too much to restrain the Managing Director of Transnational (Australia) when he burst through the police cordon and stormed off up the mountainside. But they did take the opportunity to scamper off after him, manhandling women off site "for their own safety" - and with such brutality that the zoom lenses were still pulsating weeks later.

In the melee, nobody was quite sure who got whom, how, when and where, but Sri was clearly captured by the press as she was dragged down the mountainside by her once-beautiful hair in the hands of the still be-suited Managing Director of Transnational (Australia). There was no-one to testify what transpired on the mountain top. It is, after all, a mountain top. Great for the Gods to look down from but not a lot to look up too, except in metaphor. But the Transnational boss had clearly known who he was looking for. And Sri was certainly there to meet him. Although it is said - and Michael was able later to

246

verify for himself - that Sri and Sheena looked very much alike in those days.

The Managing Director later portrayed himself in interviews as some kind of latter day champion for the rights of the individual - especially male individuals engaged in private enterprise. Sri claimed she was raped. In fact she so claimed from the outset, but none of her arresting officers would take a statement and by the time they did it was too late for physical verification.

It is distinctly possible, however, that the Managing Director had at the time mistaken Sri for someone else. Or that he had known that Sri was already involved in a relationship with Sheena, unbeknown to Michael at the time.

In fact, none of this was known to Michael at the time. He simply witnessed the entire event from his hiding place in the foothills of Mt Kalesa. And for a moment caught the chilling, grey and crazed stare of a woman he thought he had once known as the mighty hand of the earth scored itself across her back as it tore at her hair by its roots.

He heard her story later from her friends. She had stepped out of someone else's circle.

*

Ahalya

Not long after he had moved in with Bozzo and Sheena, which was in turn not long after he had moved to Sydney, a strange thing happened to Michael. Something which had moved a quality resembling life in him. Almost powerfully. Certainly disturbingly enough for him to forget it. Or rather, choose not to acknowledge it. Until another event occurred like it, a little later.

247

This first event happened like this. In order to reach the train station from where he lived, Michael had to pass through what seemed to him the ugliest area in the whole of Sydney. Of course it had a beauty of its own, and to the people who lived there it was home. But Michael was unhappy. And for the entire (if short) journey he never escaped the smell of cigarette ends and garbage - a shock to the senses after the cold, clean air of Tasmania. And Michael always seemed to be stepping over derros and mattresses spewing stuffing, which reminded him of the deformities he had witnessed so routinely in India.

Then there were the prostitutes, with their characteristic ten dollar shoulder bags and mini skirts, heroin running through their cheeks like water. (This was before he found out about Sheena and Sri.) He tried to avoid their eyes. Byzantine ladies who called men up to frolic in the biggest bed in the world by night were ghoulish and reed-voiced by day.

And from the hotel next door drunken men tottered onto the pavement twenty four hours a day to fail once more to face whatever it was they were failing to face. Even the smart brasserie on the corner, where people ate as Michael imagined people ate in Paris, was unable to lift itself from the dowd that surrounded it. And the bakery outlet next door always sold pastries that were burnt on the bottom. (Which, curiously, Michael liked.)

Everything in the Cross was like ash.

Except at the intersection beneath the giant Coca Cola sign at the William Street overpass, where in just one micro-geographical moment people, bikes, cars and vans negotiated passage with the nearest Michael had ever seen to consensus. Without even realising it. Harmony in action. For a moment, Michael could relax into being part of something natural. But only for that moment. The purity of passage was lost almost immediately in the descent into the station.

Michael hated going to the city.

And he hated coming home again. But on this day he met a man. He was passing the vacant chasm above an underpass that had never made it into a basketball court. This was a route Michael could take from the brothel belt that avoided the unstuffing mattresses until the last minute. This way he also sometimes caught a glimpse of the Hare Krishnas, who lived on an obscure dead-end crescent he was now passing. The Krishnas reminded him of the more musical, spiritual side of India, while the crescent summoned images of the sweeping terraces in a Bloomsbury Michael knew only (and somewhat inaccurately) from pages of Virginia Woolf and James Joyce.

Today, on the corner of this crescent, a little man was watering a patch of foliage on the pavement. A struggling stick of a tree which wobbled as it was watered, and some pale geraniums. In a paving stone square of barren earth. Michael was touched. Even though the parkland of Rushcutters Bay ballooned out in cumulus canopies of English green just down the road, this dusty plot of nature quivering away amongst the paving stones was somehow more heartening.

The man was Chinese. Or Asian. More Chinese than Asian, Michael thought without really understanding that most Asians he was likely to have met in Australia were of Chinese descent anyway. Michael thought it was more the round, balding pate, which made the man look like a yellowing moon. The Chinese were into moons, thought Michael ignorantly. Smiling ones. Just as this man smiled as Michael approached.

"Hallo," said Michael. And the two talked for a while about the vagaries of preserving life in such inhospitable surroundings. The man pointed to his verandah on the third floor of the terrace, where he clearly kept numerous copiously watered plants in polystyrene containers and hanging baskets. Did Michael live around here? Would he like to come up for a cup of tea? The man lived alone and would be glad of the company.

Not now, Michael replied, cautious both of the intimacy and the hope he was personally finding in the encounter. Later on, maybe. When? Today? What time? As he had said, he lived alone and it would make an old man happy. So, three o'clock it was then.

This encounter confused Michael. He could not work out what the old man wanted. Yet he did not want to distrust the apparent trust. For Michael might have been violent. Like Bozzo. Or worse. The sort who accepts your hospitality then beats you up and robs you. Even sexually assaults you. Or makes you do ugly, debasing things. And yet Michael had been invited. And afternoon tea would be a luxury. A luxury and a good turn.

        Although the man did not seem so old in Michael's memory. His smile made him look young, even though his comfortable cardigan and high-hitched trousers said he was not.

In the event, the man proved to be both young and old. He answered the door in a white towelling bath robe that hemmed at his knees. Smelt fresh-washed and hotel-bathroom. Yet still there was the balding head and white-toothed smile manners. He had just been to the gym. Did Michael go to the gym? No. He ran once, but not anymore. And, as they sat in the lounge for a moment, this was his brother's flat but his brother was away on business most of the time.

Michael began to relax with the man. He was a nice man. Open. With an aging man's head. But his calf muscles were firm and rounded. Like pears. Michael wanted to massage the man's calves. Even as he sat there and was talked to. He wanted to take a towel, pour some oil into his palms, kneel before the man, take one of the free legs so that its heel rested in his lap, and begin gently working the muscles behind the shin.

        This could have been a Christ-like impulse on Michael's part, except that he wanted more than that. He wanted to work his way up around the man's knee as he talked, gently fingering the platella and smoothing his fingertips up into the man's thigh. Gradually his hands would lift the hem of the generous bathrobe as they worked, parting the two flaps across the man's lap to allow some light into that crack of darkness he could see gathered about the man's crotch.

There he would take the man's testes in his hands, cup them gently and start to stroke the flaccid penis resting upon them. Hold it. Turn it slightly. Discover what subtle pressures gave it pleasure. Increased it in size. And the addition of saliva would help. Michael wanted to help. He wanted to take the man's penis into his mouth, draw it into him. With love. Michael wanted to love the man. And who knows, perhaps the man might reciprocate. Perhaps later the man might roll over and allow Michael to enter him. Perhaps this was what he wanted.

The prospect of this act came to Michael at once. In its entirety. As if a wave of something had broken from somewhere unknown within him, rushed from his lower back, flooded his crotch, massed against his abdominal wall and burst upon his chest in a sudden contusion of feeling. Michael had never experience anything like this. Never had such thoughts. Not about men. So why suddenly here, now? Where had it come from?

The man sat, smiling and talking as if nothing had happened. Shortly he suggested he should get some clothes on and make the tea. Michael agreed and continued sitting while the man went. Then stood up, looked around the room while the man politely chatted away, dressing in the other room. And a conviction grew in Michael that what he had experienced had come from the other man. Directly. From the man's chest to Michael's chest. Even as they had sat.

Once he was dressed in his ordinary old man's clothes, the old man showed Michael his verandah with its bevy of plants and view of the Cross, the underpass, and the glimpse of Rushcutters Bay beyond. Then the man, who had not put his socks on this time, made tea and showed Michael his calligraphy. He told Michael about the classes he conducted sometimes, and the small group of men who came around and held seances. Did Michael know about seances? Michael did, a bit.

They talked thus for the remainder of the afternoon. Michael told the man of his aspirations to become an actor, which he only really conceived in that moment, and the man told Michael

251

about his brother, who was in business. This confused Michael at first because the man seemed to be referring to some place around the corner when he talked about his brother, yet his brother owned this flat, in which the man lived, but the brother was away a lot. Then Michael realised that all three were true. The brother was a leading light in the Hare Krishna organisation - but more on the business side of it than the spiritual. The man had been banished here by his brother because he had sex with the brother's partner. It all seemed to be very naughty and the man giggled a lot. He had thought that was what it was all about: Hare Krishna, free love, sex. But the brother had been very upset. That endemic conservatism so anachronistic in men who religiously advocate change and progress in domains other than the private. They hang onto themselves.

So the man had been installed here by the brother, where the Hare Krishnas around the corner could keep an eye on him. And the brother flew in from time to time to see if his morals had improved enough for a reconciliation.

As their meeting drew to an end the man asked Michael if he wanted to join the seance group, or the calligraphy classes. Or would he come again? Michael said he would love to come again, but did not know when.

On the way out they passed the brother's bedroom and the man struck up another conversation. Did Michael like reading books? The man was reading Kerouac. A book about men who . . . if only one had the courage, the man was suggesting naughtily. And Michael was suddenly unsure if the man had had sex with his brother's partner because a photograph fell out from the pages as the man flicked through the book.

"A friend?" Michael asked, for it was a photograph of a young Asian man.

"My brother's partner," the man replied.

And for a moment a chasm opened in the man's eyes and fell away with such infinite pain Michael could have cried. But the affable face-saving smile was quickly back.

"Well, I must be going," said Michael. "Nice to meet you."

And the man put out his hand to be shaken.

"Nice to meet you too. you must come again."
"I will," said Michael, knowing that he wouldn't.
"But it's okay," he continued. "About the partner."

The man with the moon-shaped head tried to continue smiling.

"He looks like a lovely man," Michael went on, trying to reassure the man without really knowing what about. "It sounds like somebody let you down."
"Yes," replied the man, laughing.

And Michael wondered whether he had imagined his own experience. And, although they exchanged phone numbers, the man never tried to contact Michael again. Even though Michael passed beneath the flowery verandah nearly every day on his journey through the ashes, trying guiltily not to look up. Nor did Michael ever see the man again, although the tree and geraniums struggled on, and the man's calligraphy had been beautiful.

*

The Golden Deer II

After the blood run, Michael decided he was going to save Sheena. From herself, if nothing else. She and Sri were obviously locked into a vicious cycle and Michael was convinced Bozzo was responsible for their addiction. The problem was how to extradite the woman he loved from under the nose of her oppressor with out him getting wind of it.

As luck would have it, Bozzo invited Michael on a graffiti sortie with them. This would give Michael (Michael thought) the perfect opportunity to win Bozzo's trust and respect so that, when the time came for him (Michael) to make his move, Bozzo would not suspect him. Who knows, as Bozzo's confidante he, Michael, might even be able to persuade Bozzo that he (Bozzo) actually wanted to let Sheena go.

"You can have her," said Bozzo as the three sat together on the 1.45 am from Central. Michael was alarmed by the apparent transparency of his thoughts.

"Pardon?" he attempted to ask innocently.

"For tonight. D'you wanna go? She's alright."

Michael glanced at Sheena. Had Bozzo guessed? Or was he usually this generous with his female companions? Sheena sighed impatiently into her seat between them. She was wearing a greyish, leathery looking dress with slits around the edges. Her arms were bare and Michael could plainly see the needle marks, which he stoically tried to ignore.

"She loves to do it. Really," Bozzo went on.

"Fuck off!" Sheena uttered suddenly, and threw herself into a corner on the opposite side of the carriage.

Or would have done, had Bozzo not grabbed her wrist with an action so deft it hardly seemed to happen. Sheena was simply suspend mid-flounce, her arm slowly, painfully being twisted in slow motion by Bozzo.

"You won't get it," she warned through gritted teeth. "Let go!"

Bozzo released his grip, and Sheena continued on her trajectory to the corner opposite.

"I get it. Either way, I get it," Bozzo said, staring at her blankly.

Michael sat uncomfortably, trying to think of something funny to say while he tried to work out what was going on.

"It's a great line."

It could have been Michael, but it was in fact Bozzo who spoke.

"Especially at this time of night. Last train for about half an hour. Once we get the other side of Strathfield, you get even longer. And there's a channel there like a stormwater drain, you can duck down in it. Some of them just do it down there. Names of bands and things. Tags. But the best stuff's this side of Strathfield. People do pieces there. That's where we're going."

And it was true. As they approached the barrage of platforms that constituted Strathfield station, the high-banked brickwork of the cutting bore inscriptions in any number of languages, or perhaps no language at all. It was most impressive.

"We do most of 'em," observed Bozzo. "Like that one in Vietnamese. A mate of mine did that. It says, 'Communists are Cunts'. Bit serious, but. And this one here, this is a classic. Like a museum piece. Everyso-often the railway send a Dolework detail to paint it all out, but they always leave that one."

Bozzo was referring to a piece of graffiti in bold, white lettering against multicoloured, Christmassy artwork, which read:

BANKRUPTCY FOR

255

Bozzo's apparent pride indicated that he might be its author.

Although lit, Strathfield station was empty. Bozzo kicked in the front of a Coke dispenser but no-one came, so he led the way to the end of the platform, which tapered away to the large-stoned gravel on which the railway tracks lay.

There was something mystical about the railway at night. All of those gleaming strips of metal curving into the night like moonbeams setting out across the universe. Above them, nets of red and green inexplicably interchanged, as if communicating with each other. No visible cause or result. Just winking away on invisible gantries, garnering stray moonbeams into direction.

By day, of course, the signals presaged the comings and goings of urban and interstate traffic, whose intimate intercourses were mapped out in that instant on some giant integrated circuit elsewhere. But at night, as the anonymous clatterings of trains diminished across Strathfield, the silent signals winked on, as if to unseen ghosts of trains long past.

"Get going, you fuckwit!" hissed Bozzo angrily, interrupting Michael's reverie.

The latter stumbled under the weight of the speaker's shove and tripped over one of the rails. The lines were incongruously bulky and most unsympathetic to ankles, Michael discovered. Unlike the gravel, which gave way with elf-like caprice.

"I've never been on a railway line before," proffered Michael ineffectually. "Not on foot, anyway."

"We have to keep together. There's about fifteen minutes before the next train. When they see us, they radio ahead and the cops come out. Although sometimes they can't be bothered."

Bozzo pulled a couple of spray cans from his sack and gave one to each of them. As Sheena took hers, Bozzo clasped her fingers brutally to the can.

"Now you won't fuck up, will you?"

There were tears in her eyes; of pain or anger, Michael couldn't tell.

"What do we write?" asked Michael politely, hoping to engage Bozzo in conversation.

"Anything you fucking well like, as long as it's political," the man snapped bullishly, and sprayed 'SOLIDARNOJ' in red upon the dark brickwork.

"I didn't know you could speak Kurdish," Michael offered, ignorantly.

"I can speak anything," Bozzo replied. "You don't think the slavs and chinks can be bothered with this shit, do you? They'd rather be at home with their computer chips and videos."

Michael was nonplussed. He'd always admired the graffiti along this stretch of the track for its cultural diversity. Now he felt somewhat disabused. Nevertheless, he plucked up his courage and embarked upon his own contribution.

THE KING'S SHILLING
A DEADLY DRAFT

- was Michael's first somewhat cryptic attempt. But by the time he had finished it, Bozzo was onto his third. In three colours. Bozzo worked fast.

There was a roar in the railway tracks that sounded like the sea crashing on distant shores. A vibration picked up, the clatter of wheels across expansion gaps. A yellowish light began to traverse the distant constellations of red and green, a shooting star in slow motion.

"I gotta go," said Bozzo, and there was the sound of boots subsiding on gravel.

257

Michael blundered around looking for a hiding place so ineffectively that he was discovered by the approaching train with his hands in the air backed up against the low fence of insulated cables that seemed to accompany the line wherever it went.

"That was a close one," Michael phewed to Sheena when he located her further up the track. She was working quietly and quickly in short, sharp movements and did not seem to have noticed the passing train.

"Where's Bozzo?" Michael asked in search of a topic of conversation.

"He'll be back," Sheena replied without pausing. She was adding touches of red to:

LESBIANS ARE ILLEGAL
HAVE ONE WHILE THEY'RE HOT!

"We could go now, you know," Michael urged. "Just head back to the station and hop on the next train out. We could go anywhere. You could go anywhere."

"Why?" asked Sheena without interest.

"Then you wouldn't have to do this anymore."

"Suppose I like doing this? Better than have some fucking man appropriating it. And anyway, that's not what you mean."

"What do you mean, that's not what I mean?" Michael asked defensively.

"I mean you want me to go away with you so that you can love me by getting me off the heroin. Only it doesn't work like that, Michael."

It was the second time Sheena had done this to him. Floored him before he'd even had the chance to make his move. But he thought this time he could detect a softening in her resolve. Or at least, he hoped he did. So he persisted.

"But you can't go on like this. Bozzo will destroy you."

"Only if he doesn't destroy himself first. Look, Michael," Sheena rounded on Michael squarely, "You're a very well-meaning

258

guy, but we just had a screw, right? There's more to it than that with Bozzo. Okay?"

Michael could once more feel those tentacle of doubt begin to worm their ways into his entrails, but he was not to be daunted.

"Like what?"

"Like things you wouldn't understand. Or want to understand."

"Try me."

This was one of the boldest invitations Michael had ever issued in his life, had he only known it. Unfortunately (or, perhaps, fortunately for him) he never got to understand its full implications because, the next thing he knew, Bozzo's hot breath laboured about his ears.

"Where is it?" a voice rasped in lungfulls. Michael froze, frantically searching his mind for what 'it' might be. But it was into Sheena's eyes that recognition dropped, and her head that lowered submissively.

"Where is it?" Bozzo hissed again, with such menacing emphasis on the 'is' that Michael involuntarily jumped aside.

Bozzo stepped through the gap and grabbed Sheena by the hair.

"I want the Golden Deer!"

Sheena yelped in pain.

"I've seen the print out. I know it's his company. And I've fed your name onto the supply list, so it's official. All I have to do is make the call and it'll be on his desk in the morning."

Bozzo twisted Sheena's head further.

"I'll get it tomorrow!" Sheena squealed.

"I want it NOW!" Bozzo roared.

And Michael began to get an inkling of what he might be getting himself into. Then Bozzo's head turned, as if distracted by a sound off. And Michael understood even

259

better. For in the same action as he turned his head, Bozzo's hand imperceptibly flicked Sheena's head like a yoyo against the wall, using her hair as the string. Only the dull thud of her skull upon the bricks indicated the action that had been performed. Bozzo could have actually been concentrating on something else. And was.

"Lesbians are everywhere. Like cockroaches. Say it!" he said, returning his attention to her and retrieving her head to it's former position.

"Lesbians are everywhere," Sheena repeated, her voice box caught in the twist of her neck. Michael could see blood matting her hair.

"Like cockroaches!" Bozzo insisted.

"Lesbians are everywhere," Sheena reiterated.

"Like cockroaches!" Bozzo shouted. But there was defeat in his tone. "I want to see it at Macdonaldtown on my way back through!" And then to Michael, "C'mon, we gotta split."

In one movement Bozzo was up on the wall with a hand down to Michael.

"Meet you there," Bozzo said to Sheena as if the preceding exchange had not occurred.

From where he was, Michael could now see the dark, uniformed figures making their way along the railway line. It was then that he heard the dogs.

"It's okay," Bozzo reassured him, "It's me they can smell."

And he set off along the wall which, Michael discovered to his discomfort, was embedded with shards of glass.

They were swiftly back to Strathfield. Michael could see Sheena mounting the ramp onto another platform as a double decker train bolted through. Its clattering covered the yelps of the first dog to attempt to follow them along the wall.

Bozzo lead Michael across the flimsy roof of the nearest platform to the embankment, out onto the gantry that carried the overhead cables, up underneath onto the Victorian iron rafters that Michael so admired (usually from below) and down the ornate support columns onto the platform.

260

When
Michael finally found his feet, his brain remained mentally scrambling over the platform roof. But there was no time for it to catch up. The first of the policemen were ascending the ramp of the platform on which Michael and Bozzo now stood, and an old red rattler was pulling into the station alongside Sheena.

Bozzo   and Michael ran down into the subway connecting all four platforms. The police correspondingly ran to meet them, so that the two parties arrived at the bottom at roughly the same time. At that moment, Bozzo seemed to throw himself horizontally at the uniformed men, hoofing one in the groin at the same time as tearing the face of the other so that both toppled backwards, the latter cracking his skull upon the bitumen.

"Quick!" said Bozzo, up on his feet already. And Michael's body was once more hurtling after the departing form of Bozzo as fast as the sound of his thwop-thwopping feet would allow.

On   the train, which the fleeing duo jumped just as it was pulling out, Bozzo grinned hugely at Michael. Both men struggled with their ventilating lungs, breath leaping out in huge, raucous gasps.

"Alright, eh?" said Bozzo, grasping the back of Michael's neck and pulling their heads together. And Bozzo waved to the policemen on the departing platform as they passed.

"We did alright," he repeated. But Michael could still see himself hunched over the roof of the platform by the embankment, waiting for his body to return.

Then the train slowed at an anonymous set of lights and Bozzo was out onto the tracks once more.

"Got an appointment in Parramatta," he said by way of explanation, and was gone.

"Where's he going?" asked Michael as the train resumed its rickety progress north.

"You heard him," Sheena replied coldly.

261

Michael was beginning to realise that Bozzo was the sort of person who could be in several places at once.

*

"He only asked you so that there would be two of us," Sheena was explaining as she sprayed the allotted missive on the corrugated iron fence that divided one side of Sydney's most unused station from the other.

Michael had been in the process of trying to convince her once more to come away with him. He had been explaining his plan to inveigle his way into Bozzo's confidence and Sheena was in the process of disabusing him.

"But there were three of us," Michael was arguing.

"Not when the trains went by. They would only have seen two of us. You and me. We would have shown up in their lights. We would have been sitting in the carriage as other trains passed."

"So I was a sort of alibi. A stand-in."

Michael couldn't keep the disappointment out of his voice.

"Bozzo's got this thing about being watched. By satellites. He thinks he's being watched by satellites."

Michael involuntarily looked up, as if expecting to see some telescopic lens beaming down at him from the blackened heavens. Then, as if that wasn't silly enough, he looked around. So that they might wave to him, perhaps, from the blazing light of some handy bedroom nearby. "Here we are, Michael! The spies!" So Michael tried to pretend he was watching out for police.

"Why does he think that," he said, trying to sound indifferent.

"I dunno. Bozzo has some crazy ideas, maybe."

"And what was the Golden Deer he wanted?"

"When?"

"Back at Strathfield."

Sheena made no answer.

"And why Macdonaldtown?" he asked, feeling like a cue in somebody else's novel.

And he was right. Macdonaldtown was a sad case. Less than a kilometre from Newtown in one direction and Redfern in the other, its only public access was via a poorly lit, irregularly attended ticket office set into the bridge under which slid a precarious rat-tun from Redfern/Newtown to Erskineville. On the line above there were no buildings. Just this solitary beached whale of a platform that saw human occupation barely twice a day, with its dorsal fin of corrugated iron shelter, camouflaged by the occasional splash of lamplight. Against a backdrop of incoming domestic and international flights, the rooftops of Erskineville and Newtown shuffled up to its edges like men in hats and grey raincoats, waiting for something to expose itself. Like the promiscuous Sheena, spraying hot come-ons across iron in lurid lamplight, night crouching all around.

"The only thing that keeps this station open is the fact that the yuppies moved in and did to this area what the Real Estate sharks did to Paddington," Sheena was explaining as she decorated her artwork listlessly. "Drove out the workers and migrants from their low cost housing and shunted up the prices so they could never come back again. Bozzo hates yuppies. Apparently they still live around here. Can't afford to move out now. So Bozzo likes to remind them occasionally. In the mornings and evenings, before and after work, when they turn up here and wonder why."

"And the Golden Deer?"

"It's a brand of heroin," Sheena revealed with a sigh. "A very expensive brand of heroin. And a very rare one. Bozzo wants me to get some for him. I know its sole supplier. And I'm his sole supplier. I've told you all this before..."

"Yes but surely-"

"He got me into it? You're a fuckwit, Michael. Has anyone ever told you that?"

"Well, not in so many words, no."

Har-Hari

Things were not the same after the spray painting episode. It was as if they had smoked dope or eaten mushrooms or dropped acid together - all smiles and Bozzo clapping them about the shoulders, looking from one to another with a beneficent grin. He had appeared on the red rattler Michael and Sheena had picked up at Redfern after Sheena's forfeit at Macdonaldtown.

"It was alright, eh?" Bozzo said, as he had earlier that morning. He was once again talking to Michael, implying a chauvinism Michael found hard to share. Alrightness was the least of the responses he found within himself, given the demeaning penance Sheena had just been forced through (as he saw it).

To his further discomfort, Bozzo then kissed him on the lips. He almost gagged on the long, slug-like tongue that surged into his mouth from its stubbled housing, wrapping itself around Michael's retreating equivalent. Bozzo hadn't even commented on Sheena's "LESBIANS ARE IN YOUR HAIR LIKE LICE".

By the time they got home, the morning streets were still deserted. Only in the distance could the milko's bottles be heard clinking between anecdotes of door-to-door motoring. ("Fucking yuppies!" murmured Bozzo, for only conservationists had bottles delivered these days.) Even further off, the "Hoi!" of the garbos interspersed the whine of their urban battle-tank-against-waste as it stealthily avoided the irredeemable Cross as much as possible.

Sheena went straight upstairs. She looked buggered. But while Michael was cleaning his teeth in the bathroom, Bozzo came in and started taking down his pants.

"Don't mind if I have a shit, do you?"

It was unusual of him to ask.

The action once again assumed a sense of automatic male kinship long lost to Michael. We are boys together. We laugh about shit and compare the size of our penises. We fuck women. It was all alien, and Michael was vaguely disquieted by the plop-plop bouquet of Bozzo's emissions as they mingled with the peppermint sweetness of his toothpaste. When he left, Michael was too embarrassed to look at Bozzo wiping his arse.

As he lay in bed, Michael listened for the customary torture from above. For torture it had become since he had made love with Sheena. And it was with some internal conflict these days that he prepared for his customary relief.

But he needn't have worried. Nothing had happened. Michael heard the clump clump upstairs and scuff of disrobing. He heard the heavy thump on the mattress and, as he lay there with his finger and thumb on a half-erect penis, waited for the dawn assault upon the floorboards above. But there was nothing.

Instead, Bozzo started moving again. But quietly. Unusually. So that it came as a surprise when the clumsy pad pad on the stairs resulted in the pressing ajar of Michael's door, admitting the weighty breath and shivering body of Bozzo.

"Are you awake?" the body whispered hoarsely. "Shift over."

Michael tried not to move. He could almost feel the hot breath on his neck, as he had only hours before. He imagined the vertebrate rod of dick pumping savagely away at the walls of his rectum without love or care, rooting him into the barren earth of some distant battlefield, shoulders pinned by Bozzo's mighty frame, hips bounced helplessly by his violator's relentless lust.

It was to Michael's further surprise, then, that having sussed out which way Michael was facing Bozzo came around to his front and backed in.

"Shit it's cold," he said. And Michael found himself hugging this bulk of a man from behind, caressing his soft belly. In fact, once

Bozzo warmed up, Michael was amazed at just how soft his belly was. As well as being bulky, Bozzo was a bit of a podge.

After a while, Bozzo's breathing subsided, and he guided Michael's hand to his penis. This Michael found not only to be small but non-erect. Whereas the genital contact with Bozzo's bottom had already induced a modest swelling in Michael's loins.

Michael found a natural urge within him to kiss Bozzo's shoulders and neck, as he gently encouraged the larger man's penis into life. The thick muscles seemed to slide away beneath his lips. Then Bozzo himself reached around, took Michael's penis and guided it into the crack between his cheeks, rubbing it softly against his surprisingly hairless anus. Michael began to caress Bozzo's fleshy buttocks. They felt so smooth, and fell so welcomingly about Michael's erectile tissue.

Bozzo then dipped his free hand into a receptacle he seemed to have brought with him and, as Michael's glans gently pressed against the anus, applied a gel between the two. With his hand between his legs from the front, the other now stroking Michael's own bottom from behind, Bozzo pliantly worked Michael's stiffening penis into his rectum. Bozzo was evidently adept at this.

Eventually, as Michael pushed, Bozzo placed a pillow against his crotch and rolled onto his front, heaving Michael after him. He then released his hands and let Michael do the work. Michael had always found his own anus so difficult to get things out of, he was pleasantly relieved by the ease with which he got into Bozzo's. And once inside, he found himself nosing his sensile way through various consistencies. It was warm. And it was all give. It didn't open out and draw in like a vagina. But it was there to be fucked. And fucked it was.

New, unfamiliar aromas enhanced the act, drove Michael deeper and deeper. Although he started gently, as Bozzo's moans increased, so Michael's rhythm followed. He never went in hard. Just a lot. The two of them seemed joined, rhythmically. It was like magic. It was like nature.

266

Their lovemaking could have gone on forever. Michael lost himself in it. Didn't have to worry about Bozzo's orgasm or whether he was enjoying it or how he was or how he, Michael, was performing or how he'd explain what to whom afterwards or commitments . . . they both wanted the same thing and, once Michael relaxed, they worked towards it together

As the rise and fall of Bozzo's buttocks intensified, so Michael found himself vocalising his own urgency. Then a sort of yelping whine started to bound from Bozzo, like a bull on the verge of tears, and Michael found in himself a similar but deeper voice which took flight from the pit of his gut. From his very loins. Michael had never known such freedom and release. He must have hollered the house down.

As they lay there afterwards, soaked in warmth and sweat, Bozzo whimpered softly to himself, and Michael wondered vaguely about safe sex.

Once daylight came, Bozzo was gone, and Michael missed his presence in the bed. And the smell of their lovemaking wafted up from his nether regions. It was comforting.

That day Michael finally got to play a corpse as an extra in yet another war movie. So he did not see Bozzo until he got home. Bozzo was washing the grime out of a chipped mug in the kitchen, squinting over the rollie hanging out of his mouth.

"Last night," he said without looking up, "It never happened."

"Of course," Michael replied, unsure whether Bozzo meant the spray painting or the fuck.

But he felt warm inside all the same.

*

267

As Rama and Ravana Meet In Battle, Indra Petitions Siva To Relinquish His Patronage Of The Demon

After fucking Bozzo, Michael couldn't get him out of his mind. He wondered whether he should feel guilty about his infidelity to Sheena. But since Sheena didn't want him anyway, and Bozzo had initiated the act, and neither Bozzo nor Sheena seemed to value each other in any sense that could ordinarily be termed sexually possessive, such a concern on his part seemed purely academic.

Then Michael reasoned that he was substituting Bozzo for Sheena in his romantic construction of the latter. Since he couldn't have Sheena, but Bozzo could, he could have Bozzo. Or something like that. Whatever, this ratiocination was quite successful, for it enabled Michael to get on with the unmitigated pursuit of what was essentially a teenage crush on Bozzo.

He still felt Bozzo around his penis, for instance, and longed to be inside him again. He caught traces of Bozzo's odour around the house and longed to rive his tongue into its progenitor. He began to pick up articles of clothing Bozzo left here and there and smell them. Started fingering Bozzo's cigarette butts lovingly. Overflowing ashtrays became objects of devotion for him. Little temples he could maintain and decorate with petals of disused cigarette paper. The toilet bowl similarly became an erstwhile shrine. Michael ceased cleaning it compulsively as was his wont, so that the solidifying tracks of Bozzo's more explosive bowel movements could be preserved by the purifying waters of the cistern and flue.

Michael would find all sorts of subtle ways to be contiguous to Bozzo when he was around. Like being the first to follow Bozzo in the loo, or sitting in a seat still warm from Bozzo's posterior, or sipping from a cup Bozzo had drunk without washing it, or masturbating on his front when Bozzo and Sheena were fucking upstairs, so that he could pretend it was him fucking Bozzo.

Sometimes he wanted Bozzo so desperately during this act that he would sneak upstairs and complete his sublimation outside the very

268

door behind which the objects of his love were rooting - although he didn't do this too often in case he fell asleep in the bliss that followed.

When Bozzo and Sheena were out, Michael's devotions intensified. He would take relics of Bozzodom to his room - nail clippings, pubic hairs from the bathroom - and either masturbate with them, burn them, or both. He even tried to sneak a photograph of Bozzo, but the latter threatened to smash the camera in his face.

Eventually, none of these measures was enough. Michael needed to get into Bozzo's room and complete his devotions on Bozzo's bed. In the very depression in which Bozzo rooted Sheena. With, if possible, Bozzo's clothes about his person. Perhaps even something of Bozzo inside him. Once his life had resolved itself into this imperative, he began to plan. For he knew he must not be discovered.

The trouble was that Bozzo and Sheena were erratic in their movements. More often than not, when one was out the other was in. And for Michael to appear disinterested enough in their movements to remain above suspicion, he felt he had to be either in his room or in the loo when they left. Which usually meant that he never knew quite whether one or both had gone. So he'd have to surreptitiously search the house, finding some excuse or other to move through it with an air of nonchalance and purpose to check for occupancy, his excitement mounting as he went.

If he finally managed to reach Bozzo's bedroom door without encountering another, Michael would be near ecstasy. His breathing would be shallow, his ears straining for sounds within, as he stealthily avoided the creak in the last step.

Sometimes he would hear the rustle of paper or scratching of a pen. That would be Sheena. She was always writing. On other occasions he might hear the inhalation of a cigarette, or the sound of somebody playing with themselves. That would be Bozzo. Sometimes Michael was sure he could even hear Bozzo thinking.

But sometimes - just sometimes - he would hear nothing. Just the soft, silent movement of the air in Sheena's lace curtains, which hung over the always-open french doors onto the verandah, street, and city beyond.

On such occasions Michael would place his suspended foot upon the landing and creep forward, almost on all fours. His ear would telescope for telltale sounds of Bozzoness or Sheenadom in the room beyond. His face would nudge its way through bare molecules to gain apprisal of the open doorway. And always, without exception, there would be Bozzo sitting at the deco dressing table, staring at himself in the cloud shaped mirror with the two wing mirrors turned slightly in towards him.

He would always be perfectly still. Michael could barely detect his breathing. As if his sole source of being lay in the image before him. The image almost shone with the intensity of Bozzo's focus on it. Except that it was dim in that corner of the room. And the mirror seemed more like a prison. Something Bozzo was trying to see his way through, or out of, by focussing on the light behind and beyond. While a big arrow hung from the heavens over Bozzo's head saying: OPPRESSION. Bozzo, locked out of the radiance of the universe.

The problem for Michael in this situation was getting back downstairs again. Because, having heard him bash around confidently downstairs, Bozzo would know that Michael was still in the house. Yet already the silence had been too long. Michael thus had to get back to his room and occupy himself in some quiet activity, so that it would appear he had simply been reading or something.

Even as it was, Bozzo could look around at any moment, especially if he heard Michael breathing as hard as Michael could hear himself.

So would begin Michael's painstaking retreat, fortunately seldom accelerated by any eruption of movement from Bozzo.

The day did eventually dawn, of course, when an excruciatingly stealthy ascent of the stairs was rewarded by the glorious prospect of an empty room. It was like entering heaven. Michael literally felt his skin tingling, as if breaking through the dew drop layers of the clouds, as his body stretched past the door to make its final check for presences. And his body snapped back into puffy pliancy as he finally stepped inside, to find himself floating on the immanence of Bozzodom and the prospect of his sublimation in it. A pair of Bozzo's underpants lay on the bed, coyly nestled in the sheets. A sweaty t-shirt had fallen to the floor nearby. Michael couldn't have asked for more.

To illuminate the dream, Sheena had the whole room decked out in white. It seemed uncharacteristic of the hardy Sheena, and foolhardy in the light of Bozzo's inveterate messiness, traces of which littered the interior - boots, greasy denim, cigarette ends, bottles, needles and plain, straightforward dirt - but everywhere Michael looked was cloudlike. Not just the lace netting across the door but sheets, bedside lamp, cushions; even the bed, although the basic mattress-on-the-floor, was duna'd and pillowed in frilly, billowy white.

And there in the corner of the room, as if the focus of all of this heavenliness, was the dressing table that so fascinated Bozzo. Naked. Not at all the dull prison that it seemed from the doorway. But light, bright, the source of clarity in the room. And at the moment its seat was vacant.

It was an old 1920s affair, painted white. It had clearly been painted many times before, although not perhaps by its present owners. There was little on it. A fluffy powder puff in a porcelain scallop shell. An atomiser for a perfume called "Lotus", operated by a large testicle to one side which one presumably squeezed to spray the Essence of the Orient onto one's skin. Then there were the mandatory (and anachronistic for Sheena) lace doilies and an (equally anachronistic) gold dispenser containing very red lipstick. Plus a couple of Bozzo's more vicious ear- and nose-rings, one shaped like a baby's rattle with spikes on it, the other platted like a noose.

On the stool, Michael was
careful to match his buttocks to the marks left by Bozzo's. He then
made sure the stool stood pretty much where Bozzo always
positioned it. And finally, he allowed himself to raise his eyes to
embrace the experience of image that so absorbed Bozzo.

Michael
had found it difficult to look at himself in mirrors since India. It
made him feel like a clown. And now the image in Bozzo and
Sheena's cloud mirror that met his gaze confirmed that feeling. So he
decided to make himself look like one. He applied a lavish
foundation with the powder puff, created big red cheeks with the
lipstick, then couldn't decide whether the lips should be happy or
sad. So he tried both. So that his lips ended up like two red sausages
joined at the middle. Or hermaphrodite worms exchanging sperm.
Or, conversely, a couple of genes trying to separate during meiosis.
Basically, however, they looked silly, and it occurred to Michael that
he had never seen Sheena wearing make-up. Not even on the job.

Next Michael discovered that he had three reflections, one in the
mirror before him and then one in each of the wing mirrors. But only
four arms appeared. In the mirror to his right, only his right arm
appeared. In the mirror to his left, only his left arm appeared. So that
in all three mirrors, he had only four arms. Unless he moved about,
of course, which confused the image considerably. But even then,
the six or so arms he had always came back through the four.

If he sat
perfectly still and tried not to move his head, he also had three
distinct faces. For the face in the right and left mirrors took on
slightly different profiles. He realised, for instance, that his right
profile looked angrier than his left. Which confused him, because he

had thought the left side of the brain (which controlled the right side of the body) was supposed to be the peaceful, calming side.

Then Michael noticed something else in the mirror which gave him cause for further discomfort. He noticed that in the right-hand mirror, because of the angle of the dressing table across the corner, you could see the door. And through the door you could see the banisters that ran along the stairwell almost to the landing at the top of the stairs. And Michael knew immediately that on all of those occasions when he had been looking at Bozzo at the dressing table, Bozzo could also have been looking at him. He knew this because he could now see Bozzo, standing in the stairwell behind the banisters. And Bozzo was staring straight at him.

They each held their respective gazes for what seemed like an age. Michael had no idea how long Bozzo had been there, but he was secretly glad it had not been long enough to let him get to the bed. He was merely in front of the mirror, looking like a somewhat emotionally indecisive clown.

Despite this small measure of relief, Michael could not laugh as he wished he could. For he was fundamentally mortified at being discovered. And afraid Bozzo would kill him, so dark and still was the figure in the shadows. Expressionless. The mouth glum, but neither sad nor angry. Just set.

Suddenly Bozzo moved, as if a film in freeze frame starting up again.

"Great, isn't it," he called, almost incidentally. For he was already in the room, standing behind Michael. As if a couple of feet of the film were missing and Bozzo had simply skipped a bit.

"I have three faces," offered Michael lamely.

"If you move it in there and there," Bozzo said, reaching either side of Michael's head to rearrange the wing mirrors, "You have ten heads and twenty arms."

273

"I'm not sure I want ten heads and twenty arms," said Michael, still searching for something to make a joke about. "Three's hard enough to cope with, looking like this."

Michael looked up at Bozzo in the mirror with the hope of a smile, but the big man just stared impassively back. There was nothing. Not even a comment about the make-up. Or an insult. Nothing.

Michael groaned pathetically and, as if in mock faint, let his head fall against the mirror. As he did so he drew the two side mirrors in behind his head, partly in mock-execution, partly to hide himself away like a child, a little like a performer closing a puppet booth, but mostly because it was the only thing he could think of to do.

Just as the mirrors closed about his head, Michael noticed out of the corner of either eye that his image reproduced itself in increasing numbers as his head moved forward. They bounced from side to front to side and front again, replicating themselves exponentially. Within fractions of fractions of a second. It was just an apprehension, but in that moment, before what had been light became darkness, before what was visible became invisible, Michael's image was everything, everywhere, wherever anyone (namely he) looked. Infinite.

Michael didn't desire Bozzo so much after that.

*

Jatayus

Michael wasn't sure whether it was just his paranoia, but he was convinced that after the dressing table incident both Bozzo and Sheena started avoiding him. This was, perhaps understandable. Sheena, after all, had her work to do, and Bozzo had discovered Michael sitting in his bedroom at his dressing table with a face made up like a clown.

But there was also a distinct lull in hostilities between Sheena and Bozzo. This could have been for some perfectly plausible reason, such as Sheena's compliance with Bozzo's 'request' for the Golden Deer. But Michael was sure he heard the two laughing upstairs together on the night of his unfortunate unmasking. And he was equally sure he was the object of their unaccustomed and mirthful consonance. Which was hurtful as well as embarrassing when Michael was, within himself, battling out such an epic emotional conflict between his sense of bonding with Bozzo and the inveteracy of his love for Sheena.

So Michael decided not so much to turn his back on the home front as leave it where it was for a while while he pursued other life-forming activities. Like his career as an actor, for instance, which was not exactly taking off. As in, one job as an almost extra and another as a real live corpse in a war movie. It was a disconcertingly modest start, but Michael had read somewhere that all great actors started that way and so took comfort.

Not that he wanted to be great. Just someone else. But the prospect of hounding agents and selling himself around the production houses of Sydney was too much for Michael. He was, after all, once ideologically opposed to such political hierarchies and middleman (and most of it *was* men) capitalism.

So he started hanging around the studios themselves. They were as good a place to be as any until his homelife did whatever it was going to do, and he liked the melee of purposeful activity that seemed to characterise them. Like a microcosm of life as Michael would have liked it to be: everybody with their individual tasks yet all working towards one goal of common expression, communicating and interacting to that end. Consensus through practice. A nice image, if something of an illusion.

Michael was also more than a little curious about the number of war movies being made around Sydney. He had been so since, on the night of his discovery in Bozzo's bedroom, he saw himself as a corpse on some supposed news footage fresh from the

275

front. The corpse being one he had played in a film studio somewhere on Sydney Harbour.

Michael remembered seeing footage from his first almost-extra experience, also screened as news footage. He was starting to wonder if there might be some kind of relationship between activities in Sydney's film studios and the government's so-called war effort.

It was on his way to one such studio, an old warehouse in Ultimo, that Michael was able to frequent one of his favourite 'sacred sites'. Between the underground section of Central Station and the bus terminals on George Street ran a pedestrian subway that must be close to a kilometre in length. Along it, twice a day, passed crowds of faces in varying degrees of numbness and exhaustion, depending on which end of their working day it was. At such times the subway acted as a kind of multicultural fly strip for the city's buskers. They came, it seemed, from every corner of the world (if the world can be seen as having corners) to transport the drudgery of this once brightly tiled thoroughfare into a leisurely stroll across the musical globe.

An old Irish drunk, complete with flat cap and ill-fitting sports jacket, trills away at Celtic whistles like a canary, sometimes two or three instruments at once, his eyes flickering as he plays.

Next to him, a backpacker with a London accent rolls out endless barrels of cockney songs - or their choruses, anyway - melodious, sweet, nostalgic, and completely out of place in twentieth century Sydney.

Opposite, a haunted violist, possible a student from the Con, trots slavic rhapsodies out of his classical training with painful lack of rhythm. Up the other end, an old fiddler with ruddy, stubbled cheeks squeaks out popular tunes with hurdy gurdy carelessness. Neither have provision for the few coins that scatter around their feet.

Next to the student, however, a stocky folk singer with bush beard and hair

276

strums out doughty ballads of an Australian history the current dominant hegemony is systematically taking apart: ticket-of-leavers, trade unionism, selection, soldier settlers, the depression. Yet the stout nationalist seems oblivious to the fact that he is drowning out both the hippy in front of him, who has lived with aborigines and is playing a didge and selling a tape he has made with them in the Top End; and the Greek duo of middle-aged men, now presumably either retired or unemployed, the immigrant lifeblood of the country's post-war industrialisation, never fully accepted, bazoukiing it with renascent strains of rembetika.

And lastly, a little further off, a lone Chinese, who looks a little like Michael's calligrapher in the Cross, tries on one hand to pretend he isn't there but on the other plays a two stringed erhu to a pre-recorded synthesised backing such that he might as well have had an entire Chinese pop orchestra with him. And who is also selling cassettes of the music he is instrumentally karaokiing.

A Fillipino in flared trousers croons frilly messages of love from the open neck of his white, acrylic shirt to a Latin guitar while opposite two unassuming women sit on a patchwork quilt and sing quiet evocations of a Latin American oppression that catch enough on passing ears to stay with their owners in unfolding missives of meaning for the rest of the day.

A few yards further on, a kilted Scot puffs away on threadbare bagpipes with such sour-note energy that commuters unconsciously duck as they pass. Opposite a young saxophonist with saw-tooth haircut and dark, mute shades takes on the gallivanting highland notes with frenetic jazz runs. He could have been in New York.

Getting close to the hurdy Gundy man now, a couple of junkies, relics of the Hippy Trail and Magic Bus, mumble into guitars they can't tune songs they no longer understand for money no-one gives them. The money goes instead to the smiling man from Trinidad who once sang cheerful songs he had recorded on shiny black vinyl singles which he sold beside a sign that read

"SMILE! It makes others happy." Now the frizz of hair is grey, the Beatles cap dated, the sign faded, singles warped, and the New Commonwealth invasion of the UK is history. But his children smile for him. The perfect family no-one believes in any longer.

Michael aimed this morning's visit at the end of the commuter rush, so that he did not have to walk at its pace but could mask himself amongst its bodies. And today there was a new addition to the subway's cultural ecosystem. A couple of post-anarcho-punks, dressed in black with legs like drainpipes, regaled passers-by with a singularly tuneless refrain.

"I - I - I - I - I've kicked my mother to death!"

They hit the "I" roundly to begin with, allowed it to drop in tone and pitch, then drew it up and out like a skier approaching a jump. This first phrase of the refrain was complemented by a couple of spindly steps backwards, which allowed the ghoulish couple to then trip forward and boot the staccato "kicked my mother to death" metaphorically into the passing traffic of legs.

Michael couldn't help smiling at the audacity of their act, especially with a collection cloth at their feet. They too found themselves funny. As their maundy moving audience tried to ignore them, they would smile to each other as they bounded out from the subway wall like puppets on elastic with their outrageous declaration.

The crowd had thinned out considerably now so Michael crossed to the other side of the subway to avoid the same scornful invasion of personal space himself. But he still smiled as he passed. And they saw him smile.

Just then, out of the corner of his eye, he glimpsed a figure clinging to the tiles on the lefthandside. Moving counter to the flow, a mime in slow motion, crawling horizontally in a vertical plane. But glancing slightly crazed to one side, as if nervous of something opposite or, conversely, a hawk about to fall upon its prey.

No, more like a vulture in the act of doing so; for as he approached Michael recognised the scrawny,

278

sandy-haired face that turned its red-rimmed eyes towards him, and it certainly belonged to no mime. Doleful once-blue eyes. Grease-streaked once-auburn beard. Pock-marked cheeks that seemed to suck the vortices of life from the very air.

Michael had known Jamie in Tasmania. He was one of the early draft resisters to utilise the Chain. Had hung around afterwards, supposedly helping. Jamie was an addict from way back. Eluded the army because he was afraid it would kill him, but not in the conventional sense. More through withdrawal, or being busted upon enlistment. Jamie had a history of dealing. Slight, but enough to count. Enough to support those collapsing veins in their bid to become the stormwater drains for the life forces of the universe.

So that what Jamie would have seen on Michael's face in that moment of recognition was both the pleasure of meeting an old comrade and the fear that that old comrade would want more out of Michael than Michael either had or was prepared to offer. But Michael never got the chance to find out whether or not Jamie saw his reservations, for at that same moment a flurry of black came from behind him.

*

Mithila

The last time Michael had seen Jamie was at a beachside shack on the East Coast of Tasmania. The shack belonged to Michael's friend and mentor Conan, with whom he, Lachy and the key organisers of the Chain had been staying to brainstorm future directions.

During the weekend Michael had found himself in an inversely similar position to Jamie. For as Lachy, the younger of the two brothers, had been trying to rouse Michael from a desultory disenchantment with the Chain's political force, so Jamie's elder brother, Samson, had

279

been trying to instil in the younger sibling some resolve outside his self-absorption with his habit.

Michael was probably just tired at the time, but he was seriously beginning to doubt the value of pulling out a relatively low number of draft resisters when the police were most probably bagging the vast majority of 18-25 year olds in the country without so much as a murmur from the general public. Dolework simply made the age group an open vein, since just about everybody in the age bracket was engaged in the forced labour scheme in one way or another. The DSS knew exactly where they were and what they would be doing. The police simply turned up with the draft notice and took them away. The draft was supposed to random, but...

So Michael wondered what they were realistically achieving: a small pool of intellectually sensitised prols for the Golden Age, when it happened? A network of harmonious souls to hold it together when Capitalism finally thundered to the ground? Michael thought it far more likely they'd all be vaporised first. Although the much-vaunted All Out Nuclear Big One hadn't happened after Dehli, the trigger fingers would still be mighty itchy. All those Minutemans, ICBMs, SLBMs and Cruise Missiles strung in their bows just waiting for someone, somewhere, to give the signal. Or simply go loopy in the control room one night.

Such was the jeremiad of despair Michael was unburdening upon his younger brother these days. Lachy was hoping that a good rallying weekend with some of his fellow activists would rejuvenate Michael. Unfortunately, such was not to be the case. On the second morning, while Michael was out nearly drowning, Conan's place was busted by the cops. When Lachy and Michael staggered up from the beach, and their ordeal in the ocean, they found the house ransacked, Conan gone, and not a soul in sight.

Lachy and Michael immediately split for various 'safe houses' prearranged for such an eventuality. It was possible that the others might have escaped. The fire in the stove had only just been lit, but mostly the beds were as their occupants had left them. Sleeping bags upended like crumpled cocoons. Torn clothes, even. Someone had obviously been well advised.

The standing procedure in such instances was that escapees would make contact after a suitable cooling off period. But for some reason Lachy baulked at the moment, implored Michael not to leave, wept, said they could not go on like this. And ironically it was Michael who, in the end, found himself pulling his brother together, rather than the other way around. But as their paths diverged on the edge of the wild wetlands of coastal Tasmania, it was Michael who knew he had had enough, and wondered whether his brother had seen the doubt and weariness in his eyes as they clasped forearms amidst the button grass.

So Michael didn't go to the assigned refuge. He made instead for Launceston, and another safe house in which he'd been living with a young woman named Sarama. It was indeed Sarama who believed in the God Baba, of the 54th. religious sect to abscond from India with the coffers. Michael had met Sarama when he awoke one morning underneath a hedge, having spent the night hiding from police. Sarama was preparing for work in the classroom of the school separated from the suburb surrounding it by the said hedge. Sarama looked up through the window at Michael in exactly the same moment as he looked out from under the hedge at her. Which made any explanation of his predicament other that the truth somewhat difficult. Oh I was just looking for my dog. Sorry, is this the way to Darwin? I suddenly had this urge to lie under a hedge next to a school.

So the truth it was. And Sarama had taken him in. And, later, she had also taken in many of Michael's draftees, as a link in the Chain. And her relationship with Michael had remained celibate for . . . well, for a respectable length of time.

Michael's plan now was to propose to Sarama that they run away together while they could. If Conan's coastal hideaway could be busted, the whole Chain might be sprung at any moment. Michael was busily contemplating where he and Sarama might go as he approached their homey, suburban weatherboard, to find the blue flashing lights of a police car already outside.

He had walked much of the way overland, hitching only from the main highway, so he was tired anyway. But that was not what prompted him to give himself up. Yes, I am Rama Chandra, a key organiser in an escape chain for draft resisters. Yes, my real name is . . . No, the girl knows nothing.

But the police did not want to see Michael. Indeed, they didn't seem to know who he was at all. They wanted to know instead about the occupants of the house. In particular, the leaseholder. Michael confirmed that was Sarama. That he was a friend of hers'. He even gave his real name. The police then explained that there had been an accident, and asked Michael to accompany them to the mortuary to identify Sarama's body. Even as they drove through the nineteenth century streets, Michael thought this might be part of fiendish trap. But when he saw the body, it was clear that the police had no other motive. Sarama had been found naked in a paddock by a farmer who had been ploughing it. Twigs were sticking out of every conceivable orifice, and had been the most likely cause of death. Although it was clear she had also been raped, several times.

Police enquiries had already confirmed that a woman fitting Sarama's description had been dragged into a panel van by a bunch of youths near the shops just around the corner from where she and Michael lived. It was thought unlikely that she knew, or was known by, the occupants of the vehicle.

It was after that Michael left for Sydney.

*

An Abduction

In leaving Tasmania after Sarama's death, Michael lost something inside him. He wasn't quite sure how it happened, but it was as if the Medusa's head unleashed in Michael's head after Dehli, whose snakes Michael had so skilfully, if unconsciously, trained into the service of the Chain, now wrapped Michael's self up like a rope. And the effect, for Michael, was like a death. Even though he was still alive.

And it was here that Michael began to mix his mental metaphors, for he could not work out what had happened to him. He wanted to think of this snake-embalmed self as having lodged somewhere warm and womb-like; in the folds of a gut, for instance, with the serpents' heads to defend it. But he knew that the housing was far more austere. More like the underground dump in Tasmania where he and Lachy had so paradoxically 'buried' draftees. Here the walls of what Michael might have understood to be his soul were lined with quartz and salt, embedded deep in granite, a tall, tall cavern, in the centre of which was Michael's self, bound tightly, like a cannister of radioactive waste.

Would he go off? Or simply decay slowly through one half life after another, seeping out into the environment around him, infecting everything with his slow, cancerous morbidity? High above on the mountain top, demon giants stomped around in search of him. "Come up here you little bugger!" they yelled with horrendous voices. And with each reverberation of their mega-feet, Michael's volatile self shook just a few more protons out into neighbouring neutrons and beyond, into the air around. So that, as Michael's bound self worked itself towards the point of nuclear reaction, so the atmosphere around it grew more foul and impenetrable.

As Michael looked into Jamie's red-veined eyes in the Sydney subway that morning, the giants finally crashed through the mountainside of Sarama's death, grabbed the bound self by its own rope, and began whirling it around the universe like a sputnik. Meanwhile, the rocks and boulders of the Chain clamped themselves about Michael's shoulders like a mantle that had materialised out of thin air, so that he could barely move. Where the snakes went was anybody's guess.

Not that he needed to. (Move, not guess.) As Jamie detached himself from the tiled wall and reached out towards Michael's arm, Michael could see a semblance of emissary in the smacked-out eyes, as if the angels were coming at last. But the harbingers of peace were replaced by a flush of alarm, and Michael was aware of a motion behind him like a parting of oceans. As Michael moved forward against the mountainside that was growing about his shoulders, tentacles of spindly black arrested his frame at odd angles, and the snakes were back.

Disoriented, Michael struggled against whatever it was that seemed to be imprisoning him. His efforts, however, only succeeded in lifting him off the ground and rotating him through an ariel half-cartwheel. As if his own limbs were being used against him.

Jamie grabbed one of Michael's feet and pulled himself towards his former comrade, his face this time distorted with anger and contempt. One of his freckled hands passed over Michael's face like a winged shadow and pulled at the eyes of a third visage, which had arisen from behind Michael's head.

And sounds and sense began to return to Michael from another world, the one that was around him as opposed to inside him. He identified, for instance, the absence of the punks kicking their mother to death. At the same moment, he recognised his two assailants as being the same. The whole package - himself, the punks, and Jamie - was moving off along the subway like some eight-armed monstrosity, accompanied by copious "fucks" and "cunts" and the sounds of scuffle.

As they went, Michael was aware of Jamie trying to hand over hand prise Michael from his attackers. But the opposing four limbs seemed to slash with unmediated viciousness any attempt at intervention. Then a lithe black form leapt forward and delivered several powerful blows into Jamie's stomach, forcing the Tasmanian expatriate to double up against the tiles.

As the attack was withdrawn, Jamie was sliding down the wall, blood spurting from his mouth and gut. At the same time Michael himself was flying towards Jamie from the momentarily inattentive arms, so that Jamie became for a moment a rapid expansion of blood speckled with white tooth and flesh in Michael's eyes. Until the latter was seized, mid-flight, by a bat-like wing that brought a wet knife blade to his throat and words like "One move, cock, and I'll cut your throat!" to his ear. Meanwhile Jamie seemed to be spluttering "Lachy! Lachy!" through the blood as he slid to the ground, his eyes pleading.

Michael's view was then eclipsed by the crowd gathering around the receding Jamie. Occasional onlookers glanced in Michael's direction as he was hustled along the subway. Then a wave of commuters washed into the wake of the departing threesome, obscuring the scene of Jamie's stabbing altogether. Although Michael thought he might have heard someone somewhere shouting, "Call an ambulance! Quickly!" But then, didn't somebody always shout that?

*

Janaka

As he was manhandled relatively inconspicuously along George Street, Michael began to understand that Jamie had known who the punks were, just as the punks had known who Jamie was, and the two were there for the same reason: him. He also became aware that Jamie had pressed something like a piece of cloth into his hand, which he dare not examine now for fear of discovery.

The unlikely trio bundled towards the city, rather like a Hills Hoist that had collected someone else's washing in a storm. Michael found himself making such compelling demands as, "Where are you taking me?" and "What do you think you're doing?", supported by incisive elaborations such as, "I'm unemployed, you know. I haven't got any

285

money." and "I'm not going much further. Not unless you tell me what this is all about." To which he received such informative replies as "Shut yer face!" and "Keep moving!" and "You'll go as far as we fucking tell you to!"

Michael's ineluctable journey flew him up a flight of steps into one of the many tall city office blocks he'd never particularly noticed before. In the lift, which talked to them as they went, other occupants avoided the newcomers because they liked neither the look nor the smell (of which Michael was rapidly becoming aware) of Michael's companions. The latter discreetly secreted their weapons and wiped their hands, as if in preparation for a meeting with eminence.

"I hate lifts," said Michael conversationally. He was very frightened.

He needn't have been, however. About halfway up the shaft, the lift stopped at a perfectly ordinary floor and opened into the reception area of a perfectly normal business enterprise. A low, long reception desk lay opposite the lift across an expanse of predictable, purple carpet.

Behind the desk, female receptionists in blue and beige uniforms did unsurprising receptionist-type things like moving around with pieces of paper or entering data onto keyboards, answering phones. On the wall behind them a large, golden insignia sat inside a larger, equally golden circle, looking rather like a deer or an antelope. It could have belonged to an airline. It seemed vaguely surreal that, as the lift doors closed behind them, Michael's two dishevelled guards elicited no surprise from the pleasant-smelling woman behind the counter.

"This one's for Mr Joseph," said the punk who had not killed Jamie.

The woman smiled. She had the sort of grandmotherly facial down you don't notice until you get close enough to see beneath the powder.

"Thank you very much. You will be forwarded the appropriate remuneration in due course. Sit over there for a moment, will you please? Mr Joseph won't keep you long."

These last two sentences were delivered to Michael, as if he was supposed to know who 'Mr Joseph' was. Perhaps even what he himself was doing here. As for his unorthodox method of delivery, it was apparently par for the course.

The two punks relinquished their respective grips on Michael's arms, turned and left. They pressed the button for the lift and chatted to each other inconsequentially, without looking back. Michael might as well not have been there. So he wandered irrelevantly across to a selection of turquoise modular lounges and sat down.

*

Siva's Bow

Michael gazed at a slivver of Sydney skyline through a vertical strip of window at one end of the counter. Then the powdery receptionist returned and said;

"Mr Joseph will see you now. Please come this way."

She lead Michael behind the counter to an office adjoining the reception area, smiled with her laugh-lined eyes, and closed the heavy pine door behind her as she left.

The office was not unlike the reception area. The same purple carpet stretched between the same cream-coloured walls, and a long wooden counter stood beyond a suitable expanse of mauve. Except that this time it was a desk. Before which sat a couple of modular, turquoise chairs. And behind which was a longer, horizontal stretch of Sydney skyline, this time scored by venetian blinds.

Between the blind and the desk sat a man. He had white hair, which rested on his scalp in tight, almost artificially crimped waves. He wore a grey single-breasted suit which glinted with a silvery sheen when dipped into the light. And he wore a white shirt with a tie diagonally striped in blue and grey, fashioned with a windsor knot.

His face was kindly and not of the city. He had the sort of bulbous, poached nose that was used to breaking the onslaught of heavy weather. His hands might have just come from grappling with a young hefer, and his cheeks were flushed with those capillary reticulations that lace the skin as they battle with wind or grog or both. Yet here he was in a business suit on the upper floors of a plush city office block. He looked out of place.

"G'day - Michael, isn't it? Sorry about the way we had to bring yous here. Joseph's the name. Gareth Joseph. I'm from Tassie too. Here, take a pew."

And the man offered Michael the chair nearest to the desk.

"They were very rough," Michael ventured cautiously.

The man apologised with a shrug and spread his hands biblically.

"They might've killed a friend of mine," Michael continued.

"Oh. Come to that, did it? Sorry. He's been watching us, your friend. We've been watching him. We hoped he wouldn't be a bother. Was he a good mate?"

"I'm not sure," said Michael, thinking that was not the point.

"These things happen. Come on, take the weight offa yer feet. I'm sorry about yer mate."

So Michael sat down, surprising even himself. He half expected Gareth Joseph to now turn to him and say, "Now, what can I do for you?", as if this were a job interview. Although in fact the man smiled and said;

"Wouldja like a cup of coffee? Or a beer, perhaps?"

"Coffee would be nice, thanks," said Michael, surprising himself even further by relaxing a little.

288

The man pressed buttons on his telephone handset and placed his order with reception.

"I don't usually use this office," explained Gareth Joseph. "Spend most of me time down on the property. Only get up here a coupla times a year. Just to keep the business end up."

"What sort of business is that?" asked Michael, becalmed by this lapse into the familiar.

"Oh, pastoral mostly. I mean, up here we're into finance. Loans to businesses. Start-up capital and that. But I've got land down in Tassie. That's where we started. Have to lease it out these days, of course. Tobacco companies, mines, the Japs. But mostly it's still pastoral. It was one of my managers found that girlfriend of yours' - what was her name?"

"Sarama?"

Michael's gut poked its uneasy head up in surprise, and that same resonance he'd experienced in the subway now bounced again from beneath the taut drumskin of his self-composure. Giants stomping. Rocks and boulders still crashing down a mountainside elsewhere. Snakes still embalming. The story continuing.

"Sarama, that's her. Funny name."

"It was given to her by God. She was a member of a religious sect."

"Shame about all that. I was real sorry. For you as well as for her."

"Is that why you had me brought here?"

"Hell, no. It's about Sheena."

"Sheena?"

And Michael's mental orientation backflipped and span through several lots of 360°.

"Hasn't she told you about me?"

Michael shook his head. The man seemed almost offended.

"She's never forgiven me since I sold out to this lot."

man jabbed his stubby thumb in the direction of the emblem of the golden deer which, Michael now noticed, was on the wall of this room too.

"Who are they?" he asked with disinterest.

"Transnational. You must've heard of 'em. They bought Mt Kalesa, down in Tassie. I told her, yous just can't go it alone anymore. We've had mortgages as long as your arm for two generations now. Yous can't keep banking on land that won't compete in a world market. The Yanks have got machines and monopolies as'd strip a paddock from Perth to Newcastle and back. Probably do already. Daily. As for the Asians, when you've got that many people working for nicks, what hope the poor Aussie employer, eh?

"It's nothing new, you know. It was like this during the fifties too. We were just lucky for a coupla years, that's all. Able to import our own cheap labour for a while."

"Excuse me," Michael interrupted, "But are you some sort of relation of Sheena's?"

"Relation? Well, I'm not her real father but I'm all she's got, fella. I'm more of a guardian, really. I mean, it was never legal, like. But when her mother died . . . hasn't she told yous all of this?"

Michael's eyebrows must have resembled barrage balloons rising over enemy lines.

"Her mother was one of the last Tasmanian Aborigines," Gareth Joseph explained. "Well, they called theirselves aborigines. You never heard of 'em until some University professor published a book saying they didn't exist. Then up they pop. 'Yeh, I'm a Tasmanian aborigine!' 'Me too!' Suddenly the whole bloody island's full of the bastards. But Sheena's mum was the full quid. Or as close as you'd get. Come down from the whaler's women, when they used to pull int' the Derwent, before she was even a settlement. Nip off with a couple of local gins. Keep 'em up on the islands and that.

"'Course they all live in cities these days. But when they heard some white bookbasher was tryin' to write 'em out of history, they all turned out to tell him where he could shove his bloody book!

There was no stoppin' 'em. Then came the dispute over Mt Kalesa."

"I know about Mt Kalesa," Michael confirmed.

"Well, Sheena's mum was one of the five who burned. Funny, by the time the authorities got up there, all they could find was bones enough for two of 'em. Full size. But then there were two other skeletons, but shrunk. I mean real shrunk, like the size of earrings. Then a circle of skulls - not theirs', other skulls. All burnt. And around that, a circle of hands - men's hands. And no-one else went up there with 'em. Uncanny it was, the police said.

"Were you there?"

"Mt Kalesa was right next to our main property. I saw 'em goin' up. I was just out doin' some fencing. She was still pregnant, Sheena's mum. Yous could see it. Anyway, I saw the fire from the peak. Went and got the cops. I was the first one up the mountainside. Bushfire danger, y'see. And found the kid about halfway up. Just lyin' there in a little patch of earth they'd dug out for her, between the rocks."

Gareth Joseph was silent for a while, as if in awe at the prospect of it. Then, as if snapping out of a freeze frame in another film, he continued;

"Anyway, we took her in. Felt a bit guilty, I suppose. That we hadn't pitched in more. Been more supportive. But you know how it is. The pollies come round and say, 'Would you cultivate or develop this land were it available to you?' and all that kinda stuff. What do yous say? 'Course yous flamin' would.

"So we looked after Sheena. And she was fine, 'til she found out who her real mother was. She was already into conservation and that - all those dams and protests - typical fifteen year old. That was how she met the abos. And before you now it . . . they remembered her mum, see? Anyway, we had a big blue and I cut off her allowance."

Michael's disapproval must have showed.

291

"Yeh I know, not the sort of thing a father's supposed to do. 'Specially to a daughter. But, I dunno, once she started goin' on about us not bein' her real parents and ... "

"And that was when you sold out to Transnational."

"Well, that was part of it, yeh."

Michael sipped his coffee, which had long since arrived and was going cold. Gareth Joseph did likewise.

"I didn't cut her off totally. I mean, I've kept the money aside for her. Put it into a trust fund, a bit each week. And she can still have it."

"Upon what conditions?"

A tone of recognition entered Michael's voice, as if a certain code had unlocked an entire programme in his brain. His own father had made a career out of breaking trust funds.

"Well, when I can be sure it will be responsibly applied."

"How do you mean, 'responsibly'?"

"Well, when she is mature enough to put it to proper use."

"Such as?"

"A house. Or schooling for her kids. Or . . . "

"And how will she demonstrate the attainment of such maturity? By achieving one of these material conditions?"

Gareth Joseph paused before answering this question. He had obviously arrived at the reason for this meeting.

"By getting married," he said finally, carefully.

"To whom?" These questions were automatic for Michael, who knew roughly where they would be going. It was just a matter of pinning the conditions down.

"To a man. To whom she is prepared to commit herself for life."

"As opposed to a woman, you mean."

"Something like that, yairs," the man replied. And then colloqued, "Yous know about all of that then?"

292

Michael nodded simply
and said;

"So how can I help?"

"The fund is only redeemable by the husband. By contract, during the course of my lifetime, and by will in the event of my death."

"So the money in fact goes to the man, not to your daughter."

"It cannot go to a woman at all."

There was a pause.

"Doesn't that constitute a tax evasion scheme?" Michael asked tentatively, becoming his father so easily it horrified him.

"I've buried the fund," Joseph replied.

"Buried?"

"In another company. The fund is constituted through the purchase of shares in a subsidiary of my company, but the transaction is through Transnational - because it was they who insisted we take on the subsidiary in the first place. So it's a sort of - a contra-deal," Gareth Joseph found the word.

"And is this subsidiary . . . reliable?"

"Sound as a rock. Ever heard of Military Industrials?"

Michael had.

"Mega-bucks, mate! All ploughed straight back into the fund."

"So it is, in effect, interest-bearing."

"Well, not so as anyone'd know," the man reassured Michael confidentially.

But Michael did not need reassurance. He was wondering how he could best protect Sheena's interests. Perhaps this was the opportunity he had been looking for. Perhaps he could save her without her even knowing it.

"I'm still not sure how I can help you," Michael fenced.

"Well, I thought yous were . . . I mean, aren't yous . . . sweet on her?"

"I love her, yes," Michael confirmed stoutly. "But if you are aware of that, then you would also be aware that she is already living with another man."

"Exactly," Gareth Joseph replied, bringing his fingers together lightly below his chin. "I also know a great deal more about you. Activities I'm sure you'd rather nobody knew about up here. Social Security, for instance?"

Michael was quiet.

"So what do yous reckon?" asked the man after his implication had been allowed its full impact.

"I reckon Sheena doesn't attract much in the way of men. Not in the circles she mixes with, anyway."

"And you're not an addict, are yous?"

Michael shook his head.

"So, are yous interested? It's a big opportunity."

Michael looked beyond the head of Gareth Joseph to the thermal inversion layer dissipating between the office towers of the city as the day intensified.

"Do you mind if I think about it?" he asked eventually.

The man shrugged and spread his hands again.

"I'm only here for the day," he explained, "But you could call me later on this arvo. Before five, say. But listen young fella, no word of this to Sheena, right? She's not to know."

"Of course not."

"I'll find out, y'know."

"I'm sure you will."

"Well, good to meet yous, Michael. I look forward to hearing from yous presently."

And the meeting assumed an air of congenial formality. Gareth Joseph stood up in his grey suit and smiled affably. Michael took his cue and stood also. They shook hands. It could have been the end of a job interview. Indeed, Michael thought he would include it in his fortnightly job search report to the dole office.

"And don't worry about your friend," assured Gareth Joseph, closing where they had begun. "These things often look worse than they really are."

"Right," said Michael, trying to imply understanding. And then said, surprising himself for the third time during that interview;

"And who was the man who dragged Sheena's friend from the top of Mt Kalesa?"

Gareth Joseph's face turned to granite and, with an effort that seemed to come from across eons, replied;

"He's the man who might have been Sheena's father. Although she knew him as an uncle."

His visage softened.

"He gave her a little ornament once. A golden faun. When she was a girl. She used to love that golden faun."

"Deer," Michael corrected, looking at the emblem on the wall to Gareth Joseph's right. "I think it's a golden deer."

And Michael wondered why Gareth Joseph simply didn't have Bozzo killed.

Michael waved from the door as he left. His interlocutor waved back. They could have been passing time in the paddocks back home.

*

Jatayus's Dying Breath

Michael's first impulse upon rejoining the George Street throng was to go back and check on Jamie. But some quirk of contrariness he was reluctant to call cowardice impelled him to walk in exactly the opposite direction. It was his unconscious desire, he rationalised, to share with Sheena the joyful news of her impending good fortune, and his personal role in securing it for her. For Michael had in fact

295

formulated a plan to manoeuvre Old Man Joseph into resorting the trust fund to its rightful owner.

Of course he knew that he could not respond to this laudable sharing impulse because the source of the money, and the uses to which it was currently being put, were likely to likely to be met by a resounding rejection by Sheena as, along with its harbinger (vis. himself), gross manifestations of patriarchal corruption.

This was, naturally, not the direction in which Michael wanted his relationship with Sheena to grow. He wanted her to see him as a soft, feminine sort of man, opposed to violence and aggression, understanding and supportive and, simply, nice. The kind of man who would be there when you needed him.

Apart from which, if he revealed to her now his plan to relieve Gareth Joseph of Sheena's accrued allowance, he would blow the surprise of presenting her with the result. Noble, humble Michael, wanting nothing in return but her happiness, leaving her free to escape with Sri. If, that was, she and Sri wanted to escape. Somehow he was fixed on the idea that somebody should get something out of this by way of corporeal release.

In the midst of such marvellous rationcinations, it occurred to Michael than the man who called himself Gareth Joseph might be lying. He might not be Sheena's guardian at all. In which case, his motives were a mystery to Michael. Nevertheless it would be prudent to find a way of somehow subtly validating Joseph's story before he agreed to the proposal. And Sheena was the only means he could think of in the short to medium term. In fact, she was all he could think of at all.

By the time his cogitations had brought him to Circular Quay, Michael had walked the entire length of George Street without noticing so much as a bagpiping busker (of which there was always one at this time of year). So rather than choose between the discomforting prospects of seeking out the bloody Jamie or covertly eliciting verification from Sheena, he opted for a third course: continuing what he had originally set out to do that day - almost. Rather than backtrack through the scene of a crime Michael was quietly trying to deny to visit a studio in Ultimo, he hopped on a ferry for Balmain to check out Bridge Bay.

It was not until he was comfortably settled on board that Michael finally opened the loosely clenched left fist into which Jamie had pressed a crumpled note before sliding down the wall of the subway underneath George Street. It was a brief missive. Two words agonisingly scrawled onto rough, lined paper torn from a grubby exercise book. They read;

"Lachy"

and then, slightly below and at an angle not quite parallel;

"hooked"

*

Kaiyeka Persuades Daharastra To Renounce Rama As His Heir

Michael did not know what to make of Jamie's note, except inasmuch as is referred to his brother and heroin. The two, however, did not go logically together in Michael's mind, for Lachy was the last person Michael could imagine getting hooked on anything, except perhaps work. Lachy was, in a word, straight. And that was saying something, coming from Michael. Lachy was the son who studied hard, never stepped out of line, tried from the very centre of his being to fit in and got annoyed only when he failed to do so - and even then, only with himself. Lachy was so conscientious that, after shadowing Michael from the East Coast to discover the police at Sarama's house, Lachy had turned up himself at the police station. Risked identification to rescue his brother from the enemy.

297

And all Michael had been able to do was let him down. Declared his intention to get out altogether - the Chain, Tasmania, just about anything it was possible to get out of, basically. Lachy had said he understood. Said he would be there if Michael needed him. That he would carry on himself anyway. But it must have been such a disappointment to him to see the fire die in his brother's eyes. Michael could see the hero crumpling in the corneal orbs before him, dulling as they watched.

Michael could remember the farewell to Lachy before that. When the same extremity had been there, but igniting not dying. When Michael had been foolhardy enough to risk a Christmas back in Adelaide, only to discover that his first stepmother, Kelly, had persuaded his father to transfer his patronage from first son to second, Kelly's son, Barney.

Kelly wasn't even living with them anymore. Daniel was living with the actress from Sydney, Kathe, and working in private enterprise. Nor did Kelly particularly need Daniel's money. She had never surrendered her own business interests, not even through Barney's difficult birth.

It was simply that Daniel owed her. She had done all the groundwork in developing his career. And no sooner had he not only started to reap the rewards but had been borne a son than Daniel had deserted her. And Kelly had waited until now to call him in.

Thus Barney was to replace Michael in whatever will Daniel might leave and be offered a place in his corporate hierarchy. Which offended Michael's sense of justice more than anything else. He didn't particularly want the job, or the money. But once again here was Daniel failing to defend his first born against the second, and Kelly - with whom Michael had never got on.

Not that this was the actual content of the argument on that Adelaide Yuletide day that propelled Michael from his father's life forever. Any more than the capital which subsequently enabled Michael to buy his block on the North Western edge of the

Tasmanian Wilderness was a direct pay-off to salve Daniel's conscience. Daniel and Michael were simply wrangling over politics as usual. Towards the end of a traditional German Christmas dinner beautifully prepared by Kathe, Lachman's mother. The money emerged as an act almost of perversity. As in:

"If you love your bloody wilderness so much, why don't you go and bloody live in the stuff!"

"I would if I could afford to!"

The two men, father and son, locked into ill-founded threats from the furnaces of their respective inner rages by which pride would force them to stand long after the ovens had cooled and cracked. The argument had definitely not been the real issue. As Lachy had tried to suggest, staring earnestly and the angry fangs in his brother's eyes at the gate to the family home.

It was, incidentally, around this time that a similarly bolshy Australia was demanding to know of its only slightly more sagely ally, the USA, what transpired in the innermost sanctums of its satellite spy bases at Pine Gap and Nurrungar, in the centre of Australia. The Americans, however, were much smarter than Michael's father. They simply stalled the Australians long enough to move their most important secrets somewhere else and then said, "Of course! Come in! Take a look around. Cosy, isn't it?" While unreciprocal defence treaties were quietly allowed to lose what little meaning they had, and the US economy romped away with the Aussie dollar.

Ironically, it was the very technique that had made Michael's father South Australia's foremost Solicitor General which was, potentially, about to reverse this entrenched macro-economic trans-Pacific trend. For it was what Michael was planning to use to engineer an advantage for Sheena over Gareth Joseph.

Michael's father had, in his vocational youth, led his state's campaign against tax evasion. He virtually wrote the legislation that routed the trust funds and superannuation rackets and, in the process, rescued a large number of prospective retirees from financial ruin. He was hailed as a hero, and Michael was privately hoping for similar success, although on a more modest scale.

Michael reasoned that, if he threatened to dob Gareth Joseph in to the Taxation Department under the Commonwealth legislation modelled on his father's, he could force Joseph not only to release the money but to sign it and its attendant stocks across to Sheena. Sheena would thus be in a position, should she so desire it, to close down one of the world's largest military industrial complexes by simply moving the money out.

This was a comforting prospect to Michael out on the choppy harbour, as bow spray tingled his face. For the day had taken what people call a turn for the worse, and Michael was nursing a queasy uneasiness about his brother, Lachy.

*

Hanuman

Bridge Bay was one of the oldest and, now, smallest film studios in Sydney. It was basically an old corrugated iron warehouse which had been used so irregularly but lucratively by the film industry that it always just staved off that brand new container terminal or roll-on roll-off loading dock just around the corner in some town planner's brain. The aging studio had become something of an institution. If up-and-coming directors did not make a film at Bridge Bay, they really weren't in the running. Established actors returned to the furnace-hot, overgrown shed with affection. Retired extras talked of it to their grandchildren with nostalgia. Designers cursed comfortably into countless short blacks.

Once, it had commanded an unimpeded view of the harbour that brought renewal to lunchtime film crew and performers in low, flat trays of light. Or sometimes more literally, as refreshments arrived by launch. The remnants of which, in turn, satisfied the colonies of seagulls occupying the floating docks nearby.

But now those same docks were anchorage for two sometimes three once oceangoing vessels, rusting oil tankers and abandoned container ships, which rocked uneasily on keels impossibly high in the water, hungry for cargo that would never come.

Michael had noticed their numbers increasing in the waters around Sydney even in his short time in the city. Although the papers were, as usual, recalcitrant on the subject, the truth was not difficult to suss out. The escalation in sandwich wars around the world was ripping the belly out of the shipping industry. Larger shipping lines, once attracted to developing countries by lower registration fees and port charges, began to find their vessels strafed by unmarked aircraft, boarded by pirates who failed to identify themselves, hijacked mid-ocean. All in the name of one war or other, but who could tell what lengths their competitors would go to.

In the meantime, terrified crews jumped ship to claim whatever kind of asylum they could lay their hands on. Vessels entered the once beautiful Sydney Harbour and never left. Harbourfront shipping offices were mysteriously blown up in the night. Fires were lit in holds and never put out. And an ocean's entire population of ships gathered in the many bays and inlets of Port Jackson and chatted about the weather, rolled their own cigarettes upon which they drew with squinting eyes, played host to the seagulls, told old sea stories, and waited to see what would happen next. Capitalism was more reliable, it seemed, if it was transferred electronically.

"Any work for extras here?" Michael asked a young man emerging from between the two giant doors.

A take was just finishing inside. Michael had heard it. Lots of roaring noises, helicopters and machine gun fire, men shouting; the usual war movie stuff. While the rear end of a wind machine bucketed dust and debris

301

out over the car park with boundless if unwarranted enthusiasm. The crew and cast filed out to lunch to find their cars covered in subtropical effluvia.

"You got an agent?" asked the man.

He put his shoulder to one of the giant doors and began to roll it back, allowing the lunchtime exodus to straggle out.

"Yeh, but you know agents," Michael replied equivocally. "What's going on? Another war movie?"

"How'ja guess?" grinned the aboriginal, for so he was.

If there was one form of employment to which a Commonwealth clumsily straddling contradictory policies of Land Rights and Assimilation had gratefully found urban aboriginals warmed, it was the film industry. Long, unpredictable hours. Good pay. Reliable source of food. Always moving from one location to another. Companionship. Kinship. Order emerging from chaos, or indeed from nothing, as if by magic - but a magic inscribed in stories. The intelligence of consensus in action. Vestiges of a culture, anthropological reductionists conjectured, that still lingered in the collective consciousness, finally finding a place in the whitefella's world. A thesis which poststructuralists rejected, of course, as colonialist. The truth of the matter was that aboriginal people saw film as a cracking good way of spreading their own political message.

"Maybe I could come in and watch. For the experience," suggested Michael, hoping to view a section of the set he could later identify on television news.

"You want experience? For bein' an extra?" The young man was incredulous.

"Who's doing this one? Which company?" Michael tried to appear indifferent. But the man just shrugged. So Michael tried another tack.

"When's it gonna be released?"

"Dunno. Pretty quick. They're all pretty quick these days. In one day, out the next. Across that screen so fast you don't even see 'em. No-one sees 'em. I reckon they plan 'em for video these days."

302

As he spoke, Michael studied the speaker. He had one of those faces Michael was sure he knew, but which might also resemble someone else he had known once in another interface of time and place.

"Been working here long?" Michael started to fish.

"Coupla days."

"No, I mean in Sydney."

"Sydney, Melbourne, Uluru, down the track - even been to Tasmania, bro."

"Tasmania?" Michael intoned, trying to sound impressed while an internal neuronic display board lit up and the required information slipped into consciousness.

"Your name's not Hanif, is it?"

"How'd you know?" The man looked at Michael with suspicion.

"Tasmania. I think we might have met there. My name's Michael. From the Wilderness Group?"

"Hey, brother! How are you?"

Hanif broke into a broad grin and offered Michael his hands like a bird half-spreading its wings. The two men hugged spontaneously, but Michael clung on a moment longer than was necessary. It was a long time since he had had contact like this.

"Whaddya doin' up here?" Hanif asked, removing Michael's arms but still holding them joyfully.

Michael shrugged.

"Looking for work."

"Yeh, it gets that way in the end, don't it? Not much more of the country left to conserve since the Commonwealth reneged on the South West and Gippsland, eh?"

Hanif and Michael had accompanied each other on a number of forays into Tasmania's South West. They had stood side by side, aboriginal and conservationist, for land rights and human rights, as the bulldozers advanced on Farmhouse Creek and Lemonthyme. The days of affinity groups and support networks, consensus decision-making.

303

"You want some lunch?"

Hanif fetched Michael a generous plate of cold meats and salad.

"I heard about your action at Mt Kalesa," Hanif said as they sat on a bollard overlooking the oleaginous murk of Port Jackson. Hanif shook his head, laughing. "Incarcerated draftees! That was great, man. There's not much difference, is there?"

Michael was pleased Hanif appreciated the ingenuity of his and Lachy's operation, but found too much unsettling conviction in the memory to share in Hanif's mirth.

"You look strung out, Michael."

Hanif's change of tone was so abrupt that Michael couldn't help but answer from the now molten mass of unease that bubbled around the mummified cocoon of his bound self. He told Hanif about the Bomb in India, and about the Chain and its collapse, about Sarama, Sheena and Bozzo, and now about Jamie's note concerning Lachy.

Hanif remembered Sheena from Tasmania. She was one of a feminist collective who accompanied Aboriginal Affirmative on a campaign of actions after Michael had left to go bush. He thought that, yes, she might have been part of the Mt Kalesa vigil, because a number of aboriginal women had been in on that too. They said she was part koori. Which at least confirmed part of Gareth Joseph's story.

As for Lachy, Hanif said he was going down to Tassie in a day or two. The film needed some temperate rain forest. Hanif promised to find out what he could about Michael's brother.

"You sound like you've been havin' a rough time, brother," Hanif sympathised, and invited Michael in to watch the afternoon takes.

Which Michael did with a mixture of curiosity, anger and anticipation: curiosity because the movie was set in South America, and a war in South America had been in the news lately; anger because he couldn't get any work; and anticipation because his reunion with Hanif might bring him news of Lachy.

But there was something else too. A satisfaction. At being reconnected to Tasmania, and Sheena. As if he'd fallen off the island into some muddy pond in which it was situated, and Hanif had offered him a hand out.

*

Rama Wins Sita's Heart

On his way home, Michael found himself once more thinking about Sheena, and Gareth Joseph's proposal. By the time his silver elephant had deposited him at Kings Cross station, he was still no nearer to a decision. Although his conversation with Hanif had verified some aspects of Joseph's story, he felt he needed to no more. It was thus with perhaps an element of unconscious indecision that he allowed himself to be drawn from the station mouth by pedestrian flow deeper into the Cross.

Already shouldered males walked two or three abreast along the pavements, manful swaggers, walletfuls of unmarked notes jutting cutely from back butt pockets. The prostitutes, posted like sentries one to a door, could barely conceal their indifference.

Michael passed a couple of derros he recognised, and felt guilty about not saying hallo to them. Then there was a juggler, busking for homeward-bound commuters and merrymakers alike. He was juggling crudely fashioned knives of light, alloy piping flattened at one end to form a blunt but nevertheless pointed blade.

He was telling the crowd that he was juggling with the economy. If, he said, he tried to juggle Australia's international deficit with our imports and exports, the deficit just kept on growing. (And sure enough, one of the knives had a trick handle which extended telescopically each time the knife span in the air.) So the economy became unwieldy. Whereas if he balanced the

305

deficit on his forehead (which he did), he could then juggle imports and exports so that we had balance of payments (which he also did). The problem then was getting out from underneath the knifepoint of an unwieldy deficit, explained the juggler to the amusement of the crowd. He milked the joke by commenting that the best economic brains in the country weren't doing much better than he at this time. Throw money, throw money! They'd have to pay in the end anyway! (Which they did.)

Michael thought it would have made a good theatre act to illustrate an economics course, and the juggler should be selling himself to universities. But he didn't smile at the joke, or pursue the thought much further. For he knew now that he was looking for Sheena.

He quickly came to the basement bar in which he had last encountered her, but she was not there. Sri was, however. And happened to be looking Michael's way as he ducked down the basement steps. She immediately looked down, bearing her golden crown to the smoky ambience of red light, but it was obvious she had seen her former lover.

Michael's impulse was to leave. He had not been able to approach Sri since their meeting in the foothills of Mt Kalesa. Something ran so deep in her eyes that it frightened him. He didn't dare call it hatred, for that somehow figured him in the picture. It was more an ice-cold stream running through its own rain forest, and if you dared to part the leaves and look in, the sun behind your head glared back at you in frozen accusation. Barbs of litigious light were what emitted from Sri's eyes. So that, even though it was the managing director of a multinational corporation that had raped her on top of Mt Kalesa, and it was she, Sri, who had left Michael, Michael felt that he was somehow universally to blame for her being as she was. Whatever that may be. (And possibly that was simply a woman - a prospect of guilt the magnitude of which horrified Michael to his core, if only he could have seen it as simply.)

But some things had changed in Michael since that last meeting. He may have frozen his intellectual assets, leaving his guilt off the leash to gnaw out his insides, but he had also in the process allowed a basic passion to come up for air and fumble around for its own straws of reality. At the moment it was not a very substantial reality. More like a tap hole in a rather voluminous gutfull of feelings. But he was beginning to discover where his internal sea was, had some prescience of what it meant, and was somewhat (again perhaps unconsciously) in awe of its magnitude. In short, there was emerging in Michael something resembling emotional hope. And it was this compassion that brought him now to Sri's side, daunted or not.

"Go away, Michael," she said without looking up.

"It wasn't my fault," he blurted without thinking. All he could hear was the whine in his voice already seeking forgiveness.

"It doesn't matter," said Sri, with a mixture of resignation and impatience that said: oh no, not this again.

"I want to know about you and Sheena," said Michael with resolve, but changing tack.

He sat down on the stool next to her, then wondered whether she might be expecting company and looked inconsequentially towards the steps.

"Why? It doesn't matter," Sri repeated.

"It does to me," he whined again, hating himself in the process.

"That wasn't why we broke up," Sri sighed. "I didn't even know her then."

"So you did know her in Tasmania then?"

Sri looked at him in surprise for the first time.

"Yes," she replied.

"On the collective you went to. After," Michael confirmed. Sri nodded.

"Didn't you know?"

"Not until recently."

"Oh," said Sri, as if this changed things.

"I've just met her Dad," Michael continued.

"Oh," said Sri, as if that changed them again. "Did he offer you the money?"

"He does that often, does he?"

Michael felt the beginnings of a relief. If Sheena already knew...

"Yes, he's quite archaic really. Still believes he can buy her back. Even if it is through a husband."

"But he can't."

It was a question.

"I don't know, Michael. It's none of my business. This isn't a conspiracy, you know. Ask Sheena."

"I just wanted to know, that's all."

Michael was starting to feel uncomfortable. Now that he'd found out what he wanted to know, he had no real reason to remain.

"Know what?"

"What she thought."

"What do you think she thinks?"

Sri was angry now, although not necessarily at him.

"She can't do it for you, Michael. You have to make up your own mind. Take your own action. It's hard enough separating ourselves out."

She meant, broadly, from the pervasiveness of patriarchal culture. Michael understood that much.

"Sorry," he apologised. But he might as well have picked up a bag marked "GUILT" and left.

"Oh Michael, don't start all that again."

"What?" He raised his voice, trying to sound affronted, but even in the act of doing so he knew it wouldn't work.

"Look, it doesn't matter," he tried to backtrack. "I'll cope with it."

He paused.

"But you won't tell her, will you?"

"You're not going to do it." Sri looked up at him almost in horror.

"No. I just don't want her to know, that's all. I don't want to represent her father. In her mind."

"Stepfather."

"Whatever. He's her guardian, isn't he?"

"Yeh, whatever," Sri dismissed the concern as if it were an irritation, and Michael with it. "Go on, Michael. Piss off."

"I was just wondering. Does she know what he does with it? Her money?"

Sri looked at Michael once more. Her eyeballs were streaked with red, but a solid block of ocean bolted from her pupils;

"Piss - *off* - Michael!"

But she had accepted some of the responsibility. They shared that much. She wouldn't tell Sheena. Perhaps.

*

Stringing Siva's Bow

As Michael left, he realised he wanted to ask Sri what had really happened on the summit of Mt Kalesa, but it was probably better not to have pushed his luck anyway.

Back in the Cross, the young juggler had gathered a sizeable crowd.

"Look at all this money you've given me," he was saying. "If only I could stop juggling this economy long enough to pick it all up. Do something constructive and personally meaningful with it, like put it in my pocket. But there it is, earning neither of us interest. Although of great interest to us all. Like a black hole in the current account. That'll attract the foreign investors, won't it? Come on, all of you tourists! Chip in!"

309

The crowd laughed. But then the juggler took a new turn.

"But suppose for a moment that I'm not the Government. I know it's hard, but . . . suppose I'm a member of the unemployed. And this money at my feet is the portion of your taxes they've set aside for my dole. I wonder how much of it I get between juggling these doleforms, weekly budgets, Dolework assignments and applications for jobs that don't exist."

The juggler dips between somersaulting blades and plucks a solitary coin from the bitumen.

"Not even a dollar?" he cajoles, glancing at the coin before resuming his rhythmic relationship with the orbiting blades. "Jeez you're a stingey lot!"

And the crowd laugh again.

"What happens to the rest of it, I wonder? Public servants' salaries have got to come from somewhere, I suppose. And business start-up schemes, and defence budgets ... Now suppose..."

The juggler now started to systematically replace each relatively harmless blade with one of a lighter, sharper, more deadly construction.

"Suppose for a moment that the government has taken it into its head to justify all of this spending on people and projects other than you and me. We who pay the taxes. Suppose they've involved themselves in, for instance, the Third World War. Well why not? It's got to happen sooner or later, hasn't it? We have a history of involving ourselves in the folly of others in this country, don't we? Gallipoli, Pine Gap, East Timor... Goodness how readily the draft could replace Dolework in that situation, couldn't it?" the juggler asked rhetorically. "I mean, they wouldn't call it the draft, would they? But I think if I refused the so-called 'job offer' in the military I wouldn't have many options left would I?"

He glances down at the money at his feet. "I wouldn't want to have to rely on the tax free income at my feet, for instance!"

310

The crowd laugh. Michael is not sure whether they have picked up the symbolism of the knife substitution.

"But I suppose there is a third option . . . " The juggler says, and makes a comic routine out of his attempts to re-introduce the third knife into his routine. "There is a third option . . . there it is. Because they're going to drop the bomb on us sooner or later, aren't they? Who? I don't know. They reckon Indonesia's got one now. Or we might cop a stray one by mistake. The Philippines lobbing one at New Zealand on America's behalf - but they miss and, oops, there goes Tasmania."

He catches a knife supposedly falling out of orbit like a missile. There is blood on his hands from the blade as it resumes its aerial existence.

"So what? I hear you cry. But won't that be what it's like when they disarm? Nuclear weapons all over the place, like the Aussie dollar. Shipments to unarmed countries to ensure the balance. Trundling around the world like container cargo. Terrorist hijackings. Exploding satellites. It'll be like my back garden on fireworks night. One stray match is all it takes. Just one Third World nation waving a thermo-nuclear device in its neighbour's face like a sparkler..."

The crowd were becoming uncomfortable now.

"You don't believe it, do you? You believe that because the Police Powers have promised they won't let one rip, we'll all merrily trot through the ongoing prescience of world war without so much as a radioactive hiccup. Don't you people read Brecht anymore? Does it surprise you to consider that I *am* unemployed, that I *have* just received my call up notice, that I personally believe that a nuclear disaster could happen to all of us as unexpectedly as this -"

At which point the juggler tossed his third knife high into the air, arresting the wavering attention of his crowd.

"No warnings these days!"

311

He winks at the onlookers, grabs the other two knives from the air as if from stone, and points them at his stomach as if to steady himself. It is all so fast. He tips his head back and catches the third in his gullet, blade first, like a shag swallowing its catch.

At first, people thought there would be more. Some clever wisecrack. Or the blade would be revealed as fake with a flourish and the juggler would take a bow. But there was no mistake. The juggler stood there for a second, his eyes popping as he gagged on the blade in his throat. Then he dove forward onto the other two blades, forcing the blade in his throat out through the back of his neck in the process.

The effect was most ungainly. The crowd, who had been too stunned to even gasp, simply parted in disbelief as the pierced figure sprawled before them, coughing up blood about the alien metal in his oesophagus. The stench from his crudely eviscerated gut mushroomed into the air around mute witnesses while the juggler flapped helplessly towards lifelessness like a wounded seal.

Michael wanted to put him out of his misery, but didn't know how. All that the young man had said was true, and it would be cruel now to tell him that there was in fact a draft resistance movement through which he could have acquired a new, illegal identity.

Michael no longer had any of the answers.

When he got home, he saw a report on the news of Jamie's death in the subway. He also saw an excerpt from the takes he had seen filmed that afternoon at Bridge Bay. They were being shown as newsreel footage of Australian efforts on yet another front, this time in South America. So Michael was right. The Third World War was indeed happening in celluloid and cathode ray tubes across the planet, as Australia tried to cover up its failure to get real action off the ground. Or maybe it was intentional. Maybe a war economy was just what the country needed - especially if they didn't actually have to spend the money on a war.

Meanwhile, Social Security had changed their Application for Continuation of Benefit forms yet again, and Michael had forgotten to ring Gareth Joseph.

Later that night he went out to a public phone and tried to ring Sheena's guardian, but no-one answered. He tried again the following morning, only to learn that Mr Joseph had left for Tasmania the night before. So Michael took a forwarding address and wrote Mr Joseph a formal letter accepting his kind offer, but on condition that the Trust Fund was made over to Sheena, payable on her request. In return he, Michael, agreed to see that she and Bozzo were separated. He also agreed not to inform taxation authorities of the nature and location of the fund - an unfortunate eventuality that would render it of little use to anyone. He would wait upon Mr Joseph's reply and was his sincerely . . .

*

The Giant Kabandha

Not long after he had moved in with Sarama, Michael signed on the dole as the Indian refugee Rama Chandra. It was not long after that he and Sarama began sleeping together, and it was, ironically, Social Security who brought them to the realisation that they were indeed living together, in the full cohabitational sense.

Periodically Social Security would be in need of a drastic reduction in the number of clients receiving unemployment benefits. This would usually coincide with government concerns about a deficit blow-out for that quarter, which would mean an immediate loss of confidence in the Australian dollar. A sudden drop in foreign investment was always a useful tool for government in further eroding real wages, as long as it was only temporary. The corresponding drop in unemployment figures following the blow-out would bring foreign investment flooding back, but just long enough afterwards to allow the government to fiddle its quarterly adjustments accordingly.

The method by which Social Security most commonly achieved the required temporary drop in unemployment figures was known in the trade as "the de facto scam". At the appropriate time in the month, the SS would mount a nationwide campaign against de facto relationships in which both parties were claiming the dole. In order to maximise the number removed by this method, the SS would swoop on group households in which many unemployed were forced to live simply to survive, and call in anyone who could conceivably be construed as living in a 'marriage-like relationship' with someone else in the house. And that, of course, generally meant all of them. You only had to wash up someone else's cup, after all, to be in a marriage-like relationship.

Although such discontinuations of benefit were difficult to maintain upon appeal, the field officer and determining officer had sole jurisdiction in the first instance. While hordes of economically disenfranchised waifs came in a swore celibacy and sexual autism in the weeks that followed, the immediate impact achieved the effect required by government.

When Michael was first subjected to such a raid he was, naturally enough, affronted. Especially since Sarama was still teaching and thus deemed by the SS to be the 'breadwinner' of the 'family'. Michael was to lose financial independence altogether.

Now financial independence was not something Michael was going to lose lightly. He had left home rather than live with such an anathema and had almost religiously maintained his economic autonomy ever since. Indeed, even when the interviewing officer had asked him the contents of Sarama's bank account, he was unable to enlighten them. He did not even know how much she earned, and was not prepared to ask. He would not have disclosed the relationship at all had not he and Sarama been running a covert halfway house for draft resisters. (ie. He didn't want Social Security officers within cooee of the place.) But hubris had got the better of him. Michael had failed to answer certain questions

314

As soon as he left the SS he made straight for what remained of the free government legal service. The queue was, of course, already a mile long. And when he finally received attention, all he learned was that yes, he could oppose de facto classification on economic grounds - that he and Sarama shared no joint bank accounts, mortgages, loans, or wages in the form of housekeeping allowances etc. - but Social Security took in all aspects of the 'relationship'. If the 'couple' ate together, or went out together, washed up together, shopped together, combined housekeeping monies, divided up household chores, shared the same fridge, or took a bite out of the same apple, that was enough for the SS. And if they were having sex together, well that was a clincher. One of you had to pay for it - literally. (It didn't matter which.)

Michael complained that this reduced any committed, loving cohabitation to the level of casual sex, and any sexual relationship at all to little short of prostitution. It also made financial independence - the cornerstone of the free market economy - some kind of perverse patriarchal joke. The lawyer's response was that Michael was perhaps coming to understand what women had known for so long.

So outraged was Michael at being denied this basic right to self-definition that he rang the State Ombudsman (who happened to be a woman) for some redress of this invasion of privacy. The Ombudsman told him, however, that Australia had no Bill of Rights and he should have simply lied.

Sarama suggested she sign a statutory declaration to the effect that she could not have sex with Michael on religious grounds, but legal services reminded them that sex was not the sole determining criteria. It seemed that the SS had them whichever way they turned. Until they remembered that Lachy was coming to stay with them . . . .

Lachy had just emerged from the other end of the Chain and was waiting on his new i.d.. He did not thus officially exist. Sarama and Michael thus filed their respective statutory declarations of financial independence and insisted on their right to written notification of the time and date of the field officer's visit, and the list of questions they would be asked. When the field officer came, they made no attempt to conceal the full nature of their relationship. What they did do, however, was substitute Sarama with Lachy.

On the morning of the visit, Sarama made herself scarce before first light, so that the young officer arrived to discover not a man and a woman in the process of their morning rituals but two men, Lachy and Michael: two male homosexuals in a loving, monogamous and committed relationship. Social Security did not recognise homosexual relationships. Especially male ones.

Once news of Sarama, Lachy and Michael's success got out, homosexual households miraculously sprang up everywhere and Social Security were, for a while, deprived of a valuable method of cooking the books for government. Indeed, the correlation between unemployment and homosexuality was cause for no small measure of excitement in academic circles, and humanitarians hailed it as an argument for the decriminalisation of the latter in the more conservative states. But then the Grinder came back with his scapegoat campaign against homosexuals in New South Wales, and it wasn't long before Bland followed with his assault on the radicalesbians in Tasmania. Soon it became unwise to admit to being both homosexual and unemployed anywhere in Australia.

And anyway, Social Security soon came up with another method for engineering strategical variations in unemployment figures.

As sociolinguists in the 1960s observed, language was an integral feature of the inherent alienation of the working classes from the middle class institution of Education. Its alienating nature was also a skill in which middle class public servants were highly adept. All Social Security needed to do in order to precipitate a temporary drop in unemployment figures was alter the wording on the Continuation of Benefit form in a manner that the majority of applicants would not

316

understand. The backlog of re-applications took months. It was much more cost-effective than the 'de facto scam', and so simple.

It was one such seasonal purge that Michael was experiencing as he attempted to decypher changes to his most recent Application for Continuation of Benefit form. Bozzo, however, was unsympathetic to its implications.

"Bludgers!" he retorted. "Let 'em die, I reckon. Why should we feed 'em?"

Which was odd, because Michael was not aware that Bozzo actually paid any tax at all. He certainly didn't earn anything to pay tax on.

"You talk about public servants as if they're all bastards!" Bozzo went on.

"They are!" Michael wished he didn't feel so strongly about it. "How can anyone sleep at night knowing that they are structurally forcing their fellow human beings into an underclass?"

"Crap! They're just doing a job, like anybody else. Some of them like it. Some of them hate it. Some of them get a buzz out of it. Some of them feel guilty. Some of them are just plain stupid. If you don't want them to be bastards, don't let them be bastards."

The purity of Bozzo's logic sometimes confounded Michael.

"I'm not quite with you," he said.

"Jeezus," muttered Bozzo, and left.

By the following morning the computer nerve centre of the entire nation's Social Security network had been burnt to the ground. The fire had kept the Sydney Fire Brigade busy most of the night simply protecting adjacent office towers.

"I'm not sure this is moral," Michael thought to himself as he entertained conjecture as to the identity of the arsonist.

*

317

The Giant Kabandha Tells Rama And Lakshman Of Sita's Whereabouts.

The net effect of Bozzo's incineration of Social Security's data centre was disaster for the Government but a boon for the country's vast numbers of unemployed. Because of the temporary disruption to 'procedure', aided by a virus that enigmatically spread throughout the rest of their national network, the SS had no option but to pay out on whatever claims came in.

The unemployed had a field day. Nom-de-plumes and multiple dependents abounded. Parties flourished. Dope was brought in by the container load and cheaper restaurants did a roaring trade. Meanwhile Social Security staff waded through sheaves of ancient record sheets they had thought would never be used again and filed copious r.s.i. compensation claims.

Michael felt he should thank Bozzo publicly on behalf of his collective underclass. But instead he praised him modestly in private.

"It was nothing," the heavy duty anarchist replied almost bashfully, scratching his matted mohawk as if a brain were itching somewhere beneath.

Michael and Bozzo were enjoying croissants and coffee for breakfast, which the latter had allowed the former to buy as spoils of the plunder currently underway. The two dishevelled males looked out of place in the Darlinghurst coffee shop, with its wallpaper of faded boxing clippings and trophies representing a youth its proprietor had long since lost. At 7 o'clock in the morning the Mediterranean street cafe served as a general meeting place for aging Italians (who started the day as they planned to spend it: talking) and city businessmen (who were trying to preserve what precious seconds of privacy the day still held for them).

Michael and Bozzo would have been the only people in the joint actually speaking English, had it not been for the smart female executive who was attracting more than her fair share of attention on this fine morning, whether she wanted it or not. Even in this day and age, men could not get used to the idea that women had some purpose in life other than being carried off and fucked, however charmingly (and, most probably, in another language).

"They know all about you, you know," said Bozzo, almost incidentally. He was idly dunking his croissant in his latte with a surprising and probably quite unconscious flair for cultural integration.

Michael looked up.

"What do you mean?"

"They know who you are."

"Social Security?"

The intimation of discovery alarmed Michael considerably.

"No, the fucking State Bank. Who d'yous reckon?"

"Oh well . . . " Michael tried to let the idea slip by in the hope it would go away, but Bozzo persisted.

"And yer brother."

"Lachy?"

"That's not the name they give him. Lachman. German, isn't it?"

"From my stepmother. Second stepmother. Her family were from there. Originally."

"Can't stand krauts. Always make me think of Hitler."

"So what exactly is it they know?"

"Everything. You. Your lesbian friend. They greenies. They even know about me."

"How do you know?"

"Well, I didn't just burn the place down, did I? Might as well make the most of the access. Maximise the investment, as our capitalist friends would have it. Don't worry. I fed in a worm. But they'll have a back-up in Canberra somewhere.

"How do they get all of this information?"

319

As he had been once in Launceston, Michael was quietly awed by the tenuousness of his personal privacy.

"Spies mostly. I mean, this isn't just behind-the-counter stuff. It's classified. Although most of your assessors would have access to it. For your dole."

Michael was finding it difficult to understand why, if they knew who he was and what he'd done, he was on the dole at all, let alone still at liberty.

"How do you know?" again was, however, the only result of this hiatus in Michael's comprehension.

"Told you."

"Yes, but you said it was classified."

"That's right."

"On a computer."

"Very good. You should've gone to school, you know. You'd've done well, I reckon."

The notion that Bozzo knew not only how to operate a computer but also how to break into classified Social Security codes was a little too much for Michael at this time of the morning.

"What did they say about Lachy?" he said instead.

"You know they've co-opted him, don't you?"

"What do you mean?"

"Offered him a habit. Somewhat illicitly. Made him a monk in their holy order. A martyr to the cause!"

Bozzo was finding his short foray into literary extemporisation highly amusing. Michael, however, was not.

"I don't understand."

Indeed, he was getting annoyed.

"He's on smack. They've got him hooked, so they can reel him in when they need him."

"Social Security?"

Bozzo nodded, and added, looking at the occupants of the cafe around him;

"Don't shout about it. They may be dagos, but they're not deaf."

"Sorry," Michael said, restraining his anxiety. "But how can Social Security . . . I thought heroin was a black market thing. Organised crime. Drugs."

"Course. So why should that exclude Social Security?"

Understanding must have visibly dawned on Michael's face, for Bozzo said;

"Jeezus, I could drive a tank through your brain sometimes. The Government may be a bit behind the eight ball when it comes to business, but when you've got a national deficit to launder, what better place than the free market?"

"You mean black market."

"Same diff."

Michael shook his head in disbelief. Beside him, the female executive was fielding heavily accented compliments like totem tennis balls.

"I can get your bloke off, but," Bozzo went on.

"Lachy? How?"

"I do favours for people sometimes. For a modest financial return. I've got one comin' up soon. I can pull a few strings. Well, chips. Wanna come?"

"To what?"

"On a job, dillbrain. It'll be a good night. Sheena's comin'."

It sounded like an invitation to a party.

"I'm not sure I understand all of this," said Michael.

"Oh, you'll catch on. Let's just say I can help your brother. If you help me. Okay?"

"Great!" said Michael with genuine enthusiasm.

"But don't tell Sheena. About the brother bit. She'll just get edgy."

"Right," said Michael, nodding emphatically whilst wondering whether or not someone was having him on.

"You could make a film about it if you liked," Bozzo continued, as if on the same subject.

"What about?" Michael was confused.

"Your rights. I'll put it on for you. During the job. Guaranteed access to unrestricted national air time. Make a video. I'll supply the info. Get that Abo mate of yours' onto it. They know all about videos."

"Do they know about Hanif too?"

The scope of SS intelligence was about to exit Michael's orbit of understanding.

"No," Bozzo said, to Michael's relief. "I have my spies too."

"A video, eh?" Michael mused, wondering whether Bozzo was altogether the full quid.

"Yeh. I'll be in it," Bozzo offered expansively. "Expose all. That'd get 'em. Wouldn't know what to do with it if you waved it in front of 'em, some of these guys."

And he grinned, leaving Michael dwelling darkly on how Bozzo acquired his information, for whom, and whether, if he knew about Hanif, he also knew about Jamie and, indeed, the recent movements of Mr Gareth Joseph. And if he was aware of the briefly intimate relations between Michael and Sheena. And what he was going to do about them. Or whether he already was.

*

Indra's Elephant Steps On A Garland Of Flowers Offered By Siva

Such worrisome forebodings were flushed out by the chance of a train trip.

Michael loved the train. Especially on the line southwest of Sydney. There, it was as if the whole world emptied itself into the suburbs of Australia. On each platform on the journey out of town, one ethnic minority supplanted another on an Historical Guide to Australian

Immigration. Lebanese, Greeks, Italians, Yugoslavs, Vietnamese, Kampucheans - even the Kurds made a brief appearance (courtesy of Bozzo). Successive waves of migrants had pushed the rest further out, until the Poms ended up at Liverpool and the Scots at Campbelltown, and the real Australians presumably out in the scrub somewhere.

As for the Aboriginal peoples, their tide was on the turn. Once they had been driven so far out of the coastal settlements that they'd ended up in metaphorical centre of the continent, their backs to each other. It was a myth, of course. But they had got the whitefellas sussed. Moved back in and grabbed the city centre. Well, just outside it. And odds and sods in between. Refused to accept the cultural garland Europe had draped around their land's neck.

Today, however, Michael was going no further than Italy and Greece. One of the prices to be paid for Bozzo's premature Christmas was that, in their wisdom, Social Security had mysteriously relocated Michael in Strathfield somewhere. Even though he lived nowhere near the area, it was as close as the SS were going to get him while they reshuffled their virus-riven data banks.

It was one of those typical November days in Sydney. No sooner had the populace gotten used to the idea that spring had arrived than Sydney double-crossed them with a month of tropical storms. Streets were flooded, cars immobilised, and houses expired under the deluge.

Today saw the first of such storms. It had ensued as Michael's silver elephant of a double decker drew out of Central. The rain had actually drowned out the roar of the train. Then, as suddenly as it had come, it was over. One second, continuous crescendo. The next, nothing but the sound of metal wheels slowing across expansion gaps. As the doors closed, having delivered Michael onto the platform at Strathfield, rain, train, station and, to all intents and purposes, world just fell away. Absolute silence.

It truth, there were cars sloshing through bitumen shimmering in a shaft of sunlight beyond. People were talking in buildings nearby. Ants were burrowing busily in freshly moistened habitats. But for Michael, it was as if the world had momentarily come to a standstill. And he understood, for a brief moment under the oppressive prescience of a giant cumulo-nimbus, what it would be like if the world were to end. The concept was awesome. Then;

"The unions couldn't'a done it better," said a gruff voice nearby.

"Or the commos," chipped in another.

And Michael thought (ironically) how people bonded in a crisis.

Later that day, on the evening news, Michael would learn that a momentary power failure that had in fact facilitated his moment of quietude, and that it had been caused by a lightning strike on a transmission station near Parramatta. Had a bank of circuits in a nearby Telecom exchange not acted as a giant resistor, householders throughout the Western suburbs would have borne the brunt of the impact, union representatives would say. But experts would reply that the probability of such a strike recurring were several millions to one, and the city's power grid was perfectly safe.

On the same news service, a strike of a different sort would be reported alongside the lightning story, with that impish sense of hegemonic humour to which news producers were so prone. The Amalgamated Metalworkers Union was about to embark upon an illegal national strike, with two of its officials due to appear in court for addressing a gathering in a public place without permission from the Commissioner of Police.

"Workers!" Bozzo would ejaculate with contempt, chewing on a small wad of hashish. He would then detect Michael's tension across the darkened basement and say to Sheena;

"Just like boys in gangs, isn't it?"

But Sheena would not respond. So Bozzo would continue;

324

"The bigger the capitalists get, the bigger the unions get. But they never grow up. Working class kids on one side of the fence, kids from private schools on the other. But they're all men, eh?"

Sheena would at last turn her droll gaze towards Bozzo and sweep it lazily away again, like a lighthouse.

"Don't you believe in the class war?" Michael would ask, trying to sound laconically provocative, but unsuccessfully. This would be a chance to demonstrate his allegiance to Sheena, or so he would think.

"You think like mud," would be Bozzo's belligerent response. Bozzo would then explain at a length inspired by the hashish that the Transnational Corporation of America were trying to wrest a contract from the Multinational Trading Company - an Australian corporation. Multinational had put in a bid to build a new Russian satellite shuttle in Australia. A satellite-based laser was a component of the package.

While Transnational had no objection to the shuttle, they already had a laser of their own under development - one which would give the US a spaced-based strategic advantage as a Police Power. It was the US that thus objected to the Australian technology. Transnational wanted to protect their interests at home by selling their product to Australia. So they were in with a counter-offer, and engaging in whatever tactics they thought appropriate to prevent their Australian rival from securing its first venture into outer space.

Transnational's metals operation, for instance, was comfortably offshore in Southeast Asia. It was the technological development they were offering Australian employees. Whereas MTC were based in Australia, and dependent on the onshore metal industries. The strike would (in theory) threaten their potential to deliver at a crucial stage in proposal negotiations. Transnational, in the meantime, were already brokering a sweetheart deal with the powerful telecommunications and information services unions that would ease their technology into the country.

325

It would all seem astoundingly clever to Michael, even though Bozzo would begin to slur his words after a while.

"What you don't want to accept," Bozzo would conclude finally, "is that the two AMU lackeys who will be jailed tomorrow are on Transnational's payroll. You want to think of them heroically championing the anti-union deregistration cause, and the freedom of movement in the streets campaigners. You in all your indeterminate middle class glory. It offends your petty bourgeoise consciousness, doesn't it?"

Michael would be genuinely upset by this. He really did feel for the working classes. He also valued justice, and the capacity for humankind to make laws which preserved people's rights in some axiomatic way. He thought it was one of humanity's strengths, made it superior to other life forms in some way. To be able to think with compassion. In this, Michael was very conservative. Especially for someone who didn't really believe in anything.

So Michael would look at Sheena, who would be asleep. Bozzo himself would look like he was dozing off. In the silver glow from the tv his slightly flabby cheeks would appear almost babylike.

It would be time for close down, and the set would emit a persistent electronic harmonic as a black cloud gathered in the centre of the blank grey screen. And Michael would think about Armageddon. But not for very long.

*

Lakshman and Rama Defeat Bali

It was a couple of weeks before Hanif made contact with Michael again. The news, however, was good. Hanif was able to assure Michael that Lachy had not only restored the Chain but had also been active in other political spheres. Persuading the conservationists, for instance, to defer a National Parks campaign in favour of an Aboriginal Land Rights claim in the South West.

This was nothing short of a miracle in Michael's eyes. So often he had argued prior claim on behalf of friends like Hanif before fellow environmentalists, only to be told that hard won middle ground public credibility could not be endangered by alignment with extremist minorities. Michael had spent many a meeting after a 'test for consensus' in hot silence. So much so that his almost autonomic response to Hanif's news was:

"Are you sure?"

"Seen it with my own eyes, fella."

Hanif well understood Michael's scepticism. But it was his film crew that had spotted Lachy with a group of aboriginal protesters on the banks of the Pieman. Ironically, it was the Hydro Electric Authority who were ferrying them to their filming location. Up a river the HEA were in the process of damming. A process against which Lachy and his friends were protesting.

To date, their vigil had gone unnoticed. Or rather, disregarded. The considerable conservationist media machinery had not at that stage come to the party. But as Hanif set his camera rolling, despite HEA requests to the contrary ("Just testing the lenses, boss!"), Lachy shouted to the passing boat that he was there on behalf of the Tasmanian Wilderness Group, who condemned this unwarranted destruction of what was, by rights, internationally protected wilderness. They also recognised the prior claim of the aboriginal inhabitants of the island.

"I've got the film here," said Hanif, and produced a large silver disc from which he proceeded to load a reel onto a compact but expensive-looking projector. Indeed, the quality of Hanif's extensive collection of video and film equipment seemed surprising in this otherwise use-as-you-go Erskineville house.

"We were the ones who got the story out," Hanif was explaining. "Too much bother to send a camera crew in, but once they had the footage, everyone wanted it. So they had to back him up then, the conservationists. Hadn't had that sort of coverage since Lemonthyme. Even held a joint press conference with our mob. I suggested that," grinned Hanif. This was just like old times.

"Did you find out about the heroin," asked Michael. He was about to view his brother for the first time since he'd heard the news.

Hanif couldn't enlighten him.

"But he looked okay. And my mob'll look after him."

But on film Lachy looked desperate. He stood on a rock which protruded from the tree-thick bank and yelled at the camera with an untutored anger. His words sounded like fists flailing blindly at thin air. His brow was furrowed with a deep and hidden anguish which did not find resolution in words. His skin had the same watery pallor as the doped-up prostitutes in the Cross. His once-full brown eyes were glazed with Sheena's opaque dilations.

He looked like a ghoul, and Michael was glad when the next shot showed him being drawn back into the custodial line of aboriginal comrades behind a somewhat soiled red, yellow and black banner unfurled before their black japaras.

"It is raining, man," Hanif reminded him.

"So it is," murmured Michael, noticing for the first time the persistent drizzle that had matted Lachy's hair about his skull.

And it occurred to Michael that the rain he had been up until that moment absorbing through Hanif's external eye had been, in his mind, but an inversion of the tears he felt running through his brother's veins.

Michael was very worried about his brother. He wondered whether he should have ever left him back on that fateful morning on the East Coast of Tasmania. Hanif, meanwhile, was wondering how he was going to tell Michael that he had, indeed, met Michael's brother. Lachy had come out of the bush to participate in the press conference, and had shown a flair for public hectoring the movement had not seen since the Franklin. Lachy had confirmed what Hanif had feared since meeting his old comrade again at Bridge Bay: that Michael was seriously ill, and that the Chain he spoke of was a figment of his imagination, as was the Third World War with which he was so obsessed, and the bombing of Dehli he supposed to have caused it. Doctors suspected Michael had experienced some sort of mental breakdown in India, and Lachy had been sent down to Tassie by their father to watch over the disturbed son. Daniel was worried certification might damage Michael's future career prospects, whatever those might be.

So Lachy was playing along with Michael's psychosis rather than confronting it, and had so far succeeded in redirecting its considerable numinosity into the Wilderness Group's anti-nuclear "Draftees" hoaxes at the Mt Kalesa dump, and in joining an alternative-to-drugs support group run by Michael's longtime friend, Conan.

Lachy and Conan had hoped that Michael might work through his disorder without having to resort to the palliative horrors of medication and 'voltage' psychiatry, as Conan termed it. Unfortunately Michael merely transferred his delusions to the group, so that it became, in his mind, a chain of draft resisters.

It was thought that a series of events had cumulatively confronted Michael's immersion in his psychotic state with startling reality. The first of these was when he almost drowned whilst out for an early morning swim with his brother, on a weekend retreat with Conan's support group on the East Coast of Tasmania. The second came shortly afterwards when upon returning to the shack to find Conan and the rest of the group absent, Michael jumped to the irrational conclusion that the place had been busted by the cops. Lachy had lost patience and, in desperation, pleaded with Michael not to dash off to one of his imaginary 'safe houses'. He told him that the Chain did not exist, and that he should come to his senses. In so doing Lachy could see his brother disappear before his eyes. Michael left, and returned to Launceston. Only to discover that Sarama, the woman with whom he was living, and whom he had also woven into his fabric of delusion, had been savagely and arbitrarily raped and murdered by a bunch of hoons.

It was thus thought that Michael had fled Tasmania in a state of internalised crisis which might precipitate at any moment, either in a full breakdown or in self-destruction. Lachy had in fact been relieved to find Hanif. He knew he had burnt his own bridges to his brother, but now hoped desperately that Hanif might be able to forge a causeway to Michael that might yet save his brother's life.

"Have you ever thought of making a film?" Michael asked Hanif, out of the blue.

"Hell, brother, who hasn't?"

"No, but a serious film. Political. To say what we want to say. What needs to be said."

"I ain't no journalist, Michael."

Hanif's eyes were smiling but he meant what he said. Michael, however, did not take him at his word.

"I just thought it would be a good idea. I know a guy who could get it on for us."

"On what?"

"TV."

"Which one?"

"All of them. Every network at the same time. We could use your footage. And other stuff. This guy reckons he can get us material. He has access to Social Security files and everything. He's really good with computers. Just breaks into places and keys stuff in. He's amazing!"

"Sounds impressive," said Hanif with a measured tone. He was rolling a cigarette with one hand and looking down at the threadbare 1930s furniture as he spoke.

"So are you interested? We could make a video. You must have a few mates . . . "

"Hell, Michael," Hanif laughed congenially, "There are about 20,000 blokes like me workin' in the film industry."

330

But he didn't think Michael saw the joke.

"We could do Who Owns Australia? What is this war really about? Who pays for those films you make?"

"I dunno, brother. I just take my pay cheque and leave, you know?"

"But you shouldn't. The aboriginal peoples of this country have been oppressed for over 200 years. Assimilation and acquiescence is exactly what the dominant culture wants. We must take things into our own hands. Retrieve our means of cultural production!"

Hanif snuffled a laugh, shaking his head voicelessly.

"You whitefellas. Takes you a while but you get there in the end."

It was at this point Hanif could have told Michael that, in this eyes, Bozzo was a less-than-credible source of anything much, and that Michael's own zeal appeared somewhat disproportionately manic. But he let his former partisan down gently. He had promised Lachy.

"We've done films, Michael. We've made 'em 'til they came outta our ears. Films about Arnhem Land. Films about Wave Hill. Films about Myall Creek. Films about Uluru. Films about Land Rights. Films about innovative housing projects. Films about aboriginal enterprises. Films about our strong women. Films about our culture, our dreaming, our artists, work practices, natural technologies, science. tribal laws, customs - hell, I reckon the world has seen more aboriginal faces up there on that screen than there are left in the whole damn country. But they still don't understand, Michael. It's too easy to see things the way they always see them. They're still out there waiting for us to come round to their way of thinkin' in the end.

"Movies just feed people, Michael."

Michael was disappointed. He had thought the idea busting with potential. And he was also anxious not to fall back into the trough of inaction now that something resembling direction had re-entered his life. And he had to be seen to be cooperating with Bozzo's scheme is he was to have any chance of rescuing Sheena. Although how he was actually going to achieve the said rescue was as much a mystery to him as the content of the video he was currently proposing to Hanif. Hanif agreed, however, to help him produce whatever material he got together, and that, for the moment at least, would have to suffice.

*

Indra's Elephant

It was probably the prospect of rescuing Sheena that led Michael home via MacDonaldtown. To seek inspiration, perhaps. And to see whether or not her "LESBIANS ARE IN YOUR HAIR LIKE LICE" was still there.

In reality his motivation was obscure because, as he splashed his metaphorical way through the puddles of orange lamplight that punctuated the garbage-strewn Burren Street, his mind was blank. Which was probably why he was so surprised, as he was about to enter the chasm of the Burren Street bridge under which lay the entrance to MacDonaltown Station, by the ominous stillness of a diesel engine up on the line.

It was obviously waiting on the enigmatic behest of the lights on the platform side of the bridge. In reality, Michael was most probably unconsciously aware of the high whine of the dormant locomotive's engines as he approached, but it's material manifestation brought him to a standstill. For there it was, suddenly, like a ship alone on the ocean at night, visible only be virtue of the light it itself created, glowing from within.

In the steel-blue radiance of its cab, driver and engineer were chatting incidentally. About football, perhaps. Or the war they were not sure existed. Who could tell, for their mouths moved inaudible to the outside world. One was incidentally munching on a sandwich while the other was moving about, making a cup of tea or coffee. As they spoke, they casually glanced around them at the various instruments they were supposedly monitoring. They might even have had a tv on in there. But always, from time to time, their eyes would flick back to the scene beyond their windscreen, as if it would reveal at any minute some intimation of their future.

Their next act would be determined by that secret code of red and green lights known only to the inner intelligence of the State Rail Authority's computer at Redfern, just down the track. It was a code they still read, just as soothsayers once read stars and constellations; but it would only be a matter of years before they were barred from the arcanum arcanorum. Decisions in the future would be made in silence, communicated directly between engine and computer, railway line and integrated circuit. Human error would be eradicated.

Already the two men looked as though they did not belong, confined as they were to their life capsule of a cab while the engine hummed to itself in quiet readiness. And, for this brief moment in Michael's journey home, there was something deeply foreboding about the semi-dormant engine up on the line just before MacDonaldtown Station, and the implications its existence had for its human occupants. For Michael found himself wondering what it would be like to be the very last whale in the world, forever sending out packages of sound deep into the wide ocean currents only to get them back eons later, unanswered. To realise that the messages you were receiving were the ones you sent. That you were talking to yourself. Alone.

*

Ravana Threatens To Eat Siva

That night, as he lay awake on his uncomfortable mattress on the musty floor of his Darlinghurst room , Michael listened to Bozzo and Sheena fucking.

Tonight there was some sort of elastic tussle going on between them. As if they were glued together, front to front, but each struggling to be free of the other. Because of their proximity, their efforts were reduced to a sort of silly hand-smacking and face-slapping. And all the while fucking. Like wet fish.

In the midst of which Michael could hear Bozzo's gruff voice threatening;

"I'll kill myself I'll kill myself!"

Over and over again. As if he were daring Sheena to let him do it.

*

Hanuman Shows Sita Rama's Ring

For the next two weeks Michael's world took on manic proportions. His body conducted activities with a conviction always slightly out of phase with his mind, although his mind was convinced that what its body was doing was right.

Bozzo turned up daily with video tapes and floppy discs containing information and footage well beyond Michael's imagination. Politicians were linked with multinational corporations, finance companies with government departments, spy networks with underworld hoods, small business with military installations - it was bizarre.

The power structure of Australian leadership seemed to subsist in two distinct hierarchies, one governmental and the other commercial, each of which worked around the other in a sort of three-dimensional pyramid. But one with several peaks, each representing the major multinational companies operating in Australia, and of course the government (which had only one peak). This was because, Bozzo explained, each

334

multinational company had its own links with the same government departments, but of course the government only had the one set of departments. It was individual employees who created room for variation.

As if this were not enough, the whole unwieldy structure of Australian econo-politics was linked with equivalent structures in just about every other country in the world - not by government, but by the multinationals. Their pyramids also encompassed those in the other countries. It seemed logically impossible in terms of simple geometry, if nothing else, but Bozzo showed it to Michael in computer graphics over and over again, with the pride of a mastermind.

And gradually Michael's understanding of the magnitude of global politics began to grow. Bit by bit, new ideas burgeoned into each other, melded together and formed new conceptual conglomerates, until an overarching mushroom of knowledge emerged. There was no conspiracy here. The governments of the world's major nations were at virtual war with the world's major multinationals, who were of course at virtual war with each other (as indeed were the governments). So that the actual sandwich wars which dotted the earth like spot fires (indeed, Bozzo's computer graphic represented them as such at discreet pyramidal intersections) represented attempts either of the Police Powers or the Multinationals, or both, to gain some momentary advantage in the ongoing struggle.

The result, however, was simply a rolling replication of revolution and counter-revolution, coup and counter-coup, which perpetuated a titration of mini-arms races and nuclear technologies around the world. As one bright spark in some documentary footage put it, the Third World War had been going on since the end of the Second World War. It would end when somebody somewhere pressed the button. It didn't matter who. The panic response would ensure the earth experienced the full toasty benefit of its considerable nuclear arsenal.

And that could be any time really, thought Michael to himself. The whole delicate organism was like an imploded fireworks display: instead of opening outwards in all its human potential like a beautiful flower of truth, the socio-economic world was bound inwards, like an explosion that had already happened and yet was still awaiting ignition, the volatile innards of a volcanic mountain range just looking for that weakness in (or between) the peaks. It was very worrying.

For days on end Michael manually typed up and matched pieces of paper, concepts, bullet points, tables, graphs and units of information. Then Bozzo brought a video camera home and they started recording segments in the cavernous basement dining room adjoining the kitchen. Harsh quartz halogen lamps startled rudimentary diagrams scrawled on butcher's paper taped to the walls.

"They can keep us down with just their big toe," was Bozzo's favourite line. He evidently found it very funny, and said it in just about every take they took.

Secrecy, however, seemed essential. Video sessions were conducted in the small hours of the morning. Library visits during the quiet periods. Information carried in nondescript packaging or under coats. This was the documentary that would expose the governments and commercial enterprises of the world.

Every second day or so Michael would slip across to Hanif's house. He could regularly be seen on the train between Kings Cross and Erskineville with a pile of video cassettes on his knees. Hanif's housemates began to wonder who this crazy was, badgering Hanif late into the night with material that sounded like street punks reciting Shakespeare to American businessmen on top of Ayers Rock.

Hanif said nothing, but laughed nervously with his cohabitants about whitefellas on coke while he worried about how he would tell Michael that the latter was going mad. Or had already done so.

Meanwhile, in his spare moments, Michael resumed his obsessive watch over Sheena. Again. For as the project proceeded, it became essential to Michael that he preserve his greater sense of end purpose: the rescue of the woman he loved. Although fulfilling his commitment to Bozzo, Michael was still unable to trust the chimerical bully boy, despite their night of love. Mind-boggling though it was, how could he trust the authenticity of the information Bozzo gave him? Bozzo had, after all, said that Lachy was hooked on heroin, whereas Hanif had said he was okay. And Bozzo's world was pretty unlikely, when he came to think about it. As was Gareth Joseph's. The child in Michael simply didn't want to believe the conspiracy was real. Its consuming ugliness was too much for him.

So his overloaded cognition wound itself in a little tighter, and considered itself lucky it had its wits about it and was still secretly in control. And Michael wondered how his moment might come, and imagined ways in which he could push Bozzo through a gap in the cast-iron relentlessness of reality (when it presented itself) into oblivion without actually killing him. In the meantime, the least he could do was make sure Sheena remained safe.

Thus it was that Michael's form was to be seen behind the windows of coffee shops around the Cross, sipping cups of cappuccino nonsensically while staring out at some brothel across the road. Or standing just beyond the glow of a street lamp, back against the wall, gazing up at a light in the window of a cheap hotel. Or following a pinched, anaemic young woman in red high heels, mini skirt and a progression of shoulder bags, clacking her way along the chock-a-block pavements, occasionally stopping short of the metallic rush of a side lane.

Michael's shadow was everywhere.

One night, Sheena had had enough. Michael was following her home after a long night's work. They had turned off the main drag and were heading into the gentle, refuse-moist darkness of lower

Darlinghurst. Suddenly Sheena stopped, and Michael ducked into a handy doorway.

As soon as he heard the polite heels clack on, Michael sipped into train again. Only to have to squat behind a fence as they ceased seconds later.

"Michael," Sheena called wearily from down the road.

Michael tried to hold his breath and pretend he wasn't there.

"Michael, I know you're there," Sheena went on, a tone of impatience entering her voice.

They both seemed to wait for a while, then the clacking feet continued warily and Michael emerged slowly from his hiding place. Almost the instant his shoulders breached the gap in the fence before open space, however, Sheena spun round on him.

"Michael, for fuck's sake what are you doing?"

Michael decided to bluff his way out. He stepped boldly onto the footpath with a little wave.

"Hallo," he called with jollity. "Just out for a walk. Wondered whether it was you."

Then he laughed gaily, and perhaps a little nervously.

"Jeezus," Sheena growled in reply.

"Michael, why are you doing this," she continued through gritted teeth.

"What?" Michael shrugged, affecting nonchalance.

"I thought we'd dealt with all of this."

"I'm just . . . practicing. For the job."

"Well stop practicing. Especially if this is the best you can do. It makes me nervous."

"I can practice if I like. You can't stop me practising if I . . . feel I want to."

"Oh jeezus!" Sheena clenched her fists.

"As long as it doesn't harm you."

"What are you talking about?"

338

Sheena's evident anger and frustration somewhat deterred Michael from reaffirming his love for her. But not entirely.

"I'm just . . . concerned for you. That's all," he managed.

"Why don't you say it, for christ's sake? What is it with you men?"

Michael, however, was reluctant to say anything at this juncture on the grounds that it might incriminate him, whatever it was.

"Look, Michael, it's none of your business, right? Now get out while the going's good."

"It's my choice," he retorted with what he hoped was strength, but which sounded painfully more like petulance.

Sheena dropped her brow onto her thumb and forefinger for a moment and sighed.

"Alright, Michael. It won't work. Bozzo will kill you as soon as look at you. You know that, don't you."

"Of course," said Michael, who didn't, but wanted to sound like the sort of man who would take on the woman he loved with all that came with her. The reliable man.

"And you know that this video he's making you do -"

"I volunteered!" Michael protested. The responsible man.

"Whatever. It's just to protect him. From these satellites he thinks are watching him. The media exposure, don't you see?"

Michael did, for the first time. But it confused him all the more, because Bozzo must know that he, Michael, had no professional media credentials. So how could any video he made safeguard Bozzo, no matter how world-shattering its content and widespread its broadcast?

"And as for my father," Sheena continued, "I don't want the money."

"What money?"

It was an automatic response. And a foolish one. It just made Sheena sigh again.

339

"I know my father's offered you the Trust. And I know you made him sign it across to me - "

"How?"

Michael now went on the offensive. The man betrayed. The man who would take sole responsibility for his actions. But with humility. Not for his own gain, but for those he loved. The noble man.

"It doesn't matter - Oh God, now I'm doing it." Sheena turned and faced Michael squarely. "I ran into Hanif the other day."

"I didn't know you knew him."

"Sometimes. We tend to keep in touch."

Once more Sheena evinced that uncanny ability of hers' to read Michael's mind. "Not like that, Michael. As cell groups. The people from Mt Kalesa. The South West. We tend not to lose contact. We come across each other. I came across Hanif. I remembered him from Tasmania."

Michael nodded, begrudging his own relief that Hanif and Sheena were not sleeping together.

"He's worried about you, Michael." She sounded almost sympathetic. "You know where it comes from, don't you?"

It was a statement rather than a question. Michael nodded again.

"Are you sure?" Sheena now sounded almost motherly. And Michael nodded firmly again. But he was tired of being a man. He just wanted to collapse into her arms and sob. Into the arms of the mother he had never had.

"It's not just some shares, you know. It's the entire company."

Michael looked up at her suddenly.

"Yup. The whole of Military Industrials. They're responsible for some of the most advanced space-borne weaponry going, Michael. Satellite-based lasers, nuclear interceptors - it's first strike stuff, Michael, and I don't want anything to do with it."

"But you could use it. Dissolve the company. Or put the money to counter-use."

340

"They'd either buy me out or kill me before I left the bank," Sheena silenced him. "Don't you realise how much that subsidiary is worth? It's just my father's way of keeping me in the fold, Michael. Under his thumb by default. I am complicit whatever I do, don't you see?

"I don't want it. And I don't want to be rescued either. Nor do I particularly want to see the mess Bozzo'll make out of you when he finds out what you're about. Which he will, believe me. If he hasn't already. Bozzo has a knack of acquiring information."

Michael felt almost calm. Relieved of a burden. He gazed at Sheena with a distant longing, as if he were standing on one hill and she on another, a sweet-smelling verdant valley between them. It didn't seem so bad that they weren't together physically because they were spiritually. Joined by the land between them. A love that could last forever, even without consummation. If, that is, there were such a thing as spirit.

"I'd better go home alone," Sheena said softly. And Michael nodded again.

The red heels clacked off into the night with the sweetness of an orange freshly cut in half on a mouth-bakingly hot day. Michael stayed where he was for a long time, savouring the taste in his mouth where a kiss might have been. He could wait. The constant man.

*

Dasaratha Importunes Rama On Sita's Behalf

Michael had not seen his father for several years. Not, indeed, since he had left Adelaide to establish his hermit-like existence in North West Tasmania. So he was surprised now to be sitting before him in a heavily-curtained, quietly-carpeted office insulated by a library of books on law and commerce. It was lit only by a circumspect lamp

341

with a broad, pleated shade that stood on the teak desk between Michael and his father. This was the office of a man who worked late.

It had a drinks cabinet which also housed a coffee maker, crockery for any meal, even a toaster. It had two comfortable armchairs and a low casual round table which still proffered the white plate of Arnotts biscuits from (Michael presumed) afternoon tea. And it smelt of the pipe Michael's father smoked increasingly as the day wore on.

Below, on the streets of Sydney, people were setting about their end-of-evening entertainment. Up here, Daniel was still thinking. Still looking from one large volume to another, searching for a link, a hole, a nook, a cranny - some fissure through which he or his company could slip like a gas to reform again on the other side of the law.

More surprised, however, was Michael by the manner in which he had been brought here. For history had repeated itself, it seemed. He had finally made it to the studio in Ultimo for which he had been making when Gareth Joseph's men had apprehended him. Through a crack in a large weatherboard door Michael had taken some photos of the filming with an instamatic, throwaway camera. These he planned to match up with news footage that night, when excerpts from the movie were bound to turn up as the real thing.

So that when, as he made his way back to Central via the same George Street subway, he was accosted by two large Federal policemen, he feared he might have been rumbled, as it were. The Subway was almost empty. Most people were either already at shows or at home. So Michael was able to distinctly hear the two sets of well-weighted feet crunching their way towards him from behind.

He tried to pretend not to notice. Partly in the hope that their implacable purpose might not resolve itself in him, but also in the rather complex belief that, if they were heading for him and he did not seem to be aware that they were, this would someone mitigate whatever guilt they might suppose of him. Which was a bit like thinking that, if he ignored them, they might go away. Which, of course, they didn't.

Instead, two raincoated clubs of hands grasped each of his arms just below the shoulder and, without altering their step, bodily lifted Michael off the ground and carried him along with them.

Michael was somewhat perturbed. At least when the punks had abducted him there had been a sense of tussle, in which he had been reluctantly compliant. Here there was no-one to see him go or report the act. Michael was pinioned so intractably it was clear that to struggle would only cause further duress. So he coughed nervously, looked from impassive face to impassive face, and asked, almost because he wondered whether it might not be true;

"Sorry. Didn't I fill in my dole form correctly?"

They hadn't even asked his name.

"Scotch?" asked Michael's father, finally looking up from the two pages of close-typed print he was scrutinising. He was not being rude in the traditionally patriarchal sense of fathers to their sons. Daniel had already welcomed Michael warmly. A tooth-filled grin that stretched from ear to rather large ear. A brow wrinkled with forced pleasure beneath a balding pate of crinkled sandy hair. An extended hand. An expert shake. Like the suit, so much more formality than Gareth Joseph. But he 'just had to finish this' while he was 'on that train of thought'.

Michael said yes to the drink and helped himself as his father gestured the drinks cabinet.

"Would you like one?" he asked whilst doing so.

"Please," replied his father without looking up.

Shortly after ignoring the scotch Michael placed at his right hand, Daniel withdrew his pen with a flourish, tapped several times on the tome he had been studying with his middle finger, issued several 'ah's of

343

confirmation, slammed shut the book, sat back, and removed his spectacles, pretty much all in the same action.

"Well," he said at last, "I'm pissed off with you."

"Good to see you too, Dad. What's with the thugs?"

"They're Federal Police," Daniel enlightened, for it was then that Michael learnt the information.

"I thought you were out of all of that."

"I may not be Solicitor General, but one never loses the contacts. Not in my line of business. And you're in trouble. Although that's not what I'm pissed off about."

Michael did not know which issue to tackle first: the trouble, or his father's pissed-offedness. He opted for order of presentation.

"What sort of trouble?"

"What do you think?"

Ever the lawyer. That sort of ugly, smug comfort in his rational command of behavioural language. The consummate sophist.

"Do you want me to confess?"

"Not if you don't want to. I'm happy to tell you."

"Good."

"They know about your . . . anti-government activities."

For a moment, Michael appeared not to understand. He knew from experience that his father was most probably talking in code. Daniel would make some cryptic lawyer's comment. Michael was supposed to guess what was expected of him, scan his mental library of possible misdemeanours and decide which he might be guilty of today. But Michael was older than that now. He was dealing with serious things. Of global significance. And in his mind it was a question of whether it was only his anti-draft activities Daniel was referring to or, worse, the video caper. And Michael wanted Daniel to say. Which he did. After a pause.

"They know about this stupid video you're making. With that anarchist . . . clown."

"Bozzo?"

"Is that what he calls himself?"

"Why, what do they call him?"

"Well, that's another matter."

"Who are they, by the way?"

"National Security, of course. Who'd'you think? Don't know who you're working for half the time, government or business. It's all the same to them." Daniel chuckled to himself sardonically, but stopped with barrister-like precision. "So drop it. Before they drop you. You're sailing too close to the wind, Michael."

"I'm not a boat, Dad."

"Have it your own way son. It's your life. You've made that abundantly clear in the past. I'm just giving you a friendly warning."

"Thanks."

But Michael's tone was far from grateful. In fact, it was quite resentful really. For Michael would, in his child's heart, have been far more comforted if Daniel **had** cared. He had long yearned for the father Daniel was unable to be. Loving, strong, intimate, in contact. Not just a role model of rationality and success but a physical being who could hold and hug and kiss him when he was up or down, glad or sad.

Unfortunately, Daniel did not have that Mediterranean freedom from physical reserve. Not that that mattered, Michael supposed. Mediterranean men were just as likely to manipulate you. More so. Emotions as well. They all basically had the ability to turn it on and turn it off at will. Which was something Michael had prided himself on losing - that cold, rational appropriation of emotion so characteristic of men.

Although the result had never been quite what he had expected. Women hadn't loved him any the more for his emotions. On the contrary, they resented them for their rawness and relative immaturity. Meanwhile, men had continued to manipulate him. Even in so-called 'alternative' circles men had loved him, hugged him, then still done him over in the cause of healthy - if unenunciated - masculine competition.

Michael had often wished his father had been a fighter. A champion who stood up for himself, and his son. Then Michael would have felt happier perhaps about getting stuck in himself, instead of retreating into childhood fantasies of hand-to-hand combat and intergalactic victories. As it was, Daniel was the sort who stood on the side of whatever was happening, quietly positioning himself, waiting to be seen. In career terms, he had skilfully ferried himself through the channel marked "REPUTATION" and stepped onto the shore of corporate enterprise to the handshakes and admiring smiles of those who knew what it was not only to get there but also to stay there.

"You know it's my company they're gunning for, don't you?"

His father's statement plucked Michael from an internal descent that led to a rather sticky, black ugliness.

"Transnational."

"What've they got to do with anything?"

"That's who your anarchist friend works for."

"Bozzo?"

Daniel shrugged.

"I thought he was working for the Government," Michael protested. Although this was actually the first time such a thought had entered his head. Up until now, he had not really wondered who footed Bozzo's bill.

"Perhaps both of them," Michael's father conjectured. "In which case, they're both gunning for Multinational."

"And that's who you work for?" Michael was beginning to make connections.

"International Natural Resources Development is a subsidiary."

"Ah, Dad. And I thought you'd gone over to the good guys."

There was a pause. Michael tried to step back over a line he knew he'd crossed.

"Why would they be gunning for you, Dad?"

But he was unable to do so.

346

"Exploiting too many workers?"

"Too few, I would think."

"And how's it going with the Amalgamated Metalworkers, by the way?"

"Well if you know so much about it you'll know you're on dangerous ground, son!" Daniel snapped. "Anyway, that's not what I came here to talk to you about."

"Sorry, I was under the impression it was I who was manhandled here bodily by two large ununiformed police officers in the dead of night."

"I wanted to talk to you about Lachy!" Daniel cut across Michael's burgeoning tirade.

And for a moment, Michael stopped locking horns with his father and spoke from a base that was truly his own, although he wasn't aware of it as such at the time.

"I thought he was alright."

He paused.

"A friend of mine, Hanif, saw him recently. Said he was fine. I saw him on film."

"Well you can't always believe what you see on the movies, Michael."

There was another pause.

"You know he's on heroin, don't you?"

"Well, I had heard . . . "

Michael was unable to prevent the tears springing from his eyes.

"From the one killed in the subway, yes? You were there, weren't you? Just as you were there tonight."

"I'm not *on* anything, Dad!" declared Michael, catching his father's drift. Daniel looked marginally relieved.

"Well I've spoken to his brother. Of the one that died."

"Samson?"

"That's him. Seems Transnational have co-opted Lachy. And now they're setting you up too."

"Why would they - what do you mean, 'co-opted'?"

"The heroin, of course. Where do you think it comes from?"
"But Bozzo said . . . "

      Michael's last words emptied into a vat of understanding. Had he been aware of them fully, he would have seen the last of his tears follow. Despite the fact that all of the evidence should have led him to the realisation long ago, it hadn't. Transnational. Multinational. The AMU. Bozzo. Sheena.
"The Golden Deer," he murmured.

      And it was his father's turn to demand crossly;
"What?"
"Nothing. Just an emblem I saw once. In an office not unlike this, in fact."

*

Michael's father went on to lecture him about responsibility, and how he should have known better than to leave Lachy in 'that sort of situation', and how upset Lachy's mother was.

      Michael was actively bored by such pontifications. He irritably argued that Lachy had joined him of his own accord and was, after all, a real live autonomous adult now, and that if his father cared so much about it he should do something himself.

      To which Daniel replied evenly that Lachy paid more attention to Michael and that, anyway, it was politically unwise for him to be seen acting on information he ought not rightly to have. Whereas if Michael were to go down to sort his brother out, it would not seem unusual and Michael could, in the same process, extricate himself from his current precarious predicament.

      It is quite likely that Daniel was attempting a premeditated strategy with Michael. It's likely that Daniel wanted very much to encourage his son to return to the protective ambit of his younger son, Lachy. It is also possible that Daniel was telling the truth. He may well have believed that Lachy had been introduced to heroin by a rival corporation anxious to compromise him, and his corporation. Or find just one of many small ways of doing the latter.

In which case, Daniel had judged the two cathectic hooks he had deliberately placed in his presentation well. For while Michael was uninterested in his father's ratiocinations, he was disturbed by his second stepmother's suffering.

Michael had a lot of respect for Kathe. She seemed to handle her life and her children and husband with an equanimity she also reserved for herself. While she made no attempt to hide her opinions, or her politics, neither did she foist these on others. She simply constructed ways of dealing with people that compromised her principles as little as possible, and which at the same time refused to admit the compromising incursions of others.

This often led to the misconception that Kathe lacked intellect and was thus 'just like any other woman'. In reality, the inverse was true. She was perhaps 'just like any other woman', but in intellect she had, like many women, travelled far beyond such patriarchal precepts as the intellectual primacy of rationality. The intellect Kathe valued was one in which feeling was integral, logic was natural, language generative and not necessarily verbal, and the self recognised as central and intersubjective rather than as a tool of inter- and intrapersonal manipulation and suppression by the ego. Indeed, it was Kathe's very ability to elucidate such an intellect that first attracted Daniel to her - a sense of something out there that might be radically desirable, but which he never could quite put his finger on.

Not that he ever needed to. For Kathe understood his needs. And his confusion. She simply worked with and around him, at the same time. It was a form of cognitive pluralism Michael admired intensely: that ability to adapt to and generate intellectual change without sacrificing emotional attachment to the process. The kind of intelligence that left people comfortable with the experience of change and difference after it had passed through their lives almost without declaring itself.

It was also the kind of intelligence Michael felt free to enter, sit with the feelings there, without being owned by it, or threatened by it, or indebted to it. And if Kathe was upset, Michael could be upset too, without feeling obliged to. And he could want to do something about it, entirely of his own volition. Which he did, right now, on hearing of her distress over Lachy, her son.

In contrast, Daniel's intellectual gymnastics bounced off Michael's consciousness like acrobats off a springboard. If Daniel had any genuine feelings - and Michael was sure he did somewhere - they were so cunningly disguised as foils for his behavioural craftsmanship that one could hardly know them.

Michael's concern for his brother Lachy, however, surpassed both his empathy for Kathe and his distaste for his father's crude emotional politics. And to that extent, Daniel had accurately judged the capacity of the siblings' relationship to undermine the cogency of Michael's psychosis. Although Michael found it hard to believe that his brother would even touch heroin, the possibility that he had somehow been duped into it, and the threat this possibility posed to his life, called from Michael's depths a desire to act grater than anything her had ever experienced. It rang deep and long in his heart like a bell sunk in granite.

Unfortunately - and it is here that Daniel had underestimated the precarious nature of Michael's mental state - the story in which Lachy was located in Michael's psyche at that time was also the one in which Hanif, Sheena, Bozzo, Gareth Joseph and his father, Daniel, were currently characters. And it was a story from which it was difficult to extricate the younger brother. Whereas Kathe, although in a comparable internal narrative, was on another rocket (as opposed to another planet). And as Kathe's rocket took off in one direction, on a wonderful voyage of discovery and love and self-respect, Lachy's projectile fired in the other. As Kathe powered through the perimeter of Michael's mind, catching for a moment on his idealisation of Sheena and leaving perhaps some shreds there for

350

future reference, so Lachy's rocket roared into the centre of Michael's self.

It was fuelled by the realisation that the Golden Deer Bozzo was trying to prise out of Sheena had something to do with the Transnational Corporation of America, for whom Sheena's guardian worked and owned, on Sheena's behalf, one of the most lethal companies on the face of the earth, Military Industrials; and whose managing director had once dragged Sri screaming down the side of Mt Kalesa believing she was Sheena, his daughter, to whom he had once given a golden deer; and who were trying to oust his father, Daniel's firm - partly by getting to him through two of his sons - at the same time as killing Bozzo, who worked for them. Or was it the government? It was here Michael's understanding became grey. But compounded. And he, Michael, was contracted in all of this to dip his hand into this incomprehensible agglomeration of intrigues and separate Bozzo from Sheena, forever.

So Lachy's rocket plunged deeper and deeper into Michael as the magnitude of the task before him grew. And took with it such active manifestations of his personality as had presented themselves to do battle with his father to join that same mad intrapersonal panic that has caused Michael to leave Tasmania, rescue Sheena, fuck Bozzo, and make a video that would explode the entire world of patriarchal illusion.

Leaving his last few tears behind in the ether of persona, its destination was some obscure and distant crag in Michael's inner self, where he was hiding from the horror of his own ego as it rampaged, out of control, through a totally disordered universe. There Michael scrunched himself up into a tiny ball he hoped nobody would ever find ever again, while a rocket exploded somewhere above it from which it formed an outer self of platitudes and homilies to wield like lances and shields; an outer self that hauled out normative mores and stereotypes from the barren plains of Michael's socialisation and fashioned itself as a fantastically armoured, inter-molecularly mobile persona within which the man, Michael, could take on the world.

Michael was, at last, going to become the hero OF HIS OWN STORY!

*

Sita Sends Hanuman To Rama With Her Gems To Show She Is Still Alive

Sheena made one more attempt to dissuade Michael from his committed path, whatever that was. It was the morning after she and Bozzo had had one of their outrageous fucks. Bozzo had been screaming, yet again, that he was going to kill himself, while Sheena had been yelling back at him about satellites, and not if they got him first.

Michael had spent the evening over at Hanif's and was extremely bound up inside. Relations between Hanif and himself had been strained ever since Michael had discovered Hanif's treachery in meeting with Sheena. Nobody, it seemed, could be trusted.

So Michael smiled and tried to pretend he had heard nothing. And considered Hanif's attempts to talk him out of broadcasting the video as some kind of psychological doublespeak which wouldn't fool him.

So tense and exhausted was Michael by the effort of thus constantly holding onto himself that he was quite unable even to masturbate to Bozzo's and Sheena's anarchic lovemaking. Instead, he set himself to computing what Bozzo might really be saying as he rooted Sheena stupid. For it was clear the two were communicating in some primal counter-code designed to misinform Internal Security agents who had almost definitely ensconced themselves next door with listening devices.

Once he had successfully cracked the code, he fell asleep, as the muted hues of morning gradually permeated his opaque bedroom. Only to be awoken in the domestic quiet of mid-morning by Sheena, softly pushing his door ajar with a homey rattle of the doorknob, and the gently spoken;

352

"Michael, are you awake?"

It was almost as if she didn't want him to be, but he turned to look at her through the dimness anyway. So she entered with a rustle and sat down almost balletically on the edge of his mattress.

"How are you?" her voice sounded tenderly.

"I might ask you the same question," croaked Michael, and Sheena was silent. "Is he really threatening to kill himself?"

"It's a sort of challenge, I think. Part of him wants me to care, to tell him that I love him, while the other half - it's sort of political. Like his suicide would draw attention to me somehow - embarrass my father, make him take a firmer line with me, I don't know. Especially if he dies of an overdose. The cops'd be all over this place. He'd line it up beforehand."

Michael chose not, at this point, to reassert his innermost conviction that it was really Bozzo who was defiling Sheena with the drug, forcing her to tap the supply of Golden Deer her father's company trafficked against her will.

"And what might they find?" he asked obliquely instead.

"Well, you know."

"Do I?"

He was trying to sound both tendentious and light-hearted, but Sheena only laughed in disbelief.

"Well you've been following me long enough to know!"

"Well, yes, but I just thought . . . " blustered Michael amidst the sudden flotsam of his confidence.

"What?"

Sheena screwed up her eyes as if this would somehow heighten her perception, then shook her head and smiled to herself;

"Oh no, you couldn't . . . "

"Couldn't what?"

"Michael, *I* am the dealer, okay? I *am* Bozzo's supplier. Jeezus, you guys'll do anything to keep us up there, won't you."

Michael did not feel defeated. On the contrary, he smiled to his inner self. For Sheena did not know that he had uncovered the relationship between Golden Deer, the heroin, and Golden Deer, the emblem of Transnational. He *knew*.

"Look, I came down here to warn you not to go."

"Go where?"

"On the Big Job."

Michael sighed.

"Michael, I think he knows about you and me. That we've fucked."

Michael tried not to betray the absolute terror that suddenly gripped his autonomic nervous system.

"He hasn't said anything," Sheena continued, "I've just got a feeling. There's something else in this suicide stuff. Some edge. He knows I can't let him die. It's like he's pulling at basic principles, as if he wants something real, but I don't know what it is. I just think he knows, Michael. Not that he'll do anything about it. I mean, I think he'd kill me, but he just might lop you off instead."

Michael searched for a way of exuding I'm-not-afraid signals but his words, body, and the very substance of his personality managed only an intense inertia at the prospect of their imminent demise.

"So don't go, huh? Find some excuse. Tell him the video isn't ready or something."

"It isn't."

"Well, there you go."

Michael heard the familiar crack of detonators down on the railway lines nearby, warning railway workers of an impending train. Then there was silence.

"I'll be okay," said Sheena into it. "I can handle him."

But somehow she didn't sound as if she believed herself.

"Look, Michael, this is something I have to do for myself. Do you understand?"

Michael resisted any appropriation of his determined path by looking confidently complicit whilst saying nothing. The understanding man.

"So will you promise?" Sheena persisted. It seemed such a naive request to come from one so world-winnowed. "Take a coupla days off. Go bush or something. The Royal National Park's good at this time of year. Train goes all the way."

She was serious. But Michael knew better.

*

Brahma Tells Rama That Sita Is His Wife, Lakshmi

In spite of Michael's resolve to rescue Sheena, the emergence of what had seemed to be genuine compassion from the object of his desire caused a bit of a jarring of the works.

Not that he was about to surrender his place in Bozzo's impending escapade. He had only told Sheena he would think about it. But the arrival of an emotion like compassion so close to the centre of his internal commitment had called up its equivalent from the rocks and crags of his inner self. Like two flaming torches borne to a secret, underground rendezvous, his manic outer construction was brought into contact with his more fragile interior, and it worried him.

It worried him because, for a moment, a new semblance of reality leapt across the synapse. One which brought to Michael's mind the notion that Bozzo's Big Job was something slightly futile. The showdown you have when you're not having a showdown. Perhaps not even a showdown at all, but a figment of the bruiser's mind. Hanif might be right after all. The video would be a laughing stock, or not seen at all. Meanwhile Bozzo was crazy, Sheena would take care of herself, and he, Michael might be killed or, worse, make a fool of himself.

All of which were weighty considerations. So Michael took himself to Manly to think about it.

The journey from the heart of Sydney to the North Head isthmus that linked Port Jackson to the Tasman Sea never ceased to be a joy for Michael. It was refreshing just to get out on the water. The sea breeze, which so often found its way between exhaust-fume-packed office blocks, now hit him full in the face and lifted his skull to the skies. And beneath his feet, that magical, unland-like vibration. To be standing on water. And moving through it. Through the metal superstructure, the engine thumping away on the cavernous hull beneath; and through the hull, the resistant harbour building up in mass until the weight of the vessel equalled the volume of water before it, so that the massive body of fluid gave way to stream out either side in two divergent waves.

Once they started, those widening mounds of surface went on forever, criss-crossing their counterparts from other harbour traffic, meeting and re-meeting in ever-diminishing diamonds and triangles, until cosseted by the wind into oblivion. And Michael wondered: was the history of landscape like this?

Then the ferry would cross the mouth of the harbour, and the entire story would change. The tail end of an ocean current would flick the vessel up and down with menacing ease, like a plaything. Only a suggestion, but enough to remind you just how powerful was the sea just beyond those heads, wrapped around subterranean mountains to haul deep, invisible channels out through the narrow constriction of those two turtles' heads of rock which rose up from the shoulders of Sydney's north and south shores, crying out to aeons of unseen topography a planet in size. No wonder people chose to jump from those heads. They knew where they would be going.

Then there were the yachts.

Michael loved the yachts. Not only because of the ease and grace with which they wove their ways through the water, keels like blades separating cream from milk, but also because of the money they represented.

Michael was never really quite sure just how much money there was in Sydney until he got out onto the harbour. The smallest of them were worth thousands of dollars. The largest, the ocean-going racers, could float small banks. And the harbour was chock-a-block with them during summer. Hundreds upon hundreds of white triangles and spinnakers, the buntings and flags of commerce, flying on or against prevailing winds, zigzagging economies up and down the harbour. It was as if they imagined the laws of nature had been especially drawn up for them. While the ferry, with its load of passengers whose pockets would never buy them so much as the sailcloth, picked its way between them like a giant without arms.

Which, understandably, annoyed Michael. Here was a vessel swollen with the masses upon whose very existence depended the whim of those who owned the yachts. And here were the yachties, skiting around on their mother's milk in billions of dollars worth of unproductive technology, perversely insisting on an anachronistic nautical convention that power give way to sail. Michael could not believe them for it. Nor could he forgive them.

*

Agni Brings Sita From The Flames To Prove Her Purity

Manly was packed. It was Sunday, and the whole world seemed to have turned out to enjoy the summer. Kids were already excited by the approach of Christmas, even though it was only November. Saturday morning shopping. All of those scrappy manifestations of Father Christmas - the one time of the year the derros got to fulfil their dreams of manhood - popping out of every second doorway with the promise of some plastic future from a waste paper lucky dip. It was enough to make any kid crabby, to have the economy prodding away at the edges of their innocence like that. So take 'em to Manly. Day of rest. Give 'em a break. Give us a break. Or an ice cream. The fun of the fair. Marineland. Or simply turn them loose on the sea.

There was nothing quite like that walk down Manly Corso to the ocean. So many enticing distractions. Delicatessens that sold homemade pork pies. Ice cream parlours that handed out monumental Danish cones. Cake shops that sold vanilla slices oozing with creme francais. Pubs from which schooners of Hunters Old spilled out onto the pavement. And the best fish and chips in Sydney. Before you were even aware you had left the harbour, a row of Norfolk Pines visors the eyeline like a portcullis upside down.

And beyond it, bulls beyond bars, the slowly rotating hulls of the ships - oil tankers, cargo vessels, container ships, ore carriers, all at anchor, all awaiting a berth (their last?) in Port Jackson, all turning so gradually this way then that in a slow dance with the tide.

There, Michael thought politically, was where the triangle fellas inside got their pocket money. Those giant hulks, with their sterns towards the shore in some collective (if unwitting) brown eye, carried the paint peelings of the yachties of the world. No power of theirs' gave way to sail!

Michael loved observing people. He could do it for hours and never feel lonely. As long as he had his short-term goals - an ice cream at the Royal Copenhagen, a beer at the Steyne, fish and chips on the beach - he could pace his Sunday entertainment allowance through the day.

Down on the beach bronzed bodies stretched and arched in the sun like luxuriating reptiles. Renegade cellulite rippled playfully and, try as he might, Michael could not avoid lapping at the bare breasts, basting away on their host bodies like beautiful brown puddings.

And in the back of his mind, Michael thought of Sheena. He thought of her white, pinched flesh, blackened with perforations, hanging in strips from a skeleton it could barely operate. And he looked again at the wobbling bodies before him, and he thought about his desire to have something of them in his mouth. And began to understand why it was Sheena who had to kill Bozzo.

On the beachfront, a troupe of young Christians were telling holidaymakers about Christmas. Not that anyone wanted to listen. But to begin with, before they declared their faith, the Christians looked mildly interesting to the idle. A mini Gay Mardi Gras perhaps, with their saxophone, guitars, straw hats, Bermuda shorts, brightly coloured shirts and black, plastic sunglasses. Or a bit of street theatre, about militarism and the draft perhaps. But then no, they were sons of God. Or so their opening number claimed. Although how the one woman among them felt about that Michael couldn't tell. She wasn't doing much. Just holding her flower in front of her belly, like the rest of them. And singing. The Singing Christians.

Then one of them leapt up onto a milk crate and told the crowd that they didn't want money, they weren't trying to sell anything, they just wanted them to listen for just one minute. So Michael listened. The guy went on to ask him what Christmas was all about, then proceeded to tell him the answer. So Michael stopped listening. He crossed the road to the Steyne for his beer and watched from the comfort of a seat by the window.

What then impressed him about the Singing Christians was their use of space. They were only young, but they had already learnt that if you stand apart in a space yet still appear unified and ordered, you are much stronger than you are individually, or just standing serried in a bunch. It's an immediate testament to your commonality.

If you then move together, clapping and singing in unison for instance, you get pretty impressive. These guys had gone a step further. They stood in an open swastika which, on one hand visually invited you to enter but, on the other presented you with four walls. Armies, thought Michael, must adopt similar principles in inculcating obedience amongst their cannon fodder. Except the clapping and singing is replaced by rifle slapping and mindless hollering. So that, when they go into battle and are told to run, they run. And when the tridents of missile-fire pick them up and turn them over to roast in eternity, they can fly with pride. As the blood in the bodies boils like lava in the moment before vaporisation, they can still hear the voice of the RSM ringing in the ears: *that's the way!*

Michael was aware that the swastika formation was open, and was thus unlike a military formation. But he couldn't close his mind to the metaphor. On the contrary, as one Singing Christian started to leap up onto the milk crate after another, all hectoring the audience about the meaning of

360

Christmas, Michael thought more about Hitler than he did about Christ. There was lots of arm waving and pointing at the audience, or to heaven. Like some vaudevillian cosmic dance. Or, after a while, simply a hard sell. Their product could have been motor cars. And most of the olds were just walking past, ignoring them; they had it every day of the week.

A foursome of bikies passed in front. All grimy jeans and slumped necks, and that characteristic stoop of the shoulder from which helmets hung on permanently limp arms. They too moved in space, but as one body. Like one eight-armed embodiment of anarchy. Nobody was going to tell them the meaning of Christmas. Their mere presence was proof of their potential. The warrior caste.

Then there came the surfie, his board in its cover under his arm, mouth agape, obviously disconnected from what was going down. And why shouldn't he be? He was unemployed. He'd been having it out with the sea and the shells, throwing his designer mansized discus against waves and wind. It was his lady by his side who lingered to listen to the Singing Christians.

Michael couldn't identify with any of them. Least of all the Singing Christians, bobbing up and down one after another, mouths flapping meaninglessly beneath black sunglasses. Arms waving frantically like so many angels learning to fly. It began to seem like a competition. Who could spruik the longest and get to be the most faithful Singing Christian of the day? For all their pure white teeth glinting in the sun, none of them seemed to be mentioning the wars Christianity had condoned, or the role it had played in the rise of Capitalism, the endorsement of usury and the creation of the Protestant Work Ethic. They were just interested in being the first to get to heaven. Christians aren't perfect, just forgiven.

It wasn't until the males had finally exhausted their reserves that they finally let the woman have the guitar. And she started singing. And, even though Michael couldn't hear a single note she uttered beyond the glass, he

361

knew she was singing beautifully. Because suddenly people stopped ignoring the Singing Christians and listened. Gathered around. Adopted attentive body language. They did what the male Singing Christians had wanted them to do all afternoon. Whereas the woman hadn't asked them to do anything. She just sang to them. Like a river. And they drank. Like the sea. And the truth of her voice flowed into them, around them, and out again. And even if they did not agree with what the voice said, they understood where it came from. It washed them.

And Michael wished for all his worth that, in that moment, that woman was Sheena. Sheena stepping out of the flames of Hell.

Of course the guys quickly cottoned on to what was happening. With due humility, they fell into supportive poses in their swastika of strong, Christian spaces, and earnestly tapped their toes and gazed meaningfully at their fellow (female) Christian. And as soon as she had finished, the winner of the testament-of-faith contest leapt up on the milk crate and began teeth-showing and arm-waving all over again. And to the day they die, thought Michael, none of them will ever understand what had happened. They will duly praise the woman when they get home, humbly defer to her success as is meet and right. And in the future, at the apposite moment in their beachfront busks for God, they will trot her out to draw in the crowds. But they will never understand what it is she does that they don't.

Because basically, they all want to be leaders. So that they can use their own self-sacrifice as a paradigm, and thus make factory fodder out of the masses who follow so that a few can win. And be forgiven for it. By a conveniently transcendent authority whom only they can understand. What could be better? If we could all be leaders without really being leaders . . . it was sublime.

It was around about then that Michael decided to go on the Big Job. Not, he told himself, to protect Sheena. (Although he *would* be there for her.) Nor, necessarily, to kill Bozzo. But so as, fundamentally, not to be a leader in any shape or form. Not a male one, anyway. Not

362

the leather-blacked, multi-armed bikies, nor the beautifully-haired, white-skinned, lotus-bearing Christians. Nor even, perhaps, the discus-riding surfie. Let alone a draft resister in a Third World War that might not even be happening except on celluloid. He didn't know what there was outside the opposites of Heaven and Hell, black and white, right and wrong, man and woman, but he knew there must be something . . .

*

The Attack On Lanka

Bozzo did not give Michael time to dwell any further on his determined course, for it was that very night the mega-punk announced the job was on.

Michael and Sheena were sitting in the basement lounge watching a news item about an American oil magnate who claimed to have discovered the graves of King Arthur and Queen Guinevere on his Texas property. The President of the United States was heralding it as proof that the US was the Isle of Avalon, the Promised Land, in a bid to exhort national confidence in his latest trade initiatives against France for their monopolisation of the plutonium market. The news commentator was saying that no-one had the heart to tell him that King Arthur was, in all probability, of Gallic extraction when Bozzo brought his awesome bulk into the room.

There was no time to strategise. Not even a chance to dress. They must go as they were, there and then. In a beat-up old combi-van Bozzo seemed to have acquired. Michael with his video camera for some live-to-air additions to the broadcast, and the unfinished, hastily edited cassette. Sheena with her soft canvas bag of gemmies and housebreaking paraphernalia.

From Darlinghurst they rattled down to the Cahill Expressway and north. The evening sky was beginning to accumulate heavy clouds at the end of an almost tropical spring day. As they trotted up over the bridge, Bozzo told them about the sinking of the Titanic, and how there were only enough lifeboats for a certain proportion of the passenger list, the difference being the number of berths in third class. As the epitome of Western capitalism sank, the hatches of all third class quarters were battened down. Since these were below decks, it was likely that their occupants never knew quite what was happening to them until they either froze to death, suffocated, exploded with pressurisation, or simply drowned in darkness.

"But when the carcass of the ship was finally discovered four kilometres below the surface of the North Atlantic, do you think the general public wanted to know their fate?" Bozzo rhetoricised. "Bullshit, they did! All the media were interested in was the oldest, coldest collection of vintage wines in the world. There were pictures of them, photographed with the best in underwater technology, strewn about the decks of the world's deepest cellar."

Bozzo evidently thought this was extremely funny. He was in fine form tonight.

Michael was subdued, still straddling his various states of mind. Although he had come to some decisions, he had been unable to share them with Sheena. He had arrived home only minutes before Bozzo. Now she sat between the two of them without comment. They might have been off on any of their nightly jaunts. A spray painting adventure. A foray into the urban catacombs of law enforcement. Yet Michael felt a foreboding sense of bonding between the three of them, as they sat so slightly above the already red-and-white-eyed cattle of homewardbound traffic on the bridge.

Below them, one of the chosen oil-laden few was being admitted to the arcanum arcanorum of Sydney's inner harbour, ceremoniously parading its dull, high-masted navigation light under the watchful eye of the Harbour Bridge. In the sky to the West, the early evening salvo of incoming domestic flights picked their ways between the amassing clouds on descent into Kingsford Smith. It was twilight, yet the sky already seemed to have decided to go to bed.

It was a remarkable phenomenon, the Sydney Harbour Bridge. Built in the four years spanning the turn of the decade into the 1930s, it was a testament to the Keynesian economy. Its massive girders defied winds of up to 110 kilometres an hour during construction. The investment in local industrial muscle and technological self-sufficiency served as an inspiration to a nation of disempowered workers wallowing in the trough of a US-led depression. It was literally as if they had built their way out of the doldrums, as the mighty metal hands of North and South Shores, Sydney's rich and its poor, reached out towards each other.

It was ironic that it was a relatively unknown cultural imperialist and militarist, De Groot, who should have the honour of cutting the ribbon, gazumping the official opening ceremony with his sabre and horse, breaking from the ranks, stealing the thunder from the hero of the working classes, NSW Premier Big Jack Lang. Now the once great national symbol had more significance overseas, characterising Tourism Australia, while its exorbitant and rising toll made money for a New South Wales Government fending off corruption allegations.

Once they were on the other side of it, Bozzo, Sheena and Michael entered the domain of the newest of Australia's nouveau riche. Behind them, the lights and towers of the insurance brokers and financiers of the post-industrial boom were shrouded in the gathering gloom. Before them, the squat square fortresses of the information generation were on the rise, heralded by neon logos in primary blues and reds.

The slopes of North Sydney marked the gateway to a new metropolis, this one for micro-technology's global economic barons. Those Australian larrikins who'd cut and run with the international share market and returned home with armfuls of sunrise industries and 'tax haven'

365

foreign citizenships. Their towers contained fewer windows, employed fewer people, demanded less fealty, and paid fewer taxes than any enterprise before them. But they made much, much more money.

Their affiliation was less with any one economy as with the interdependence of many. With their grip upon the transnational marketplace they could, if they so chose, bring about a redistribution of wealth across the boundaries of nationhood, class and gender unprecedented in the history of what Western commentators called civilisation. Instead, they served only to line their own pockets at the expense of those very same divisions, to boil their constituents down and render them residual, powerless. All in the name of electrons, who knew nothing of either labour or wage.

It was outside one such mausoleum to equality that the positively ebullient Bozzo brought their post-war chariot of hippydom to a halt. It was into this very same fortress that the punk led his accomplices without so much as a blow, a blast, or even the merest jiggle of a lockpick. Bozzo simply inserted a small, embossed plastic strip into the entry decoder and had access, it seemed, to virtually the whole building. Lift doors opened and closed for him. Elevators rose and fell. Infra-red secure corridors admitted him passage. Doors slid gracefully to one side and back again. And deep in the bowels of the tomb-like building, without the slightest tremor of an alarm anywhere else in the wired-up world, a large vault received him. Them. All three. Together.

The vault contained a computer the size of which Michael could not have imagined. Metal spools whirred behind glass compartments. Multiple banks of red, green and purple lights exchanged obscurities with laser printers and vacuum discs while facsimile copiers beeped, buzzed and poured out information into the long and silent night about them. And this, Bozzo assured them, was just the bit that was for show. Most of it happened on silicon chips you could barely see with the naked eye.

"What is this place?" asked Michael with childlike wonder. It could have been a line from Jules Verne's *Journey To The Centre Of*

The Earth. Or, more probably, the film of the same.

"This is where the cleaners live," explained Bozzo tendentiously. "Where's the cassette?"

He had stopped in front of one amongst a number of indistinguishable visual display monitors. Michael looked to Sheena in askance, but she just shrugged. He was on his own.

"It's not really ready," he offered weakly.

"Fuck it, do you want your brother out or not?"

This was obviously the first time Sheena had heard this intimation. She glanced warily from one male to another. Michael reluctantly handed over the video cartridge to Bozzo.

"And start shooting," Bozzo commanded incidentally.

Obediently, Michael set the video portapak rolling and started immortalising Bozzo on magnetic tape. The anarchist depressed a couple of illuminated keys in the console and elicited from the screen what appeared to be a list of every television station in the country. He then keyed in a set of coordinates, including a time which was, according to Michael, about ten minutes away. The cartridge was then inserted and OK'd on the VDU.

Bozzo then set to work on a fresh set of keys which summoned a new display of information, in which Michael recognised the Transnational Corporation of America as the holdings company for a hierarchy of media, metals, minerals and software subsidiaries based in cities throughout Australia. Bozzo selected one of these and input what looked like a mathematical formula alongside it. The company was Military Industrials (Aust.) Ltd.

The next corporate hierarchy brought to the screen was the Multinational Trading Corporation, and among its Australian subsidiaries now appeared Military Industrials (Aust.) Ltd. A few more keyboard operations and the words "Golden Deer Asia Imports" flashed up beside Military Industrials. This produced an involuntary cry from Sheena.

367

"No!" she screamed, and threw herself incomprehensibly at the back of the multifingered Bozzo.

The latter's dexterity, however, simply transferred its attention to Sheena who, within a fraction of a second, was lifted bodily from the ground, rotated in mid-air and hurled brutally against the base of a nearby magnetic relay unit, which coughed a few sparks in protest.

Michael found himself stepping between Bozzo and the latter's momentarily disoriented room mate.

"Bozzo, you don't need to do this," he was saying.

"Michael," Bozzo intoned reasonably, "Do you want to save your brother?"

"Yes, but there are other ways."

"The other ways are already happening. In eight minutes your programme will go to air across the nation, and in another two I'll have your brother out of trouble. In another one, every satellite in the world is going to be focussing on this little joint. So get filming. Got it? It's the best hope you have."

"This is between Bozzo and me, Michael," warned Sheena from behind him.

"Yeah," sneered Bozzo, "Between the lady and me."

Michael stepped aside.

"You can't do it, Bozzo," Sheena continued painfully. "You're betraying your own company."

"Yeh, but if they know about each other . . . " Bozzo was automatically working the keyboard again.

Michael now realised that the letters of the two transferred companies were emboldened, which meant that the transfer had not yet been accepted by Multinational's system.

"There are twenty one companies which control 98% of the world's economy," Bozzo was explaining to the camera, rather like Batman to Robin back at the Bat Cave, "And these two are amongst the top seven. Between them they can move 10% of the world's wealth at any one time, and have access to two thirds of it."

368

BOZZO

had now brought both Military Industrials and Golden Deer alongside International Natural Resources Developments - Michael's father's company.

"That's a conservation initiative." Sheena protested. "You promised not to touch those."

"It's a tax bucket to offset Multinational's sales to the commies, you dickhead," Bozzo replied, "They want to manufacture a Russian rocket here, Michael."

Bozzo was clearly trying to draw Michael into the argument as honest broker. But Michael couldn't find any honesty to broke with right now. He was busily wondering whether Bozzo knew that his father worked for International Resources. Bozzo, in the meantime, had his back to both of them, and fed a new set of instructions to the computer. The code name "Rough On" appeared on the screen.

"Shouldn't there be an 'e' on the end of that?" Michael asked, more out of curiosity than anything else.

"Tape it!" Bozzo snapped back, and Michael ducked behind the viewfinder again.

"The programme won't accept the final character," he relented in a language Michael did not really understand.

"Bozzo, you can have it," Sheena said from what sounded like a defeated distance.

"Sheena, I've got it," Bozzo replied. "I just don't want you to have it now."

Michael deduced that by placing Golden Deer Asian Imports - which he presumed was their mutual source of heroin - outside Transnational, he had removed it from Sheena's guardian's, and therefore Sheena's ambit. How the transfer to Multinational gave Bozzo control over supply was, however, unclear.

Bozzo, meanwhile, had switched back to Transnational's corporate hierarchy and was picking out certain personnel. These he aligned

369

with their equivalents in Multinational's management structure. Both were cross-referenced with a network of Asian cereal and grain exporters and certain government officials. Bozzo worked with lightning hands. His fingers seemed to multiply as the information network emerged. Michael was familiar with these patterns from his work on the video. Bozzo was setting up an automatic electronic exchange of information. Memo by computer.

"That's not fair!" yelled Sheena.

"They're all doing the same thing, Sheena," replied Bozzo insouciantly. "And you would've done it to me in the end. Don't think I don't know, lady. You and that lesbian bitch."

Michael was once more unsure what Sheena's concern was. He had realised it was possible Gareth Joseph did not in fact know of the activities of Golden Deer Asian Imports. And that it was thus Sheena's knowledge of the same that got her the supply. It was possible that it was with exposure of this knowledge to her guardian that Bozzo had been threatening Sheena back at Strathfield. He had, after all, slipped off into Telecom heartland with alarming alacrity that night. And the ease with which he now encrypted the incriminating information into Multinational's acceptance of transfer indicated how much was electronically within the realms of possibility for Bozzo. Sheena was silent.

"Now for your brother," Bozzo went on, and keyed in the term INDRAJIT, which was accompanied by the VDU sequence, "Target: Space Research Launch Project; Multinational Trading Corporation." To this he added the subscript, "Golden Deer Transduction Targets." A list of names appeared on the screen, from which Bozzo expeditely removed three - his own, Michael's, and Lachy's.

Into the viewfinder Michael saw Sheena's silhouette creep.

"Sheena, no!" he cried, stepped forward and wrestled the gemmy from the raised hand.

"Whose side are you on?" she hissed, although whether to him or the camera perched upon his shoulder was not entirely clear.

"It's my brother!" Michael protested with painfully familiar petulance. He was getting sick of himself again.

"And you!" retorted Sheena before Michael had time to even apprehend the implication. And there he was, grappling irrelevantly with Sheena's wrists. His own life saved. Bozzo found it all somewhat amusing.

"You people are such worms," he derided, and dropped his index finger on the appropriate key with such dramatic aplomb that Michael expected the whole place to detonate instantly.

It didn't.

But what followed remained unclear to Michael. He was aware that Sheena hurled herself at Bozzo. And that the read out on the screen had transferred the Golden Deer Transduction Targets from INDRAJIT to a new operation, RAVANA, for which the target bore the title "Military Industrials Strategic Space Defence Initiative". He was also aware that Bozzo was shouting at him -

"Press the button Michael! Press the blue button."

- as he whirled Sheena in the air above his head. And -

"No!" Sheena hollered in reply, rather like a police siren subject to the Doppler effect as her voice was rotated through 360°.

It wasn't chauvinism that impelled Michael to follow Bozzo's advice rather than Sheena's. Unless concern and deep love for his brother could be construed as chauvinism. But there was some atavistic intelligence that told him that, whatever the operations Bozzo had executed on the computer screen had meant, for whom, and how, directives concerning both Sheena's legacy from her guardian and for his and Lachy's demise were about to be extinguished in one press of a button. So Michael pressed the button. Instinctively, almost. While still videoing the bi-human gyroscope before him.

"You fool!" Sheena gasped as the multi-armed Bozzo brought her to a standstill but continued to hold her aloft. "International Resources are government. They redistribute resources and production technology to the Third World. They're *good guys*, you fuckwit!"

371

Michael had not realised that his father had maintained any of his more altruistic links to government and, indeed, humanity.

"Whereas now they are going to be discovered as a cover operation for an international drug syndicate," Bozzo said, and he began to laugh. "They were getting hot anyway, Sheena."

"And that," Bozzo's laughter was starting to come in large, guttural lungfuls, "is a laser."

He was pointing at a newly flashing button on the console.

"A laser that could knock out the lot of them. The bastard that pressed that button could end the war before it even started!"

Bozzo now opened his throat to its full and horrific aperture. His laughter started to bounce off the silently computing facades and multiply in a crescendo of human resonances that filled the entire vault. And with it, Bozzo began to stomp. As the sound fed itself and amplified, the body from which it originated began to stomp from foot to foot in a slow circle of celebration. And as it stomped, the woman held aloft by its arms began to shake, helplessly, with it.

And it began to occur to Michael that he had been had. He wasn't sure how, but Bozzo had won out over Sheena. Perhaps it was that, if Sheena had been tampering with her guardian's company's heroin ring, she would most certainly be found out herself in the transfer to Multinational. And if Transnational overlooked that transgression, perhaps they would most certainly be after her as, they would assume, the main beneficiary of Military Industrials. Especially once they discovered that Gareth Joseph had signed the legacy across to Sheena's signature. Perhaps. Whatever it was, it seemed that her future was on the line. And Michael's own attempts to safeguard her had, in fact, been used to get her there.

As Michael watched Bozzo stomp through a perfect circle, he saw a man impregnable. No matter what you threw at him, even political intrigue and ideological abstraction, Bozzo could key it into a computer and return it as a missile or aim it as a laser at your best friend. For each wound you attempted in his extensive defences, he'd grow ten fresh electronic strategies for dealing with the likes of you, each more deadly than the last. He was a monster. On the streets of Sydney he tore people physically limb from limb. Amidst the computer banks of the patriarchal world, he was supreme. And Michael was in awe of him. In awe and deeply afraid.

So afraid that he had to refocus his glazed eyes as Sheena, who had managed to wriggle free of Bozzo's outspread palms, dropped onto his back like a monkey. A cumbersome struggle ensued in which Bozzo tried to reach over and wrench her off, like an awkward pullover, while Sheena fought to retain her grip yet evade his. Her hands seemed to be everywhere. She had many arms. All of which seemed to converge at once upon his eyes yet, at the last minute, change their collective mind and clasp his forehead.

Bozzo's reaction to this last encumbrance was something Michael would remember for the rest of his numinous life. To begin with, it could have been a fit. He could have been an epileptic, or an apoplectic, straining his head forward, eyes protruding. Then he grabbed Sheena's wrists and prised them ineluctably apart. At the same time a strangled grunt that had replaced the demonic laughter became a roar which, in itself, immobilised Sheena. He then flipped her over his head and twirled her in the air as if she were a fighting staff. She span above him, and he began once more to dance. And as he danced, a scar in the middle of his forehead Michael had barely noticed before began to glow with a bright red centre. It came ablaze with rage. And in its rage, Bozzo danced. He danced with a verve the horror of which Michael could not comprehend. It came from a bottomless well of hatred so deep that it beamed in hot red from Bozzo's forehead. It came from a rage so terrifying that the world would shrink from its mere unleashing. Bozzo danced a dance that could shake the very world.

"Press the button!" Bozzo howled in words that Michael had never heard a man utter before.

"If you want to save your pathetic, fucking brother, press the fucking button!'"

Michael could not believe someone could have so much anger in them. When the boulders of his own inner self were torn away from the sun-stopped entrance to its feeling centre, where his soul had pumped relentlessly all along weeping for love, where was *this*?

Michael involuntarily depressed the blue key, and the screen instantly displayed the message:

"CODE NAME: Rough On
EXECUTION: RAVANA - confirmed."

In the same moment, Michael's cartridge was swallowed up into the video machine, the screen of which sparkled into life and ran through the same list of television stations Bozzo had initially fed into it. And as it went, it seemed, the current transmissions from each station Bozzo was intercepting flashed up on the screen. And for a second, or a fraction of one, Michael thought he saw his brother amongst a group of Aborigines protesting in some sort of bush setting. Michael thought it might have been Hanif's footage, but in the micro-second before the link-up moved on the shot zoomed out to reveal the foothills of Mt Kalesa. So Hanif's friends were, indeed, looking after Lachy.

As for Michael, he felt like a shell slammed shut inside the barrel of a shotgun that was about to be fired. But by whom, he really didn't know.

*

Garuda

A silver dart skips across cumulus canopies as they column heavenward. Above it, the world is indigo. The deep, deep blue of heaven. Below, usually, fishbones were picked of their white flesh by its twin-finned technology. Today, there was a storm brewing. Today its routine pattern over the North West Cape, Jim Creek and

Cutter triangle was subject to a minor variation.

As far as its pilot knew, the Australasians still believed North West Cape - and, indeed, the whole Australasian sub-triangle - had been phased out. Political fall out of the seventies. So nobody expected him to be here. But Garuda normally terminated the VLF pattern over the Cape then crossed to link up with the SDI grid. Today, he was making a small and dangerously low-level detour over the continent's Eastern coast. Sydney, they called it. After some guy, he guessed. It had a Harbour Bridge, apparently. And an Opera House.

He was only 31.5 seconds from the intercept point and pulling a tight circle over where the city should have been. He would have to get straight out. Since the Australians had gained limited access to Pine Gap, you never quite knew what they knew. And anyway, it was approaching evening. Their incoming internationals would be due in around now. He didn't want any mysterious "UFO" sightings today.

He had never seen a cloudscape as voluminous as this over the barren continent before. Perhaps he had never been in the right place. He never ceased wondering at the way nature reproduced itself in so many varied yet similar forms. His world, for instance, was confined to the white, blue and various shades of indigo of the heavens. He took off at night and landed in the dark. Or emerged from anonymous airborne tubes into bright sunlight and returned to them again. He had been born to this. Yet whenever he got down amongst the white, it was like returning home. Or home as he remembered it. A home he might not have had. Horses galloping through the forest, their manes afire. A deer leaping from bank to bank, pierced by an archer's arrow. Those bones of fish, from which the world seemed to spiral out as sunset approached, or a horizon. But always in white. Quite white.

Then he would run into this stuff, and memory would run wild. A tortoise from his youth, but the size of a mountain. Carrying a mountain. Or was it a boar? Yes! A boar, spinning a ball on its tusks as if it were the very world itself. And it changed again. Always changing. So fast, as urgent, furious winds rose from the ungainly conflagration of atmospheres. A lion's mouth leaping up from the body of its tamer. And in he'd zip. The world was indeed churning over Sydney today. Boy, would they be wet down there. And he was helping them get that way.

Twenty seconds to contact. Undetected as yet. He pulled through another torque to avoid an Everest of nimbo-cumulus. Red lightning. That was a new one.

He began to key into the satellite grid over Pine Gap. S-$\underline{IV}$-A was the co-ordinating barrel, and INDRAJIT the target. Apparently we had a friend down there. He had connected with this contact before. One of their Transnational operatives. Slick. About to knock the guts out of some poor sucker's economy. He had no idea whose. Or where. Never did.

It was funny, when the 747 went down over Russia, nobody thought to consider the fact that the Migs were still twenty thousand feet below their supposed target. And the Ruskies never mentioned the two of theirs Garuda got as well. The Koreans never knew what hit 'em. Shame we had to down one of our own.

It was the same when the Hegg went down off the Philippines. Nobody really believed two unmarked prop fighters could do a job like that. Not in this day and age.

CONTACT!

The plane automatically flipped over and span on its own axis before rocketing heavenward. Too much for the body, despite the G-suit. But the on-board had it. Locked into S-$\underline{IV}$-A and Pine Gap. It was over in seconds. Two on-board lasers keyed into the satellite grid and the target was out before Garuda had broken seventy thousand. And who'd notice? Except some aspiring fascist next time he turned on his underground console to plot the next step in his global apotheosis, to find his funds gone and his network

376

decimated. They hate it what they get dumped, these guys.

But, as long as it kept the sandwich wars going, he'd keep slipping between the stars and the world would remain a safer place for the majority. He was a preserver, not a destroyer. At least, that was the way he regarded his role. And that helped him sleep at nights, in the white plastiform bunker that was his only contact with Mother Earth.

Garuda was back on course for North West Cape before he knew it. Although, upon checking the on-board he discovered that the Cape leg had been cancelled by Jim Creek, and he was in fact heading for Nurrungar. The computer also showed that the signal had, at the last minute, been altered. The actual target had been RAVANA, not INDRAJIT. Which was strange, because he'd understood RAVANA to be their latest; the one with first strike capability. But he must've got it wrong.

There had also been a couple of ancillary strikes against operatives elsewhere on the continent about which he'd not been briefed. So . . . these decisions were so often made upon last minute intelligence. It was history. Twilight was nigh, the sky above him indigo, and soon the shadows deepening below him would plunge his world into a snowbound forest floor of moonlight . . .

*

The Death Of Ravana

As they hit the Harbour Bridge, the rain was coming down by the boatload. Michael had never seen anything like it. It was as if the clouds had dispensed with the pleasantries of physics and dropped their collective bundle. Gone were the meteorological niceties, the gathering of droplets from inland trees or harvesting of evaporation from the seas for the occasional precipitation over coastal tumescences. Clouds from every tarn and puddle in the world, it seemed, had gathered over Sydney this night, in a show of global counter-meteorological solidarity Noah would've been proud of.

And as the oceans egested themselves, so the earth went out in sympathy. Silicon chips, carbon derivatives, metals, and all the precious elements men had ripped out of the planet spat their proverbial dummies as cars and electricity gave up the ghost across the city. The people of Sydney rediscovered the tyranny of distance (in its more metaphorical semiotic location) as batteries gave out, distributors failed, and tyres lost their grip in the deluge. Those who dared to leave their homes were ambushed at corners or in surprise dips in the road as stormwater drains joined the revolt, disgorging their contents at every conceivable orifice.

The bridge itself was littered with scuttled vehicles. Their occupants had either fled or were awaiting rescue by lone NRMA service units, banks of refugees cowering ineffectually under iron girders against the merciless onslaught of weather.

Bozzo thrashed the van through the congested concourse, but the angrier he became, the more he seemed to drive himself into cul-de-sacs of dormant cars.

"Christ! We could spend all fucking year up here!" he spat. "Mind you, we could live in this thing."

His tone changed completely.

"The guy I ripped it off was some kind of hippy. You've got everything back there. Primus, saucepan, bed, bottled water, even food. All vegetarian of course. The shithead even fed his fucking dog vegetarian."

Michael wondered under exactly what circumstances Bozzo had 'ripped it off' the said hippy, given his intimate knowledge of the owner's habits. Perhaps Bozzo had been planning to make himself scarce for a while.

"He used to travel around getting into it. Lived up near Lismore somewhere. Had lots of meaningful relationships with women. Mostly," Bozzo continued, as if reading Michael's thoughts. Sheena sat once more impassively between them.

For himself, Michael was bound about the arms and torso by a length of rope Bozzo had produced from Sheena's gemmy bag. He hadn't explained why, but as soon as they had completed their 'live broadcast' Bozzo had taken the portapak from Michael and tied him up. To Bozzo and Sheena this seemed routine, but as the three left the computer centre Michael couldn't help wondering whether he was hostage or a condemned man; Bozzo's surety against the satellites or the about-to-be victim of a cuckold's revenge. But since he didn't seem to have any say in the matter he tried, like them, to carry on as if nothing out of the ordinary were happening.

After several abortive attempts to bludgeon a pathway through the barrage of deserted vehicles, Bozzo brought the van to a halt and banged on the dashboard petulantly.

"Can't see a fucking thing in this!" he sprayed, and Sheena suggested she drive.

"We'll need to head out West," she said. "The Cahill'll be chocka."

"Do what you fucking like," retorted Bozzo. He was too angry with other things to take it out on Sheena. So she took over the wheel.

Bozzo then sat sullenly snuffling coke while Sheena indomitably and expertly picked a path through the chaos. Once she was in control, Michael was able to relax a little. As much as his ropes would allow. Across the Quay to his left he could see the Opera House in all its rain-shrouded, quartz halogen glory. Like a conglomerate of giant shells whose occupants had long since deserted it. Those who scurried from their urban habitats to these carapaces of some dimly remembered past were more like hermit crabs, naked, looking for another home in that sad and long lost Australian artefact, the artist. Whatever had happened to the arts in this country, these days its exponents were like urban oysters. They

379

spent a lifetime sifting through the dregs of the oceans, distilling the essence of the sea from its edge, only to be dropped down the gullets of middle class bureaucrats, entrepreneurs and politicians as if they were somehow unclean. Yet still the population who remembered what it had once been like came out to inhabit the shell of remembrance with sad, if unflagging, hope. The possibility of consensus in action . . . ah!

In the face of such an onslaught from real Gods as tonight's, the steps of the Opera House were empty. Except, Michael noticed, a young couple with a child. One of them was dancing. Dancing under the one plaza lamp left alight. Dancing in the rain.

It looked surreal. They could have been for all the world the sole cause of the current deluge. Dancing a dance that shook not the earth but the heavens, and all the water from them. And the Opera House was not a collection of shells but a brace of sails, ready to catch the next prevailing wind, detach Bennelong's Point from the rest of Sydney and carry these divine protagonists out through the Heads and into the commanding swell of the oceans beyond.

Of course they were just a couple dancing really. Michael thought it was the guy who was dancing at first, but as the van passed through its perigee he could tell it was the woman. She danced from her centre. With everything. None of those elbows and shoulders and earth-weighted feet you see with guys. He was holding the child and looking on. And for a fleeting moment Michael wondered whether the Holy Spirit was a woman. As was God. The Biblical scribes had simply misheard the personal pronoun.

When they reached the city end of the bridge, the outlet to the Eastern suburbs was indeed as Sheena had predicted. Lone sets of orange and blue flashed out from the agglomeration of traffic, beacons of authority stranded like the rest. Whereas the flyover to the West lay before them like an open jaw. The Mouth of Hell. For its lights were out.

"Watch the fucking road!" yelled Bozzo as Sheena slewed the van upstream into the blackness.

"I feel like a salmon," Michael said limply.

As they climbed into the darkness Michael thought that they might as well have been leaving the planet. The storm now had such control over the city that the lights were dropping out by the suburb. The world seemed to be simply falling away below them. But Sheena seemed to know where she was going. Yawing against the tide, she steadily steered the Combi up over Pyrmont Bridge, left into Ultimo and then right into William Henry Street, such as it was.

The deeper they drove into the darkness, the more Bozzo's coked out eyes tried to widen.

"Where're yuz goin'?" he asked.

An edge of gruffness could not conceal the fear in his voice. Bozzo was worried. With half a dozen microchips in his pocket, removed from one of the computers at the last minute 'for safekeeping', he felt every bit the target.

"I thought we might cut across to Leichhardt," Sheena explained dispassionately, her eyes on the road. "To some people I know. Lie low for a bit."

Michael understood the logic of it immediately. Leichhardt was where her collective had once lived. Sheena was making for home ground. Glebe, maybe. Just the other side of Wentworth Park. Bozzo had not the wits about him to realise. Just a vague unease at the edges of his senses.

Suddenly it occurred to Michael: Wentworth Park. And at that moment an unworldly surge of power through the city grid revealed them to be at the crest of an almighty descent into the Ultimo vale, at the base of which a lake of swirling stormwater covered the small, green oasis of Moreton Bay Figs in the heart of Sydney's warehouse belt. It was as if Sheena had planned it. Right down to Bozzo's panic.

381

"What the fuck . . . " he cried, grabbing the wheel as if he would do something about their impending plummet. He couldn't, of course. Sheena had her feet so firmly planted on the pedals that the van rose on a mounting wave of water and surged down the dramatic escarpment out of control. They were surfing. But there was no beach to break their fall. No gentle length of strand onto which they could roll out from the foaming tunnel. Just a fomenting mass of water, populated by yet more vacated shells of the once socially mobile.

The light only lasted for a second. It might as well have been orange lightning. Then the van was dropping like a stone into murky blackness. Michael was aware of a struggle for the wheel beside him. He sat on the edge like a gooseberry at the Drive In, hoping that the movie would start soon. The van swayed to the left then thwumped into what must have been the body of water. Or another car. Michael couldn't tell.

Then there was light again. And Michael could see Bozzo slumped across the wheel and Sheena, groggily trying to right himself. But Sheena's elbow jabbed. And jabbed again. As if she were hitting him to Get off! Get OFF, you oaf! So Michael reached over to help, discovering in the process that his arms were free. Had been for some time, it seemed. The ropes had been cut. He made to lift Bozzo from the wheel, but Sheena screamed at him.

"Fuck off!"

And Michael withdrew his hand to find it sticky with a black fluid that could have been tar in the orange light, but was in fact blood. Bozzo's blood. Sheena had struck. And was still striking. Michael could see the violent metal of the blade as it pulled and tugged the life out of Bozzo's pale blubber. Sheena was killing Bozzo.

"Get out!" she screeched at him. "Go on! Piss off!"

"But I have to help you," he shouted back pathetically.

But it was already too late. Bozzo was pawing at Sheena with mud-bloody hands, his head lank and spewing at the mouth. And Michael was already scrabbling at the door, wanting to run as he had in a dream once. But this time he could not simply bolt. Metal thwarted his fingers. Water swirled around his legs and waist. The van was listing like a wounded ship, as if the waters would at any moment cause it to capsize.

Michael tried to support the van against the current, as if this would do some good. But it righted itself anyway, shifted downstream and then was lost to the current. Then the lights went out again. And Michael was alone in uncertain waters. His own life at stake, as it had been once before, in a dream.

*

Dasaratha Entreats Rama To Accept The Purity Of Sita

Now that Michael was so suddenly out of the central action towards which he had and yet had not been moving for so long, reality did not seem to be particularly relevant. It was just as it had been once before, when he had almost drowned. Instinct did the job.

He was wading waist-deep through water towards the nearest shelter, which turned out to be a warehouse at the foot of the hill down which he, Sheena and Bozzo had aquaplaned. There was a half-open doorway in the lowermost portion of a large wooden roller door, and Michael blissfully entered a world of total darkness and peace. The rain receded to an asbestos roof several floors above him and, although the water was knee-deep in the loading bay through which he had gained access, he quickly found the first level of storage above the waterline. There he settled amongst sackfuls of soft somethings and relaxed to the aroma of old hessian, musty furniture, and a home he had never had.

As he became accustomed to the clammy dampness of his clothes and surroundings, it began to dawn on Michael that he had just been witness to a murder. And he wondered if he shouldn't be doing something about it, although he couldn't think quite what offhand. He'd gleaned the impression that, in redistributing the targets on the computer, Bozzo had issued his

383

own death warrant anyway. Although Michael still did not really understand what had transpired in the vault of the North Shore information technology centre, he gathered there was some sort of battle over spy satellites and who would get them, and that Bozzo and Sheena were somehow caught up in the political machinations of two multinational companies who were in competition for Australia's confusion about its global allegiances. And that his father was in there somewhere, perhaps now politically on the line. But that he and Lachy had been saved. Maybe. Frankly, Michael was content to be marooned on the oasis of a very dim present, with a nostalgia for something that might have been once. A home with Sarama, perhaps. Or beyond.

For there was indeed a certain amount of light now entering the warehouse. A couple of street lamps winked at the multipaned windows high above him and Michael could clearly read the labels printed on the sacks in foreign ink around him. Indeed, he even fancied he recognised the initials, although he wasn't sure where from.

He also became aware that the sacks upon which he was sitting in cell-like solitude were growing, as if by osmosis. Perhaps Bozzo had slipped some acid into his tea (and he would wake up to discover it had all been a bad dream), or he was suffering some kind of post-trauma psychosis, but he was certain that his improvised armchair had changed in size as the shadowy scallops of sacking around him expanded.

Before he despaired of his sanity, one of the sacks split to reveal that its contents, rice, had been absorbing moisture from the rising waters. Each grain only slightly, but collectively enough to produce an effect of some magnitude.

As he thus rose towards the floors above, Michael wondered idly who was going to pay for this lot. Then he remembered where he'd seen the acronym before. INRD. One of the subsidiaries of Multinational Trading Corp Bozzo had flashed up on the screen not half an hour before, and against which he had aligned the elusive Golden Deer Asian Imports. His father's company. And, from the rest of the information printed on the sacks,

384

it was importing rice from Thailand.

And Michael wondered what his father was doing importing rice from Thailand, since Australia had its own burgeoning rice industry. One which was turning an agriculturally inhospitable Northern Territory in a minor goldmine in the process. Unless this was an example of what Sheena had intimated whilst whirling above Bozzo's head: that INRD was into redistribution of world food resources. Although that sounded rather too altruistic for a capitalist enterprise, even if it *was* a tax bucket.

It occurred then to Michael that neither Sheena nor Bozzo may have been right. What his father's parent company might be into was multinational macro-economics. It had been one of the models Bozzo had thrown into the video. By buying up resources in Southeast Asia, INRD could sell them back to their original producers at a profit by channelling them through an Australian importer and inflating the price along the way. Meanwhile the Southeast Asian worker, just as they thought they had gained a foothold on the rungs of economic mobility, finds their newfound income going not on improvements to their standard of living but on its maintenance against inflation. They are still struggling to buy the staples. Thus the progress of the Developing Nations towards the status of Developed Nations is kept in check while the capitalist growth spiral is able to spiral on - around the world.

It was to do with redistribution alright, but not of food resources, thought Michael cynically as he watched another couple of sacks split like distended stomachs. And he lay back on his billowing bed to dream of fluffy white clouds of corn-popping rice bursting through the roof of the warehouse and dispersing across the nation on the winds of change. Sydney would become the rice paddy of the world while Asia starved . . .

*

The Almighty Sire

When Michael awoke, the storm had abated. Well, locally. He could still hear it in the distance, like two amorphous Gods hurling boulders of atmospheric pressure and spears of electrical discharge at each other, battling out some ancient and irresolvable feud.

Closer to hand, however, it had been replaced by another sound which brought Michael out from the disgorging sacks of rice into what looked, by all accounts, to be the golden dawn of another day.

The sound that had penetrated Michael's slumber was not, as he had imagined in his dreams, a baby's scream on exiting the womb, but a car alarm. Or rather, lots of them. Hundreds. Possibly thousands. For, as the storm had struck, the percussive trigger of perhaps one or two cars had been set off. Or perhaps a circuit had shorted in the downpour.

In an ordinary storm, this was not unusual. Neighbours would try for a while to resist the yelping and whooping of this small, mechanical device writhing in the grip of the metallic despot it was supposed to protect. But eventually one or two of them would come out in their dressing gowns, exchange grumbles, wander up to the offending vehicle, establish that it wasn't theirs' and wander away again. They might even return to bed, only to rise angrily minutes later to telephone the police, who would say that they couldn't do anything about it but would turn up anyway, illegally enter the vehicle and shut the howling beast down.

On this night, however, so volatile was the tension between atoms and atmosphere that the merest quantum leap would send stray electrons flying absurd distances in unlikely directions. With the result that one car alarm tended almost inevitably to set off another. Which would in turn set off another. And another. Until what began as a palliative mating call between solitary vehicles stranded suburbs apart became a veritable love meet. Alarms throughout the city chattered to each other maniacally, freed at last from the factitious constraints of

386

vehicledom to explore the unleashed capacity to replicate themselves endlessly. The car alarms had taken over Sydney, liberated by the avenging turmoil of the storm.

Outside, the warehouse looked to all intents and purposes like a Chicago Gothic movie set in the early morning glow. At its base, however, Michael was still in shadow. It was understandable, then, that as he raised his head to take in the heavenly cacophony that so commanded the city's airwaves, he did not notice at first the waterlogged body that gently bumped against his legs in the retreating flood. But once he became aware of the sensation and looked down, there, jammed between a lamp post and a fire hydrant, Bozzo's pale face glowed in thinning lamplight.

Michael had never seen a dead man before. Bozzo's skin looked like it had turned to water. Bluish and lifeless, like old wax. His eyes had somehow closed and he seemed almost at rest with himself. The scar on his forehead, which had blazed so brightly during the fight with Sheena, had actually reopened. The skull was dull and grey beneath the rubbery skin, and puss wept from the edges as from an old wound.

Bozzo's at-once flaming at-once matted mohawk spread out in the water now in three long, sad dreadlocks, unravelled it seemed by the exeunt of life from Bozzo's body. And for a moment, as Michael looked perhaps a little too intently, the swirling torrents themselves looked as if they flowed from Bozzo's head, in three expansive rivers.

Michael felt little, gazing on the already inanimate form. Except relief. That he no longer had to be part of what Bozzo was part of. And a sort of residual, sweet amazement that this body, floating to and fro in the floodwaters like seaweed, could have been capable of such fantastic violence and destruction.

He waded off towards where he hoped the path across Wentworth Park lay and began to make his way up into the Glebe. The distant applause of car alarms was already fading from its sonic cosmos like stars from the night sky. The police and the NRMA, it seemed, were back on deck.

*

Visvamitra Gives Rama The Wisdom To Plan And Skill To Act

The Pie Shop provided a real sanctuary for Michael that morning. Not the more esoteric oasis offered by the warehouse during the night but, by the time he had clambered up through the lower Glebe into the early hours of daybreak, a practical, rich and welcome relief for his cold, wet legs and trauma-torrefied throat. A huge glass of freshly squeezed orange juice. One of the best *cafe latte*'s in Sydney. Crusty, almost pastry-like croissants, as only the Pie Shop could make them. Breakfast on this day was like a holiday.

But the cafe's restorative qualities were not confined to its four walls. They spilled out into the suburb that it fed and which, in turn, fed it. The Glebe had started out as one of the original working class suburbs of Sydney. Deserted for the middle ring suburbs by the materialism of the 50s and 60s, it was bought up by the government to make way for a freeway to the west - a freeway that proceeded as far as Ultimo and stopped, both tiers of it.

Which made the vacated Glebe a prime target for squatters. It also became a home for the gays, lesbians, unemployed, and others displaced by the gentrification of Paddington. And while Annandale and Newtown were falling to the economic rout of their low cost housing by the Grand Knights of Real Estate, Glebe had somehow managed to contain, if not altogether avoid, the thrust of private enterprise. Between the city and its service ring of inner city suburbs for young, upwardly mobile professionals, Glebe was a haven for the marginalised minorities.

The Pie Shop was a focal point for this mixed and matched community. It had been run by collectives since its inception. One seemed to grow out of another. As a result it offered the sort of food its patrons wanted at prices they could afford. Posters and write ups on local goings on adorned its walls. An ancient juke box thrust out its dated chest from a cramped corner, offering a selection of songs from times its denizens remembered and loved. Daily specials were flamboyantly extemporised on an overhead blackboard with coloured chalk. People left messages for each other on the cork board, or roamed from table to knee-knocking table to chat with friends, or simply sit quietly and read.

Even at this hour, two lesbians came in and ordered huge plates of bacon and eggs. They talked as though their mouths were full after a night of long and languorous lovemaking. Michael gazed at their sidelong glances and carnal smiles with a longing of his own. He lusted after the freedom of their relationship, as they razzed the grouchy old woman serving them. She gave as good as she got, and probably didn't resent them, or the morning, as much as she seemed to.

Then there were the man and his son, dressed for what was obviously a rare day out together. The man was awkward, unsure, unaccustomed to the proximity of his child. Allowing him to eat ice cream at this hour. Perhaps it was his access day and he was, like so many men of his age, working through the discovery that he had not been brought up to share intimacy with his children. Especially his male children. That, even when the intellectual defences were stripped away to reveal the vulnerable parent within, there were still those deep, deep cultural imperatives that made him want to be the provider, the authority, the leader, and want the emotional support of others he had been reared as a man to expect.

Every image and pattern that presents itself to his waking self is channelled again and again by that masculine mould. But he loves his child desperately, and wants to change. And even now he is beginning to understand the earth-shattering catastrophe that seems to have befallen him. But oh so slowly.

In contrast, a couple of travellers who had also followed their noses from the bus station remind Michael of the inherent conservatism that can be found as readily amongst marginalised groups as any other. Backpackers had always seemed to Michael the pioneers of subculture, pushing themselves through the barriers of their own conditioning to walk amongst the world in all its difference. But when these two donned their packs and left, it was the woman who bore the heaviest. It was the woman who fell in six paces behind the man, and had worn a headscarf all along. Somewhere along the way the pioneering had become too much, and the Koran had been the only dogma strong enough to sustain them.

So Michael sat on the periphery of an ethos in which people were, in their various ways, simply getting on with the lives in which they had found themselves. And it didn't seem to be so hard. What they minded, they changed as best they could, and lived with the rest. The bomb might drop tomorrow, or even today, but at least it seemed less likely than it did last night.

And Michael wondered whether he shouldn't move here. Get away from the Cross. It was like living in an ashtray. For it was beginning to dawn on Michael that he had recently been party to something that was very much bigger than him. And that he himself had been ill, possibly very ill, for some considerable time. Quite probably since India. Perhaps even before. Prior, even, to his birth. And beyond. As long as history had been recorded by men, most likely. And longer still.

Walking up through the Glebe that morning had been like emerging from a movie. But one he had been in rather than one he had seen. And as the dawn strengthened around him, so did the understanding in Michael that he might not have been entirely correct about the bomb having dropped on Dehli. And his convictions about movies around Sydney being made into news footage might well be delusionary, albethey grounded in fact. And as for the Chain, it might never have existed. Not as a movement of draft resisters anyway. Perhaps in some other form. A mutual support network, maybe. That was what Lachy had called it. Still convened by Conan, of course. He was definitely not an illusion.

Conan had been a mentor to Michael, albeit an unwilling one. The father he'd never had. Conan had had just about every job imaginable. From twisting together metal bracing for reinforced concrete on a subzero building site in Hobart to running a small dairy farm in the highlands of Northern Tasmania. And, somewhere in between, had spent time with mystics in the Himalayas. By some quirk of fate known as Rural Relief, Conan had ended up studying law. His friendship with Michael had formed during the anti-logging campaigns of the late '70s, when Michael had worked as publicist on the law suits Conan engineered.

It was logical, then, that Conan should be the person to whom Michael turned upon his return from India. It was to Conan's shack on the East Coast of Tasmania that Michael and Lachy had gone one weekend to discuss the future of what Michael understood to be a resistance movement in which he saw himself as a key figure. And it was an argument Michael had been having with Conan that had remained unresolved from the night before when Michael and Lachy had gone out for an early morning swim and nearly drowned. And returned to find the shack empty.

Michael suspected now that Lachy might have been right. The occupants might simply have gone to another beach for a swim too. There were, after all, no tell tale 4WD tracks of intruders or signs of any real scuffle. Michael may well have misunderstood his brother when the latter said, almost desperately;

"Michael, there *is* no Chain. Don't you understand? There *is* no Movement. It's a delusion."

He may also have seriously mistaken his brother's weariness on parting for his own. For it was Michael who had argued the night before that what they were doing was futile. The rate at which what he called the Movement was able to erode the hierarchy was minimal in comparison to its own messianic expansion.

And it was Conan who had replied with characteristic equanimity, as he would have done if Michael had not been ill. For it was his policy not to patronise people. He said he believed that capitalism, as a hierarchic ordering principle which currently governed the Western world, was doomed to failure. It was based on an economic growth spiral it could not possibly sustain in a finite world with a finite capacity for population given its finite resources. It was already building structures to shore up structures to shore up structures. And eventually it would collapse under its own weight. All individuals had to do was gnaw away at one or two of its supports to help it on its way.

Michael had retorted tersely that all the hierarchy then had to do was replace the eroded member, which was exactly what they did. To which Conan returned, with nettled composure;

"Well, Michael, I believe there are times in people's lives when they have to make certain decisions. Decisions that may turn out to be life-forming. Or they may not. What I've always found, for myself, is that you make certain choices in these situations not because you have any high opinion of yourself and what you might achieve, but simply because they are what you can do best in the circumstances. Not all you can do, but *what* you can do, given what is available to you at the time. But these choices you make are enhanced and become yours - your *actions* - if you have a belief system which gives them value. If you don't believe in it, Michael, I suggest you stop doing it."

Michael would have wished for any response than this. He would have wished for an event - anger, a hot rebuttal, a defence, an accusation or exhortation, a pulling aside and personal entreaty to hang in there mate we need you. Some demonstration of personal bonding that attested Michael's value to the moment.

Instead he was left with the profound possibility of simply not belonging. Not even to Conan. With his deceptively wizened face and that twinkle of Gaelic impishness handed down through seven generations of Irish Tasmanians.

It was thus, Michael realised, not Conan's anger he remembered but his own fear. Somehow the child inside him had always expected that his efforts would eventually be rewarded somewhere along the line; with love and respect, honour and obedience, recognition and kindness. In reality, this was not the case. Possible, but not inevitable. He was in there swimming with the rest of them. You had to do it for yourself.

So it was that Michael fled the sanctuary of Conan's mutual support group for the psychologically disturbed, the East Coast, and any supportive links his past may have had to offer. To pursue some mythical state of individuation. Only to be confronted by Sarama's senseless, inhumane and brutal death. It was with that last reality Michael was beginning to realise he had to come to terms. He had to face his grief, awesome and self-shattering though it might be. And embrace the possibility of a new beginning for himself. And, perhaps, for his brother Lachy, who might really be hooked on heroin . . .

*

Sita Returns To The Earth That Bore Her

Michael never saw Sheena again. Not that it mattered. In his heart she was already receding towards some distant birth. He found out later (from Hanif) that she and Sri had gone underground. The fight was, apparently, far from over. Indeed, it seemed to be just beginning.

In retrospect Michael felt cheated, in asmuch as he had somehow been prevented from culminating in Bozzo's demise. Even Hamlet, after all, had his revenge in the end. (Even though he snuffed it himself in the process.) Moreover there was something profoundly ideologically unsettling about the method of Bozzo's death. Sheena and Sri (Michael assumed they had both been in on it) should have devised some astoundingly clever, non-violent strategy to defeat their age-old tormentor which somehow deposed patriarchy

393

forever. But perhaps that was asking a bit much. The equally patriarchal desire for wit, order, intellectual panache, and universal and idealised outcomes. In reality, the knife that killed Bozzo had also cut Michael free - literally and metaphorically. Although even that smacked of patriarchal determinism. An eye for an eye. Tooth for a tooth. A blessing in disguise. Out of the lion came forth sweetness. A phoenix rising from the ashes.

There must be some getting away from it, thought Michael as he toyed with the empty *latte* glass. Although perhaps it was happening anyway. As the dominant order started to fall - for Michael was sure it *was* falling, that much was real - so masculinity perhaps slid ever so gently down the sluice. And out along the tail race into the rapids? Oh no, my lumberjacketed friends! Out to the sewage farm, to be thoroughly treated and reintegrated with the land in proper ecological soundness.

Not even inflicted on the oceans. They'd had their share.

What worried Michael was what happened when the East and West went, as they inevitably would. Every binary stereotype has its day, after all. Even if some of them are rather long. (The days, that is.) It was clear there was going to be no great final clash. With sandwich wars in every second country, masculinity managed to contain the rage at its centre with a global network of release valves. But as the hollowness at its centre grew, the more desperate would become patriarchy's attempts to shore itself up from without with buildings built, things done, people won, absolutes affirmed . . .

Meanwhile, the developing countries were capitalising (or being capitalised) on whatever rafts emerged from the fluctuating economies of capital's major protagonists. And what happened when Islam became as powerful as East and West combined? Would the heathen hordes run throughout the land knifing lesbians, wimps and gays alike, throwing women behind yashmaks and hurling anyone who showed so much as a bare leg behind bars, handless? Was there indeed a more horrifying and barbaric brand of masculinity on the rise in the reunification of God, Capital and Politics? As Christianity falls one way and Capitalism the other, like the gantries of yet another abortive Challenger mission, does a new, sleek, thoroughly refoundered phallus of absolutism emerge in its place? Or is this too just another convenient metaphor to fashion the illusion of a future?

Whatever the case, Michael thought that perhaps Sri and Sheena were right to go bush, or wherever their collective were regrouping. As men increasingly found their hands behind their backs against the wall, the next stage of the battle was going to be harder than the last. And, quite frankly, Michael hadn't a clue what he was going to do about it. His dishearteningly comprehensive masculine conditioning had led him to expect some sort of linearity. An end point. A climax. A revelation. Whereas all he found was a man who knew what he didn't want to be. And that was just about everything on offer, in normative male terms. He was still without much idea who he was, but at least he felt more hopeful about his chances of getting there.

He knew he was still worried about the world. And he knew he no longer hated his father; but he didn't know why. He was a man who had once narrowly escaped drowning. He was a man who had lost a friend he had, despite his illness, loved very dearly and tenderly. And he wanted very much to do something for his brother Lachy, who had helped him once.

So he thought he might go down to Tasmania soon. But for the moment, he supposed, it was back to the old adage of taking each day as it came. And perhaps finding a few men who felt the way he did. For in the back of his mind there was still a juggler who had impaled himself on a set of knives in the Cross one night. He hadn't imagined that. So he turned to the Pie Shop's cluttered notice board to see if there was any joy there.

Meanwhile, the city began to clean itself up after the torments of the night before. People unstuffed tissue paper from the cracks around their windows, or emptied buckets and took draught dogs away from doors. Others sprayed WD40 into distributor caps in the hope of reviving waterlogged electrics. Businessmen staggered to their feet, opened shopfront shutters, and searched for ways of making a buck out of the current crisis.

Down in Wentworth Park, the police were booking cars deserted by their owners in the flood. Roll on the Golden Age, eh? thought Michael, tearing a phone number from an advert in biro seeking a man to share an all-male household (non-smoking, counter-sexist, vegetarian)(pity about the vegetarian, Michael mused).

*   *   *

BRAHMA - AN EPILOGUE

Why would a woman write this? A literary conceit strung between two continents dangling mythological appropriation over the culture of origin like so much dirty washing.

In reality, I am the other half of the lesbian relationship Michael was observing in The Pie Shop that morning in Glebe. I have been living here with Belinda for over a year now, after returning from the women's action at Black's Bluff (Mt. Kalesa in the story). We worked down there with a Dance In Education team for a while, the one Weiner once worked with, but that's another story. Back home, Brook had an abortion, but left Janaka anyway. (She isn't living with Aidan, as far as I know.) Fleur is studying fine arts and Verda is talking about coming out here for a spell 'away from herself', as she puts it. Dad is still living with Stella and, at last report, they were planning marriage.

I eventually had a letter from Savithry, via a circuitous route that took in the best part of the globe, written for her in someone else's spidery English. With it came a press clipping from the local paper about a 23 year old woman who was burnt to death when her husband offered her the choice of death or divorce. She insisted on death by his hand. So he poured the petrol and set the match. The man is only being charged with manslaughter, even though it is clearly a dowry death. Beside the item is a photo of the grieving Savithry being comforted by her youngest daughter.

In the letter, Savithry says that her youngest daughter graduated 'with honour' from business management school and they are setting up a fruit wholesaling business together in Trivandrum.

Belinda and I are still very much in love, and that remains something new and wonderful for me. She has forever berated me about Michael's novel. Says I inversely idealise women by offering them as

397

the only resort for other 'us' - a sanctuary from the ineluctable onslaught of patriarchy. But at least she concedes that in the end it is my bazzar to write my way out of, or re-write as a non-bazaar. I'm not wiping men off as an option. Part of me still loves Aidan, heaven help me. And there are so many men we both know around here who are good friends, and goodness, there's even a Men's Movement these days. Which was the hope I wanted to offer Michael, I suppose. I don't know where he came from really, but it certainly wasn't The Turd, as we have canonised Weiner.

I ran into him once, at the Paddo Markets. He was back for a while to earn enough money to return to India. That same measured eye and easy hand. It was one of those real heart-in-mouth moments for me. As in, a sort of red electric something floods my body from my womb and tingles at my extremities as I recognise the face before me and think: oh god, not this again. But it isn't long before the I'm-together-now edges of his persona start to luff in the wind of a flagging self-esteem. He jokes that he has well and truly become the Indian equivalent of a Sinophile, if there is such a thing. And the fear glimmers at the back of his eyes as he stands before the Hindu flame and thinks: I cannot become a Hindu, I have to be born one. And I remember how many more Australians I have met now with the same ease of eye and hand; how characteristic it can be here of so much more. And so I slip away from the encounter into the newer, softer recesses of myself, where I know a different kind of love. And a girl joins Weiner anyway, and he smiles and introduces her boldly, affably, with aplomb, trying not to seem 'discovered'. And of course, she's not a girl. She wouldn't be much younger than I was when I first met him.

Sadly, I never did find my mother. I had thought that was the purpose of "Boys With Bugs", or that would somehow be it's outcome. But I think I farewelled my mother in blots of salt on a page of a journal in Kanyakumari. Here I have found another 'black lady' entirely, and find more of her every day, and that has become something of a pleasure for me - a nice surpise, as they say!

And I still feel guilty for shamelessly commandeering Indian mythology in order to re-inscribe my own. But in the meantime, the Wall has come down, the Soviet Union collapsed, and along with it some of Eastern Europe's great socialist experiments, and Asia has emerged as the largest growth point in the global economy - China leading the charge (over its student youth in Tiananmen Square). People are talking nuclear disarmament like yesterday's news, and who could have known that my novel, even as it was written, was being made artefact by the very history that created it. Narrative dead in its tracks. Although the wars, in whatever power configuration, continue. As does the pervasive and persuasive influence of patriarchy. Men still running through the thought bazaar, grabbing ideas as they go, hoping one of them will stick. And if one thing remains sure in my mind, it is that if real change is to occur in our world, it is the men who will have to effect it. And they will have to start with themselves. Deeply, ineluctably, rigorously, and without resistance. Our future is not an idea they can simply have.

Rhea Barnett

www.ingramcontent.com/pod-product-compliance
Lightning Source LLC
Chambersburg PA
CBHW071148020726
47502CB00002B/324